PEACEKEEPER

MELINDA BROWN

With thanks to:
Character Design by: Rachel (Raena) Matthews
The following team at Stardust Book Services:
Cover design by Natasha Ali
End papers by Jonas Spokas
Formatting by Sara Vertuan
www.**STARDUSTBOOKSERVICES**.com

ISBN: 979-8-9986219-0-1 (paperback)
ISBN: 979-8-9986219-1-8 (hardback)
ISBN: 979-8-9986219-3-2 (hardback special edition)
ISBN: 979-8-9986219-2-5 (e-book)
FIRST EDITION 2025

To my daughter Kimberley.

Always follow your dreams and never
give up.

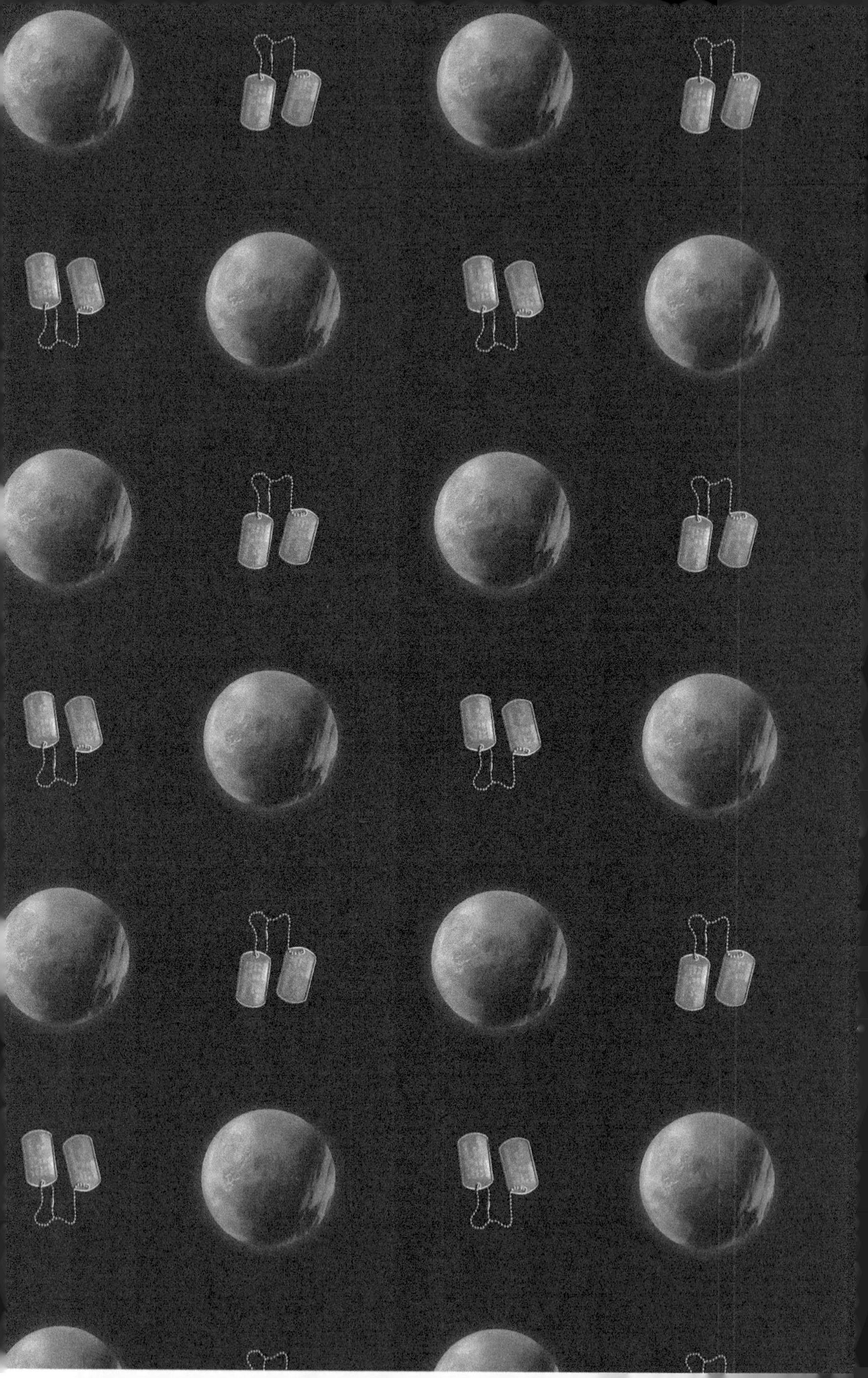

Colony Enlightenment, Aether B
June 6, 2220
Population: 56

John Evreux held his breath, his eyes fixed on the holo monitor's video feed of the aliens outside. The director and security team were speaking to them, but John could only make out several armored, ivory-skinned beings. He reached beneath his shirt and clutched the wedding band on a silver chain, the cold metal grounding him in his desperation. His gaze locked on the alien, its amethyst eyes gleaming coldly under the colony's lights. "It will be okay. It will be okay," John repeated under his breath over and over.

"Humans, you have trespassed on our territory," the aliens announced, the words conveyed through an AI translator tool. "Choose quickly: annihilation or servitude. If you serve us, you will obey the laws and customs of the Achli. We are beyond your primitiveness."

John's breath sped while his cloudy brown eyes spied the colony director and the head of security, arguing about how to respond. The security leader's hand rested edgily on the butt of his pistol strapped to his side. "Please don't. God, please no."

Seconds later, glowing spheres burst from the aliens' gauntlets, cutting down the security team and the director in a deadly instant. The building shook with the blast, and John gripped his wedding band tighter as screams filled the air.

"Everyone, get to the far side of the building. Stay together!"

Taking a shuttered breath, he released his death grip of his chain and pushed towards the rear side of the atrium. The entire room was thrust into chaos as he crawled towards the front while a gigantic mass of humans squeezed their way through the one doorway. Electrical sizzles followed by explosions caused the lights to flicker and the stampede transformed into a free for all. A hard shove in the back caused him to stumble. An older woman hit the ground ahead, and the mass did not halt to come to her aid while she struggled to get up.

"I got you." John pushed through the crowd to assist her up, then held her hand to drag her along behind him. "Stay with me. We need to get away from the front entrance."

The far back room filled up quickly with the colony workers and they wailed, holding onto one another for some hope of a savior.

Spotting the row of respirators hanging on the back wall near the exit door, John hurried to flag a few colonists that he passed by. "Come with me. We can't stay here." John snatched a mask off its holder and then tossed a few more out. "Put these on, quickly."

The woman fumbled with her mask. "We can't go out there! They're outside!" She dropped the mask and then pulled away into the sea of civilians.

"Don't go that way!" he called her through his mask.

Another civilian worker picked up the dropped item and fitted it on. He turned his attention back to John for guidance. "You sure we will survive out there?"

"I have a wife and a young daughter at home that I want to see again. We have more chances outside than we do here right now. This place is like packed cattle waiting for slaughter." Screams of dread towards the front of the room seized his attention, and he jerked his head to see four Achli rushing in with their crimson armor. John opened the door behind him. "Let's move!"

He stormed ahead, his legs pumping, mind racing with images of his young daughter smiling at him with her blonde hair flurrying around her. He ignored the shrieks from those he left behind, not daring to look back. His family's faces remained inside his mind, reminding him grimly of the safety he left behind on Earth. A mirage of Earth hung in the background as his eyes desperately searched the sky.

"Charlotte, Krysta. . . I'm coming home to you both. You hear that, baby girl? Hang on. Daddy's coming home!"

Chapter 1

Krysta Evreux ran her fingers down the cool metal sides of the dog tags underneath her obsidian-colored body armor while she reviewed the specs of the mission. Her holo watch projected a small image of a ship's interior layout. A strand of her blonde hair tickled her face as it draped along her skin from her tight bun, and she wiggled her head from side to side to rid herself of the distraction. Her brown eyes sharpened on the image in front of her, refusing to break focus.

"Mam, docking with the Martian mining freightliner in two minutes," said a gentle voice.

Krysta turned away from the ship's schematics to the younger man before her. His dark fingertips reached out and gently brushed the rogue hair strand away from her face.

"You alright, Krysta?"

"Yeah, Grim. Just mulling over how to handle this one. Can't believe that a bunch of pirates commandeered a Rubex freightliner for aluminum deposits. It makes little sense. Why does Rubex want it back so damn bad?" Her eyes flickered over to a red-bearded burly man sitting with the rest of their team of five. Their full-body armor was identical. "Taking lead is a huge deal to me. Bad enough that Bear's over there grading me."

"Well, he *is* your mentor, Lone Wolf." Grim smirked. "Is it nerves or something else?" He motioned to her hand on her dog tags. "It's not like I don't know you."

Her eyes retreated to the holo. "My first space mission—too many ghosts out here."

Grim sat next to her in their small spacecraft. "Nothing out here differs from what we have faced before. Earth has a lot of ghosts too."

"Colonies that disappeared from hostile aliens?" she countered with a lift of her eyebrow. "They have *that* too?"

He chuckled. "Off to battle already, Krysta? Ease up. You gotta let the past go. I know losing your dad was rough. That was what? Fifteen years ago? Humanity's first encounter with extraterrestrials and we lost bad."

"Nineteen years ago."

"Docking enclosure in range," Bear flagged their attention from where he sat.

Krysta moved over to where a teammate was sitting behind his portable terminal. "Any scans coming in off our pirates, Switchback?"

"No logos. They've scrubbed their identification marks."

"Damnit." Krysta sighed. "We're going to have to work today, aren't we? Get us hooked, Raven."

"On it." The pilot acknowledged behind the ship's controls.

"Lone Wolf," said Bear, beckoning her from where he sat. The tension in the air thickened and a chilling silence filled the close quarters. All eyes leered his way. "No two-bit pirate group has the tech to do a full scrub." His eyes moved ominously towards their hatch door. "Maybe I should take lead on this."

"Relax, Papa Bear," Grim chimed in. "I know Lone Wolf is only in her late twenties, but she's not a kid. We're going up against pirates, not the Hell Suns. She has this one in the bag."

Bear's jaw tightened underneath his beard. "Don't even joke about that, Grim. The Hells Suns are one mercenary group you don't fuck around with." His emerald eyes fell on Krysta. "I don't give a shit about your age, Wolf. If you need to tap out, do it. No points deducted on this one if you do."

"Roger that." She nodded. "Okay, Peacekeepers, listen up."

Wolf projected the holo image of the ship from her watch. "The ship's layout is simple." She pointed to the projection. "Our docking port will lead us into the cargo bay. It's wide open but should have the containers for any cover. The pirates will know we're coming in as soon as we latch on. That's where they'll wait for us. It *will* be hot."

"Any workers they can use as hostages?" Grim asked.

Krysta shook her head. "No, Rubex divulged the ship's navigation is purely an AI interface and all the working crew are box mechs. No humans onboard. If any of the robots get in your way, you have my permission to take it down." A jolt soon followed, causing her to slightly lose her balance.

"Latched on," said Raven.

Krysta was the first to slip on her helmet. The brightly lit heads-up display flashed to the right of her inner visor. She could hear her breath through the respirator. A quick double check to her assault rifle clip and she made her way over to the hatch entrance. The sealed door stared right at her, though her black-gloved fingertips hesitated over the switch. She inhaled slowly. *I got this.*

"Let's move, Peacekeepers. Go! Go! Go!" Lone Wolf pressed her fingertip against the button and the seal zipped open, bolting through the doorway as klaxons wailed ahead, signaling their attack. Shouts of disarray were met with weapons being cocked. Her boots echoed on the cold smooth floor, teammates right behind her, until she stopped as her eyes widened at the tribal sun insignia on her opponent's armor ahead. "Peacekeepers, fan out!"

She dove to the right, seeking shelter behind an open container. Gunfire deafened her surroundings. With her hands gripping her rifle to her chest, Krysta kept her head low, the bullets pinging the container from all sides. Frantically, she tried to shift her body to gain sight of her team. She spotted Bear to her right alongside Grim.

With one arm, she pointed to him and Grim, then held up two more fingers. Bear gestured towards a crate at his side. This allowed her to let out a sigh of relief. All were accounted for.

Bear tipped his head toward the Hell Suns, then he pointed over to her. She chewed her lip and nodded. The firing finally let up and before the hijackers could throw out a choice of words to the newcomers, Krysta sprang up from cover and began opening fire back to swiftly eliminate a few unlucky enemies. Feeling a light tap at her side, she knew her mentor had safely made it to her during the fray.

Returning to cover, she tapped her earpiece. "Hold."

Seconds later, silence fell upon them again. Krysta held her breath and looked at the bearded man next to her for insight.

"What are the Hell Suns doing here, Jack?" she finally whispered. "Why did Grim have to bring them up earlier?"

"I have no clue, and this is bad. We're seriously outnumbered. We can't leave Raven and Switchback down here alone." Bear's eyes dodged away from the pirates.

"I'm not aborting this mission," Krysta spat and checked her rifle clip. "I still have half before I'm empty. You and I can crash the party upstairs. Grim should be capable of assisting Raven and Switchback."

A voice crackled over an intercom system above them. *"What a treat. The Peacekeepers have come to say hello."*

"Jones," Bear muttered. "This day keeps getting fucking better and better."

"*That* asshole? Why couldn't I have a simple mission?" She glared at the ceiling to address Jones. "We are here because Rubex wants their ship back."

"*You want it so bad, baby? Then come and get it,*" the man chuckled. "*Kill them.*"

Seconds later, the hold erupted into a frenzy again as gunfire came in their direction, nailing the containers. Lone Wolf and Bear exchanged silent looks, and with a finger, she motioned Grim to their teammates.

He nodded, the look of worry in his dark eyes. *"Be careful."*

Krysta shifted towards the corridor. They had to be smart about this. "Papa Bear, we have a three-minute window to get up there and gain control."

"I was going to say the same thing. I've got your six. What's the plan?"

She peered around the edge of the container. The mercs concentrated most of their attack on where Grim and the others were. Fortunately for her and her mentor, a box mech offered a small obstruction. They could use this, slipping back towards the corridor undetected if they were quick enough.

"Follow me," she said, pushing ahead and keeping her head down amid shouts of alarm, then the ping of rounds hitting the floor and wall that they just got behind. She trudged ahead with her rifle barrel pointed down as the sounds of gunfire faded. Yet this quiet felt out of place. The tiny hairs on her neck crept up. She peered down the hallway, expecting some type of trap. Oxygen levels were adequate, so she removed her helmet for a better view. A camera was ahead, and she took it out with a few rounds.

"So much for the element of surprise," she murmured back to her partner.

Coming up to a bend, she placed her back flat up against the metal wall and peered around the wall's edge, the control room ahead. The door was closed, and three heavily armed Hell Suns stood guard. She held up three fingers to Bear, and he tossed back a nod. Just as she was about to make the move, Jones' voice came over the speakers ahead.

"Krysta Evreux. You finally made it to space. Surprised that you did after what happened to your father. Did you think we were some big bad aliens?" He bellowed in a mocking laughter. *"Sorry to disappoint."*

"Facial recognition," Her mentor grumbled beside her. "The scan from the camera must have pulled up intel on you. Should have kept your helmet on." His dark visor stared at her. "Something about this is not right, Wolf. Why would their employer want Martian freight? What's the plan?"

Krysta's chest tightened with Jones' disclosure and her fingertips gripped the handle of her weapon tighter. She closed her eyes, her younger self's cries over the loss of her father echoing in her mind. That and a fading image of her mother's voice beckoning her back from the void, like a siren singing out to sailors in the moonlight.

"Krysta!" The man next to her grizzly snapped her back to reality. Disoriented, she glanced around to get her bearings. "Get it together, soldier. We need an order. Don't let him get inside your head like that."

Wolf shook her head and blew air from her lips. "Sorry. Get ready to move on my signal."

She cursed to herself silently as she slipped back on her helmet, having cost her squad fatal seconds. She tossed a quick nod, then bolted out of cover with her assault rifle clutched tightly in her hands. Krysta squeezed the trigger, taking out two of the mercs in rapid succession. Jack finished the third, leaving their bloody bodies on the floor in front of the Peacekeepers' destination. The area clear, Krysta flagged her teammate to follow her forward. She stopped at the closed metal door. "Locked. Bear, let us in."

"My pleasure." He reached into his armor's utility belt compartment and retrieved a slim, rectangular object. He pressed the device on top of the control panel to the right of the door. Within a few seconds, there was a chime, and the door whisked open.

With a racing heart, Krysta moved first. Her eyes locked on the four Hell Suns inside the open-area control room with the man, most likely Jones, standing boastfully in front of them. Each of the five mercenaries had the same assault rifle.

"Jones, I presume?" she asked, spitting the vile name out of her mouth as if poison. Her eyes narrowed at the coal-black-haired individual in front of them.

The man grinned from ear to ear, stretching out the large, jagged scar on his right cheek. "Jack, you let a girl lead you around like a dog? Did you lose your balls after our last bout?"

"That's Bear to you, asshole. Since when were the Hell Suns freight runners?" Bear countered.

"Heh, is that what you think this is? A simple run?" Jones cackled. "Surprised that Rubex is crying over their precious ship. I may have to destroy some more of their toys for the men you cost me."

"As long as I take you down, kill all the bots you want."

"Take 'em, boys," Jones said to his men. "Leave the girl for me."

Krysta and Bear bolted behind one of the server boxes. The Hell Suns opened fire in the direction they went, and the rounds thrashed the server box, breaking bits of the circuitry boards away with smoke pouring out of the structure.

"Don't shoot there, you idiots!" Jones screamed. Alarms wailed inside the control room from the damage.

Wolf smirked at her mentor. "One server node down the old-fashioned way."

"These assholes are doing our work for us," Bear chuckled. "Two more to go."

Krysta spied their next query. "The one on the opposite end may be our best shot. Lure them there?"

"Doubt those guys will make the same mistake twice. Want me to stay here and hunker in? Give them something to shoot at?"

Suddenly, Krysta's comm crackled to life as Grim said, "*Lone Wolf, we have a problem! Switchback and Raven are down, and I'm pinned with four remaining mercs.*"

"Shit. Hang on, Grim. I'll send Bear after you."

Damnit. I have already lost two under my command. I'm not losing Grim.

"You can't handle Jones alone," Bear said. "You would be seriously outnumbered."

"I have to complete this mission," she protested. Her brown eyes darted around, the helmet's H.U.D. barely keeping up.

"There's a time to hold the line, Wolf, and then there's a time to fallback. The objective for this one isn't worth it. We save Grim and get our asses back on the shuttle."

She shook her head. "I have to do this, Jack."

Popping out of cover, she opened fire on the mercenaries in the room. Unexpectedly, Bear yanked her back into cover just as the Hell Suns volleyed. He cried out and a splash of blood erupted onto the server tower glass cover that they were hiding behind.

"Jack!" she gasped, noting the hole in his left upper arm.

He hissed. "Damn armor-piercing rounds."

Her eyes grew wide, breath quickening as she gaped at the crimson blood on the server glass. *This is it. I'm going to lose Jack and Grim. It's my fault.*

She gritted her teeth and fought back the tears. "Let's move out." She tapped her communications link. "Grim, standby. We are coming down." With one flash of her hand, she and Bear bolted for the doorway and squeaked through just as the door closed behind them in Jones' unsuccessful attempt to lock them in. After racing down the ramp to the first room, she nailed two unsuspecting Hell Suns in the surprise attack. "Grim, get to the ship! We're out of here!"

She backpedaled, firing her rifle as she went along while Grim and Bear made their way to their ship first. Just as she reached the ship's hatch, a clicking noise came from her rifle. Empty.

Grim switched places with her and opened fire, allowing her time to get inside with Bear before he followed suit. The hatch closed as bullets pinged into the exterior shell. Krysta made her way to the controls and disengaged the lock. She felt their small craft shift as it released its hold and soared into space. Using her fingertips on the holo console, she engaged the thrusters to make their getaway.

It was only when they were safely out of range that she allowed herself to move away from the controls. The ship seemed empty to her with the loss of two members. Her eyes fell upon Bear as the larger man was tending to his bullet wound.

"Fuck!" she snapped, punching the inner hull with her fist.

Chapter 2

In the aftermath of the mission, sleep eluded Krysta. The sound of Grim's soft snores drifted out from behind her. Rolling onto her back with a heavy sigh, she fingered her dog tags. A compulsive habit. All she could hear was Jones' voice nagging at her thoughts. Images of Switchback and Raven's corpses lingered in her mind. She could almost feel the stickiness of their blood on her fingertips. Holding up her hand in the near darkness, she sighed. It was all an illusion.

Defeated, her eyes fell back over to Grim's backside in the oval-shaped pod. The sleeping arrangements made it barely manageable for them to sleep together in the same pod, despite how wide its circumference was. She tapped her holo watch to note that dawn approached shortly, before slipping soundlessly out of the bed with a shiver as the room's cool air caressed her naked form. After putting on her panties and sports bra, she heard Grim turn to look at her. "You up this early?"

"I want to hit the trail right at light." Without looking at him, she finished pulling on her workout clothes, adding, "I may go farther on my run this time."

"Okay." He yawned and moved into an upright position. "I'll go with you. Just give me a moment."

She shook her head. "Not this time. I just want to be alone. Need to clear my head."

"Krysta." Grim rolled out of the pod and reached across, gently cupping her chin, drawing her closer to him. "You tossed and turned all night. Don't let this mission spook you. You held it together. Heck, better than I would have, given the Hell Suns surprise. If you want to place blame, put it on the intel. Not yourself."

"A leader knows how to adapt to change. Jack even called it. I should have listened and backed away or let him resume command." Her fists tightened at her sides. "I thought I could do this. Now, Raven and Switchback are dead." She jerked her face away from him and crouched down to slip on her boots.

Grim jostled with his pants as he slipped them on. "Jack said you crashed out back there. Something about what Jones said?"

"Yeah, facial recognition scan. The bastard got a blurb on me. Brought up the shit that happened to my dad and the Achli. I just let it get to my head. That's it." Unwilling to dwell on her father, she made way out into the cool morning air of Manitoba. The gentle breeze brushed her skin lightly, creating a subduing effect.

Grim hopped along behind her, his feet sloshing against the wet grass and mud. He pulled his shirt over his head while moving to her side. "That was the trigger?"

She detected skepticism in his words. "Yeah, that was it."

He scratched the back of his head. "I don't get it, Krysta. When will you get past it?"

"Never."

"Dwelling on the past is not healthy, you know?"

"It's not something I can just switch off, Xavier," Krysta growled before adding, "I thought we were going for a run, not a therapy session."

He sighed, taking her hands in his and giving them a light squeeze. "It's the missions that make it hard for you to move on, Krysta. Look around you." He gestured to their naturistic surroundings with his eyes. "Isn't it better to be down here? Space missions are new to us, and I know it bothers you. Space reminds you of the Enlightenment massacre. So why do we do it? We could stay grounded, right here in Manitoba."

"It's not like we get a choice on what contracts the captain picks up."

"That's not what I'm getting at. You and I both served in the armed forces and then in the Peacekeepers for years. When our luck runs out, we may not return from every space mission. Raven and Switchback were not the first to be killed." Grim's hand moved up to her face, and he gently grazed it. "I don't want you to be next." His voice softened. "I'm afraid that one day you won't make it back. What if we just pull out and find a place here? We can take on-the-ground contracts and be our own captains."

"Grim," Krysta leaned back, letting his hand slip off her face and linger briefly in the air. "Did the Hell Suns frighten you that much?"

"I've been wanting to withdraw from missions for a while, Krysta," he admitted. "And I mean… with you. This one made me reflect. Don't you want to be more than what we are now? I want more with you than just the occasional shared sleeping pod together."

"I…." Her body went rigid. Her gaze desperately searched the horizon, toward the direction of her jog. Grim's concerns anchored her down like weights and she felt like a prisoner unable to run ahead. "I can't do anything serious," she finally answered.

"So, you never want to stay?" His voice hitched.

"Stay for what?"

"Love."

She found her bearings. Without hesitation, her eyes directly met his. "I don't think I could love anybody, Xavier."

"I don't want to be just a fling, Wolf," Grim's words soured with obvious hurt mixed in. "I told you; it's your past. You've been this way with others. But I thought it would be different with me." His voice suddenly hardened, sharp and cold, like the crisp air around them. "Let it go, Krysta. Let me help you let it all go. Learn to let someone be close to you. What will it hurt if you do?"

Krysta's jaw tightened. "Everything."

Grim sighed as his fingers raked through the short hairs on his head. "You're right. Settling down here was a pipe dream. Well, you know what, Krysta? Word on the camp is that Captain Masters just sealed the deal on a new space contract. I hope it's long term. I may volunteer for it so I can just get away from all of this. Maybe that will give you time to deal with whatever you have to deal with."

She blinked at him in disbelief. The announcement was so sudden and so out of character for him that it took her several seconds to even process it. "You're just leaving my team, then? Just like that? You just said you were done with contracts."

He shrugged, defiant. "You lost someone close to you on an exo-planet in the middle of nowhere. Maybe if I go out that far, you may eventually learn to give a damn about me, too." Grim pivoted sharply on the heel of his bare foot and stomped back inside the bunk.

"Xavier...." She stared at the closed door and then shifted her eyes up towards the thin stratus clouds that stretched across the sky like a cotton ball. "Why can't I let it go?" Krysta broke her gaze from the bunk and moved towards the designated trail for her run. A tug inside her chest made her pick up her pace toward the direction of the sunrise that crept over the mountaintops. *Why can't I just love somebody? Do I really want to fight for the rest of my life?*

Chapter 3

Eight months later…

A chime from her private bunk door made Krysta sit up more in her sleep pod. "Computer, music off." Engaging the room's AI, she waited for the rhythmic tone to fade before welcoming her guest. "Enter."

Seconds later, after the doorway whisked open, her brown eyes fell upon Bear as he stepped inside. She sat up straighter in her black sports bra and workout sweats. "Sorry for my appearance. I was about to hit the shower after my workout." Her words were barely audible as she tossed aside her personal tablet back onto the sleep pod.

"Of course you would squeeze in a jog after training," Bear pointed out. "I miss the crap you used to give me about Marines versus the Army."

"I just wasn't feeling it today," she shrugged. "Can I go over the new roster in the morning?"

"Krysta, don't isolate your team out there." His eyes lingered on her. "Especially me."

"I'm not, Jack." Finding her courage to meet his gaze, she tipped her head upwards to look at him.

"Don't give me that shit." His tone turned prickly. "It's been awhile since Grim left and you have been moping around. I don't know what the hell went down, but he's gone, and you need to focus. You still want to lead a team, right?"

"Of course I do, Jack," she shot back. "But after what happened with Hell Suns last time, I don't-"

"Don't even," He cut her off. "I've seen you out there in our training sessions. You're the only person who gives more than a hundred percent and still, you're hard on yourself. Nobody expected the Hell Suns that day. Things could have been a lot worse."

"How?"

"You could be dead."

Her eyes flickered to the floor and a soft breath escaped out of her chest. "Don't give me that, Jack. Raven and Switchback were killed on my watch, and you were shot. I fucked up. Just say that."

"I healed," he answered, flatly. "Fine, I'll get to the point of why I really am here. The captain assigned my team to another space contract." He paused and his abrupt silence provoked her to lift her eyes back up to him. "I want you to come along."

"What type of contract?" Her anxiety slowly seeped out like a dormant volcano.

"No specs yet. I came to you first so you could come along for the brief. I know you have what it takes to lead Krysta." Then his serious tone cracked, and a playful smirk slid across under his mustache. "I'm getting too old for all this traveling."

The change up made her chuckle. "Too old? Jack, are you feeling ill or something?"

"I'm fifty-four, Wolf."

Folding her arms, she leered at him. "By the way, it sounds like you're whining."

His expression turned resentful. "Ease off. I know you're young and in your late twenties, Krysta, but this shit wears you down after a while."

"Are you suffering from testosterone dropping? I hear that it hits around your age."

He threw his head back in laughter. "I love having you around, Wolf, although you are a pain in the ass most of the time."

"Only most of the time?"

"Wash up quickly. Masters is waiting."

After her brief shower and a new change of clothes, Krysta followed Bear out of the bunk. They moved through the grass strands towards their destination as the sun set, eventually disappearing behind a faraway mountain. Krysta remained silent in her own thoughts while the two walked towards their destination. The idea of going back out into space was a notion hard for her to swallow. The reassurances from her teammates fell upon her deaf ears. In her mind, she failed her test. She wasn't cut out to be a leader and losing Grim soon after was the final insult. Though losing Bear to a space contract was somehow worse, his invitation brought her comfort that she wouldn't be left behind.

Minutes later, they entered the Peacekeepers' outpost and found the conference room. The balding, gray-haired man inside flashed them both a smile when they entered. "Bear and Lone Wolf," he acknowledged the two of them, then motioned to their seats.

"Captain." Krysta fired off a salute before taking her seat.

Her mentor glimpsed down at his holo watch. "I apologize for our tardiness, sir. Had to wait on Wolf."

As he sat beside her, Krysta elbowed him in the ribs. "You are such a kiss ass."

Masters sipped from his coffee cup and slid a digital interface tablet over their way. "Dhank Trust out of Dubai is one of our new clients and let me start off by saying this: they have deep pockets." His hollow eyes panned directly over to Krysta. "I assigned a team, including your old squadmate, Grim, to our first contract of its kind with them; exo-planetary security."

"Exo-planetary?" Krysta's eyes widened and her breath hitched in her chest. "You mean off-world somewhere else? Not a space cruiser?" Trying to withhold her apprehension, she glanced at Bear. She didn't like where the conversation was already leading. Wolf couldn't stop thinking about what her former lover got himself into.

"Let me step back. Dhank Trust gained sole rights to the discovery of the latest exo-planet, al Sufi-C." The captain gestured toward the tablet before them. "There's all the information you need on the planet."

Bear picked up the tablet and read out loud, "Distance from Earth: Twelve light years, size: Four thousand kilometers with nearest star size: Over a million kilometers. Evolution: Two hundred fifty days. Rotation: Twenty hours. Tilt: Twenty-eight degrees." He snorted at the facts so far. "Spare us the boring details, sir."

"It gets better." Masters waved his hand for him to continue.

Bear and Krysta exchanged doubtful eyes before her mentor complied. "Surface temperature on the warmer side for the day is around thirty-two degrees Celsius with night temps at eighteen degrees Celsius." He chuckled without humor. "A perfect getaway temperature. It has two connecting land masses: the warmer side boasting over eight hundred thousand square kilometers, and the cooler side has a third of that."

With a touch of sarcasm, Krysta finished the read, "Six bodies of water, two moons and a partridge in a pear tree. Jesus Christ, sir." She tossed the tablet back down. "Don't even tell me."

"I know what you're thinking," the captain's voice softened by her rejection. "This isn't like what happened to your father on Aether B."

"Corporations failed him and every poor bastard on Enlightenment, sir. They cut corners and expenses so they could put their name out there in bright lights. In our first encounter with aliens, they shredded us to bits. Chretien Incorporated hired damn mall cops for security." Krysta shifted in her seat by the predicament the captain placed her in.

"A fatal mistake," the older man in front of her agreed. "Dhank Trust seems to know what they are doing. They hired us as security for their colony, Bakht."

In disbelief, Krysta quickly rose from her seat. "Sir, Bear and his team can handle this. I'm not a good fit." Her eyes avoided her mentor's. "Sorry, Jack." Inside her head, the room spun like a centrifuge and her heart rate climbed with it. Krysta slowly backed away as their faces remained glued to her. The room felt like it was closing in. For a terrifying moment, she could even hear screams of agony inside her head.

"Krysta, easy…." Bear called to her in a soothing voice.

"I need to get out of here." Ignoring him, her back bumped against the room's door and her right arm blindly reached out to find the control panel. With the door open, she bolted out of the conference room into the cool air of the hallway.

"Lone Wolf." Master's voice boomed after her.

"I can't. I can't do this." Her legs wobbled like jello, and she struggled to take a few steps. All she could think of was her father and the rest of the poor people who lost their lives at Enlightenment. Their fate was prophetic of what would become of Grim, and it was all her fault.

"Wolf!" Jack hurried up to her with his dog tags clanging together.

"No way, Jack." Tears burned in her eyes. "No way in hell!"

Jack's sharp voice cut through the air. "Get it together, soldier."

Biting back a furious retort, she scanned her surroundings for something to strike. Her fists clenched at her sides. "Why the hell did Grim do this? What was he thinking?"

"Lone Wolf." The captain beckoned to her from the doorway. "You want to continue this meeting?"

Bear held up his hand slightly to their leader. "Give her a moment, sir. I got this." He turned back to Krysta. "I don't know what the hell is going on, but Grim's out there with the rest of us. We stay together. Remember our oath?"

"Peacekeepers to the end," Krysta muttered under her breath. She could not look him in the eye.

"Damn straight. Dhank Trust wants another group out there. It's going to be us whether we like it or not. I need you there with me."

"Shit probably hit the fan. Just like Enlightenment." Krysta cursed under her breath. "Damnit, Xavier."

"He's a hired merc. We all are. If they are in trouble out there, then it's up to us to save them. No one else is going to give two shits about mercenaries. Now let's go back in there and finish this meeting. We get our bearings, then tear the place apart on this al-Sufi C."

Chapter 4

"Good to see you again, Captain Masters. Are these the next group leaders?" A man with coal black short hair in a pristine, plum suit walked into the conference room twenty minutes later with a digital interface tablet tucked securely under his arm.

"Jack Tighe and Krysta Evreux." The two Peacekeeper mercenaries rose to be introduced one by one by their leader before retaking their seats. The captain smiled at their guest. "I must say, Mr. Kumail, that you caught me off-guard with that ping in the middle of the night."

"I apologize for the time zone differences, but this matter must secure top priority in your schedule, which is why I sent the meeting request as I did." The man found his seat across from Krysta's.

"This is Yusef Kumail, the CEO of Dhank Trust." The captain introduced the well-dressed man before them all. "The floor is yours, Mr. Kumail."

"Two days ago, our colony, Bakht, implemented the code, '020-875'. Hours later, the entire connection to the colony went offline." Mr. Kumail explained with a tight tone, while he swiped the tablet in his possession, then flipped it around so everyone could see the screen. "Our security cameras detected several unidentified organic subjects that somehow bypassed our perimeter alarms."

"Let me guess. Soon after the unknown subjects arrived, someone flashed 'your code', and the colony went dark." Bitterness laced Krysta's words.

"I am afraid, miss, that is accurate."

"And my men?" Despite the heavy despair in the air, the captain's voice remained steady.

Krysta stared at the CEO, her mouth grew arid. What was going to be the fate of Grim? When Yusef didn't answer fast enough, she urged him on, "Well?"

"Undetermined. There has been no word, and we hoped the colony would regain its connection before now. When it didn't, we reached out to you," Mr. Kumail replied, still calm but rigid.

"Dead men don't reach out," Bear bluntly put it. He pounded the table violently with his fist, and the others seated around nearly jumped. He jerked his head furiously over to their captain. "What was the name of those aliens that hit Enlightenment again? Abli?"

Masters held the palm of his hand against his forehead with irritation. "Don't go there, Jack. We don't-."

Krysta corrected the burly man beside her with a hollow voice, "The Achli. Those fuckers are back. We are marked, and we were stupid to even try again."

"Stop it. The both of you." The captain's voice drowned theirs out, and the room fell silent. His face turned beet red as his eyes angrily met theirs. "I will not sit here and listen to this nonsense. We don't know if these were aliens."

"That may not be entirely true." Mr. Kumail timidly disclosed from his seat. All eyes returned to him. "An unidentified species had already established a colony on the opposite side of the planet. They remained docile during our early development stages, and we had no reason to assume hostility."

Bear gave Krysta a side-long look full of worry. "*What* species, Mr. Kumail?"

"You didn't tell me the planet already had aliens on it when you offered the first contract," Masters pointed out. "What of my men?"

With rapidly increasing breaths, Krysta dug her nails into the faux leather of the chair until it created long scratches. The urgency of Grim's fate was at the tip of her tongue, but words escaped her. A demonic, invisible hand seemed to squeeze her throat, tightening its grip to silence her.

The lavishly suited gentleman held up his hand to calm the room. "I regret terribly for the lack of transparency, Mr. Masters. The board believed it was necessary to keep that information confidential to not panic our investors. I assure you that I have examined all documents pertaining to the planet and its inhabitants prior to moving forward with this ambitious project, and there is no reason for alarm by these details."

"Says the man who didn't go up there himself," Krysta's edgily spat. "You still haven't told us what these guys look like. Is it the Achli or not?"

Mr. Kumail fidgeted with his tablet again, then slid it across the table for all to see. "These are the scans from our satellites. As you can see, their colony is at a safe distance from Bakht."

Bear shook his head in astonishment at the reveal. "That's not a colony, Mr. Kumail. That's a goddamn city."

Krysta observed the different overhead still images of bipedal life forms walking around on the pristine white ped ways. The city's skyline was quite impressive, with structures that resembled twenty-story mega apartment complexes and various towering skyscrapers with designs unlike Earth. Compact vehicles traveled upon metal highways woven throughout the metropolis landscape, while others loomed in the air in between buildings. Krysta quickly snatched up the tablet and used her fingers to zoom in on the life-forms. "From what we know by the Enlightenment's final reports, the Achli had ivory colored skin and were slender. These guys are green, but it's hard to tell what their bodies look like from these angles. A different variety?"

Bear nodded as she slid the tablet over to him. "Yeah, I agree. Any direct communication with them? I mean, if you can get a handle on whatever language they speak."

The CEO replied, "They have not reached out and have ignored all our requests. As I said earlier, they appear to be passive, so we assumed they just wanted to be left alone."

"Not the Achli's M.O. that we know of."

"Any other scans on their body makeup? What was our first group up against?" Krysta redirected the conversation.

"Our software identified them closely with our class of Reptilia. They have similar body compositions with two sets of eyes. Our research team believes they chose the warmer side of the planet because they are cold-blooded, just like reptiles back here."

"Reptilia?" Masters blinked.

"Correct." Their guest continued. "Our raw data suggests that their population on the planet is around minimum three hundred. This is most likely not their home world."

"Okay, so maybe not the Achli, but three hundred fucking Reptilia." Scoffing, Bear rested his forehead in his hand. "Three hundred lizards and you guys thought it was okay to send one team of us to deal with them?"

"This is not good, Mr. Kumail." Krysta frowned at her colleague's response. "These guys are not reclusive since your scans picked them up near the colony's perimeter. They wanted to see what we would do. We can assume that they did not like the fact that we built on a planet that they've settled on. They found out we were barely armed and dealt with us." She closed her eyes, as if in pain. Was Grim truly dead? Her heart lurched in her chest as guilt bathed over her. They ended things on such bad terms. What if she didn't push him away that night? Would he still have considered taking the off-world contract?

The CEO of Dhank Trust argued against her words. "I beg to differ. We have processed all the legal paperwork for our investment. By law, we now own the land."

"Yeah?" Bear butted in. "Tell the lizards that. I'm sure your lawyers can work it out with *their* lawyers."

"So, what's your plan for getting my men back?" The captain went straight to the point. "And we're still getting paid. You violated the contract terms by hiding the Reptilia from us."

"With the colony offline, we do not know what we are up against." Mr. Kumail calmly leaned over the table to recollect his tablet. "Your men may be in trouble. We need a second Peacekeepers team for recourse. Bringing in world leaders would only delay any hope of a positive outcome."

Masters snapped up straight in his chair, glaring at the man. "Let me get this straight. You lie to me and hide the knowledge of hostiles in the area. Your colony gets wiped out and you expect me to just relinquish another team to you? This has to be a joke."

"We will compensate you for the second team. As before, it will take seven months for the journey out there in cryo stasis, then six months to assess the situation to provide stability or evacuation."

"No," Masters flatly rejected the new offer and rose from his chair. "We are finished here."

"I'll go, sir," Krysta blurted out her words before she could stop herself. She held her breath tight in her chest. What was she saying? What was she thinking? Every portion of her prefrontal cortex urged her to stop.

"Wolf." Bear gently put his hand on her shoulder. "You don't need this shit. Look, if anyone is going to get the others back, it will be me to lead."

"Bear, I got this." She pressed her teeth together tightly. "I won't sit here and let our friends be out there alone. I can deal with the aliens."

"Quiet, the two of you," Masters barked at them. "Didn't you hear me? I'm not sending another team."

"You want more compensation, Captain?" Bear countered. "Take my pay if you have to. I'll do this gig for free. The Peacekeepers are all in this together."

"Same here." Krysta concurred. Her eyes remained glued to Bear as she silently pleaded with him. She had to do this. Break up or not, Grim was her friend, and she wasn't about to let the aliens wipe him out, just like her father. Not again.

Mr. Kumail politely bowed his head at both of them. "You humble me with your devotion to your comrades." His dark eyes panned over to their captain. "I have inquiries already out to other companies in the same field to go soon after you. We want Bakht to thrive for humanity at all costs."

The captain sighed hard, and his aged eyes moved upon the two of his group in the room. "You two okay with this? Wolf? You sure you can deal with it? Things may not be good news when you get up there. I don't need you to go into shell shock."

"She can handle it, sir. I'll be there," Bear butted in.

"Six months upon arrival, Mr. Kumail, then that's it," Masters gave in.

Krysta released a pocket of air from her mouth. *Grim, you better be alive up there.*

Chapter 5

"Krysta, you want to hit the mess hall?" Bear tossed out as the pair exited the meeting.

She paused outside. "Sure, why not? I skipped ration packs this afternoon, and I'm starving." She took note of the blackness that ate at the sky. It was night fall. The perimeter lights illuminated their path and surroundings.

"I'm surprised you agreed to go. You sure you're good, kid?"

At hearing the label, she frowned. "You know I hate it when you call me kid, Jack. If something happened to Grim out there, then I want to deal with it."

"If something happened to Grim out there, then it's on Dhank Trust, Wolf. Don't take the fall with that one." A gruff mutter escaped his lips as he walked beside her. "Just like Chretien Incorporated, they cut corners and played loose with those poor bastards up there." He entered the mess hall first with Krysta following him in. The doorway opened to a large room littered with bench tables where the mercenaries sat with their trays, while serving AI bots delivered the food or cleaned away empty plates. Arriving at the bench first, Jack sat down, Krysta taking the seat opposite. Right after they sat down, a bot with one large wheel and plate tray on top approached them. Bear held up two fingers. "Meal Ration Two and none of that dehydrated crap." The bot chirped and scurried off to the task. A mischievous smirk spread across his face. "I feel like drinking after that meeting, Krysta."

"Ask the server for a beer?" she said impishly with a shrug.

He shook his head. "What if I told you I smuggled some of that Brazilian ale in on the base? Arm match right here and if you win, I'll hook you up." He winked playfully.

"Don't mess with me, Jack. You know that stuff is good. You really have some stashed?"

"Do you think your old mentor would lie?" He produced a wide, seemingly innocent grin.

"And what if *you* win?"

"If I win…" He rubbed his thick red and speckled gray beard in thought. "Then, when we get out there in the lizard utopia, I am in charge, and you do exactly what *I* say." Jack laughed at his bet. "That shit eats you up the most. Doesn't it? Taking orders from me."

Krysta scowled teasingly at his suggestion. "Well then, I better not lose."

Bear busted out laughing. "That's the spirit, Wolf." He then flagged everyone's attention around. "Move aside. I'm going to show up Wolf here—again." The mess hall erupted into cheers for the proclaimed match. The gathering mercs moved from their seats and circled around the table.

Krysta propped up her right elbow on the table. "Steady now, Peacekeepers. This may get ugly when Papa Bear loses his crown." A few jeered her remark, while others took to Bear's side to defend the renowned earlier winner.

The older man placed his opposing arm on the table in front of hers and smirked. His fingertips lined up and then locked into place with her own. "Get ready to be kissing my boots, Wolf."

"Ha." She tightened her grip around his larger hand. "Your hands are smoother than usual there, Jack. You gettin' hand massages off base?" Her comment made the nearby crowd erupt in laughter. A few whistled to egg him on more.

He rolled his eyes. "At your signal, Wolf. Unless you just want to bore me to death."

She seized the moment and pressed hard against his hand, hoping to catch him off guard to finish this fast. The man didn't flinch and easily braced to keep their hands in the center; not even moving a millimeter. She gritted her teeth as his hand pressed against hers and immediately, both their arms shifted in her direction.

Without cracking a bead of sweat, his eyes stared into hers knowingly as he kept moving the needle. "Tell me something, Wolf. What made you really volunteer to go? I know it wasn't to please me."

"You said it yourself. We don't leave our friends behind like that."

"Bullshit. Be straight up with me."

Krysta froze as flashes of her father screaming in agony streamed into her mind, snatching her attention. She felt her elbow slipping as he overtook her arm. Angry that he stirred up cold memories, she gritted her teeth and pressed back against his grip. "Stop it, Jack."

"Good. I got in your head, and you are losing. Get ready for Boot orders on that planet, Wolf. If you think camp was hard with those sissy marines, wait till you see what I have in store for you."

"Fuck off." A snarl escaped her lips, though her teeth remained clenched. "You remember what A.R.M. Y stands for, right? 'Ain't Ready to be a Marine Yet.'" She eased her arm in deception, allowing him to take her own lower to see if his guard would drop. The look of triumph in his eyes and the slackened grip meant that he succumbed to the bait. She just had to wait a few more seconds to snare the trap. The mercs eagerly watched and cheered louder for the expected winner to be Bear. Krysta narrowed her eyes in determination and then pressed as hard as she could against his arm, surprising him. With a giant swoop, she slammed his arm down, leaving the echo of a satisfying smack on the table. Bear's bottom lip dropped in disbelief and the group of mercs nearby cried out at the deception.

"Wolf! Wolf! Wolf" They chanted, and a few gave playful cele-bratory slaps on her back.

Bear stared at her in disbelief, then burst out laughing. "It worked." He leaned over and tapped the center of her forehead with his fingertip. "Don't let that get the best of you. Use it to strengthen your resolve like you just displayed. I believe in you, Lone Wolf."

Chapter 6

Krysta strummed her fingers along the tiny desk that she was sitting in front while she waited for the technician to see her. On her desk she noted a large terminal screen that had Dhank Trust's logo with a sign-in prompt. "Let's just get this over with." She scowled and crossed her arms across her chest.

"Not causing problems here, are you?" Bear teasingly walked up to her. "It's been three days since that Kumail guy talked to us. Why the hell have they not shot us up there yet?" He whistled at the large bright white room they were in. "Fancy."

"Each passing hour makes the chance of the others up there being alive slimmer." Krysta couldn't take her eyes off the cryo capsule that was on the floor one meter in front of her. Its length and width strangely reminded her of a coffin, and a shudder went down her spine. "I've had three long days to prep my mind for this one, Jack," she gulped hard. "Still scares the living shit out of me just looking at this thing." She watched the Dhank Trust technician pacing around the perimeter of the capsule with a tablet in her hand.

"What's the big deal?" Bear plopped down on a chair at the next station over. "Those years in the frigid hell of the Manitoba wilderness are all the prep you need." He shrugged at her uneasiness. "Think of it this way: at least you will get some shuteye."

Krysta scrunched up her face at his dismissal. Her eyes remained on the obstacle in front of her. "What about our gear, Jack? Our weapons? Are you okay with someone else holding onto it?"

"Ease up, Krysta. I bet Grim didn't do all the bitchin' and moanin' like you are when he went under first."

"Miss?" The technician called out in a soft, polite voice. "We are ready. Let's get you in the pod."

Krysta cringed at the sound and a shudder escaped her lips. She forced herself up from the chair; her legs felt weighed down. "Here goes nothing."

"You got this, Krysta. I'll be right behind ya. See you on the other side," her friend cheered her on from his chair.

Timidly approaching the capsule, Krysta's heart pounded inside her chest and her eyes locked on the cryo capsule while the technician moved behind her. "Miss Evreux, give me a minute and I'll activate the privacy shutters. Disrobe completely before entering the capsule."

As the floor shutters ascended, creating a temporary enclosure, Krysta waited for Jack to make a joke, but the only sounds were her breathing and the busy technician concluding the final preparations. Inhaling slowly through her mouth, Krysta removed her clothes and slowly stepped into the capsule. She winced as her bare skin touched the cool metal. "They couldn't keep it warm for a little?"

"Relax. You are in excellent hands during your journey to al-Sufi C."

The feeling of the freezing metal outlining her body didn't sit right with Krysta and she wiggled her hips a bit to make an adjustment. "I'm sure," she murmured under her breath.

"Sweet dreams, Ms. Evreux," the tech smiled down at her warmly again and then the capsule door slid shut, creating complete darkness all around Krysta.

A faint hum generated at the back of Wolf's skull and she heard a series of chimes and beeps coming from within the pod. A rapidly intensifying chill crawled up her spine, making her shiver. *I can't do this! I can't do this!* Fatigue smashed into her and her eyelids felt extremely heavy. She forced them open, but no sooner than she did, they dropped back down into place. The void snatched her subconscious, and she drifted off.

Kaleidoscopic memories poured into her dreams with no logic or connection to one another. Her mind floated like a dandelion seed in the wind from dream to dream; a passerby drifting between each event, unable to stop. Then an unfamiliar gentle masculine voice called to her from the far depth of her consciousness, "Krysta Evreux, it's time to wake up."

A bright white light burst through the void and her eyes popped open. Startled, she reached out with her right hand instinctively and patted around the bed for her weapon. "What the hell? Where am I?"

"Easy." A warm, gentle hand touched her arm. "Disorientation is a common side effect to cryo sleep. It will pass."

Her vision acuity adjusted, and she glimpsed down to notice that she wore a typical medical examination gown. Wireless electrodes protruded from her arms, legs, temples, and upper torso. Her mouth tasted gritty like sand in the desert. "Cryo sleep? You mean to say, I'm at Bakht? Already?" Her brown eyes flickered back up to the older gentleman sitting next to her bed in a sky-blue medic uniform.

"It's been seven months," he gently explained before patting her arm. "That's one advantage with cryo technology. It makes the time pass so fast for travel." A soft, amused chuckle escaped his mouth. "Though I'm afraid you are still on the ship. They have not yet given us clearance to arrive at the colony."

"Why not?"

A familiar red bearded face sidestepped around the medical staff. It was Bear dressed in full tactical gear. A grave sheen was in his eyes. "Wolf, the colony is on lockdown. That's why. Suit up, Peacekeeper. Grim's team shot up a distress signal as soon as the ship was within orbital range. There is a report of more casualties and hostiles in the area. One fine wake up call."

Chapter 7

Krysta watched the sleek shuttle craft lift off after she and the rest of the Peacekeepers were ground side. Workers offloaded their supply crates nearby. "They are not sticking around?"

Bear shook his head before he slipped on his helmet. "The ship's only a runner. They're bogeying out to Earth for the next shipment supply. It's not large enough for a wide-scale evacuation."

Krysta's eyes settled on the colony that lay ahead. Blaring alarms punctuated the darkness that fell over the area. The outlines of buildings blended in with the fast approaching night, making it difficult for her to see. She slipped on her helmet and allowed the interface to scan for any potential threats in the area. She checked her rifle's ammo count in the upper right of the screen. A distant bone-chilling howl pierced the air. It was unlike anything she heard before on Earth. "Bear, what the hell was that?"

"Not good, *and* we are out here in the open. Let's move to the colony and connect with Grim. Keep comms open. Single file, everyone." Bear seized the lead with his assault rifle clutched to his chest.

Krysta fell in line with him. Her heart rate rose with each step in the dark colony. There was no sign of life anywhere—no voices. She activated the commlink in her helmet. "Grim, this is Lone Wolf. We are in the vicinity. Do you read?"

Only silence responded.

"Grim, this is Bear," Wolf's mentor picked up next. "If you can hear me, activate your tracking beacon. We will find you."

There was a brief few seconds of unease until a blip appeared on Krysta's helmet display. "He pinged." An immense weight lifted off her chest.

"Southwest inside the colony. Stay tight, everyone. Comms are open, but he may not speak." Bear paused right outside the entryway. "What the heck?" Moving closer, he reached out to touch something.

Krysta noticed what he was looking at. Three perfect parallel lines, deep and rugged, cut straight down the metal as if it were butter. A chilling howl echoed nearby, intensifying the already frightening discovery. "Claw marks, sir?"

Bear's helmeted head swiveled in each direction after the howl dissolved in the air. "Whatever it is, it's moving in. Let's get inside." He turned to one of his men in the back of the group. "Specs, you and Relic stay here. Work to get this gate closed. Something is out there, and it may return for us. The rest of you follow me."

Just a few footsteps closer and a scream of agony followed by tears of flesh erupted in the same direction as Grim's beacon. Feral snarls echoed through the darkness. Then a shattering of gunfire. Krysta's mouth gaped open before she ducked and charged ahead. "Move it!"

"Wolf!" She heard Bear's boots pounding in the dirt behind her as he called out, "I said stay together!"

"That may be Grim, Bear! We need to pick up the pace!" Krysta rushed onwards. Her eyes picked up on an elegant dome structure ahead and the blip inside her helmet became larger with each step. "He's in there." She bolted inside first, followed by Bear and the rest of the group. The area opened into a large room that contained sitting areas and terminal stations, then it narrowed to a corridor. Her eyes fell upon two bodies on the ground. Upon closer inspection, she saw one was missing limbs which were strewn a meter away, and the other had a severely mangled face. "Colonists." She recognized the uniform they had been wearing.

"What the hell happened to them?" Bear kneeled next to one corpse.

The distinct sounds of clawing and heavy paws followed a sudden burst of snarls from the hallway. Red eyes glowed ahead. "Hostiles!" Krysta alerted the others. Bear sprang to her side.

A black-furred dog-like beast leaped in front of them before targeting Bear. Krysta squeezed the trigger on her rifle, tearing the mutt apart with her rounds while the rest of the mercs fired away. The lone threat was no match, and it whimpered piercingly from the multiple direct hits before it collapsed to the floor with a thud. She heard a break in Bear's breath and the man kicked the animal hard before he fired one more shot into its corpse. "What the hell is that thing?" his voice trembled.

The larger man's fright ignited panic within Krysta. If he was terrified, then something was wrong. She slowly stepped toward the animal and glanced over its body. "No idea, Papa Bear." She noticed short brown hair strands covering its body and guessed that it was double the size of a typical coyote back on Earth. "Some type of wild dog? A fox or wolf?"

"That's no damn wolf."

From down the hall, a familiar voice called out, "Peacekeepers!"

Krysta lifted her head and watched Grim limp into view. His armor had seen better days by the assortment of scratches and chips. Dry blood caked the right of his face. Two more mercenaries fell in line behind him, whose armor appeared just as bad as his. "Grim!" Krysta flung off her helmet and rushed over. She wrapped her arms around his neck. Tears seeped into her eyes. "I thought you were dead." She could still smell his familiar aftershave coming off his skin.

"Nah," he chuckled and lightly pecked the top of her head. "I wouldn't let those bastards take me down that easily."

"That was the last one?" Bear called out.

"So far. There's another pack moving in. The smaller ones ambushed us."

"Smaller ones?" Bear tapped his ear communicator. "Specs, what's the ETA on the gate?"

"*Two minutes. Just re-syncing to start it up.*" Krysta heard Spec's voice come back through.

"Make it one. There are wolves out there. Keep your wits about you." Bear urged, and he turned back to Grim. "Where are the colonists?"

Grim shuddered as he pulled away from Krysta. "Most of them are in the atrium. We barricaded the place with what we could find after the first attack. There's a few others back here with me that acted as a security skeletal crew."

"Skeletal crew?" Krysta listened in closely.

Grim pointed to the two next to him. "This is all I have left after the first attack."

"Two?" Bear's jaw dropped. "Intel showed the captain released a team of ten. We lost eight?" Grim nodded solemnly. Bear patted him on the shoulder. "I'm sorry, Grim."

"How many colonists?" Krysta's mind flurried with questions.

Grim scratched the side of his head. "We started off with seventy-five, but now we are at sixty. Lost ten from the first attack and five a few days before you showed up." He glanced nervously at his group, then back. "There's more to this than wild beasts. Someone orchestrated it. The complex thought process definitely isn't derived from an animal."

Bear held up his hand. "Hold that thought." He then tapped his comm piece. "ETA, boys?"

"*Just got the gate locked in place,*" Specs' voice crackled through Krysta's earpiece.

"Good. Hold it tight and alert me if we have hostiles." Bear re-diverted his attention back to the team. "Which is it, Grim?

Intelligent dogs, or are you saying that someone attacked the colony intentionally with them?"

Grim's lips parted open, but no words came out right away. "I don't know, man. It's not making any sense."

"Neither are you. Quit with the damn riddles."

"A few months after we first arrived, everything was going well. No sign of any Reptilia interference. Though, we quickly found out that Dhank Trust didn't divulge all the facts to us."

"How so?"

"Drones picked up a reptilian base near this place."

"A base?" Krysta sighed. "Wonderful."

Grim continued, "Then one night, a scout from my group swore they saw movement in proximity to our boundaries. We placed the colony on lockdown to be on the safe side, and I went along with two others to check it out. There was no trace of our guest, and all alarms were still active. Nothing breached."

Krysta stroked her chin. "False alarm?"

Grim moved his eyes over to her. She could see the disturbance inside of them. "That's what I thought, but that wasn't the only time. A few nights after that, one colonist swore the same thing. Nothing came out of it. To ease the tension, we mockingly called it our 'ghost.' Soon after that, our first attack came. It caught us completely off guard."

"That's when the colony went dark and Mr. Kumail called the captain," Krysta explained to Bear. Inside her mind, she was fitting the puzzle's pieces together to create the timeline. A pit formed in her stomach. There was more to the story than the CEO of Dhank Trust let on.

"Was the attack planned, Grim?" Bear repeated, recalling his teammate's words. "How do wolves just take a colony off the grid like that?"

"I know it sounds crazy but hear me out." Grim held up his hands. Krysta noticed the surety that had once resonated within him was completely absent. His demeanor mirrored that of a shell-shocked veteran. "The pack hit us right at sunset. There were six of them, two large black ones and four smaller brown ones. They hit a few night crew workers just outside the gate, leaving nothing of the colonists' bodies. Then they breached the gate before we knew what was happening. I yelled for a lockdown, but it was too late. It was a massacre." The man paused as he exhaled. She didn't recognize him.

"Keep it together," Bear reminded him. "Tell us about the grid."

Grim's trembling eyes met his and then Krysta. "The wolves then broke into two groups. One stayed back to deal with us while another diverted to the far back of the colony. It was as if they knew where to go. We took down the three after some heavy fire, but before we could hunt out the others, the damage was done and they fled."

"How would they know where to go?" Krysta pressed at the space between her nose and eyebrows in frustration. "This doesn't make any damn sense, Jack."

Grim shrugged. "The ping we had a few nights before may hold the clue, but hell if I know what it is."

Bear raised an eyebrow at Krysta, then looked back at their colleague. "Ping? What ping?"

"Bear, this is Specs!" The earpiece chimed again inside Krysta's ear. The deafening sound of gunfire made her cringe from the torture to her eardrum. *"Those canines are back! They are charging into the gate!"*

Ahead of the others, Krysta sprinted toward the two remaining Peacekeepers at the colony's entrance. Just as she entered the main courtyard, a brown blur flashed into view. One of the feral beasts climbed over the wall. It pounced down to the ground next to the two mercs, as they opened fire on it rapidly.

Krysta skidded to a halt when she was close enough to take aim and squeezed the trigger. The beast whimpered loudly before it collapsed. Specs tossed her a thumbs up for the assist. She approached again, but this time Bear and Grim were with her. Seconds later, a larger mutt leaped over the wall and landed in front of them. The midnight-colored fur creature's crimson eyes fell upon Krysta. She noted it was significantly larger than the previous brown one. Its height was nearly one and a half meters tall, and its legs were wider than a human. If she had to guess, the creature weighed well over one hundred kilograms with its muscular mass. Its deadly jaws opened wider as the wolf salivated. A vicious snarl rose from its mouth and then, in a flash, it turned onto Specs. "No, you don't!" Krysta squeezed the trigger on her rifle along with the others, but the direct hits did not deter it.

Within seconds, the wolf lunged and knocked Specs onto his back. Then, with its powerful jaws, it latched onto the man's torso, rocking him from side to side while its razor-sharp teeth pierced into his armor. The man wailed in agony. Krysta watched in horror. "Specs!" She continued to pummel the beast, pressing her finger firmly against the trigger. The wolf slumped over, with Specs' body still in its jaws. Dark red blood mixed with the man's brighter shade streamed along the ground.

There was a stillness in the air outside the gate. "Specs! Shit!" Bear raced toward their comrade, pumping a few more rounds into the dead beast. Krysta kept her gun poised for cover while she looked on. Bear pried open the red stained jaws of the beast while Grim gingerly removed Specs' impaled body.

"Holy shit," Grim quickly released the body once it was free. Their comrade's entrails dragged along the nearly severed torso. Grim vomited right where he stood.

Krysta fought back the tears in her eyes and angrily clenched her teeth. "Who the hell is releasing those things on us? It has to be the Reptilia from that base!"

Wiping his mouth clean, Grim stared at the two. His chest rose quickly as his eyes jumbled over the bloody landscape. "I should have never come. You guys should have stayed back on Earth. Why the heck did you take the job?" He hysterically cried out, "Those reptiles out there are hunting us. These beasts attacked soon after our ghost appeared."

"I don't believe in ghosts." Krysta met Bear's eyes. "Instead, I think it's time we hunt some reptiles. What do you say, Papa Bear?"

"Right there with you, Lone Wolf. Grim, show us where you first encountered your ghost. The rest of you stay here with the colonists. Keep it locked down. These bastards can climb walls, so don't let your guard down for a second."

As Bear explained the next plan of action, Krysta's eyes drifted over to the horizon outside the gate, and she breathed hard through her nose. "Jack, belay that order. We have little visual right now with it being dark and there may be more of those hounds out there. I say we hunker down here. We hunt in the morning."

Bear paused to consider her recommendation. "Good idea, Wolf. Let's find a place that keeps casualties to the minimal and defensible. Grim, come with me. Krysta, secure the colonists. I just finished a seven-month nap so I'm wide awake. We'll move out at first light."

Chapter 8

Krysta swatted a tiny insect that fluttered in front of her face as Bear and Grim trudged alongside her, through the grass that early morning in their black and gray full body armor. The lavender sunrise created a deceptively peaceful visual of their surroundings, depicting a tropical paradise with crystal blue waters to their right and tropical plants all around. The sunlight allowed her to see the colony's exquisite design. It mirrored an expensive Polynesian resort with large windowpane curved living pods and a few smaller buildings off to the left that housed the colony's administrative offices. In the middle was the atrium that resembled a rotunda building. Tranquil artificial waterfalls trickled down posts just outside the atrium's entranceway. Deep down inside, she knew the safety and calmness of the colony was a farce compared to the horrors that stalked them at night. A chill crept down her spine like a spider descending a wall. Her eyes anxiously skimmed about. "Is it me, or do I feel like I'm being watched?"

"I'm getting that too." Bear sounded off first beside her from his helmet. "I've seen these movies, and they always kill the last person first."

Krysta quickened pace to put her ahead, next to Grim. "Well, sucks to be you then, Jack."

Grim held up his fist to signal them. "This is the spot."

Krysta gazed around. "Are you sure? How do you know? This entire place looks the same. Did anyone toss out breadcrumbs?"

Her former lover pointed to a mark on the tree in front of him. "That's the notch I etched in with my knife. I've been here longer than both of you."

Bear slapped Krysta playfully on the back as he walked ahead. "Genius move, Grim. Krysta, you didn't see the cut in the tree? I did."

She rolled her eyes at his jab. "Sure, you did, Papa Bear. Did you get your spectacles out to see it?" Krysta crouched down and brushed away some of the foliage to see the ground more clearly. "It's hard to determine if our mystery guest was even here." A garble of birds to her right grabbed her attention, and she slowly rose back into a standing position. "Guys."

Bear slowly cocked his rifle. "Is it the direction of their base?" He turned briefly to Grim, then back toward the disturbed birds.

Grim pulled up a holo map on his wrist gauntlet. "Yeah, southwest from this point. Fourteen kilometers roughly."

"A very short ride on a hover skid or a terrain vehicle," Krysta tightened the grip on her rifle. "We are not alone out here." Her eyes passed over to Bear. "How do you want to play this out, Bear? Two-man approach?"

"Yeah. You and Grim move ahead, and I'll be our seeker. I'm not here to play games with a fucking lizard." Bear slowly stepped backwards until the flora hid him.

Krysta exchanged a glance at Grim and moved forward towards the direction of the birds. Tiptoeing across the dirt floor, her heart pounded in her chest. Grim was at her side, his helmet darting left to right. When they were only a few meters away, she halted and aimed her scope in the thick foliage ahead. "Identify yourself now," she called out to the shadows. "No more hide-and-seek. Friend or foe?" There was no sign of Bear nearby, and she hoped he was close. The trees only answered in silence.

In a hushed tone, Grim informed her, "They're watching us. Could be another setup. I don't like this, Wolf."

Gulping, Krysta spoke out again, "We are armed. Identify now or we will treat you as a hostile."

Ten seconds later, a voice called out to them from the hiding spot, but its words were not audible and sounded more like a series of clicks and growls. Krysta pressed two fingers to her earpiece. "Dammit. He didn't talk long enough for the AI to translate."

"At least you have one talking. Try it again," Grim encouraged. His rigid demeanor showed her that the man was on pins and needles. He had been through hell and back before their arrival.

"Please, step forward and we can talk." This time, there was no reply. Krysta called out to the voice again, "Come forward and show yourself."

Seconds later, a bipedal being emerged out of the shadows. It sported black light-weight, body armor that shaped to its form. A color-matching helmet with a single horizontal thin crimson visor hid its face, and its right upper arm displayed a white upside-down triangle. It stood about two meters tall, and Wolf picked up that it only had four fingers bilaterally. Silently, their disguised guest stood. Krysta instantly noted two pistols attached to both sides of its hips. "Grim, it's armed."

Grim kept his arm poised with his pistol drawn on the figure. "So am I." The entire area grew still as the standoff ensued. It had to understand her by stepping out upon request, but would it speak again so she could activate their translator? The one-sided conversation made even a single misunderstanding extremely dangerous.

Moments later, the creature repeated its series of clicks and growls. A chime beeped in her ear to notify of the translator's activation. A shape suddenly burst from the dense foliage. All Krysta first saw was a black blur. It was Bear! The brawny man lunged at their spy, but the reptile was quick. It side-stepped to avoid the tackle, then did a low sweep with its boot, tripping Bear to the ground. Grim moved in next and swung with his right arm. The reptile blocked the hook with his opposite forearm, before yanking Grim's extended arm. With a hard twist, it flipped Grim onto his back.

"My turn." Gritting her teeth, Krysta threw a right punch, but the reptile jutted its forearm up to block the hit. She recoiled her hand and delivered a left front kick to its exposed torso sending it stumbling back from the sheer force. She kept her guard up and waited for him to make his next move. Out of the corner of her eye, she saw Bear and Grim bolt to their feet. "Three on one, pal. You want to keep talking, or shall we continue this?"

Instead of pursuing another attack, the Reptilia crouched, then sprinted into the plants.

"After him!" Bear barked.

Her mentor didn't have to tell her twice. Krysta pounded the dirt with her boots as she followed the scout through the thick tropical foliage, breaking away branches with her body. Eventually, they reached a small clearing surrounded by more trees. Krysta's eyes instantly fell to the dirt floor to look for any type of tracks that they could follow. The scans inside her helmet were not picking up any-thing. Bear groaned behind her. "Where the hell did that thing go?"

"Maybe they have some type of cloaking technology?" Grim suggested. "It would explain the stealth of their scouts."

"Scouts don't talk," Krysta stated matter-of-factly in her crouched position. Her eyes fell upon dents in the dirt to their left. She ran her gloved fingertips near the impressions. "We have tracks. This way." She jogged toward the tracks, busting through another clump of undergrowth. After she cleared the area, she saw the scout sitting on what looked like a wheel-less motorcycle. The cycle itself hovered less than a meter from the ground. The Reptilia's helmeted face stared at her for several seconds before it reacted. As it turned to take off, Krysta put all her energy into her legs and leaped forward. Her body slammed into it, knocking both to the ground off the getaway vehicle. She heard it groan, then hiss as they rolled before Krysta managed to wrestle her way on top. Krysta pressed her weight to keep it pinned and glared into its visor. "That is far enough, pal."

The reptilian spat shortly back at her in its language, and she heard the chime beep into her ear from the translator program. Then, a knee struck her abdomen, causing intense pain. It then threw her off it and she rolled away to put more distance between them. Just as she scrambled to her knees, she caught it striking out at her with a fist, but she blocked it with her left forearm. Twisting back to her feet, she narrowly avoided a kick to her face, and then seized the exposed area to maneuver a heavy uppercut to its face with her right hand. The scout stumbled a few steps back from the hit. It then jerked its helmet off, revealing its identity.

Krysta's eyes widened at the close-up appearance. The reptilian being stared crossly at her with its four yellow eyes. Each eye consisting of two diagonally parallel amber irises with black sclera. Though it was reptilian, it appeared very… male.

His body looked almost humanoid but with distinct differences. His nose was more predominant than a human's and pointed downwards. His bony, broad cranium shaped more like a fringe towards the back. The reptile's skin was scaly and shiny, like a snakeskin, a mossy color with a few patches of black. He spoke while baring its sharp fanged teeth.

The AI chirped again, and it translated its words, *"Arlandr, state your business on this planet. Are you one of the Children of Sani?"*

The questions stumped Wolf, and she shrugged while maintaining her guard. "Listen. I'm not really following you. What is an Ar-land-er? Who are the Children of Sani?"

As the reptile reached for his sidearm, a gunshot rang out, causing the dirt near his boots to explode before he could draw his weapon. Both sets of the scout's eyes widened at the near hit and Krysta followed his gaze to see Bear and Grim with weapons fixated upon him. She turned to her friends. "Hold up. I got him talking again."

The Reptilia sped back to its cycle. As fluid as water, he gracefully flipped onto the bike. "Shit, he's getting away!" Bear lunged after him, but the reptile quickly sped off, leaving a blast of dirt in his wake. Within seconds, he was out of sight and the sound of the cycle quickly disappeared.

"That guy moved like a damn ninja," Grim grumbled. He glanced over at Krysta. "You said he spoke? What did he say?"

"Nothing that made any sense. He called me an 'Ar-lan-der' and mentioned something about the Children of Sani." Krysta pushed her strands of hair back into place. "Jack, scouts are normally for recon. They normally don't engage. Would they send an officer instead?"

Jack shrugged. "Doubt it. That's a risky move."

"May I suggest we move back to the colony?" Grim fidgeted with his hands and glanced nervously around. "Every time one of those reptiles gets near us, the hounds attack. It's their M.O."

"I agree."

Lost in thought, Krysta's gaze followed the fleeing reptile. His words repeated in her mind over and over again. "At least we now have something to work with." She furrowed her brow. "I can't say I'm too thrilled that they can bypass our security measures. They have some fight in them."

"Some fight?" Grim griped through his helmet. "This guy almost broke my arm."

"He didn't fire his weapon at us," The oldest of the group pointed out. "Don't know what armaments they have." Bear turned to Grim. "When the hounds attacked the colony, did the reptiles join in?"

"Negative," Grim answered.

"Cowards."

Pulling her gaze away, Krysta tapped Bear on the shoulder as she walked past him. "Let's head back. I hate to say it, Peacekeepers, but this is an opponent unlike any we have ever faced before."

Chapter 9

The early following morning, cool air hit Krysta's face as she exited their designated sleeping quarters in Bakht. With her body armor in place, she hoisted her assault rifle over her shoulder and secured her pistol in its magnetic holster attached to her right hip. The sunrise bled to a swirl of tangerine and pink lemonade. The gentle breeze parted the hair strands on the right side of her head. "Dad, was this what it was like?" She whispered to the wind. She squatted down and placed her gloved hand against the sienna-colored grainy ground. Her other hand reached underneath her armor's collar and touched her dog tag chain, reassuringly.

"Always the first one awake." Grim approached from behind in similar gear. He yawned drowsily. "Shouldn't be out here by yourself. That thing could lurk out there."

Rising to her feet, she glanced in his direction. "And you always snooze, soldier." She flashed him a teasing smirk. "I kicked his ass last time."

"Did you?"

"He retreated, didn't he?"

Grim took to her side and the pair moved along to the colony's hangar. "Wolf, when I first arrived, my intention was to stay. Even if that meant leaving the Peacekeepers."

The revelation made Krysta look his way. "On a colony? In the middle of nowhere?"

A soft chuckle came from him. "Yeah, I found a spot near the shore that would be perfect. Of course, hanging around lizards is not ideal, but I just didn't want to return to Earth." He gently touched her arm and paused in his step. "I shouldn't have left like I did, Krysta. We left on bad terms, and so, I didn't want to see you anymore."

Krysta sighed. "Grim, the choices in your life shouldn't revolve around me. You know who I am. I just find it difficult to be in a relationship with anyone." Up ahead, she spotted Bear in place at their destination. His gaze raked over them. She motioned Grim to pick up their steps again. "No matter what, Xavier. I still give a damn about your life, and I would blame myself if you died."

"I beat you, Lone Wolf. That's a first." Bear's loud yawn greeted their approach.

"The only time, Papa Bear," she teased back before moving inside the garage to see two land rovers awaiting them. The rovers were roughly eight meters long, five meters wide, and four meters tall. She whistled in appreciation at their sleek design and walked up to one to pat it on the front hood. "Not too shabby."

Amused, Bear approached her. "Six-hundred-mile dual battery life. I checked the specs while you slept in, princess. Top speed one hundred kilometers per hour. Titanium plating all the way around. Those Reptilia won't mess with us."

"What's the agenda again today, boss man?" Grim inquired. "We hunt more scouts?"

"I wish," he murmured. "The colony director doesn't give two shits about what's out there. Dhank Trust wants the colony expansion to go forward as scheduled. Our objective today should be light: Escort civilians to the site of Phase Two for whatever they must do out there while the rest of their crew remains here to restore all functions to get everything online again. I can't say I'm too comfortable in the open with a reptile base parked near our asses. I'm leaving most of our group here to make sure those lizards don't get any ideas."

"Agreed." Krysta turned to her ex-lover. "Did you bring your sniper rifle, just in case?"

Grim happily patted the strap on his shoulder. "Black market special, as always. I never leave home without it."

Twenty minutes later, both rovers rumbled their way to the Phase Two site. Bear unexpectedly stopped the vehicle that he and Krysta were in, and she turned her head to him, "What's up, Bear?"

"*You saw that too, huh?*" Grim's voice popped through the radio from the other rover next to them.

Bear tapped the radar screen in front of him. "About time the paparazzi showed up."

Krysta clenched her jaw when she saw the blip on the radar at their starboard side. She rose from her seat. "Open the doors, Bear. I'll flush out the game."

He gently stopped her by placing a hand on her arm. "Negative. It appears to be a small vehicle. One manned? Maybe two? Figured some movement would spark their interest," Bear regarded the radar. "Now it's a staring contest to see who blinks first." He studied the equipment intently. "Aye, there," he said, deriding the screen. "What's your move, greenie?" A moment later, as if the unknown being heard them, the blip moved away. "Hah," Bear jested. "He blinked first. Too bad we're in these big things, or I would have raced after him."

"*Now what?*" Grim inquired over the link. "*I don't think it's a smart move to head on up to the site when we have eyes watching us. Could be an ambush.*"

The Peacekeepers' bearded leader turned in his seat to peer back at the group of civilians behind them seated in the cargo hold of the rover. "Your show. We have one lizard out there… maybe two. Right now, we outnumber them, with my team of six. They could come back with more soldiers or even release their wolves."

The man sitting closest to Bear and Wolf glanced back at his compatriots and then motioned with his hand. "Proceed. Dhank Trust wants the markers down today."

"Fair warning, if we have to fallback, I'm not carrying any of your asses with us." With a worried expression at Wolf, Bear complied with the request, turning back to tap his comm. "Grim, they want to finish this. Let's keep moving."

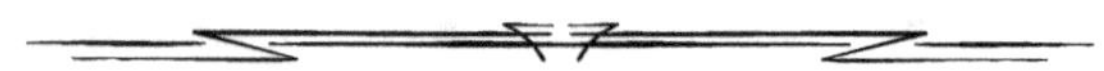

Ten minutes later, they arrived, with Krysta being the first to hop out of the rover with her helmet on. "We're here. Everybody out and I want a thirty-minute window for this only."

"Thirty minutes?" One colonist griped while he and the others filed out. "It will take us that long to just get all the equipment in place."

"Thought you guys were only placing markers to outline the perimeter?" With his helmet on, Grim watched them set to work.

"We also need soil samples for potential farm plants. Hydroponics won't sustain us forever."

Bear signaled a few members of his team to take various points to surround the area. Krysta moved over to him with her eyes skeptically watching the colonists set out their markers. "I wonder if Dhank Trust called ahead to the Reptilia to tell them of the expansion."

The muscular man huffed in his helmet, and crossed his arms. "Fucking doubt it."

"Watch our six. I'm heading up," she slowly replied, then motioned Grim with her head to follow. The two hiked up the small ridge that obscured their view ahead. Out on the horizon, about sixteen thousand meters from where they stood, she noticed several protruding rocky cliffs that prevented her from seeing beyond its horizon. The planet appeared darker and menacing there, and a chill crept up her spine. She pulled up geographical scans of the planet, downloaded onto their wrists' holo amplifiers. She held her arm out further for Grim to look at. "Ok, we are about nine klicks out. Your previous drones showed a Reptilia encampment roughly twenty-two klicks away." She pointed to a red flashing light on the holo that indicated the structures. "There are several buildings, none of which appear to be hangars. No aircraft was spotted. We need to get more eyes over there to see what we are up against."

"An army of reptiles, that's what," Grim mumbled through his helmet. He removed his sniper rifle and checked his scope out in their field of vision near the towering cliffs. He slowly shifted the barrel from left to right and down to up. When he raised the rifle, he froze. "Oh, shit."

"What is it?" She viewed him uneasily, and her eyes followed his rifle barrel pointed toward the upper part of the cliff. There was a visible black speck beside it. The object was too far out for the target assist inside her helmet to queue it up.

"It's a drone."

She clamped her teeth and instinctively seized her assault rifle. "Is it inbound?"

"I barely got it. Scope detection shows its velocity is fifty k-p-h."

"I knew that lizard earlier wouldn't just leave." Krysta's fingers tightened on the butt of her rifle. "We don't know if this thing has a package for us. Keep it in your sights, Grim." She tapped her comm piece in her helmet. "Bear, we have an inbound drone! Get back to the rovers now!"

Down below, she watched the distressed colonists panicking and dropping their instruments as Bear flagged them to the rovers. Out of impatience, she saw him grab a few workers by the arm who were lingering out to finish whatever task they had assigned to them for that day, obviously ignoring the Peacekeepers' order.

Grim turned his head away from the scope. "It's inbound. ETA: I would say three minutes. It is almost in range for me to get a clear shot."

"All civilians accounted for," Wolf informed him. "We scatter in two. Is that clear?" Her eyes moved from him towards the sky. "How am I not surprised this thing didn't get detected?" She checked her wrist apparatus. "Systems are functionally normally and no alerts from the colony."

"Got a closer visual." Grim's finger moved down to the trigger of his rifle and paused for the order. "No armaments detected by the naked eye. I can't say if this thing has anything hidden or if it's a kamikaze. Permission to take down?"

"ETA?"

"Two minutes."

Krysta debated on what order to give. If she assumed it was hostile and they shot it down, it would spark an intergalactic war that their group alone couldn't handle. Then again, if they were friendly, and she was wrong, it would cost them more casualties. The colony had already suffered a great deal. There was a strong possibility that the drone was gathering intel for some mass Reptilia army waiting nearby. "Lone Wolf?" Grim pressed urgently, his focus still on the scope.

"Dammit," she cursed under her breath. "Hold fire and scatter to the tree line! Draw them away from civilians!" She skirted down the knoll. Grim followed. Wolf tightly braced against a palm tree trunk and watched to her right to see her sniper acting in kind. She inhaled and waited as her eyes peered around the obstruction to see the drone as best as possible. Shiny metal reflected the sunlight as it soared across the sky above them. The target assist program in her helmet outlined the drone's perimeter while her display's right visual outlined trajectory coordinates for optimal hits. The object appeared to be around two meters long and one meter wide. It moved soundlessly like a cloud. Krysta remained frozen as it passed over and beyond the location of the two rovers. The drone made no change in its path toward the colony. Following the all clear, Grim moved back up the knoll again with his sniper rifle, but the airborne device swung wide to the right and disappeared into the horizon. Krysta went to his side and watched on. "It's going back home."

"There's a good chance they know we are here."

"I agree."

The dark visor on his helmet turned toward her. "Lone Wolf, these guys are not happy with us building on this planet. There's another attack coming soon. I can feel it."

"Can't disagree with you there," she sighed. "But I don't like being spied on and letting them have the advantage. We need to reconnect with Jack and return the gesture in kind by sending over our own drones. Let's see what *they* are hiding." Krysta stared at the horizon and mulled over what she knew about the planet and its inhabitants. "It doesn't make sense. This is not their land."

"What, Krysta?"

"The Reptilia's city is on the opposite side of the planet. Why leave this area so bare?" She tapped the activation button of her earpiece communicator. "Bear, this is Lone Wolf. Do you read?"

A few seconds later, Bear's brawny voice came over, replying, "*Present. I know what you are going to say. I'm calling drones to our location. Now those lizards are just pissing me off.*"

A bone-chilling howl erupted from the wooded area to their right. "Shit!" Krysta's adrenaline kicked in, and she charged down the hill with her rifle in place, blood pumping through her veins.

Grim followed suit. Seconds later, more howls, then vicious snarls. "Not good!"

"Get your bloody asses inside the rovers, now!" Bear yelled at a few of the colonists that straggled back out after the drone passed by. The snapping of twigs and the sound of multiple creatures charging closer made everyone panic. Some civilians raced into their designated rover while a few stayed behind to gather their gear.

Wolf dashed to the nearest person and jerked them hard away from their task. "Get the fuck in there!" She whirled to face her team. "Grim, cover the rear and get the scope!"

"Anthony is not in yet!" One of the frightened staff inside a rover yelled in protest.

Krysta's eyes darted to see a worker running toward them holding several containers. Just as she was about to tell him to lighten his load, a massive, black furred creature burst out from the woods and pounced on him. With lightning-fast speed, the wolf clamped its jaws around Anthony's neck, shaking its head violently. The jaws were so powerful that they severed the man's head entirely from his spine. Anthony's body quit jerking before he went motionless on the ground. Two brown wild beasts tore through the tree branches into the clearing. By their positioning, Krysta deduced that the black one was the alpha. aimed her rifle at its right exposed torso without hesitation, then pulled the trigger. The high-grade modified rounds bore deep into its flesh; the canine yelped in pain, then it released its prey. It made a sudden turn towards her, snapping its jaws before the charge.

She didn't flinch and fired again relentlessly. "Wolf!" Grim moved to her side and shot at the charging beast. The creature let out a faint whimper before it slid onto the ground, blood draining out from all of the bullet holes in its head and body. The impact was less than four meters from where the two stood. Krysta switched out her clip within seconds before spinning to address the other two mutts.

One of the smaller ones charged at Bear with the others. The mercs let out a barrage of bullets from their rifles pummeling its body, before the creature wailed sharply and collapsed onto the ground. The remaining hound skidded on its paws and changed its direction toward the tree line to break off the attack.

"Bear, we need to take it down before it comes back!" Krysta pursued the hostile creature.

"Wolf!" Grim shouted in alarm, "That's not a good idea!"

"I got her. Stay with the others!" Krysta heard Bear yell out.

Krysta pushed through the dense plants and vines, her legs pumping hard as she chased the canine. It halted unexpectedly ahead. She trained her weapon and fired a shot, aiming at one of its limbs. The round hit the creature's back leg, and the creature whimpered before it tumbled onto the ground. Within seconds, it picked itself back up to retreat. Krysta used its slowing pace to gain upon it quickly. She leaped over a downed tree and continued her advance. She overheard Bear entering the overgrowth from behind. The beast quit running and turned to face them. It bared its fangs viciously and barked threateningly. Its red eyes detected the two mercs eight meters before it.

Krysta gambled a daring second to glimpse her surroundings to make sure they were not brought into an ambush by more wolves like that one or the Reptilia. There were no signs of movement. In fact, the jungle was strangely silent. The creature locked its sights on Bear and charged in his direction. Both Peacekeepers fired their weapons in unison before it collapsed. A gush of blood seeped through its wounds. Krysta slowly crept toward it with her rifle pointed, should it have one last fight left. Moving to its backside and further away from its mouth, she kicked its body hard with her right boot. There was no response at all, and the body just fell back down, lifeless.

Bear shuddered in observation. "This entire planet is crawling with these things."

"Bakht has a science team here, and they are going to examine one." She flagged the way they came. "Let's go grab the alpha. I want to know how the hell the reptiles are controlling them. No more surprise attacks."

Chapter 10

"Hunter Carson, Colony Director of Bakht. I believe we met at orientation," a sandy blonde-haired man addressed Jack and Krysta in a private conference room of the main facility. The youthful director shook both their hands like an eager politician and motioned for them to be seated at the conference table across from him. "My apologies for being late, but I needed to contact Anthony's family before word got out about his death." A weary sigh escaped him as he reclined in a rose-colored chair. "It's never easy to deal with these types of conversations. The colony has lost so many as it is." Krysta found his lighthearted chuckle inappropriate for the sensitive situation. "I'm sure you guys dealt with that a lot in your line of work. Am I right? Rough, for sure."

Krysta glanced sideways at the merc beside her. She wondered just how competent this guy was for the job he was chosen for and if he was fresh out of some ivy-league college. Silent and arms folded, she wore a short-sleeved black athletic shirt, combat pants, and boots with her dog tags displayed above the collar. Bear wore similar attire. Taking another breath, Hunter looked at his tablet, then raised his eyes to them. "Do I have your report yet?"

Bear leaned in and said, "That's why she and I are here. We are giving you the report right now."

"Ah, yes," Carson returned to his tablet. "You brought one of the feral canines back?" He lifted an eyebrow at the duo. "I mean, the thing is dead, right? The last few incidents traumatized the colony, and nobody wants to see one of those things near us."

"It's dead," Krysta broke her silence. "I want your staff to study it to know what our team is up against. Somehow the lizards are controlling them." She returned to her previous pose; this time, her old friend in the room gave her a cautious stare. She knew his look was a warning not to cross the line.

"A pack of three ambushed us and your staff just after a drone flew over." Bear steered the conversation back to himself.

"Drone?" Carson blinked.

"We believe the drone originated from the nearby Reptilia base. We also had a blip en route to the site; one reptile was keeping tabs on us."

"Not to mention the scout we entangled with at the first sighting location," Krysta added in.

Carson looked up from his tablet. "Did the drone shoot at you?"

"Negative. The Reptilia have been spying on this place since day one. Your scans nor ours can detect these guys or their fancy hardware. We were completely blind to this one until one of my men spotted it." Krysta leaned over, in the same position as her friend. She knew where she wanted to go with this and had to sell it to Carson. The guy was clearly following the codebook that Dhank Trust gave him on day one, but she presumed he was too green to be completely brainwashed by the corporate mentality.

"What do you think they were watching us do?" The colony director's lips trembled.

"Everything from security rotations to worker shift changes," Bear freely murmured.

"They could have watched the entire construction of this facility." Carson's face grew pale.

The man before them was hooked and Krysta needed to reel him in. "They are picking us off one by one—a battle of attrition."

Carson jumped up from his chair, before roughly running a hand through his hair. He stared at them both in disbelief. "I mean, I know the military uses dogs for situations, but not so savagely. Are you sure?"

Bear held up his hand to soothe him. "Remember, this is *not* Earth, and these people are *not* human. Different laws and regulations govern them. If we don't act, they will continue to bleed us slowly."

"This colony cannot survive another direct attack. I'm low on staff as it is. What recommendations can you offer me before I report back to my superiors?"

Bear leaned back in his seat and exhaled loudly while he stroked his beard, deep in thought. "We know there's a base a few hundred kilometers away from us. Let's send a drone over there to collect recon."

"Two," Krysta piped in firmly. Her mentor grunted under his breath by the raise of the stakes but said nothing against it.

"Two?" Hunter gasped at her request, and she almost thought he would hyperventilate.

Wolf's eyes flashed over to Bear, and she silently pleaded for him to support her fully. There was an awkward pause of stillness before he broke his gaze. "Lone Wolf is right, sir. We need to show the Reptilia that we are not screwing around. If we give them any sign that we are weak, it may make things a lot worse." Krysta couldn't help but smile with relief at his agreement.

"Yes, but wouldn't the action be a sign of aggression?" The head of Bakht returned to the table, an edge of exhaustion to him.

"Damn right we're aggressive. Look at what they are doing to us." Krysta's fist pounded the metal table to emphasize her point.

Carson's solid mentality was completely shattered within those few minutes. "What are you telling me to do? I mean, this entire thing could backfire and prompt more attacks here," he stammered his words.

"A risk we will have to take. It's time to show them we have teeth," Krysta countered.

"Make it happen." Carson rose from his seat and gathered his tablet. "I better go follow up on the analysis of the canine that you brought in."

"We'll go with you," Bear stood to follow him out.

Krysta eagerly trailed behind them. In her mind, she saw the face of the reptile they encountered. His sharp yellow eyes glowered at her while his piercing fangs glistened. What did he mean by the Children of Sani?

An overpowering smell of a sanitizing solution mixed in with a sweet, cheesy odor hit Krysta's nostrils when she, Bear, and Mr. Carson entered the pathologist's examination room in the designated medical ward on the east side of the colony. She coughed before lifting her arm in an attempt to block the stench; Bear and Carson had almost the same reaction. The cold room held the dissected body of the black beast they'd brought in. Its open body cavity rested on a white sheet atop the metal table. The colony director gagged as they approached, "Oh my God." By his reaction, Krysta presumed Carson was not familiar with seeing corpses, but rather, he'd spent his entire life cooped up inside safe office walls. The physician waved at them to continue. Carson kept his mouth and nose blocked, then staggered back to the comfort of the hallway entrance.

A pleased grin spread across Bear's face as he looked at Krysta. "I guess the wee lass couldn't handle this." She cracked a sneer at his remark.

"Is he okay?" the doctor questioned them, while her dark eyes peered over their shoulders in the direction of the vacated director.

"Weak stomach," Wolf shrugged indifferently.

"I apologize for the odor. We use peracetic acid for sanitization, and the body has already begun rigor mortis." She gestured for them to follow as she slipped on a fresh pair of latex gloves. "The name is Dr. Ersoy," she introduced with a thick Turkish accent. "I'm Lead Pathologist. That is my assistant, Sanchez. You brought in quite a find for us. I'm not accustomed to necropsies."

"Give us the 411, doc. How much of a threat are these guys?" Jack leaned his hip against the medical table.

"First, an overview. I haven't dissected all its vital organs nor weighed them. Before I peel back some of the epidermis to go over the incisions, I will review a few findings. First, this animal is anatomically close to our wolf species on Earth, and I can go over that conclusion during its skeletal structure. Second, she's a female and weighs about one-hundred fifty-eight kilograms. Her age is inconclusive, and she has bred before; the milk sacs are dry. No sign of pregnancy at the time of her death." Her hands moved over the head of the beast, before she lifted it. The creature's lifeless eyes stared hauntingly back at them.

Dr. Ersoy continued, "As you can see, her skull size has a large brain capacity; this shows the beast is intelligent and could potentially solve complex problems." Her gloved fingers moved down to the oral cavity of the beast, and she pushed the upper lip to reveal sharp, deadly teeth. "Her muzzle and jaw belong to a wolf family." Ersoy gingerly placed the head back down and moved to the torso cavity. "One of the biggest contrasts between the two species is its fur composite. Wolves have thick fur to adapt to harsh, inhospitable environments. This species has a very thin layer of coarse fur, most likely to protect it from predators and tree limbs they may encounter. The thin layer prevents overheating, given the tropical habitat. The paws slightly differ as well." She lifted one leg. "The front paws have five toes, while the back has six. A different genetic makeup, and fascinating."

Krysta thought back to the doctor's earlier finding and interrupted her, "Doctor, you said she had cubs. How long ago do you estimate it?" She did not know if the two other wolves in the attack were her cubs.

"Hard to say for sure. A year? Without a comprehensive study on this new species, it's difficult to determine their breeding cycle and whether it mirrors the Earth wolves."

"Any control chips?" Bear cut straight to the chase.

The doctor's eyes widened in surprise at his question. "I'm sorry?"

"The Reptilia are controlling these freaks, and I need to know how."

The doctor shook her head. "My preliminary inspection of the body boasted no signs of neurological implants for control. Without a live subject, we cannot test brain wave patterns."

"Live subject?" Krysta scrunched her nose at the statement. "That's a pretty tall order."

"Another issue I must point out." Ersoy lifted a gloved fingertip. "When I examined the stomach cavity for food digestion, I found remnants of small prey, close to a rodent." She peeled back the layer of flesh with her forceps to reveal guts and organs. A putrid stench arose that caused tears to form in Krysta's eyes, and she coughed. Unfazed, the doctor continued with her analysis. "Their size makes them one of the more dominant species on this planet, but why hunt small game? I'm hesitant to state without a doubt that they hunted this colony for the main primary food source."

Bear faced Lone Wolf. "We will need to tell Carson to pause operations outside the colony's boundary until we get a handle on this."

A boasting smile spread across Krysta's lips. "We have killed three, including their alpha. I think these wolves now know not to deal with us."

"I didn't want to come out here just to hunt a pack of wolves."

"We need to hunt *someone else* first," she reminded him in a crisp tone.

Nodding, Bear turned back to the examiner. "Thanks for the intel. Please send us the results of the tests immediately after you get them in."

"It will take a couple more hours, but I will send it as soon as possible," Dr. Ersoy answered.

Bear signaled Krysta to follow him out to where Carson was waiting for them. The lack of color on the man's face told her he was still pale. Relief turned quickly into unease. "We need to head to the main security room and activate our drones. I recommend placing the colony on high alert until we have a handle on the situation," The red bearded merc walked on, not even giving the director a second to discuss the topic anymore. Krysta glanced back at the young man and trailed her mentor while Carson pursued.

"What did you guys learn in there? Is there a way to kill all those things?" The man struggled to keep up with their pace.

Bear and Krysta remained tight-lipped while they rushed through the medical wing of the colony's enclosure and back to the security facility's central control room. Bear moved over to one technician operating a terminal station. "I need two birds set to go." He used the holo touch interface to expand a large area map. "The computer is set for a four-hundred-kilometer radius." His eyes honed in on the site of the Reptilia base. He tapped the screen and then expanded it out. "That's our target. Speed: One hundred and twenty k-p-h. I want a sweep and then R-T-B."

"Affirmative." The officer touched his terminal screen to begin the order. "I got birds going out hot."

"Good. Keep visuals up. If we get pinged, I want to know about it."

Silent and with folded arms, Krysta stood next to Bear behind the technician's chair. Her eyes remained steadfast on the large wide monitor in front of them that displayed a split screen of the feeds from both drones. "Get cozy, Mr. Carson. This will be a long introduction."

"Wait! Wait!" The colony's leader jumped in front of them, panic etched on his face. "Shouldn't we discuss this more? Are we going to shoot at them? I wasn't aware that you had any intention of starting a war."

"Don't piss yourself," Bear dismissed his accusations. "The drones are weaponized should the need arise. The Peacekeepers received payment to protect this colony. I know the ramifications of firing first." He looked at Krysta. "We should probably hit these guys with the infrared scans. Just in case they scurry."

Krysta glanced his way. Papa Bear, these are reptiles. Wouldn't that make them cold-blooded?"

The bearded man huffed in irritation. "Damnit, Wolf. Don't school me." A chirp notification soon followed from the workstation in front of them. "What's going on?" His head snapped toward the sound.

"Weather system alert. There's a storm cell moving towards the Reptilia base," The technician explained from his seat.

Bear glanced nervously at Krysta. "How fortuitous for them. One lightning strike may end our drones. Please don't tell me these guys can control the weather."

"Doubtful. But think about it, the cloud cover may help by providing the element of surprise," Krysta argued. "Their radar may detect us, but they will lose visual with our cloud cover."

He grinned. "I like it."

Suddenly, a klaxon wailed like a banshee from the terminal. "Both drones are locked on," the technician shouted from his seat.

"This far out?" Krysta looked at Bear with a dreadful expression.

Carson stammered, "Now what?"

"They know we are armed," Wolf admitted. "They want us to make the first move."

Bear brashly tapped the tech's shoulder. "Continue the present course and no deviations. Let's play chicken with these lizards."

Chapter 11

Twenty more minutes dragged by as the group remained transfixed by the drones' live video footage. The feed shook back and forth as the drones sliced through the rough wind shear from the passing storm. Lightning created temporary whiteouts.

"Navigation is becoming disrupted by the storm's electrical charge. Taking over for manual guidance," the technician proclaimed from his seat.

"No intercepts yet." Krysta watched on eagerly.

"They know what we have packing," Bear's chuckle broke through the tension. "Or they lost us because of the storm."

Krysta sighed lightly, "If only it were *that* easy. I fear that we are in the Bronze Age compared to them."

"Target queuing up," the technician said when the terrain flattened to a more developed region. Structures came into view. Everyone squeezed together, crowding around the screen.

"They still have us locked on?" Bear inquired.

"Affirmative. They never let go."

"Slow up Drone Two, in case we must take evasive maneuvers."

"Good idea," Krysta had to admit to herself she would not have arrived at the same idea. It was good to have her mentor around on the planet with her.

The base came up into full view. It was smaller than she expected compared to standard military bases on Earth. There was no sign of any aircraft on the tarmac. Bear pointed to a break within the base's primary roadway. "Underground hangar doors?"

"Clever bastards," Wolf concurred. "Protect their craft from any bombardment or attack from within. A few armored transports of some type near the outer buildings." She stepped next to him and pointed to the visual. "Barracks?"

A scurry on the ground seized their attention. Fully armored figures dashed out of the barracks while a few came ground side by circular doors stationed nearby. "Zoom in," Wolf's mentor ordered the pilot.

The visual flashed over to the specified target. "Looks like the same armor that our spy wore the other day. Love the design of the assault rifles." Krysta focused tightly on the group of reptiles rushing out at the threat. "Maybe twenty of them?" Her eyes flickered over to the heavy artillery cannon. "That's a welcoming sight."

"Drone One to the cannon," Bear ordered the pilot. "Watch those guys with the second."

"They could see this as a threat. I don't like playing chicken with the cannon," Wolf cautioned him.

"Yes, I agree," Carson's voice wavered. "What if they fire at us?"

"Simple," Bear answered flatly. "We find out just how durable their armor is."

"We are still locked on, and the cannon is in position," the pilot's voice quivered with alarm. The Reptilia had their rifles pointed right in the drones' direction. The camera tossed side to side, and an alert chimed out again. "Wind is picking up velocity."

"Hold course and don't deviate," Bear pressed with his eyes glued to the screen. "These guys should know by now that we don't have a weapons lock." Despite the storm becoming more violent, the Reptilia remained in place.

"They know we are *armed*," Krysta interjected. Following the drone surveillance, many images filled the security room monitors. The enlarged images revealed soldiers branded with a single white stripe on their left arm, while two had an upside-down triangle. "Different rank markings and one just like our friend had the other night." She directed Bear's attention to the picture.

"Heh, can't be officers. They don't do recon. Can we cue up the audio?"

"Capturing audio in three.... two...one..." The technician steadied the drones after their flyover. A few faint, untranslated conversations came through the speakers, and a sterner one shouted soon after. Lone Wolf recognized the sounds to be very similar to the scout she encountered the night before. The sounds were mainly sharp clicks, with a few growls mixed in. The voices faded out when the drone's range drifted further away.

"Circle back and get as close to the base without flying directly overhead. I want to know which one is giving out the order," Bear directed their next move.

A second later, before the tech acknowledged the command, one display completely went white, before the feed shut off. "We lost a drone," the pilot confirmed. "A lightning bolt struck it."

"Keep going." Bear ignored the danger.

A few seconds later, the new feed was displayed. One of the two upside-down triangle insignia Reptilia produced a flat across-hand signal to the others. The troops didn't move or follow the drone with their rifles. "One of them," Krysta pointed out. "They are calling the shots. Our lizard was no mere scout there, Jack."

"Interesting. Looks like he ordered a hold fire," Bear considered out loud.

"Agreed."

"Rerun it with the translator." He kept his eyes glued to the screen.

"It will take a minute or two for the AI to interpret," the worker reminded them while his fingers swiped away at the screen.

Krysta's eyes widened at the live feed from the drone flying past the base toward the colony. A group of seven Reptilia broke formation and sprinted fast with weapons gripped in hand toward an armored rover. "Shit!" Bear's gaze followed hers. With the reptilian group inside, the armored vehicle's hover mode engaged, accelerating rapidly towards the colony's direction.

"They are coming here!" Carson's face went white with panic.

"Give the order to lock the colony down!" Lone Wolf flagged Carson with her hand to get him out of the way. They needed a plan, and this guy was about to pass out. She moved over to the central holo projection console in the middle of the room and activated it. Seconds later, there was an oversized image of the colony from a bird's-eye point of view. She used her fingertips to adjust the image to expand to cover more terrain. At a side glance, she noticed Bear walking over to where she stood. "It's best that we intercept them. Can't risk another wolf incident."

"We need one team to go in and one team to remain in defense, to guard the colony should they try to ambush us." Bear remained composed and studied the map. "Only problem is that we have one hell of a storm heading here."

"A little wind and rain won't scare me. I'll intercept. I'll take a team along with Grim. He's my sure shot."

Bear tossed a side-eye of annoyance at Carson pacing behind the tech's chair. "Fine. Go armor up. Keep your wits about you, Wolf. This is not Enlightenment. You got it?"

She tightened her jaw muscles. "I know the contact protocol."

Bear returned to the holo image flickering before them. "They'll need to navigate that mountain range to get to us. That will be our intercept point." He homed in on the coordinates.

Krysta recognized the mark well. "That's near where we were the other day when those hounds attacked us. This is no coincidence."

"Easy." He picked up on her statement. "We are not one hundred percent positive that those mutts have anything to do with these reptiles. Presumptions are dangerous. I'll split the Peacekeepers in half. I'll escort one half to the midpoint to act as a buffer should you need backup. We can fall back if necessary."

"Sounds like a game plan. Heading out now."

"Lone Wolf?" His voice beckoned to her softly when she turned away.

"Yeah?"

"Stay safe out there."

"You too, Bear." Adrenaline soared through her veins. "It's round two for the lizard."

Chapter 12

"ETA: three minutes," Grim announced from the rover's helm as Krysta's team made their way to the cut-off point. "Rain ban is picking up. Diagnostics show the storm cell bearing down on our position."

"Any marks?" Wolf asked. She saw large droplets of rain pummeling the vehicle's exterior, and the rumbling thunder dampened any other noise.

"Negative."

Wolf tapped her earpiece to secure a connection with the other Peacekeeper group. "My screens are dark, Bear. Did these guys double back?"

"*Damnit,*" the man on the other end griped. "*We lost them in the mountains. They went in, Wolf, then went off the map. Could be another cloaking trick. The storm is going to make you lose visuals quickly. Pull back.*"

"Interception point." Grim stopped the rover.

Krysta ignored Bear's warning and moved out of the transport first; she then signaled Grim and the other two members of her team to their strategic positions. "Negative, Papa Bear. I'm here. We'll kick their asses."

"Or they could kick your asses." The loud boom of thunder deafened his voice, followed by a crackle of lightning that spread across the cloud top like a spider web.

The heavy rain droplets poured over their armor and made the ground muddy within seconds. The winds howled and shook the treetops, throwing rain into Krysta's visor. "Anything?" She called out to her group. Everyone shook their heads. "They should have been here by now, Jack." She lowered her voice to him to avoid detection. They were exposed out in the open. She didn't like this. Bear was right, it was too dangerous. The wind velocity increased, and she struggled against the sheer to go the direction they came. "Fallback to the rover!"

"Sniper!" Grim's shout rang an alarm, and his rifle focused on a cliff to their east.

"Fan out and take cover! Grim, keep a bead on them!" Wolf ushered her team to jump out of the way. She darted behind their vehicle and pressed her back squarely against the metal. Her heart pounded in her chest with her boots digging into the murk. The torrential rain, similar to a waterfall, drowned out all other sounds.

"Movement on the hill," Grim's voice cracked through the comm.

"How many?" Krysta lost track of her men and had no clue where they had dispersed. "Everyone okay?"

"Clear," their voices responded to her, one by one, over the link inside her helmet.

"Grim?" Krysta fell back to her first question.

"I got four on the cliff," he finally answered.

"I'm getting fucking tired of being the seeker," Bear moped over the comm.

The same unfamiliar language sounded from a hidden location in front of them, near the entrance of the mountain pass. Wolf estimated it to be around nine meters away. A commanding Reptilia spouted out orders again in his tongue. It took a few moments for her translator earpiece to analyze the words pouring in. *"Arlandr, please identify yourselves and your intentions here."*

"Before I say anything further, can you understand me?" Krysta called from where she remained covered, her back pressed tightly against the rover's hard exterior. Another clap of thunder soon followed; it appeared as if the storm grew by the tension in the air. As lightning briefly lit up the surroundings, she saw Grim positioning himself near a tree.

"I can comprehend you seamlessly. I will repeat myself. Please identify yourselves and your intentions on this planet." The apparent leader of their squad barked out a command over the storm's raging winds.

"They are a threat, Hosir Matelija. A prophecy foretold Sani's creations would challenge us. They have weapons," another Reptilia contradicted the other.

"So do we," the one named Hosir Matelija insisted.

"What the hell are they chattering about?" Bear intently listened to the translation. *"Who the hell is Sani? Is it the same bullshit that one said the other day to you?"*

"Yeah, at least we have one of their names." Krysta switched her conversation briefly to her squad. "Anyone got a visual?"

"Arlandr, this is your final warning before we consider your actions here on Ljosa to be hostile. Identify yourselves and state your intentions," the Reptilia unit leader ordered them.

Krysta tapped her fingers around her rifle barrel and contemplated how the scenario would pan out. "We are humans from Earth, not 'Ar-lan-der' or whatever you are calling us. Our objective is to settle and be peaceful."

"Hu-man," the being spat coldly. "Lower your weapon and make yourself visible to us. If you comply, we will consider what you say is the truth." The rain whipped around her violently as the large storm cell was directly on top of them. Krysta worried it would disrupt communications as it approached the colony.

"*Wolf*," Bear warned in her ear.

"Like hell am I going to expose my team to slaughter." Gripping the barrel tightly with gloved fingers, Lone Wolf breathed out in frustration. "I will order my team to stand down, but they will remain hidden for their protection. Are you the one in charge? If so, I would like to meet you. Can you guarantee me safe passage?"

There was a brief pause on the other side until Hosir Matelija finally replied, "I am Hosir Eski Matelija. No harm will come to you. If this is a trick, then deadly force will be used, human."

Krysta kept her weapon pointed in a neutral downward position but did not discard it entirely. Instead, she moved out of cover in their clear view. Her helmet's H.U.D. queued up two armed reptile creatures emerging from a hiding place near the base of the cliff, and it was only due to a lightning flash that spotlighted their visual appearance. The helmeted figures didn't react to her, and she couldn't tell who she was addressing; however, she noticed the figure on the left had an inverted triangle on his left shoulder. "My call sign is Lone Wolf. My colleagues and I are from a security group called 'Peacekeepers'. A corporation contracted us here to provide safety for our colonists. I take it, you were not too fond of our drones?"

"They violated our airspace—"

Krysta corrected harshly, "You were spying on *us* first. I'm sure you were watching us from the very beginning." Thunder roared overhead.

"Ever since humans moved toward our planet." Eski removed his helmet to show his face. Both sets of his yellow eyes stared down at her.

Her eyes widened at his facial appearance. Her mind thought back to their run in with the scout just outside Bakht. "Jack?" She mumbled under her breath to her comm link.

"*Yeah?*"

"It's our guy from the other day. His pals around him have rifles, but he has two pistols."

"*Easy, Krysta, do nothing rash.*"

"You could have just said hello." Wolf removed her helmet in kind. "It's rude to snoop on your new neighbors, or is that what gets you off?" She shivered, feeling the chilly rain hit the top of her head and bead down her face. The reptilian being before her was unlike anything she had seen before. Streams of water moved down his rigid body. His guarded disposition made him difficult to read. He kept his eyes locked on hers. An uneasy feeling settled within her.

"*Wolf,*" Bear prompted in her earpiece.

"Your species used drones around our boundaries, including our city, before your group's arrival. Are we still considered impolite?" Eski countered. Krysta cringed inwardly. She figured Dhank Trust gathered more intel than they let on when they negotiated the contract for Grim's team. What else were they hiding about the planet? Eski continued, "We set up a base close to your camp for our protection. Two of your vehicles were located further out from your colony. I presume your goals include expanding your borders. How much territory are you acquiring?"

"One of your scouts followed us out... or maybe it was you again." She backtracked. "You are aware of our previous position. For now, that is the newest boundary of our territory."

"I remember you, Lone Wolf. You are a formidable opponent." Eski surprised her by the reveal. "And I was the one who followed your group. Your statement is open-ended. It is safe to assume that your company's plans are ongoing beyond these mountains. If that is your intent, then you must cease all further operations. For the Hlinan prohibit you from entering our territory."

"I'm sure my contractors were unaware of your claimed land. I will convey your concerns to them immediately, and I hope our interactions will remain diplomatic. Am I to assume the land our colony is established on is not disputed?"

"For *now,*" Eski replied vaguely, emphasizing the phrase she used a few moments ago. "Our city is called Heofen, and this planet is called Ljosa. Does your colony have a name?"

"Bakht." Krysta's mind then switched to the wild canines. "Are you using those beasts to attack us? They conveniently show up when you are lurking around us."

This time, there was a reaction from him; his slanted eyes widened, and she wasn't sure if he was surprised that she figured it out or if he knew of the creatures she spoke of. As if on cue, a familiar and haunting howl erupted in the trees to the west, followed by multiple alarming howls after it.

"Hosir Matelija! It is the hata!" One of the Reptilia called from the cliff near Eski.

Eski slipped on his helmet and signaled his soldiers. "With me in staggered formation. Activate shields."

The sudden turn of events made Krysta's heart leap to her throat. For a moment, the mud trapped her feet before she recovered. "My team, stay alert and confirm visuals!" She slipped her helmet back on. Her gaze drifted to the Hlinan, whose bodies emitted a flickering light. "They have personal shields? Great."

Bear's panicked voice came through her comm. "*What the hell is going on?*"

Wolf checked her magazine stock before moving closer to where Eski and his men were. She didn't see them as allies, but against the savage canines, there had to be a temporary alliance. Grim and the others joined her closer with the Hlinan on the ground. There was more chance of survival in significant numbers. "Those damn wolves are back! And these guys know what they are!"

"*Shit! I'm going there.*"

"Negative. Stay back until we can reach our targets. Last time, there were only three. These things may be in small packs; at least eleven of us are armed here." She visualized the bearded man fuming on the other end at the rejection.

"*Just watch your ass, Wolf. Do nothing stupid.*"

"Affirmative." Her jaw tightened. The howls and vicious snarls came nearer. The animals charged in their direction. Their feet sloshed through the muddy ground.

"That's over three this time, Wolf," Grim's dark visor turned her way. "It could be a larger strike, like the first time they hit Bakht."

"That's what I'm afraid of. Keep your marks!" Krysta aimed her rifle at the approaching beasts. The Hlinan, unlike her team, remained still and quiet.

Seconds later, two large black wolves leaped through the tree cover, with one instantly moving in on one reptile. The soldier fired his weapon at the beast, and the rounds pierced its thick hind and torso, but the creature was upon him within seconds. The reptile grunted as the hound lurched into his shield, creating enough inertia to knock him back. His comrades fired on the beast, but the large canine acted faster, slamming into his prey again. It broke the barrier, and he victoriously chomped through the lizard's armor within seconds. A terrible wail escaped the reptile's mouth, then silence fell around them. Krysta gasped inside her helmet at the gruesome sight. "So much for shields."

Six smaller brown beasts emerged from the trees and squared off with the Hlinan. As if it was a planned strike, one of the black alphas broke off from the large group with three others in tow. They ascended the rocky mountainside towards the cliff where the Hlinan fired from fifteen meters above. The creature's large, clawed paws tore at the wet rocky surface, with no trouble with traction. The Reptilia aimed their rifles at the approaching group and fired mercilessly at the hounds. Two beasts whimpered in pain when the bullets struck vital organs, and blood burst from their trunks before their bodies tumbled down the side onto the floor, dead. The other brown one and the alpha continued their trek.

Krysta peeled her eyes off the corpses, when the alpha on the ground formed a group with the other three brown-furred ones. It bared its lethal fangs. Its chilling red eyes bore into her, her team, and

Eski, with his two other Reptilia at his side. With a menacing step, the alpha advanced into the mud.

"Open fire!" Wolf squeezed the trigger of her rifle. The alpha snapped its head before leaping towards Eski and the two Reptilia while the three brown ones moved on to Krysta and her squad. Screams of agony echoed around the clearing as bones were crushed and flesh was torn apart high above. Wolf cringed at the pieces of the Reptilia's remains draped along the mountain cliff like a bloodied tapestry while a few fell down the side in a gory crimson trail. The alpha and the remaining brown beast descended back down the mountainside to join the fight below. She knew their odds of surviving this battle were slim, even if they regrouped. With one brown hound down, she signaled to her comrades. "Retreat! Get back to the rover now! If the reptiles with the shields are not surviving, then we don't have a damn chance out here!"

The alpha pounced on one of the retreating mercs, cutting off his path. Its massive jaws tore into the man's back armor, treating it as if it were butter, before severing his spine. The other Peacekeeper stumbled in the slick, mud and fell onto the ground. The alpha made short work of its next victim.

Krysta had no clue if the reptiles had any rides nearby; if they did, it was not visible. "Hell." Wolf stormed to Eski and his team to assist. With both pistols drawn, Eski used his agility to evade the beast's attacks. He hammered the alpha on the side as the creature lunged at him. Frustrated, the hound changed its target and unsuspectingly pounced on one of his men nearby, stomping on the lizard's body relentlessly with its enormous paws till the shield phased out. The other Reptilia stumbled to escape its next kill and nearly fell back on the ground. Matelija aimed carefully at the beast, but the alpha positioned Eski's comrade in his line of fire, making Matelija hesitate. With a flash of lightning, the big black hound swiftly chomped into the last one.

Wolf winced at the brutal kill. She aimed her sidearm at the reptile's head and fired several rounds to end his suffering. She then tugged on Eski's arm. "You got too damn cocky with those cheap shields. Your men are lost and I'm losing mine. Get your ass back to my rover! We need to get out of here!"

The Hlinan squad leader remained frozen in the rain, before he staggered a few feet. Based on his reaction, Krysta suspected he was suffering from shell shock. He was the last remaining soldier of his kind; the rest were slain, with some scattered in several pieces. Their rich, dark red blood splattered along the ground and cliff sides. Eski raised one of his pistols and fired multiple times at the nearest brown hata, right in the center of its skull. The creature whimpered loudly in pain before it collapsed.

After they saw their fallen comrades, the pair of brown wolves snarled at Krysta and Eski. "Well, that just pissed them off more," Wolf grumbled to the reptile next to her.

Just as the left one pulled ahead, a bullet hit its right rear leg, sending it crashing to the ground. Following the shot's path with her eyes, Krysta spotted Grim with his weapon poised on the beast. "I got you, Lone Wolf."

"Thanks for saving our asses, Grim." Krysta flashed him a thumbs up from where he stood next to the rover, then her smile faded fast when the remaining brown creatures and the alpha charged him "Grim, watch out!" The man dove into the rover and shut the door just as the hounds pummeled into the vehicle with their bodies, causing minor damage to the hull exterior. "Get away from him." Krysta leveled her rifle at the black alpha. Just before firing, Eski scooped her up, carrying her over his shoulder into a narrow mountain pass. The movement caught her off guard, and she watched Grim's rover grow further and further away in the rain. Eski held her tightly with one hand as his other clutched one of his pistols. She struck his arm hard with her fist while she held her weapon with the other, careful not to drop it in her disarray. "What the hell are you doing, lizard? Put me down!"

Eski skirted along the mud path through the passage until he reached a tunnel that was just wide enough for a human to squeeze through. He set her back down. "Get in there, now."

She eyed his helmeted face suspiciously. "No way. I'm going back." A clap of lightning in the sky echoed her defiance. She heard vicious snaps near their vicinity; more hata. Darting into the passageway, she moved far back before daring to look to see if he was still trailing her.

Only seconds after he entered, the alpha located the way they slipped in. The beast clawed ferociously at the rock. "We have time; move!" Eski ordered through his helmet and engaged a light from the top that lit their way deeper inside the rocky, dark, cavernous abyss.

Krysta risked a quick glance backward. "You think it will break in?" The hound's thick, sharp claws scraped the rock in desperation.

"You want to wait and find out, Arlandr?" He motioned her along.

The end of the narrow passage opened to a broader space with a labyrinth of tunnels. "Quit calling me that. I don't know what that is. Any idea which one we need to use, or should I find a Minotaur?" Only the gentle sound of distant water dripping from the cave ceiling to the floor was audible above the storm's faint roar.

"An 'Arlandr' is one that is not part of the Hlinan society. What is a Minotaur?" Confused by her mythological reference, Eski stood at her side.

"Never mind." Panic filled her mind. She needed to get back. Krysta tapped her earpiece to communicate with the Peacekeepers. "Grim? This is Lone Wolf. Come in." There was static on the other end, and she clenched her teeth to try again. "Grim, do you copy? Over." The same result. Exasperated, she exhaled in defeat. "If you can read me, rendezvous back to Bear. Do not bring those hounds to the colony. There's an alpha right outside of my location, so do not attempt a rescue."

The Hlinan remained motionless at her failed communication attempt. "The rock inside this mountain may impede your transmissions."

"*Now* you tell me," she complained. Krysta heard the beast snapping violently at the passage entrance. "Lead the way, Hlinan."

"This way." He gestured toward a nearby tunnel to their left. "That is the one to take. Once we are on the other side of this mountain, you will need to warn your colony. The hata do not hunt like normal predators that we are accustomed to."

She clamped the grip around her rifle tightly at his menacing words. While she walked, the vivid imagery of those monsters tearing two of her men apart haunted her. She was incapable of saving her own, and she hated herself so much for it. *Lost more men under my command. This is the second time. I don't have what it takes, and this asshole in front of me is not helping.* "Your fancy shields fizzled out like black-market parts. Catch them on sale?"

Rotating on his boot heel, he peered at her through his opaque crimson visor. "Our shields are for artillery rounds. I was hoping it would provide some layer of protection against them. Yes, I was wrong in that. Shall we continue this volley, hu-man?"

She squared her jaw and glared hard at his hidden face. "Did your beasts get out of hand? Every time you are sneaking around, they hit us. I wonder why that is."

"If you insinuate we can control such terror, then you are mistaken, Lone Wolf. The hata are not native to this planet. We suspect that Sani's creations released them after they wiped out our first colony two hundred years ago. In fact, we theorize they are the ones who guide them. When another team arrived to claim our dead, those monstrosities mauled them. We did not return until fifty years ago. By then, the hata population increased by fifteen percent. Thankfully, they kept to your side of the mountains."

"These things hunt in packs. Couldn't you locate their den and bomb it from above?"

"They are difficult to track. The packs divide when their numbers grow; they never stay in the same territory. They are clever and create multiple false dens."

"You said they were Sani's creations. The first time we saw one another, you referred to us as 'Children of Sani.' You know what I'm going to ask next, right?"

"Sani is my kind's mortal enemy, Lone Wolf. There is speculation that you are his creation set to harm us." He nonchalantly tossed out, "And that was not the first time that I saw you."

Krysta tilted her head with a wide eye expression on her face. "Come again?"

The far-off sound of the creature on the prowl froze both of them into place. Hosir Matelija glimpsed back, "We need to hurry." He grabbed her hand to usher her toward one tunnel. Pulling her hand away, Krysta followed Eski into the darkness, his helmet illuminating the path. There was only the sound of their steps on the terrain and their breath in their helmets as they moved. How far would she flee into the mountain with him? They needed to find a way out soon. If the hounds broke through, she suspected all the zigzags and false tunnels would not fool the feral creatures' keen sense of smell.

As she stumbled through the narrow passageways, her mind switched over to Bear and Grim. The canines could have moved on toward the colony. Would Bear and the others be able to go up against them? Even if she made it out of the labyrinth with her lizard guide, would she enter a world of chaos and death? *I'm stuck for now. I feel like Dante from humanity's old texts in this hell. If that's the case, lead the way, Virgil. I wonder which layer he's taking me to next.*

Chapter 13

The rock formations blurred together as Lone Wolf rounded another bend with the Reptilia. She couldn't cling onto any distinguishing features to remember. "Do you know where we are going, or are you just guessing?" Krysta trailed the armor-suited reptile through the tight, dark corridors inside the mountain pass. As they distanced themselves from the entrance, their fear of the beasts finding them vanished. Krysta activated her wrist gauntlet's navigation program. *Shit. Navigation is down in this place. Too far in. I've been walking for almost an hour. How the hell did these guys pull off coming through here earlier? Something isn't adding up.* She paused in her tracks on the rocky path. "I know damn well that we have been in this place a lot longer than you were earlier. Enough tricks. Where's your ride at, Hlinan?"

Pausing, Eski turned to face her. He leveled his visor on her. "Due to the unexpected skirmish with the hata, I had to choose another path instead of the one that I used previously. We could go the shorter route to where my transportation is, but it would lead us right back to the alpha. Do you prefer that way, human?"

With a scowl, she motioned him on, "Long way, it is."

Eski removed his helmet and put one of his four-fingered, slender, gloved hands against the rock wall beside him. "I have navigated these tunnels many times, just like the ones before my arrival."

"Did your kind create these?"

"The tunnels were in the mountains when my ancestors first arrived on this planet. There are many paths with many dead ends. I believe only three come to an exit point, and one goes deep within the planet's core, which bans all Hlinan from entering."

"Definitely staying away from the banned one. We near one of *those* exit points soon? I need to get to my team." Her jaw stiffened. The thick rock layers of the pass disrupted her comms, and she wasn't sure if her armor beacon was transmitting. Both sets of his eyes stared soundlessly at her. "I hate how you look at me like that. The whole four-eye thing creeps me out."

"I know you lost some of your own today." His gentle words brushed aside her pointed insult. "I will mourn their deaths with the loss of my own."

His unexpected sincerity startled her; she watched him cautiously, then gestured for him to continue. "Just get me out of here."

The Hlinan soldier placed his helmet back on and continued the way. "The tunnel concludes ahead; then I can order a pickup from my base. It will be safer to do that than for us to walk to locate mine with the hata lurking in the vicinity."

"*Your* base?" She stopped dead in her tracks, redrew her small pistol, and cocked it. "You believe *I'm* your prisoner?"

Creating more distance, Eski retrieved one of his pistols. Unlike hers, his gun was a few inches longer, with a black and crimson color scheme. "Is all of your kind this pugnacious?"

"Just know that I don't trust you." She kept her arm tight aiming the targeting bead on his chest.

"Your conjecture is a mutual feeling," He pointed out with his weapon still drawn. "My back has been to you the entire journey. I expected you to fire one shot at least." His words were coarse, like rough sand.

"I still have time."

The jibe prompted a delighted chuckle from within his helmet. "You are quick to strike. Perhaps the others are right. You are a Child of Sani." He harnessed his side-arm. "Though I have my doubts, for if you were, there would be no hesitation in your mind about killing me."

"If you believe I'm not a Child of this Sani guy, whoever he is, then why am I here?"

"Would you rather be with the hata?"

"Quit with the cryptic shit."

His helmet faced her again, and she saw the distorted reflection of her face in his visor. "I am very curious about your species, Lone Wolf. The Children of Sani plagued this world years ago, and you do not look like them. Your existence should not be according to our religion and yet you are here among us. My first conversation with you did not go as planned. I hoped for another chance."

"Spying on us is not how you start a conversation."

His helmet resonated with a soft chuckle. "You stunned me by knocking me off my hover cycle, Lone Wolf. I admit I did not expect your resilience. Going back to the matter at hand, you are not my prisoner, despite how you perceive it. I need to consult with our leader on how to proceed. Your action puts us in an interesting predicament." Eski switched on his helmet lamp, illuminating the dark path ahead. "We have a little further to go. Shall we?"

"*My* action?" She would be damned to allow him to have the final say. "*You* are the one who grabbed me away from my team." She directed her argument to the rear of his helmet.

"I saved your life against the hata." He reminded her indifferently before turning her way slightly, with the light barely coming into her eyes.

She continued to follow him. "So, your name is Eski Matelija?"

"Your perception is sound, Lone Wolf." His words dripped with mockery. "That is correct. Your name is Lone Wolf of the Peacekeepers."

"My callsign is Lone Wolf. My real name is Krysta Evreux."

"Factitious nomenclatures?" A chuckle escaped his lips. "Interesting."

"Military normalcy; sort of like nicknames based upon something personable."

"What is a wolf?"

"A wild canine that lives back on Earth," she chortled softly, "Sort of like the hata, but not as large nor as vicious."

"I see," he pondered aloud momentarily. "You are alone? Yet, you were with others when we met. How does that formulate your callsign, Lone Wolf?"

"Reference to my past. Let's leave it at that."

"Do you have a lounge? A family?"

"The Peacekeepers. Is the interrogation over?"

"This is not a formal proceeding, Krysta Evreux. I wanted to provoke more cordial conversation while we forge ahead."

"If I were you, I would just hurry it up. You made a big mistake kidnapping me, and Jack will be seriously pissed off." A boastful beam crossed her face. "He probably has a target sheet with your ugly face on it."

His head turned sideways slightly to respond, "Jack? Is he your mate?"

A blush rose on Krysta's face as she looked at him in disbelief. "My what? Whoa there, pal. No way, and that's getting way too personal."

Eski simply shrugged at her scolding. "Very well. You are a soldier, yes? What is your rank?"

"The Peacekeepers are mercenaries with no rankings. If you are looking for a line of succession to figure out how valuable I am, cram it."

"Very well, Lone Wolf. I am one hundred and seventy-eight years old. My species' lifespan goes to an average of three hundred. What about you?"

Her eyes broadened at the knowledge. "One hundred and seventy-eight? I wish we could live that long. I'm twenty-nine and have another ninety years, give or take. We used to live no longer than around a hundred, but medical advancements have prolonged our lifespan."

"One hundred and nineteen?" This time, he didn't look at her while he walked. "That is piteous. Your kind does not have a lot of time to fulfill anything."

She ignored his remark. "Now it's my turn for the questions, Hlinan. This can't be your home world unless your population is that scarce. Why are you guys here and who attacked you before?"

"Your metacognition processes are sound, Lone Wolf. My home world is Emble, and this planet is a gift from our god, Hlidar, for knowledge and understanding of the way of things. We established our first colony two hundred years ago." His gaze drifted to the distance. "Until the Children of Sani, the Achli, arrived."

The mention of the alien race made Krysta tense. Under her armor, her chest heaved as her breaths quickened. "The Achli?" She could barely utter the words.

Their stares locked again. "Yes. They gave my ancestors two choices—"

"Choose slavery and religious conversion, or face annihilation," she finished his explanation for him.

Eski's stance turned rigid. "Do you know them?"

"Same kind of bullshit that they gave our first colony, Enlightenment." She recalled what she scavenged in her searches on the internet when she was old enough to truly understand what happened to her father. There was an audio transcript of the Enlightenment's director's last words and what the AI translated from the Achli speech. The pain of the loss seeped through her body like nutrients being sucked into the roots of a plant. She suppressed the urge to divulge too much of her past to a stranger, an alien nonetheless, and inwardly hugged herself for comfort.

"Then I am sorry," He steered her gently back to their conversation. "I hope your ancestors fought like mine did."

"They didn't have a chance."

"Then we share something in common, Krysta. A bond that is unusual and I do not wish to have that connection to you, yet we do." Eski removed the right glove and gauntlet from his forearm armor, and placed his bare scaly claws against the rock wall. "Because of the words of our ancient texts, we believed the occurrence was a prophesied war to determine our fates. Fear paralyzed us for centuries in the belief that our failure meant our doom until fifty years ago, when there was a mission to come here to finish what our ancestors left for us." He put his glove and gauntlet back on. "We were alone and free of fear until your kind arrived. Now, you see where our distrust lies. There are many that believe that you and the Achli are the same. You have simply changed your form to deceive us all."

She narrowed her eyes at his words. "We are *nothing* like the Achli."

"My kind has no intention of violence against yours if what you say is true, Lone Wolf. *I* have no intention of harm to your kind."

His words caused a small, soft smile to play on her lips, but a sudden insect-clicking sound disrupted the silence before she could reply. The disturbance of rocks quickly followed. Eski held up his hand to signal her to be quiet, while turning off his helmet's light. He drifted his hands down to his sides to retrieve his twin pistols. His action made her retrieve her primary weapon. She eyed him uneasily. "What is that?" She whispered to avoid detection.

He remained guarded and didn't flinch away to answer her. "Ikol. I hoped that our passage would not disturb her."

Struggling against the darkness, a tense whisper escaped her, "What the hell is that?"

Chapter 14

"How many shots do you have left?" Eski positioned himself against a jutting boulder. He held both pistols ready, aiming one at the source of the demonic screeching ahead.

Wolf checked her weapon supply. "I have one clip left in my pistol and two left for my rifle." She held her modified military-grade assault rifle in the ready posture while she kept the pistol still in its holster for backup. Whatever they were about to face would need more to take it down than a pistol. "You never explained what an 'Ikol' is."

"An underground arachnid that stays in the deeper tunnels of the mountain pass. She is rarely seen in the upper levels of the mountain. My kind encountered her here after the first pilgrimage to honor our ancestors. Many were killed during an attempt to subdue it and they wounded one of her legs. She remained dormant for years after. We almost believed that she died, but no one dared to travel further to verify the fact."

"A spider? That thing ahead sounds bigger than some damn bug, Eski." Krysta gnashed her teeth as she heard the creature picking up the pace. "This news could have been useful before I blindly followed you in this cavern. Only one?"

"The rest of her breed remains well below the cavern surface." Eski gazed around. "We need to move forward. The tunnel opens to a wider cavern. If we stay here, she will pin us." He switched his helmet light back on to forge their path ahead and grabbed her hand to get her to follow him. "This way."

Lone Wolf struggled to keep up with his faster pace. "Isn't that where she is?"

Eski paused at the cavern's mouth and fired his pistol at an unknown foe before he darted to the right. Wolf heard a loud screech, and her eyes sprung open when she came to the opening. There, poised at the far side of the cavern, was a monstrous spider. The grotesque beast stood around six meters tall and roughly nine meters across with its legs. Its head was jagged, with bright sky-blue eight eyes, and its fangs were half the size of Krysta's whole body. The spider detected the two intruders and hissed ferociously. Its front legs pushed out like spears to capture its intended prey.

Near the cavern's right corner, Wolf braced herself against a rock formation, jaw clenched tight. She momentarily lost track of her Hlinan companion. A gunshot rang out to her right, followed by the creature's howl. Risking to blow her cover, Krysta bobbed up and saw the spider turning its large abdomen towards where Eski was. The reptile kept firing with his dual pistols, but the rounds only scuffed the spider's thick outer layer of its cephalothorax.

"We need more punch than that," Wolf called to her counterpart and aimed the sights of her rifle onto the creature's abdomen underside, then pulled the trigger. A barrage of bullets hit their mark and tore through the skin. Foul-smelling, putrid green liquid blood gushed from its gash. The odor was so intense that it penetrated her helmet's filtering system. Alarms rang inside her in her helmet and a message popped up on her display, revealing high toxicity levels.

Eski yanked her aside while the spider curled in to attend to its injury. He removed his helmet and placed it as best as possible over Krysta's head after removing her own. The helmet was loose fitting because of their different head structures. "Careful," he cautioned. "Ikol's blood is poisonous. We will succumb to it if we linger here. My helmet's filtering component blocks the lethal air."

The extra eyes made it strange, yet she tried her hardest to see him through the eyeholes. He held his hand over his nose and coughed a little. She returned the helmet to him after a few breaths of fresh air and placed hers back on. "Take it. I'll be fine." Her eyes quickly shifted to the spider. *Can't shoot this bitch. Now what, Wolf? Think!*

The spider redirected its focus back to the duo. This time, it scrambled toward them. "Have to risk it." Krysta aimed her rifle at one of its back legs and pulled the trigger. The bullets caused the spider to collapse to the ground and shriek. The putrid scent of the insect's blood broke through her helmet's respirator and hit her nasal passages inside. She coughed hard enough that her lungs burned between each movement. "Bad idea."

Eski aimed one pistol and fired toward one of the creature's eyes. The bullet punctured through it, and a spray of blood gushed outward. The spider's wild screech boomed through the cavern. "I think we are just pissing her off!" Wolf choked out to him. The creature endured so much, and each strike caused more toxic blood fumes to pour out. Poisonous gas saturated their cave. Krysta couldn't take it. Coughing violently, her knees buckled, and she fell to the ground. Her lungs burned like a napalm blast, with her eyes watering so badly that she struggled to see.

Eski was at her side within seconds and switched her helmet with his own again. A few breaths later, the burning stopped, and she looked up at him. He pointed toward a tunnel to her left. "You will not survive here, Krysta! Go on and wait for me. My helmet will keep the toxic away. You need to clear the room!"

Wolf slowly stood and glanced back at the spider. "There's no way you can take that thing on! And wouldn't it just follow us?"

The spider lashed out at them again. Ikol's right leg struck between Krysta and Eski just as they dove in opposite directions onto the ground. Krysta rolled onto her back and sat up quickly to locate the Hlinan fighter. He was already on his feet to square off with Ikol. "Eski!" She removed his helmet and threw it back at him, then slipped hers on. "Take it!"

With his helmet back on, he faced Wolf's direction. "Do as I say, human!"

"Dammit." Scrambling up, Wolf fled in the indicated direction, staying low to avoid the arachnid's sight. After she reached the spot, Krysta whirled around on the heel of her boot to see that Eski climbed on top of the spider's body. He ran up to the top of its head and relentlessly fired rounds into Ikol's cranium, while he remained far back enough to avoid the spider's blood onto his own body. The same vile fluid erupted, along with brain matter; Ikol thrashed violently from the elevated pain. It screeched so loudly that Wolf held her helmet's sides.

Just as Eski leaped from the creature's wounded body, one of Ikol's legs whipped out and caught him off-guard. His body flew wide before smacking hard onto the ground, and the spider lurched in. The arachnid raised one of its legs and pierced Eski's armor near the right upper arm. He let out a faint groan with his body pinned down onto his back.

"I'm going to regret this." Krysta stormed toward him, aimed her rifle and pulled the trigger. As the spider turned to eat its prey, the bullets tore into its rear. "Not this time, bitch." She clamped her teeth tightly together.

Severely injured and in pain from multiple gunshot wounds, Ikol let out a final threatening hiss before her massive form retreated down the tunnel, trailing blood in her wake. Only when the creature's sounds were gone, did Krysta move in to check on Eski. The Hlinan sat up and favored his injured arm. She observed that the attack cracked his armor, which exposed his scaly skin. The creature's leg broke the fleshy surface, revealing ligaments and seeping blood.

"More fun down here for me to enjoy?" she joked in an attempt to lighten the dire situation. The lingering toxic fumes overcame her, and she started coughing uncontrollably.

Without a word or hesitation, Eski scooped her up in his arms and hurried toward the exit tunnel. "Human, you should have kept going like I said," he hissed through the helmet. "Why did you come back to save me? I said I would handle it."

"Yeah, being pinned down was really handling it, Hlinan." Her watery eyes blurred his hidden face. She honestly did not know why she saved him. "You spared me from the hata. Now, we're even. That's the only one you get."

"Fair enough."

The outside light greeted them ahead and Krysta found the air easier to breathe, yet her lungs still stung between breaths. As he carried her, she glanced over to his wound and gingerly touched his arm near the exposure with her gloved fingertips. "You probably need to get that looked at soon." Her fingertips lightly lingered on the hole. *This guy could have died trying to save my ass.*

His red visor bowed slightly down at her. "I am. You will need to have a breathing treatment to prevent further respiratory damage. Ikol's toxin causes only temporary irritation in our lungs, but the discomfort eases once the inhalation stops."

"How fortuitous." She winced again with a sharp breath. "I love this place. Five stars all the way around."

After they reached the sanctuary of the outside world, Eski slowed his steps and then steadied her on her feet. "Are you injured anywhere, Lone Wolf?" He removed his helmet.

"Nothing that Jack can't patch up." She removed her helmet to flash him a smile. "You're not too shabby in your combat skills, Eski." She extended a handshake of acceptance, but the Hlinan stared blankly down at the gesture.

"Your skills, Lone Wolf, are up there with some of my top operatives at the base. Another reason I would prefer to be your ally and not your enemy." His eyes rested on her for a moment; then, he retreated a few steps. Krysta overheard him talking to someone. She glanced at his base, then looked back at the mountain. A shudder coursed down her body. She never wanted to see that ugly Ikol again. Shortly after, the Hlinan returned to her. "A ride from my base is on its way. We should be safe here."

"Are you sure there are no more beasts out here for us to battle? I haven't filled up my card yet," she kidded while still trembling. "Hell Hounds, Monster spiders…what's next? Hydra? Leviathan?"

"Creatures from your world?"

"Only in myth."

A crooked smile touched his lips, followed by a chuckle as he walked off. She watched him detach the damaged armor piece from his arm. Guilt washed over her. Moments before they crossed paths with the spider, she was aggressive and curt with the Reptilia. Her attitude was reason enough to fall victim to Ikol or the toxic fumes that exited its torso. Yet, he risked his own life to make sure she lived.

Squaring her shoulders, she walked toward him; her face creased with regret. Her gloved fingertips gently prodded at his upper arm as she inspected the wound. "I didn't deserve what you did back there. You know nothing about my species."

He hissed low from his throat, and he squarely set his reptilian eyes upon her. His arm did not recoil at her touch. "You could have abandoned me there as well, Lone Wolf. If you did not, I would have been Ikol's next meal," he admitted lightheartedly. "Your communications should work now if you would like to use it before my kind arrives."

Embarrassed that she forgot to check them, Krysta scurried over and tapped the link. "Bear, this is Lone Wolf. Over?"

"*Wolf! This is Bear. What's your status? Where are you?*" His familiar voice poured into her ear. It sounded so refreshing to hear him.

"I just made it out on the other side of the mountain pass. I lost comms in the tunnels. The Hlinan have transport en route for pickup to their base. I'm with one of them. Did Grim make it back?"

"He made it back. Heard it was a rough one, Wolf, and that those slimy reptiles kidnapped you. Did they hurt you? What the hell do they want?"

"A misunderstanding, Bear. This one saved me the first go round when we squared off against the hata. He hasn't tried to hurt me and you know damn well if I got that feeling that he would be dead by now."

"The h-a-ta? What is that?"

"Sorry, it's what they call those hounds. I've been through hell and back inside the mountain. We fought a gigantic spider, Jack. It wasn't pretty," she taunted. "You would have screamed like a girl."

"I hate spiders. I'm on my way to get to you. Place a beacon and hold your position."

"Negative. I'm going with this guy to his base to learn more. I don't think they have any desire to hurt me or any of us; there's more to them here than we know. The Achli invaded their colony here too, years ago. I need answers."

"Krysta," he said, his tone growing firm. *"Don't go down the rabbit hole. Not alone. And certainly not because of your father's death and your past."*

"My beacon will be transmitting. Level head, I promise."

"Three hours tops and if you don't check in, I'm coming there, Wolf."

From the background, she heard a man yell angrily, *"What is she doing?"*

"Who the heck is that?" Krysta questioned.

"Carson. Turns out that the stiffs here just wanted us to ditch you. The director just showed up with his friends at our abode."

Krysta narrowed her eyes. "Patch me through."

"I got you through, Wolf." Bear confirmed a second later. She imagined a leer on his face on the other side. *"Mr. Carson is now listening."*

"Hey, asshole. Thanks for sending a search party. I really appreciate it." Krysta emitted a growl. She desperately wished she could reach through the comm and strangle him. She noticed Eski's stare at the raise in her voice.

"*With all due respect, we don't want an incident to come up. You are dabbling in intergalactic affairs that our politicians should handle. Each step can put Earth in jeopardy. I will not be responsible for it,*" The colony director argued.

"I will be diplomatic," she countered sternly through a clenched jaw. A burning sensation crept up her chest, and she held her forearm against it for support.

"*You have no approval to negotiate treaties with the Reptilia.*" Carson lashed out.

"Who says I was going to negotiate?" Krysta severed her connection and huffed loudly at the exchange of words. Her chest constricted more and the stinging sensation intensified, causing her to swear under her breath from the pain.

"Something the matter, Lone Wolf?" Eski moved to stand beside her.

Hissing through her teeth to work through the electrifying stinging sensation in her lungs, she feverishly shook her head. Krysta took a few slow breaths. "There was an ass on the line." The reptile said nothing in response and turned back around to watch for his compatriots. "I guess there are some words in our vocabulary that don't translate for you too, huh?" With the reptile's back turned, she wondered if he'd ignored her question intentionally or hadn't heard it at all. He held his arms stiffly at his sides, deeply focused on his base's direction. "Eski?"

With a slight flinch, he glanced in her direction. "Yes, Lone Wolf. I apologize. You must not speak and rest. Ikol's toxin lingers throughout your respiratory system. I will ensure your treatment. The amount you inhaled won't be lethal if you receive our medication within the next few hours. However, exertion will only exacerbate it."

"Just a few hours? That's all I have left?" Worry crested her brow, and she yearned for the direction that her colony was in. "You better not be shitting me, Eski. My life is in your hands." A part of her wanted to contact Bear and tell him to pick her up pronto, but nobody at Bakht had the medical means to treat her without the luxury of time and a sampling of the venom itself.

"Shitting you?" Eski's eye ridge lifted at her words. "Your species has an interesting set of semantic phrases. You must trust me, Krysta. My words are not deceitful."

Ignoring her pain, she pleaded, "I have some questions about the Achli that I need to ask."

"After you recover, then we can have an open exchange. I would like that very much."

"Hey, I may die in a few hours. I need answers. Who were the Achli?" She sat down on the dirt floor, taking slower breaths to divert the discomfort. The constriction around her chest was slowly dissolving.

"The Achli were the evil ones, the Children of Sani, Krysta. Why do you want to know about them?" He sat down by her side.

She noted he didn't slump, and his right fingertips rested guardedly on his pistol. Her first reaction was mimicking the position with her own pistol, but she suppressed the unease and moved her eyes back up to his face. She didn't fault him for his distrust. They were both soldiers from opposing races and neither had anything to prove they were safe from the other. Her focus strongly met his. "Because my father was a colonist killed by them. That's why. Nobody reached Enlightenment after the destruction of the colony by the Achli. So please, tell me everything you know about those bastards: their language, their appearance, and their weapons."

Pausing before answering, she noticed the uncertainty clouding his yellow eyes. "What drives you to acquire this information?"

"If I live, then one day I am going to find those bastards and I'm going to kill all of them." Her past's distorted memories surged into her mind, fueling her rage. Her fingertips resting on the dirt at her side tore into the ground as she felt the anger boil within her. She looked away to hide the moist tears that rested just at the surface of her eyes.

No words came next from Eski's mouth. A neutral expression rested on his face. He rose and avoided her gaze. "Krysta, rest first, and I swear I will tell you everything once you are fully healed." He walked away, putting more distance between them.

Wolf's jaw tightened at the sudden change in him. A door was closed on the openness they once had. Her hand reached underneath her armor to clutch her dog tags, and she squeezed the cold metal. What was the Hlinan hiding?

Chapter 15

Time ticked away as Krysta coughed and flipped her dog tags through her fingers from where she sat. Every so often, her eyes lifted to where Eski paced distractedly ahead of her. His movements were stiff and jerky. The sound of an incoming hover vehicle made the Hlinan freeze in his step. On cue, Krysta rose from the ground, tucking her tags underneath the skin of her armor. She observed that the inbound hover vehicle had a more streamlined and curvaceous shape than human-designed vehicles and was significantly less massive. Eski slipped on his helmet and kept his distance. "I will handle this matter."

"How come I don't like the sound of that," Wolf muttered under her breath.

The vehicle slowly descended to the dirt floor upon reaching its destination; a door in the middle of the vehicle opened laterally. A line of three armored Hlinan exited swiftly with weapons in hand. They moved past Eski and to Krysta's position with their weapons drawn toward her. Another Hlinan that bore the same rank insignia as Eski exited the craft more gradually. Unlike him, Krysta noted this one had a more petite body shape. Its helmeted face turned slightly to look at its fellow kin before leering Krysta's way.

Alarmed by the weapons aimed on her, Wolf pulled out her pistol. "Back off," she growled. "This is not the welcoming party I was expecting, Eski."

The Hosir Matelija rushed over to place himself between her and the others. "This one is not a threat. Stand down!" The three armed reptilians ignored the order, making Eski look at his counterpart for an explanation. "What is the meaning of this, Hosir Madu?"

"After you left the base to follow their drones, Hosir Matelija, I transmitted a report to High Command. We are taking all necessary precautions," Madu replied, in a more feminine voice, Krysta noted.

"Report? What did you tell them?"

"That enemy drones intentionally invaded our airspace. I informed them that you led a team to intercept a potential scouting party. They were very unsettled that you had brought an Arlandr back with you without the order given. We will interrogate this prisoner further." She motioned to one of the three standing by. "Secure her weapons."

"Like hell you are," Krysta spat venomously. "Try it, and the only thing they will be securing is a nice, friendly bullet."

Eski's claws curled into fists. "It will make things easier if you comply, Lone Wolf."

She struggled to keep her pistol poised as her lungs burned. "This wasn't part of the deal." A cough broke her words and heard her own self wheezing.

Eski stepped again to put himself between his soldiers and her. This time, he focused on her directly. "Krysta, you are not well. At least trust *me*."

"You are with *your* race now. Why should I?" She glared accusingly at his visor. Her watery eyes from the coughing bout made her vision blurry and she barely made out the shape of his face.

"Because I *trust* you so far," he urged without hesitation. "I will make sure that no harm will befall you. You also need treatment right away."

Wiping the tears from her eyes in defeat, Wolf lowered her weapon and turned it to where the grip faced him. She then removed her assault rifle and handed it to him as well. She was no match for Ikol's toxin. "Fine. Just give me the damn antidote."

"Remove any communication devices you may have and your armor," Madu instructed firmly.

Krysta complied, begrudgingly, and handed her comm to Eski. She unfastened her armor joints and removed each piece to reveal her black smooth pants and shirt that perfectly shaped her figure. "I'm keeping my dog tags on before you ask further, and my translator earpiece, if you expect me to understand." She noticed Eski's eyes lingered on her new appearance before he cleared his throat to hand the articles of gear and weapons to the three soldiers. One soldier moved to take off her dog tags, but she swatted his hand away hard. "Back off, lizard. I said these stay on. This is not negotiable."

The female leader grumbled at her aggressive stature. "Hosir, this one is contentious and should be restrained."

"That will not be necessary," Eski interjected quickly, before Krysta had an opportunity for a rebuttal. "Are we ready to head back to base now? Lone Wolf has been exposed to Ikol's toxin, and she requires lung treatment immediately. We must not linger any further."

Madu sneered knowingly. "Correction, Hosir. She is not staying at the base. High Command wants her transferred to the Hevding. Our divine ruler has requested to see her without delay."

Glancing at Wolf a second time, Eski then responded, "Then I will go as well. I will directly provide my report and my recommendations on an alliance with the humans. She will need a portable lung treatment along the way."

"Alliance? With humans? You mean the Children of Sani." Madu scoffed at his hasty suggestion. "Do not be so naïve, Eski. This is a very dangerous matter. You will not accompany her further. She is no longer of your concern."

Unable to keep quiet any longer while they decided on her fate, Krysta blurted out, "If you take me without my consent and without *him*, then you will throw your kind into a war with mine." She stepped firmly around Eski to put herself just a meter away from where Hosir Madu stood. She couldn't see into the Hlinan's helmet but knew the female Reptilia was more than likely glaring at her. A fiery pain seared Krysta's lungs, causing her to flinch.

"Our Hevding has given his order, Arlandr. You do not have a say in this."

Krysta glowered at the response. "Well, then, if I have no say in the matter." She whirled on her heel swiftly and delivered a hard punch to one of the other soldiers nearby. The hit knocked him off balance and sent him reeling to the ground. The jerk of her body aggravated her burning lungs, and she winced loudly, clasping her arm against her chest to suppress the sharp stabs of pain. "Son of a bitch," she clenched her teeth.

"Lone Wolf!" Eski grabbed her arm to prevent another strike. She caught him off balance and flipped him onto his back. She glared down at his hidden face. He yelled to her, "Don't do this, Krysta!"

"You lied to me, Hlinan," she growled out with her fists clenched. "I will not be your prisoner." The feeling of the needles inside her lungs poked at her and her breaths became sharper. It was becoming more difficult for her to draw breath. With her knees buckling, she staggered a bit, resisting the urge to collapse.

"She's a threat, Hosir." Madu turned to the other three soldiers. "Shoot her on my command."

"No." Eski ascended swiftly to his feet and removed his helmet. He faced Krysta. "*I* will pacify her."

Krysta sized up the Reptilia in front of her as her eyes hardened on him. He made no movement towards his weapon. She collapsed to one knee, lightheaded. "I knew I shouldn't have trusted you—all that honorable talk was fake," she spat with acid in her tone.

"Lone Wolf, I do not desire to fight you. Everything I said to you was not duplicitous," He kept calm. "If you continue down this path, you will die."

"Heh, like you care," Krysta heard her words slur. His response was muffled. Then her world turned black.

Chapter 16

Krysta awoke to unfamiliar surroundings. The entire vicinity was dark with a red hue glowing from the light bars that outlined the perimeter of wherever she was. When Krysta felt something on her face, she touched her mouth and nose, finding them completely covered. Alarmed, she sat up with her fingers, moving around the apparatus to find that whatever it was; it was completely wireless. A voice cried out next to her. "Hosirs!"

She jerked her head and saw an un-helmeted Hlinan soldier that wasn't Eski standing on guard nearby. This also enabled her to get a better handle on her surroundings. She deduced she was in some type of transport by the enclosure structure. The driver's station had a large panoramic window, but the rest was shuttered. Eski sat three meters across from her in another row of black attached seats. He had his injured arm exposed with a strange black topical on top of his wound. He sprung up at the announcement and rushed to her side. Madu soon followed from the transport's driver's cab. "Easy, Lone Wolf." With his dark claws bared, Eski gently touched her arm. "What you have on is a respirator to provide the necessary levels of the breathing treatment. Your oxygen levels have stabilized, and there is only a small percent of inflammation left. It should not take much longer now."

Krysta noticed a significant improvement in her breathing and the painful stings within her lungs vanished. "Where are you taking me?"

"To see our Hevding," Madu flatly interjected. With a sideways glance at Eski, she added, "That is all that you need to know, Child of Sani."

Eski's face tightened at the title. "Hosir, it is presumptuous to make that conclusion. The human has denied that they are affiliated with them."

"And you just believe an Arlandr, Eski?"

"Her kind bears no resemblance to the Achli. Are we that paranoid? Will every race besides our own be one of the wicked?" His eyes held Krysta's. "I sense no deception within her." His voice became quieter.

"It would be wiser for you to hold your tongue, Hosir," Madu snarled. "Your words run parallel to those of a Slaroar."

Krysta silently observed Eski's silent responses. His jaw clenched, and his gloved fingers fidgeted, curling and uncurling in his palm. "That is a bold claim, Hosir. I will speak no more in protest. That is not my intention here and like our god, Hlidar, I merely want peace. Not bloodshed."

A tiny victorious smile spread across the female's thin lips. "I am pleased to hear this, Hosir." Her slender arm moved across the area of the transport towards the squad of Hlinan, observing the conversation. "The Slaroars have poisoned our home world, and the Hevding will be most displeased to learn of the infection's spread, Hosir Matelija." Turning swiftly, she disappeared back toward the driver's seat.

Eski moved close to where Krysta was seated on the small oval-shaped makeshift cot. "Here, Wolf, let me adjust your respirator." As he leaned over to fix the apparatus, she felt his warm breath lap along the top of her shoulder, neck and ears. He whispered to her, "Remain close to my side, Krysta. You may have been better off with Ikol." He delicately readjusted her apparatus, then stood over her. "Your treatment is nearly complete, human. Stay still."

Krysta watched him closely as he moved away to his seat across from her with his attention diverted to his wound once again. Her fingers touched her exposed dog tags. "Hosir Matelija," she called back to him as he spread a weird black ooze onto his wounded arm. "I need to alert my team of the change up before things go south. How about turning over my comms?"

His eyes dashed over to his own kind, then back to her. "I cannot allow that, Lone Wolf. You must relinquish your possessions until after you speak with our Hevding."

Ripping the respirator away, she glared coldly at him. "You are playing a dangerous game. If you don't let me connect with my team to tell them what the hell is going on, then you will have some pretty rude guests on your doorstep."

He paused in his task and she hoped the reaction meant that her remark rattled him. "Arlandr, we are strong enough to handle any threat."

Surprisingly, her chest stung at his apathetic reaction. Fuming, she threw the treatment device onto the solid metal floor beneath her feet. This provoked some of the other Hlinan soldiers nearby to stand up.

Her eyes narrowed at Eski, ignoring the other threat nearby. "Assumptions are dangerous, lizard. You are no friend of mine." His contradictory behavior baffled her; she felt manipulated. One hand extended to cohesion and trust, while the other revealed deception. She felt so foolish for telling Bear and the others to hang back. She dug her fingernails into the cot's thin material. Attacking now would be unwise. She had little room to maneuver and had no clue about her bearings. As much as she loathed to admit it, Krysta needed to wait for their arrival at the Hlinan's city thousands of kilometers away from the safety of the other Peacekeepers. The first step would be to get her gear back, especially her comms. She faced the problem of no longer being able to depend on Eski. It would come down to the Hevding. How persuasive could she be with him?

Chapter 17

"Hosirs, we have arrived," the driver called from his position.

Krysta stood from her seat and watched while the rest of the Hlinan moved toward the exit. Eski motioned her forward without directly looking at her. Madu moved to seemingly block Krysta's view of Eski. "Arlandr, remember that you are not free to go as you please. You will remain with our escort and do not talk to anyone unless spoken to. Is that clear?"

Eski confronted Madu. A low, feral growl emitted from his chest. "Zorainine, Hosir. Lone Wolf is not our prisoner and we will not treat her as such. The Hevding has not made such a proclamation and your authority cannot supersede his."

Judging by the intensity of his tone, Krysta figured the word was like a curse word in his native language. His reaction puzzled her but then she recalled her earlier dialogue exchange with him which made it difficult for her to take his side.

The pause allowed Madu to respond. She cackled at his outburst and cooed rather smugly. "So poignant, Eski."

Krysta leaned in with her finger pointing right up against her chest plate. "Back off, bitch. I am doing your Hevding a solid, so be a good escort and lead on."

Madu's lip curled up to reveal a glistening pointed incisor and Eski gently took Krysta's hand to lead her in the opposite direction. "This way, Lone Wolf." She thought she detected a faint, amused chuckle from him.

"Let's make this quick," Krysta griped as the door parted open, causing bright sunlight to pour in. She shielded her eyes momentarily from the glare until they could adjust. "Your leader will see that I'm a soldier and not a politician, Eski. I won't play nice." A push from behind sent Krysta stumbling, and her training kicked in, causing her to swiftly turn and face Madu, the clear culprit. Wolf stopped, her face only millimeters away from the other Reptilia. "You're sorry for tripping me?"

"Move forward, human." Madu showed no reaction.

"Lone Wolf, with me." Eski called to her.

Letting her eyes linger a few seconds longer on Madu, Wolf turned to head out the exit. A couple of Hlinan armored guards greeted them outside the craft, and curious Hlinan bystanders formed a crowd in anticipation. Krysta kept her forearm up to block the sun's glare, then slowly lowered it to see the apparent civilians of their species murmuring and conversing about her arrival. A few kept their distance while others moved along hastily, with fear or trepidation, she couldn't tell. A line of armed guards held back the crowd, creating a passage to the skyscraper's plaza via a single flight of stairs. Many eyes fell upon her while she followed her escort. She glanced around to note her surroundings. The city was a sprawling metropolis with exquisite architecture and tall, slender, turquoise glimmering skyscrapers. Their design was unlike Earth. The pathways were composed of pristine white metal. Patches of tropical palms outlined the dirt-paved paths. There were no signs of graffiti, no trash, not a stain in place. "This place is too clean," Krysta joked under her breath, "Where's the smog? The noise pollution? At least 'one fuck you' lash out?" She smiled to herself as the warmth of the planet's sun kissed her skin.

Flying vehicles that varied in size moved about, whisking away occupants to and fro on laser-guided highways that weaved along the city. The grandeur of the city made Krysta stop in her tracks to marvel at it. Nothing on Earth topped this. The building in front of her appeared to be one of the tallest she'd ever glimpsed. She barely made out the pointed end. "Keep moving, Arlandr." Madu huffed behind her.

"This is our city, Heofen, Lone Wolf, my city. Here you will speak with our Hevding," Eski explained while he walked in front of her. He led her inside the building's front large oval shaped automatic door. The inside of the building was the exact opposite of the outside of their city. Her body quivered by the warm, humid air radiating down over her as if she were under a sunlamp. Glass-darkened panels composed the flooring, and the walls matched them equally. There was just enough lighting for her to see. Just like her transport over there, red fluorescent light panels outlined the baseboards and connected wall lines to the ceiling. The Hlinan were now basking in a red aurora by the lights as she followed them. Her escort team halted at a set of elevators. Unlike those she was familiar with, the translucent doorways protruded outwards in a half-sphere shape, and the elevator shaft was also clear.

Part of her guide remained back while Eski and Madu entered the cart next to her. She rolled her eyes at the female. "Damnit, I'm stuck with you this whole way?" Seconds later, she felt a strong inertia while the cart shot upwards. Krysta saw the ground below recede further away as they sped hundreds of meters upward. Her eyes widened in surprise till the cart finally slowed seamlessly to its destination. The desired level revealed the same dark path before them, opening up to an overly decorated area where a seated Hlinan behind a very thin opal-colored desk greeted them.

The Hlinan adorned itself with a loose-fitting silk blood moon-colored long-sleeve top and dress pants. The shirt was embroidered in turquoise with an unrecognizable tropical design pattern. The Hlinan rose from his desk and calmly walked around it. He paused a few steps away and greeted her with his left arm across his chest. Curling his fingers into a fist, he bowed slightly. "I have been expecting you, Lone Wolf. I know you are only one Arlandr, but can you speak for all that arrived? This meeting is overdue. It needs to be a matter of unity and plans for future harmony between our two races."

"Let me save us all a headache. If you are hoping to speak with a diplomat, then you kidnapped the wrong person. I'm a former Marine and a hired gun for Dhank Trust. They own our colony and I'm just here for security. Simple enough?" Krysta hoped they would see their error and return her items. She did not know what the Peacekeepers were doing back at Bakht and it wouldn't be long before they would tear the place apart looking for her.

"Kidnapped?" His eyes widened at the term. "That was not the intention. That is very harsh to allege. By my request, I advised Hosir Madu to bring you here for a meeting."

She crossed her arms stubbornly. "Call it whatever you want, Hevding, but it will look like a kidnapping to my group. Your pal, Hosir Matelija, over there snatched me up. That was the first mistake. Then, you bring me here without allowing me to notify my team. That was mistake two. Don't make another."

Madu retorted, "Show some respect!"

The Hevding raised his hand politely to calm Madu and returned his focus to Wolf. "Are you saying that you do not affiliate with the others of your species?"

"Nope. I'm just with the Peacekeepers." She defiantly held his gaze. "Hired mercenaries, not with Dhank Trust at all."

The Hlinan leader stepped closer, as if eager. "If you are not truly associated with the ones behind your colony, then you can speak freely about their intent without repercussions. Is that veracious?"

"I don't know all their dirty little secrets," Krysta admitted and relaxed her arms lightly. "No offense. I don't know you and refuse to be a pawn in whatever game you are playing."

The Hevding moved around his desk to take his seat. A lengthy, tense silence filled the space as his thin fingers laced together under his jaw. One set of eyes peered over the taloned tips at her. "We are aware of the discord at our base. Your military formed just outside the perimeter and demanded your swift return. They wanted to escalate this misunderstanding further into war." He unclasped his hands and pushed back from the desk, with all four of his eyes studying her. "I do not know what to make of all this. You say your colony's intentions are diplomatic, yet you threaten war over something so trivial."

The uncovering made Krysta's eyes widen. She was speechless. *Jack, what the hell are you up to?* She then addressed the leader's remark. "I *thought* I could trust Hosir Matelija." Looking over at Eski, she noticed his quietness. "I don't think you want to continue this façade further, Hevding."

The Hlinan leader rose from his desk. "Please, human."

"Lone Wolf."

"Lone Wolf." He opened his arms in a non-threatening universal gesture. "I am utterly captivated by your species' progress on this planet."

"I will share this. I know that the Achli or what you call the Children of Sani wiped your first colony out. You think we are them, but I assure you, we are not. The Achli hit our first colony too on Aether B. We share a common enemy. Does that help?"

Shocked, he looked over at Eski. "Hosir Matelija has informed you of this sensitive history?"

Madu stepped hastily around Krysta to address her ruler directly. "The Hosir has compromised our integrity. A formal inquisition must take place." She gestured towards Eski's location.

The Hlinan leader lifted an eye ridge with her outcry. "And do what, Hosir Madu? Excommunicate him? Execute him? For what charges? For conveying the truth of our history? I believe Eski has the same mindset as I do and wishes to build a bridge of trust between us and these humans. He placed the first link, and I hope we can build upon that."

With a slight bow, Eski stepped forward in a dutiful salute. "I have the same hope, Your Excellency."

"But Hevding I must object—" Madu broke in.

"You may remain reticent during this meeting, Hosir," their ruler shot sternly back at her. The Hevding sat back down in his chair. "If Matelija revealed our dark past, he must have told you about the Children of Sani's imminent return. We came to this planet two hundred years ago to preserve our civilization should our home world ever fall. For fifty years now, we have remained isolated on this planet. At first, you merely scanned our world and sent probes down to the planet's surface. Then, years later, your species returned with ships and built a colony. We established the base on the other side of the planet within reach of your colony to keep a careful vigil. Now, you speak with us."

"Look, you don't get it." Krysta let out an irritated sigh. "You are wasting your breath. If you want their plans, then talk to Colony Director Hunter Carson. He's your guy."

The Hevding's eyes gleamed with renewed vigor, and a smile touched his thin lips. "Then *he* will come here?"

"I can't speak on his behalf, but I will inform him that your kind wants to talk. I'm sure the company has someone nominated for that role. My job is to guard and shoot things. I don't think you want that here." Wolf glanced over to Madu to see the female Reptilia still stewing in the background.

The gleam in Hlinan's eyes died, his expression wavering. "How not fortuitous." He rose from his seat again. "Then I invite you to stay here until this matter is resolved."

Krysta gave a shake of her head. "I have to reject that but I do need a ride back to my colony. I hate to walk the whole way.

Besides, my team is right outside your base and making them wait is not wise."

The Hevding fixed his eyes on her. His friendly demeanor morphed into a callous one. "That was *not* a request. I will dispatch a messenger to your settlement to beckon your leader here, this… Hunter Carson. It shouldn't take too long. I'm sure your team will comprehend the fragility of the situation and exercise devout patience."

Wolf vehemently shook her head again. She was not about to be whisked away another time without her consent. "No way. I'm not staying here a minute longer."

Eski stepped in, his voice filled with alarm, "Hevding, I must oppose that–" Madu shifted from her position to Wolf's right. Turquoise armored guards entered the room. They surrounded Lone Wolf. With a furious jerk of her head, Krysta glared at their ruler.

The leader remained neutral in his pose. "Please, Lone Wolf. We do not want violence."

With a hardened look, she readied herself against her oncoming opponents. Her lips curled into a cynical smirk. "Looks like you'll get it." She saw panic in Eski's eyes. "I failed Diplomacy 101."

Chapter 18

"No weapons on her." The Hevding shouted to his soldiers.

The closest guard stashed his gun away and then lurched forward with a left hook; Krysta braced her right arm across her face to block the attack and bore through the risk of lacking armor. Using the momentum, she delivered a strike with her left hand, catching the Hlinan right in the center of their armor. He stumbled backward, so she shifted to a right uppercut, which landed squarely on his face. The guard staggered away, and his companion swung several blows at her. Although she blocked most of his attacks, he was too quick; a blow to her left cheek sent her spinning through the air before she hit the ground. Despite the stinging pain on her face, she was on her feet seconds later, ready to try again. "You will not get a second one, bastard." She backed up her guard.

Eski deliberately positioned himself in her line of sight. His stern gaze met hers. "Lone Wolf, you must refrain yourself from pursuing this action any further. I do not wish to fight you."

"I am not staying here, Eski. I should have never listened to you." She swung at him with a right punch, but he stopped the damage with a cross left block. He used her momentum to his advantage, grabbed her left arm, and flipped her onto her back. Despite the sharp pain in her spine from the metal floor, she was up in seconds, ignoring the discomfort.

"Will you not yield, human?" Eski kept his guard up.

"Not yet, lizard." Krysta tried the same punch again to throw him off. After he blocked it, she grinned and shoved his arm up higher, exposing his entire front torso. She then delivered a left cross hook, catching him dead center in the abdomen. The force of the blow made him stumble back. His eyes widened at her strike, and then he hissed loudly in irritation.

Without hesitation, Krysta charged and tackled him to the ground. The reptile was fast, and he bucked up to throw her balance off, then used that to his benefit. He rolled on top and held her down with the weight of his body. His gloved fingertips pinned her wrists. She could almost feel the claws beneath the material. His face was millimeters apart from hers. He displayed his sharp incisors. A low growl rose from his throat as his four eyes stared right into her. She jerked to free herself but failed to move.

Wolf sharply met his glare. "I won't be your prisoner any longer, reptile. You may as well kill me," she whispered, ensuring only he could hear.

Eski's sharp breaths slowly receded, and his tight grip loosened up slightly. He leaned in, his mouth close to her ear. "If I wanted to kill you, Lone Wolf, I would have done so." His words and the tickle of his breath sent a shiver down her spine, creating goosebumps along her skin. Her mouth parted slightly open, breath ragged, as his yellow eyes slowly drew away.

Just as she could get back to her feet, Madu's voice shrieked like a banshee in the night wind. "Guards, detain her at once."

Krysta pivoted and spotted two of the Hlinan guards moving in from her left. Unexpectedly, Eski charged at the nearest one, kicking him with his right foot, knocking him hard on the ground. Then he stood in front of Wolf to shield her from any further onslaught. He growled threateningly at his own species. "No, that is unnecessary, Hosir Madu."

"Hosir!" The Hevding yelled at him in alarm. "Stand down." But Eski held his ground.

The sudden change dumbfounded Krysta and she stood frozen with her bottom lip drooped. Disbelief washed over her. Was he going up against his own species for her? Before she could grab his attention, an arm wrapped around her neck and pressed against her skin like a vise. She barely turned her head to get a good look at Madu. Krysta dug her fingers around the armored arm to relieve the pressure against her windpipes. She did not know how far the Hlinan would go, but fight-or-flight mode kicked in. Madu hissed, maintaining a firm grip despite Krysta's struggles. "Es-Es-," she struggled to flag his attention.

"You are pathetic," the Hlinan soldier said in a harsh whisper. "I should just end your life."

"Madu!" Eski spun around. "Release her now!"

Madu didn't respond and tightened her hold. Krysta was getting lightheaded because of the oxygen deprivation. Either Madu was going to continue until she fell unconscious long enough to be subdued or killed. To deceive her opponent, Wolf relaxed her muscles, making her body appear limp. A few seconds later, the female seized the bait and released her hold faintly. Krysta used the loosening to her advantage and repositioned her body so that her right leg swung back between Madu's legs. Her foot then hooked around the Hlinan's right foot. She pulled her right leg back in one solid motion, caught Madu's boot, and the Hlinan tripped back. Wolf was completely free.

She then reached around and grabbed the Hosir roughly with both hands, then threw her over her shoulder onto the floor in front of her. Krysta coughed hard and inhaled a few times to recoup the oxygen she lost. Her knees buckled, and she staggered to maintain her gait.

Eski swiftly caught her and propped her up. He gaped at her in terror, his voice trembling. "Krysta, are you alright?"

Krysta glared hard at Madu standing back up. "How'd the floor taste?"

Madu growled loudly and stormed toward her, but Eski slid right in front of her and held his ground firmly. His face leaned right into Madu, with their eyes heatedly locked on each other. Eski clenched his fists tightly at his sides with his two front fangs showing. "You will not harm her anymore, Hosir Madu."

"Why do you protect her?" Madu lashed out. "She is a Child of Sani. Are you a Slaroar?"

"Hosirs!" The Hlinan leader's voice boomed over them. "I will not have us fight one another. Is that clear?"

Eski instantly dropped his pose and bowed before his leader. "As you will it, Hevding."

Madu begrudgingly followed suit. "Yes, Hevding."

The planetary ruler exhaled hard in dismay. "This is not how I wished this to go at all." His eyes flitted Wolf's way, sorrowful. "It is a pity that we could not agree on cohesion. I will attempt to speak with Colony Director Hunter Carson. For now, I ask that you leave my office. Hosir Madu, see that she is settled into an accommodation. Hosir Matelija, a moment?" Krysta flashed Eski a dreaded look, but he did not show any remorse or fear. How he defended her left her astonished, but what were the repercussions of his unforeseen actions? Her eyes never left him standing there silently while the guards led her out. It was only after the doors closed that she lost sight of him.

Would it be the last time they saw one another? What would be his fate?

Chapter 19

Isolated in a small windowless room, Krysta sat in a curved chair while the same red light rained down on her from above. She apprehensively faced the door, her fingertips intertwined with her dog tags' chain. She mulled over the logistics to come up with the next plan of action; there was no way she would simply be their prisoner. She quickly noted no devices inside the room which meant no way to tell how much time passed since the Hevding's meeting. Eski was nowhere to be found. Resting her fate in Carson's hands was out of the picture.

She kicked the floor hard with her boot. How was she going to contact Bear without her communication device? What were the others up to? If he confronted the base, the Hlinan forces outnumbered them. Was she relying on ghosts to save her? Suddenly, a chime from the door made her rise from her seat. The door whisked open and Eski stepped in. He remained quiet until the door shut completely behind him. "About damn time you showed up," she snapped at him ferociously. "What took you so long?"

"Bringing you here in this manner was never my intent, Krysta. Though I failed to predict that you'd resort to violence. If you have remained reserved, then perhaps the Hevding's opinion of you would not be clouded. You did not make a good first impression."

"Oh, I'm sorry. Next time, I will just allow myself to be captured like a good little Arlandr." With a loud scoff, Krysta threw up her hands. "How is this my fault? What about you kidnapping me? Is that okay in your culture?" Miffed, she slanted her eyes away from him. "Your friend Madu wants to kill me, yet I am the hostile one." His silence made her lower her tone. "I don't get you, Eski. At first, you play along like a dutiful Hlinan soldier, then do a complete one-eighty and defend me against your own men, er, lizards."

"I must adhere to my Hevding's command, but Madu had other intentions than just to pacify you, Lone Wolf. She wishes for your death to end this matter."

"No shit. Moving me to your city without my consent was not cool, Eski. I know your Hevding is just using me as leverage to get some deal worked out, but I'm telling you now that he's messing with fire."

Eski rubbed the bony ridge just above his eyes and muttered under his breath, "I did not wish for this to happen. Your kind are not the Children of Sani, but I do not understand your origin or your existence. I wanted to learn more about you."

"Hell of a way of showing it." Krysta clenched her jaw as she watched him work through his own transgressions. "Can I leave now?"

Rushing over to her, Eski lowered his voice to a near whisper. "The Hevding has lost patience and insists that he speaks with your colony's leader. A group of your Peacekeepers have positioned them-selves right outside my base. They are threatening violence if we do not send you back."

"And I'm supposed to care?" Krysta responded with a frigid voice. "I knew the Peacekeepers wouldn't just sit back and let you guys keep me away." Then her tone turned somber. "Your Hevding is messing up royally, mind the pun, if you do not get my ass back over there. I need my comms, Eski. I can end the bloodshed that you fear." Her voice was thick with contempt. "You have lied to me over and over again. Your Hevding had no intention of releasing me."

"Your friends must not resort to aggression over this, Wolf." Eski's expression darkened. "There are many innocents in the city, including our offspring. This must not spread!"

"It wasn't *my* choice." She glared back. "You know damn well who you should blame for all of this."

"Zorainine!" Jerking away, Eski paced with rigidly held arms. "You are sound, Krysta. I should have never taken you from the fight with the hata. What was I considering?" He stopped and whirled again her way. "Hosir Madu gave your possessions to the Hevding, and he is withholding them at his discretion. I will try to convince him to hand them back to squash the tension back at my base."

Exasperated, she threw her hands up. "Try? Damnit, Eski. Get my things back. At least you admit you were wrong. Now, fix this mess." Krysta moved away and leaned back against the wall with her arms crossed across her chest. "By the way, what is Jack exactly saying at the base? Or is he already doing fisticuffs?"

Eski paused in his pacing and blinked at the question. "The one with the red hair on his face? Your colleague is threatening swift violence if we do not promptly return you. My soldiers have tried to assure him that you are safe, but like you, he does not believe us."

"Can't blame him there," Krysta snorted under her breath. Her fingers tapped along her folded arms and her eyes glanced his way again. "Jack doesn't bluff. I've played him way too many times in poker. What is Madu saying in all of this?"

"Hosir Madu does not agree with me. She perceives you only as a Child of Sani and a threat to all Hlinan."

"Good. She should fear me," Krysta snickered with a leer. "Glad I knocked her to the ground." She observed the troubled expression on his face. "I still don't get why you went up against your own kind for me."

His eyes didn't falter from where he stood. "You saved my life, Lone Wolf. I do not see you as a peril. I believe in my heart that Hlidar sent you here as an ally in our war against Sani."

"Hlidar had *nothing* to do with this. I assure you," Krysta shrugged his words off and walked up to him. "How's the arm? I see you that they swapped your armor out with a new one." She reached out to inspect his wounded upper arm, but as soon as her fingers touched his armor gauntlet, he recoiled fast with a low hiss from his mouth.

"I am fine. My species have good regeneration properties, along with our advanced medicine. It will take time, but once I shed the old skin, there will be no markings at all."

"That's pretty useful for combat." That impressed Krysta. "I'm not too keen on shedding skin, though."

"Humans do not have that ability?"

"Not as fast." Her head roved up from his arm to his face. "Ok, maybe I understand why you defended me back there, but why did you take the spider's blow to allow me to live? You knew you wouldn't be able to survive that."

"Why did you come back to save me?" he countered with both sets of his yellow eyes bearing down on her.

Her bottom lip dropped slightly by his gaze, and she swallowed hard to regain her composure. "Because what you did was suicidal, and I wasn't about to get blamed for your death." Then she shrugged, "Heh, didn't make any difference. I'm still here at this place and they all hate me."

He chuckled at her words. "They do not all hate you, Krysta. They do not comprehend your species. You are an anomaly to our understanding of the way things are, even the way of our religion."

"What makes you think I'm not some ancient enemy of the Hlinan race?" She pursed her lips teasingly. "What makes you believe I'm not hostile at all? You should call yourself the anomaly. No one feels about me the same way as you do."

"Because I have seen images of the Achli, the true Children of Sani, from their first attack on this planet. Your characteristics do not match theirs. As you said before, we share a common enemy."

"Tell me about them. I'm not going anywhere soon, it looks like you owe me an explanation at the very least."

"The archived data revealed the Achli spoke two languages. Their frequency and phonetics were dissimilar. They presented very limited choices for our colonists here: submit to them or be annihilated. We saw them as the Children of Sani and knew that we must fight to protect Hlidar and our own existence."

Krysta felt a hard lump form in her throat at his words. "Enlightenment could only send audible transcripts, but what you are saying sounds very familiar. The feed showed two times that our translator software failed. Bastards. What about their weapons?"

Eski reached down and undid the holster of one of his pistols. His eyes scanned over it thoughtfully. "They did not have weapons like you and I, Lone Wolf. Their wrist gauntlets released energy spheres that were fatal upon direct impact. Over time, we constructed our shield technology to protect ourselves for their return."

She watched him tuck his pistol back in. "I'm glad your colony fought back. I'd rather be dead than a slave."

"Some of the Hlinan's bodies were never located, Lone Wolf. Not all can face their own death without breaking."

"Why do you firmly believe that I am not a Child of Sani, Eski? Perhaps your god, Sani, enabled the Achli to shapeshift to make you let down your guard. Don't deny that many of your friends see it that way. It's in their eyes, especially with Hosir Madu."

"Hosir Madu has many faults, Krysta. She will believe what she desires. The theory that you present is not valid to me. Deception can only go so far." His claws reached out, and he gingerly scooped up her dog tags into the palm of his hand. "What do these signify? You guard these quite possessively."

Krysta watched his black claw tips move down one of the dog tag's sides and then she clutched them away. "I received these in the military. It's a reminder of what made me strong and how far I've come."

"You are very rogue, Krysta," He chuckled again lightheartedly. "I do not believe you were ever weak. You are a formidable opponent. I hope that fate will not pit us against one another."

She smirked as he moved back to the door. "For your sake, Eski." With a returning leer, he silently tipped his head at her before pivoting back on his heel to head out of the door. She called to his back, "I'm surprised that Hosir Madu let you visit me after what happened."

He halted at the door and kept his back still towards her. "She is not here. She returned to the base while the Hevding has asked me to remain for the meeting with your Hunter Carson. As Hosirs, she and I share responsibilities."

The unsettling news made Krysta's spine go rigid. "Eski, I don't like the idea that she is at the base to call the shots when my friends are at your doorstep. It may not end well for her."

Bitterness laced Eski's voice as he replied, "Lone Wolf, although Madu and I are no longer bonded, the pain remains deep within me." He glanced at her over his shoulder. "I remain concerned for her well-being, and I hope what you said doesn't turn out to be true." Following his departure, the door closed silently.

His last words caused her jaw to drop. She stared at the metal door in disbelief "What?" She stumbled a few steps towards the door as she struggled to get herself to move, frozen by the shock. She slammed her hand on the door and slapped it hard a few times more. "Wait a minute! Eski! Come back here!" There was no sound at all on the other end. She pounded the door harder with her fist. "Hosir Matelija!" Grinding her teeth against one another, she punched the door hard with her fist, ignoring the throbbing pain after effect. "Dammit! What the hell did he mean by he and Madu no longer-bonded? Ugh, this day keeps getting weirder and weirder. Come on, Jack, where are you?"

Chapter 20

Fortunately for Krysta, shortly after Eski's departure, two Hlinan guards arrived, and she was already on her feet when they entered. She eye-balled them carefully. She had a decent chance of getting away.

"Arlandr, the Hevding has requested your presence at once. Your colony director has arrived. Please follow us," a guard ordered.

Krysta unflexed her muscles and decided not to ambush them. She needed to be at the meeting with Carson even though she didn't like the idea that her only intel would come through him —it's not like she had a choice. "Lead the way."

Following an escorted route through two hallways, she arrived at a larger room. Eski was already present, and he rose from his chair to greet her. Krysta sat down on the opposite side of the large, oval, jasper-colored rock table that dominated the room. The puzzled look on his face revealed his confusion over her seating arrangements. She mouthed to him, "I'm going solo." The Hevding entered next and Hosir Matelija immediately stood from his chair again for a salute; the other guards inside the room mirrored the same action. Following tradition, Krysta mimicked their movements, eliciting a warm smile from the Hevding before he took his place at the head of the table. Next, two Hlinan guards sporting the turquoise-colored armor entered, followed by the Bakht's leader. A mocking shrug from Krysta drew an icy stare from the man.

The Hlinan leader motioned for Carson to take the empty seat beside Krysta. "Thank you for receiving the invitation and coming without reluctance, Colony Director Hunter Carson. I hope your travel accommodations were adequate to your liking."

Never taking his eyes off Krysta, Carson nodded at the speaker with a sideways glance. "They were adequate. Thank you for the arrangements."

Wolf attempted to study his unspoken body movements to figure out what was happening. Krysta contemplated and then beamed in joy, when she concluded that Bear must have done something spiteful.

Carson leaned over to Krysta's seat. "I stupidly believed I could trust you all." The words sliced through the air like daggers.

Wolf scrunched her nose. "What the hell is eating at you? Isn't this what *you* wanted? I figured you would be happy by finally putting those ivy league skills to work."

Carson's face broke into a sly grin. "You haven't talked to your team, have you?"

"Um, hello? Where have I been? You tell me," she harshly whispered. The man dug under her skin. Every fiber of her being ached to reach over and punch him.

As Eski cleared his throat, it became apparent to Krysta that the Hlinan were paying close attention. The Hevding briefly looked at each of them. "Is there a problem? You both know each other, correct?"

"Hevding, if I may?" Carson rose to greet the ruler. "I am not accustomed to your formal proceedings, so please stop me if I need to clarify anything." The Hevding motioned for him to continue with a wave of his hand. Carson moved to the front of the room, his hands at his sides. "Before we discuss a beneficial partnership between your city here—"

"Heofen," Eski corrected him.

"Ah, yes. Heofen and our colony, Bakht," Carson continued. "I think I need to handle a private matter foremost." His eyes then shifted back to Wolf with intent. "I would like to request the removal of this woman from the meeting."

"What?" Krysta sprang up. "I have every right to be here!" With the sudden commotion, Eski reacted quickly, drawing his weapon to shield his leader. The two Hlinan guards did the same.

"Incorrect," Carson snatched his interface tablet off the table and did a few vigorous swipes on the screen. "I know you may not be up to speed on current events, but your organization ignored a direct order. Instead, they left to rescue you with the threat of violent means. As colony director, I tried to intervene to remind them that their sole contracted duty was to protect the colonists' lives and the colony's interests. They broke their agreement when they left Bakht without permission."

"They left to find me. The Hlinan stole my comms, preventing me from warning my team. Peaceful resolution would have been possible if they had known the Reptilia's intentions," she argued in a tone of acid. If only the Hlinan listened to reason.

"Lone Wolf," Eski called out to her firmly. Krysta paused. He shook his head at her derogatory words toward his kind. Her jaw tightened. Was he really going to take Carson's side over her? She pressed back against her seat with her arms crossed sharply, fuming inside. It appeared diplomacy wouldn't resolve her predicament.

Hevding entered the dialogue. "I see there was a misconception."

Carson turned from Krysta. "I apologize for the housekeeping details, but because of the Peacekeepers' breach of contract, my employer, Dhank Trust, has severed ties and exiled them from the colony. She is part of that group and has no interest in this meeting."

"Exiled?" Krysta lashed out at him. "You bastard! What the hell are you doing? You're an idiot for even disclosing that you're defenseless out there."

"For a moment," the director jumped in. "Your contract was short-lived as it was, and Dhank Trust has already dispatched the new permanent force to arrive in the weeks to come. Bakht will be completely fortified." His eyes flickered over to the Hevding. "However, I'm hoping with this open dialogue that the Hlinan will not become the aggressors."

The Hlinan ruler rubbed his forehead in what appeared to be frustration. "This gravely worries me. There has been tension on the border of our base near your colony, and I was hoping we could come to terms to live peacefully as neighbors, but now you state that what is currently happening is outside of your control."

Eski moved back to his seat. "If I may, Your Excellency, the solution to the problem outside my base is simple. There was a misunderstanding about Lone Wolf being present here; Hosir Madu declined the use of her communications with her kind. Once we adjourn here, we should immediately allow Krysta to speak with her organization and return her. That will quash tensions. I will make it my priority." His hands flattened on the smooth tabletop, eyes locked on his leader.

The Hevding gave each one a wary look before he addressed Eski's proposal. "I am not persuaded, Hosir Matelija. Their colony's leader admitted that there was already instability in the humans' colony and that these Peacekeepers were acting on their own accord. How could any terms with him rectify that?"

Krysta let out a loud huff in her seat. "Fuck's sake. I said I wasn't a diplomat, but I'll make a deal with you."

The Hlinan ruler shook his head at the advice. "No, Lone Wolf. How can the Hlinan here remain neutral and make peace with two warring sides?"

Furrowing his brow, Eski then turned back to his leader. "Virtuous One, Krysta has spared my life from Ikol and proven herself worthy through her combat skills. I let my guard down intentionally several times in the mountain pass to test how she would react, but she never acted in hostility. Kindness and trust have always been your words, for that is how Hlidar taught us. We should display our beliefs by letting the Peacekeepers come under the protection of the Hlinan at my base until the fracture within their own colony is healed."

Stunned, Krysta turned her head to him. His eyes flickered to her only for a microsecond before back to the leader of the room. His words were like rope-a-dope. Earlier, he acted like he was turning his back on her by defending Madu and disciplining her when she lost her cool with Carson. Now, he was at her defense again and proposing a bold move by suggesting that exiles be permitted to stay. She heard Carton snort under his breath at the Hlinan's words.

Eski's superior slowly sat down, and his eyes moved to the large pane window that overlooked the city's skyline for a few brief seconds before his focus returned to the table. "You speak like a true believer, Hosir Matelija, but that is something that I cannot allow. If these two groups are in conflict, we must remain neutral. As the chosen Hevding, I must protect our species."

Bakht's director clapped irritatingly hard at the Hevding's response. "I concur, a sage and noble idea. To avoid war at all costs is beneficial to all. Whatever harm emotionally or physically, the Peacekeepers have caused your people-" A wide smile spread across his face. "I humbly apologize for and assure you that's not what Dhank Trusts wants out here."

"What do *you* want, then?" Eski challenged back, unmoved by the display.

"Me?" Carson brushed the rhetorical question away. "I am speaking here for my company."

"Edify me then," Eski pushed him.

A nervous chuckle escaped the man as he settled deeper into his chair. "Well, if it were me, to be honest, I wouldn't have hired combat-worn ex-military mercenaries to be sent out on this planet. After all, we are here to build partnerships to enhance humanity which includes all species, and Hlinan. You come in with weapons, and it sets the wrong precedent."

Krysta heard enough. "You do *know* what happened to our first colony on Aether B, Mr. Carson?" She scowled hard; her nails dug into the table by the resurrected memory. "Enlightenment? What about my father?"

Carson rolled his eyes. "Yes, a very tragic tale, but one that we must accept when we take shortcuts. I assure you that Dhank Trust has outlined many scenarios for success here."

"Bullshit," Krysta grumbled. "Which scenario was it when you exiled your own security group and your shit came apart at the seams? Was it A, B, or C? Or S for 'screwed?' Hevding, all corporations are greedy, and dealing with them will not end well. They will make a deal with you first and shake hands on it until a better one comes along."

Carson stewed in anger next to her and he craned his head her way. "So, do you want these people to believe a highly unstable gun-slinging ex-soldier instead? Violence is all that you know."

"Lone Wolf has proven herself to me. You are mistaken," Eski disputed. "I would put my life on the line with her rather than with you. I do not believe your company would save anyone in your colony from the creatures of this world." Wolf's eyes widened at his admittance, and she displayed a rare, but tender smile to him. He was still by her side, after all.

The Hlinan's planetary ruler rose from his seat, prompting all of them to do the same. "I need to take a short recess. Hosir, please escort them into the hallway. I will call you back when I am ready."

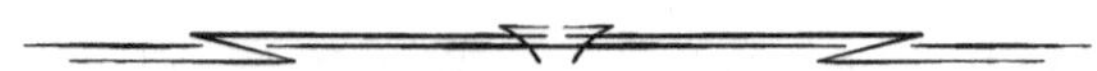

Both sets of Eski's troubled eyes loomed on Krysta when she turned to face him upon entering the hallway. He clenched his jaw, and she

saw the tension in his posture. "Remain here." The door then closed behind him, blocking her and Carson from entry.

Krysta fought off the uneasy feeling inside her by jabbing her finger into the director's pristinely pressed shirt and jacket. "You need a good punch in the face, not just one time. Maybe two. Anybody tell you that?" She spat before glancing over at two Hlinan guards nearby. She needed to be tactful and restrain herself from allowing her emotions to take over. Being locked out there with Carson after his position was not helping her.

Carson huffed as their eyes met. "I rest my case about your type, straight to violence is your natural instinct."

Wolf diverted her eyes to the dimming sky outside. Her fingers curled into the palm of her hands by her sides to suppress her rage. "Who did your team hire to replace us?"

"That's confidential."

"Amateurs, I'm sure." His unwillingness to turn over information felt like a jagged fingernail slowly moving over her skin. "Maybe exile was the plan all along to stop paying us. A fucking loophole in the contract. Are your employers that cheap?"

"You're unbearable," Carson groaned, rubbing his temple. "Look, when we get back in there, let me do the talking to work out something. You play the game, and I'll see how I can get you guys back. I didn't like that one's tone in there. Did you brainwash him?"

"Eski just knows what the hell is going on. I can't help it if he doesn't like you." She smirked proudly with her arms crossed. Carson slid his hand through his hair. He scurried closer to the door and pressed casually up against the wall; his eyes frantically moved over the tablet he kept close to him. Krysta watched on curiously, "Hey, how is Dhank Trust handling the situation back home with the captain? You told him yet?" In the back of her mind, she feared what the repercussions would be back home on Earth. Would there be some political fallout or raid? She didn't plan to make her trip to the planet permanent, but she may have to face it. Carson grunted a response and kept his eyes on the task at hand. She flipped him off. If getting back home by Dhank Trust was a no go, who else could the captain rely on? Her brown eyes darted eagerly back to the door. If the Hlinan sought to destroy them, would they find their way to Earth? Could her planet's forces be enough to save humanity?

Chapter 21

A long and difficult wait ended with Eski's hasty exit from the conference room. "The Hevding is ready." He then stepped aside to allow Carson to rush in while Krysta dragged back. The Reptilia used his hand to stop her, his eyes nervously flitting between her and the conference room. "Stay calm in there, Krysta, no matter what happens." His words were ominous, and she didn't like how the conversation was already starting.

"No promises," she mumbled.

With a motion toward their seats, the Hevding's lips curved into a narrow smile. "Thank you for your patience. This is a keystone for future partnerships, from which I hope we can both prosper." His gaze first fell upon Wolf. "My sincere apologies for any inconvenience you experienced during your stay here. I offer you my blessing from Hlidar for your brave action in saving my Hosir. I will take the obligation to ensure your safe return to your people."

Krysta bowed slightly in her seat. "I accept, Hevding. Thank you." Immediately, she observed Eski sitting perfectly still, devoid of emotion. Discipline steeled his gaze. She wondered about his fate. Would he face consequences for his actions? This might be their last meeting. Reluctantly, she admitted she enjoyed Eski's company despite their short, adventurous mountain trek. She no longer desired solitude. He gave her so many answers about the Achli, that she wasn't sure if the companionship was a mask for intel to learn more about her past, or something else. Something she didn't want to think about.

Carson radiated proudness in his chair as the Hevding turned to address him. "Colony Director, I believe today was very beneficial and I want to cement our alliance with Bakht."

"A pleasure, and I hope our next meeting will be at my colony. Your city is exquisite, and I'm certain my employer would love your help." Carson stood and extended his hand. There was an awkward pause in the room as the Hevding and Eski exchanged looks of confusion by the gesture, then Eski shrugged. Carson grimaced at the rejection and sat back down. Krysta stifled her snicker.

A wide, gleaming smile graced the Hevding's face. "May Hlidar watch over you all during your travels."

As soon as the meeting was over, Carson seized the opportunity to leave quickly. Krysta increased her step to catch up with him. "Hey Carson!"

The colony director glanced her way with reluctance. "Yes, what is it? Make it quick."

"Are you going to admit to your *superiors* that you were wrong about the Peacekeepers and reverse our exile status until our ride to Earth gets here? I'm sure your colonists don't want to be left alone in the dark with the big dangerous monsters in this place. You think those hounds are frightening? Try a big toxic spider crawling out for you in the dead of night."

"What big spider?" He merely chuckled. "You are a piece of work, mercenary. "

Krysta grabbed his arm, roughly. "You have seen nothing yet. What's the ETA on our departure? You gotta know that. When your mall cops arrive, we should get their seats for the return."

Carson recoiled and angrily shoved her away. "You are no longer welcome in the colony, Peacekeeper. Check with the Hlinan for any updates."

Before Krysta fired back a response, a green blur flashed in front of her; Eski was at Carson's face within seconds, and he shoved the man hard against the wall. "Touch her again, and you will deal with me, human." The Reptilia's forearm dug hard into the man's chest, and he hissed loudly with his sharp incisors poised to strike. Krysta was stunned by his protectiveness.

Carson's jaw dropped at his predicament. "You again. I should have known."

"The Hlinan will welcome the Peacekeepers and it would be wise for humans to withhold any threats toward them." With a low snarl, Eski finally freed the trembling man.

Carson shot him a fierce glare. "I don't believe you are the one calling the shots. Should I ask your Hevding in there? You created this mess to begin with."

This time, Krysta thrusted Carson back into the wall with her hand pressed against his shirt. "Back the fuck off, Carson. Do not threaten Eski. In case you forgot, having an open dialogue to improve relations amongst one another was not a good time during the hata attack. If it wasn't for Eski, I would have been in pieces on the ground by those wolves and most likely your company would have extended the colony right on top of my corpse. So take your sniveling little ass back to your colony and don't bother leaving the light on for us." Eski's touch on her shoulder caused her to relax and withdraw her arm.

"This won't be the end, Peacekeeper. Dhank Trust will remember your shrewd loyalty."

"Screw them and screw you. Eski, I'll ride back with you."

Eski motioned her to follow him. "This way, Lone Wolf. The Hevding will send your possessions to my personal craft."

Krysta glowered once more at Carson as the man stormed down the hallway with another Hlinan escort. "Good." She strolled along Eski's side. "I didn't expect you to slam Carson." With a devious grin, she laughed. "That jerkoff deserved it."

"He did not have the right to shove you." His focus shifted her way, then a tiny smirk appeared on his face. "Looks like you and I think alike, Krysta. Well done back there. I did not expect you to come to my defense as well."

She punched him lightly on the arm as the two moved down the corridor. "We make a good team. It's good to know that the feelings toward Carson transcend species."

A seriousness entered his tone. "It is dire that you now return without further delay. Hosir Madu lacks the compassion that I have toward the humans. I fear she will force me to take sides if she intervenes further."

She tilted her head. "What do you mean? Like a setup?"

"Fate brought us both to the base as Hosirs. We must work together. She does not approve of my handling of the situation. Her tainted feelings toward me may make things more personal. I fear the darkness inside her will create pain."

"Shit. Your Hevding seems to think like you, though, Eski. He has your back, right?"

"I am afraid that the decision I made to rescue you from the hata has altered the course of many things. Your existence on this planet sparks debate and the Hevding cannot control the minds and feelings of the Hlinan." He glimpsed her way. "Even now, I question the validity of my faith, though I must resist the urge to reflect at the present moment."

She touched his arm to stop him before they rounded the corner toward a set of elevators ahead. "Hold up. Eski, this is a big deal. If shit hits the fan, you will be their scapegoat. You know that, right? Madu is playing that hand strongly. I saw it earlier when I first met your Hevding. She was out for blood."

Without a word, Eski drew her into a room to their right and shut the door. Krysta observed it to be a much smaller conference room. Crimson light illuminated the area, creating an aurora-like effect on their faces. "It is very dangerous to be speaking such things in the open, Lone Wolf. In the Hlinan's hearts and minds, we are pure creations of Hlidar. His brother Sani created our home world, Emble, but grew jealous of what Hlidar made. Sani then made his own children to pit against us and the winner of that battle will determine the fate of all. Just as the prophecy foretold, the Children of Sani, the Achli, came to this planet to take revenge against our god's creations. We lost the battle and feared our end would soon follow, but it was only a test in which we failed. Sani's children, the Achli, have not yet waged the epic war upon us, but we must remain vigilant and true to our faith. To my religion, humans should not even exist. Either you are false, or you are another creation of Sani."

"The Achli hit our colony, Enlightenment, and killed everyone. They are not the Children of Sani. They are just a bunch of imperialistic assholes hellbent on domination," Krysta argued. The constant reminder that she was something she wasn't, was grueling. "Just accept it. We exist outside your religion's parameters. All of you will have to get over it."

With his gloved claws, Eski gingerly scooped up her dangling dog tags in his palm. His yellow irises' focus dropped upon the cold, hard metal. "Perhaps, Krysta, your kind is another creation by Hlidar to help us in our war. That is what I want to believe and the most likely explanation."

Krysta possessively removed the tags from his hand and held onto them. "No, Eski. Look, I'm not getting theological with you on this, but trust me, Hlidar did not create us. We just exist and it's as simple as that." She snatched his hand and placed it on her cheek. "I'm assuming that your god, Hlidar, made you guys in his image. If I was a creation of him, would I not look like a Hlinan to you?"

A breath escaped his lips and his hand rested on her face while his thumb gently stroked her skin, creating a chill down her body. He averted his gaze and withdrew his hand. "It cannot be. To question our faith is to be deemed a Slaroar."

"A what?"

"A radical; one that does not accept the true Hlinan faith."

"It sounds like there's more than one radical out there."

"Yes, there is a mounting number of Slaroars in my home world since your kind's presence came to this system. Some believe that Hlidar is the false god, and, in fact, Sani is the true one that we must worship. They shout Hlidar created us in deception to shun Sani and that our current belief is a veil over our eyes. Others dare to question our faith altogether. They fear deception by our leaders; they encourage a rebellion. To date, no Hlinan on this planet is part of those groups and the Hevding worries that their venom will spread here."

"If he's afraid, then why befriend us? It makes little sense."

"My devout leader does not fear you, nor does he find you made of evil. With our friendship, he hopes that this will quash tensions that are fiercely growing like a wildfire. I am afraid my rash action in bringing you to us created an unstoppable event." He swore under his breath in his native tongue. "I blame no one other than myself."

Krysta reached out with her fingers and gently turned his head back to her. The roughness of his scales brushed abrasively against her skin. "Eski, get it together, soldier. Blaming yourself will get you nowhere. The Hlinan are going to have to deal with this, eventually. But for now, you need to focus on the dangerous game you are playing with Carson. Dhank Trust won't just stop at their current boundaries. They claim to own the entire planet, and I'm telling you, it will not end well with the Hlinan."

A low hiss emerged within the reptile's chest and he firmly removed the hand from her face, again. "I will ensure that does not happen."

"The Peacekeepers fully support you. Trust me, if Carson is true to his word and exiled us, then it's game on." A smirk played on her lips.

"Thank you, Krysta," He whisked the hair strands from her face. "Perhaps Hlidar controlled what happened that day when I removed you from the hata attack. I can see you in my fate." His fingertips rested on her hair. Then he leaned in closer and his lips gently met hers. Her mind raced and intrusive thoughts paralyzed her. His cool, moist lips remained on hers and her fingertips hesitated right on his forearm. A part of her wanted to snap away and demand to know what his intentions were. But it was small compared to another part that longed for the relationship that never worked before in her life, despite the form being non-human. Her fingertips relaxed on his forearm while she pursed his lips to return the affection; she chose the latter of the two warring sides within her.

Eski withdrew slowly till finally his face was fully in her view again. The memory of his kiss lingered, their faces a few centimeters apart. His warm breath and gentle touch caressed her face. "Krysta, I do not know what this means." His eyes tore away from her, for the third time. "I cannot do what Hlidar asks of me."

Krysta pursed her lips together while her own mind soared. Her heart pumped frantically inside her chest. The notion of what had just happened seconds ago startled her. It was as if she was dreaming and could not control herself.

Before she could speak, Eski pulled further away with a guilty expression on his face. He held a finger next to his communication device in his ear. "This is Hosir Matelija." Krysta remained silent, straining to hear the other's conversation. Eski's eyes widened and then alarm filled his voice. "Hold further action against them, Hosir! The Hevding has asked me to return Lone Wolf to her kind immediately. We are on their way now. Please alert the humans outside the base." Without a single word, he grabbed Krysta's hand and dragged her behind her in a frenzy toward the door. "We must hurry."

"Care to explain what the hell is going on?" Krysta stumbled behind him as he led her out into the hallway and toward their earlier destination. Her face still felt flushed from their kiss.

"That was Hosir Madu. She informed me that your group has their sights set upon one of our bases. I fear she may act before we arrive. When we get to the garage, grab your items and send word to them. We must stop the bloodshed."

Krysta broke out in a jog past him. "Then move your ass, Eski! I need to speak with the Peacekeepers." She inwardly begged that Bear do nothing crazy until she got there. Eski increased his step to move along beside her. Her mind relentlessly poked at her to ask him about what happened earlier with the kiss, but the words stumbled right at the tip of her tongue. The idea was so far-fetched that even she didn't come to grips to admit that it occurred. She noted several Hlinan guards standing nearby as they neared Eski's vehicle and figured it was not the ideal place to bring up kissing. Krysta peered over at Eski. His expression was so neutral, like usual, that she couldn't read it. What did he make of all of this?

Chapter 22

Eski piloted the sleek, two-seater hovercraft as it zipped across the terrain. Restrained in the passenger seat, Krysta felt the velocity press on her chest. The acceleration of the vehicle was unlike anything she had ever seen back on Earth. Krysta glimpsed at the flickering holo display of the map. "Comm's in range, I'm calling them." She tapped her earpiece. "Grim, Bear, this is Lone Wolf. Do you copy?"

"*Krysta? You're alive!*" Grim's voice came over the call first. "*I knew those lizards couldn't kill you.*"

"*Better tell us some good news,*" Bear grumbled. "*I was getting tired of those greenies' excuses. I wanted to knock down the front door.*"

"Yeah," Krysta teased her friend. "I heard you were making quite the stir outside their base."

"*Locked and loaded,*" the older man grunted.

"Director Carson made a deal with their Hevding. They finally sent me back."

"*Hevding?*" Grim piped in. "*What is a Hevding?*"

"The one calling the shots on this planet. Heard you got us exiled, Jack. What did you do?"

Bear snorted at the question. "*I told Carson we were going to get you back from the Reptilia. He told me no, and I told him to go fuck himself. I guess he didn't like my response.*"

Krysta chuckled. "Always rough around the edges, Papa Bear. You heard about the replacements?"

"*I figured as much,*" Grim sourly put. "*Who is it?*"

"Carson wouldn't say."

"*Mall cops?*"

"*I don't care. Return here, Wolf, and then we are leaving this piss-hole.*" Her mentor interrupted.

Krysta cringed. She figured he would want to leave after what had happened so far. "Easy there, Bear. I think Dhank Trust is going to do the Hlinan dirty. We should hang back to make sure that it doesn't happen."

"*Wolf,*" He started. "*If they made a deal, then it's two sides against one.*"

"Just wait till I get there and hear me out," she pressed. "Heads up. Hosir Madu is calling the shots right now at the base. Eski told her to stand down. I don't trust her, so stay alert."

"*The bitchy female? Yeah, she came here a few hours ago, making some demands. Who the hell is Eski?*"

"The one that took me. He's on our side."

"*He's coming? Good. Because I want to have a word with him,*" Bear growled. "*No one snatches one of us like that.*"

"*No offense, Krysta. Even if he's on our side, it's one against what? Thousands?*" Grim pointed out. "*Not good odds. Don't think we can trust anyone right now besides our own people.*"

"Hang tight, guys. I'll see you soon." Krysta pleaded with them. After the call, she contemplated what had happened while she was gone. Bear was on edge; she'd never seen him this half-cocked before. Grim made a valid point. Even if Eski fully committed to the Peacekeepers' aid, it would be him against his planet. Would he be that extreme? The weight of his religion was already buckling on him.

Her almond eyes shifted over to him uneasily as she watched him guide their craft in haste. His right forearm remained locked; his grip tight on the crescent-shaped steering wheel. He heard every word that she said to her team and could possibly piece it all together: The Peacekeepers did not trust him. Becoming uneasy in the silence, she glanced around the small craft; it was large enough for the two of them with a snug storage space behind their seats. She doubted if a single person could fit into such a small area.

Her eyes fell back upon him and her mind flashed to what transpired in the room earlier, prior to leaving Heofen. In an attempt to break the awkwardness, she teased lightly, "I still haven't forgiven you for kidnapping me."

This provoked a chuckle from his mouth, and his guarded posture relaxed. "Understandable. I hope Bakht holds up their agreement with my Hevding. To fight off the Achli, we will need allies. I fear they will return to this place, although their absence over the years has deceived everyone into nonchalance."

"Believe me, I would love to hunt down the Achli with you." She punched her left fist into her right palm. "Payback is a bitch and I'm the one to deliver it."

Eski gave her a warm smile. "You amuse me, Krysta. I was hoping to know more about your species, and… you."

"We have some time before we get to your base. Ask away." She still found it difficult to look his way without being heavily reminded of their kiss. Her fingertip stroked the doorframe next to her and she hoped the casual conversation would get her mind off things.

"Very well. I have shared my religion with you. What about yours, Krysta? Do you also have two deities?"

She tossed the question around in her head for a bit before she replied, "Depends on the person, really. Some people on Earth worship one god, some worship many, while others don't believe a deity to exist."

"What do you believe, Krysta?" He completely pivoted his head her way. "How can one species believe contrastively?"

"How long is it to your base again?"

"Not too much further. Why?"

"Then remind me to explain later. Religion was never my strong point."

"Which do you believe?"

"None."

"Why not?"

"Because I'd rather choose my fate." She hugged herself and steered her gaze to the scenery outside while they traveled along. As dusk settled, a deep lavender sky darkened the entire scene. As the sun sank behind a distant peak, the ocean's waters appeared inky black. The entire conversation brought the uncomfortableness to a whole new level.

"Krysta," His voice softly beckoned her from where he sat. "I apologize if I offended you." When she didn't answer him, he continued, "Be assured that the Hevding is more open-minded than our chosen leader back on Emble. I hope he will persuade the overseer to provide passage for the Peacekeepers back to your own world."

"Hopefully," she muttered glumly under her breath. "Eski, you want to talk about what happened earlier?"

His gaze diverted over to her momentarily before snapping back into place. "I apologize for my actions, Krysta. I do not know what came over me to act in such a manner."

"Not sure what kissing means in your culture." She knew her words came out to be blunt, but she needed answers. The feelings inside her whipped around like a tornado: violent and uncontrolled.

"I have to admit, Krysta. In the few hours that I have been at your side, I find myself curious about your species. In the time I am spent apart, my mind longs to be near you." He removed his armor glove to expose his clawed long slender fingers and then gently reached over and delicately brushed one claw tip against the top of her hand. "Though I must be mindful of my feelings and actions. If I am careless, then my race will label me as a Slaroar."

"What will happen to you if they deem you to be one of those Sl-araors?" Krysta tried to repeat the term as sound as the Hlinan said in his native tongue, but she struggled in hitting it just right. Dread filled her even while she asked the question.

"I do not know."

Krysta grumbled in her seat. "Typical religion. If you walk their path, they treat you like gold, but if you question anything, they cast you out like a demon into hell."

"Where is hell?"

"Nothing," she muttered sourly. "Sounds like you care for me."

"I do, Lone Wolf."

"I won't let you take the fall for this, Eski." His hand remained on top of her, causing her to pull away.

Eski too withdrew his own hand. "I apologize." He cleared his throat before jumbling out, "The director of your colony should have not spoken to you in such a manner."

"Eh," she shrugged. "I'm a mercenary. There have been a lot of jerks I have had to deal with. Carson is only a mild case, just annoying."

A chirp from the console in front of them cut into their conversation sharply. "We are almost there." Eski leaned forward and pressed a lit-up button display. "This is Hosir Matelija. I am inbound to the base from Heofen. Please patch me over to Hosir Madu."

"*Welcome back,*" a male Hlinan answered on the other end. "*Hosir Madu is not at the base.*"

Krysta's eyes went wide by the news and she sat straight up in her seat. "Where the hell is she, Eski?"

"Where is the Hosir?" Eski restructured the question.

"*The Hosir left with a team of five toward the armed humans. She has placed the base on a heightened alert system.*"

Eski severed the connection in a frenzy and punched the side closest to him. "Feon!" His native tongue flowed in a sharp, hissing curse. He then pressed an adjacent button on his console. "Hosir Madu, this is Eski Matelija. I am inbound with instructions from the Hevding to reunite the human with the others so they may part from our base."

There was silence on the other end. "This is not good," Krysta contemplated out loud. "Kick it into high gear!" She reached down to unholster her pistol and checked its clip. Then she tapped her comm link. "Bear, this is Wolf. Do you copy?" Her body pressed hard against her seat as Eski yanked the craft's throttle to the max. "Come on, Jack, pick up."

Seconds later, she heard a voice breathing heavy on the other end. "*I'm a little busy right now!*" Bear snapped and then groaned. "*The lizards know nothing about extended check-out times! Where the heck are you?*" Gunfire flooded the comms' line, causing Krysta to wince and remove her earpiece. "*Crud!*" He grunted again. "*I don't need to bleed out here.*"

"Bear!" Krysta yelled at him in a frenzy. "Are you hurt?"

"*I'm getting too old for this shit! Just get your ass here, Wolf! We are taking fire and casualties!*"

Krysta cocked her pistol after he disconnected and jerked her head towards the vehicle's driver. "Eski, move your ass! My friends are dying out there!"

"I will have my soldiers stand down once we reach our destination."

"Think you can bypass Madu's hold?" Krysta questioned, skeptical. "Doubt it."

"I *can*," he fired back. "You must give me time."

"Order a ceasefire and we are in agreement. Light us up and we are enemies." She already regretted the words that flooded out of her mouth. Her curt attitude was a bit too much, and she could see his demeanor stiffen. "Eski?" Guilt and regret washed over her.

His stoic appearance fractured. "Very well, Lone Wolf."

A chilling coldness overcame the interior of the craft. The taste of death loomed in the area. Her fingers wrapped eagerly around her pistol's handle. Krysta hoped that the new heightened tension in the air was not a precursor for events about to happen.

Chapter 23

Eski's vehicle came to a grinding halt minutes later on the Hlinan side of the discord. On the craft's monitor, Krysta saw a heated gun battle with both sides taking cover. Several mercenaries and Hlinan soldiers lay dead amidst the fighting. Placing on his helmet, Eski grabbed his twin pistols. "I will calm things down with Hosir Madu. Stay here."

"Like hell I am. My friends are out there," Wolf protested before opening her door. With her helmet on, she darted out in her body armor, sprinting fast toward her team with her pistol clutched tightly to her.

"Friendly!" Bear spotted her first, and the Peacekeepers steadied their hands until she took cover behind a tree beside them.

Krysta braced her back against the turn, then glanced around it slowly to see the dead Peacekeepers on the ground. "Damnit. Lost three." She sighed hard and pressed her head against the tree trunk, swearing to herself. "Bear, what happened?"

The bearded man gritted through his teeth while he applied a quick patch on his leg from his personal medic kit. "I got shot, that's what happened."

Grim frowned at her. "That same female showed up with more of those lizards, claiming to have orders to remove us from here. They turned their guns on us first." He pointed to where Eski was dealing with his kind. The Hlinan was too far away for Krysta to make out what he was telling them, and she wasn't sure if the translator's range would even pick up that far out. "That him? The one that grabbed you?"

"Yeah, that's Eski." Krysta stayed focused solely on the Hlinan on the far side. *What the hell is he telling them?*

"Check clips, everyone, while we have a breather." Bear's call to the nearby mercenaries broke her concentration.

"Something is up, Papa Bear," Grim stated in a low voice. "They are chattering way too long."

"I know that."

"Give Eski time, you guys." Krysta allowed her fingers to tap around the pistol's handle while her mind darted through all of the scenarios. "If the Hlinan weren't so warped by their religious delusions, then I would have been here a lot sooner." She strained her head to catch the Hlinan's eye. Was he going to double-cross her? He was taking a longer time on his side of the fence than she thought was necessary.

"Wolf, that guy is bad news. I don't like the way he keeps looking over at us." Grim came to her side. "We are on their turf. They are stalling till their reinforcements get here."

"Give him time. I trust him," Krysta forced herself not to be in denial. She could trust Eski. She had to.

"How do you know that for certain? What reason do we have to trust them? Krysta, they approached us with weapons drawn. That's not friendly."

"Quiet! Eyes up!" Bear drew their attention. "Wolf, your friend is approaching."

Wolf saw Eski jogging toward them from his group. Madu sprinted to catch up to him. Fortunately, they were near Krysta's translator to capture their words. "Where are you going, Hosir Matelija? They are the enemy." With a violent hiss, Madu lashed out at him.

Eski sharply turned toward her. "Who gave you the order to come out here? Did the Hevding?"

"My duty is to protect our city and our kind," Madu launched back, clearly on edge. "These are the Children of Sani. Open your eyes. They do not belong here! They intend to destroy us."

"The Hevding brokered an alliance with the humans, Hosir Madu. They are not the Children of Sani. They are not our enemy, and never were."

"Whose side are you on?" Madu shrieked sharply. "Even if they are not the Children of Sani, the agreement is only with *their* colony and not with these exiles. The Arlandr are beneath us. I ordered their departure, and they refused." She then pointed over to where Krysta and the others stood. "Hosir, are you loyal to us or are you a Slaroar?" Murmurs rose from the accompanying Hlinan.

Pivoting his helmeted face her way, Eski calmly replied, "I have always been loyal to my race. These humans did not violate us. If you want to pass judgement, then it must be on me first."

"And why is that? Because you are weak and someone deceived you so easily? You should have left them to the hata." Unexpectedly, multiple gut-wrenching howls sounded from the southern direction, followed by savage jaw snaps. Madu cackled, "How ironic. Here is your chance to redeem yourself, Hosir. Perhaps Hlidar desires your salvation, after all."

Eski shouted out in a panic, "The hata! Activate shields and retreat to the transport!" He gingerly picked up one of his fallen comrades and ushered the others to the only means of cover.

"Shields? These guys have shields?" Bear griped at the order.

Grim patted him on the shoulder. "Trust me. They don't work too well against these wolves."

Disobeying the order, Madu advanced on the Peacekeepers, rifle in hand. Krysta heard Eski shout to the female to stop, but she did not. "Hostile!" Wolf alerted her team with a raised pistol and aimed at the approaching female. But just as she did, a pack of four hata broke through the tree limbs near them. She spotted one alpha and three smaller pack members.

"Round two." Krysta fired at one of the small canines. The round from her weapon hit the creature's thick hind, causing it to whimper, then snarl. "Bear! We need to get our asses out of here!"

"You included!" Bear unloaded his rifle against the feral beasts. "I'm not starting this shit over again! Peacekeepers, back to the vehicles now!"

With a crack of its powerful jaw, the alpha hata signaled its pack, and they broke apart, with two bounding toward the Peacekeepers, with one staying behind the leader to focus on the Hlinan. "Bear, you're wounded! Get your ass to the vehicle! Grim, on me!" Wolf shot at one of the incoming wolves. The rounds affected the beast's front leg, severing the ligament and causing it to whimper loudly in pain before it collapsed to the ground, tumbling end over end by the inertia until it finally stopped.

Grim crouched with his sniper rifle steadied before pulling the trigger. Several rounds hit an approaching hata, striking it multiple times in its neck and upper spine. With a wail, the creature crashed to the ground, lifeless. Wolf charged ahead to the one she had wounded and fired two quick rounds into its head before she paused. Glancing up, she took in how the Hlinan fared this time.

Eski and Madu had their backs against their craft squaring off with the alpha while the others fought the smaller one. Krysta overheard Eski pray out loud, "Hlidar, our creator, watch over us as always."

Madu yelled at him, "He is disregarding you, Eski! You will not fight with his blessing any longer!" She fired at the hata's front legs and struck her target. The alpha snarled louder, without flinching. Saliva dripped off its fangs. Lowering itself, it pounced with a lethal strike.

Eski shoved Madu hard to shift her out of harm's way. "Move!" The beast slammed against the vehicle's outer shell right where she had stood previously. Eski forcefully kicked the dazed beast in its head before he shot a round into its right eye.

In agony, the blinded creature thrashed and snapped, desperately trying to attack its unseen attacker. Blood soaked its face where its eye used to be. Madu jumped up and then fired upon its backside; her rounds shredded its side torso. The hata cried out, then fell to the ground, its body wracked with violent spasms until it finally ceased moving. The other Hlinan made short work of the other dog.

Once the hostiles cleared out, Krysta jogged over to Eski and the others. She gave Madu a look of disappointment. "Too bad you survived."

"Same for you, Child of Sani," Madu spat. Slipping off her helmet, the Hlinan base leader glared furiously at Eski. "These Peace-keepers killed several of our own, Hosir. We must notify the Hevding of this transgression."

"Shall I tell him you broke our banner of peace when the order was to release Lone Wolf to her group?" Eski countered as he removed his own helmet.

Madu bitterly scowled at his counter. "She has now returned. We are finished."

"Not yet." Eski faced Krysta and the others. "Peacekeepers, I want to ask for forgiveness for Hosir Madu's prejudiced actions toward you. I know it cannot restore those who lost their lives today, but not all Hlinan have the same viewpoints. Our beloved Hevding wishes for peace amongst everyone on this planet."

Bear folded his arms indifferently and leaned on his good leg. "You mean he made a deal with Dhank Trust. Thanks for what you did, mate. We have been exiled. We are stuck here and losing people one by one. I don't think your words will fix any of this mess."

Eski glanced at Madu, then replied, "Our base will offer you refuge until you can return to your colony or home world."

"You do not have the authority, Eski." Madu confronted him. "I will oppose this."

"As Hosir, I have the power to grant such a temporary motion, and I will send confirmation to the Hevding. I know the rules and abide by them, Hosir Madu. I appreciate your apprehensiveness," he passively said.

Krysta crossed her arms smugly, hiding a snicker at the other's defeat in the verbal battle. She playfully nudged Bear beside her. "Better than staying out here with the hounds. Besides, you need that leg tended to."

Grim glared distrustfully at Eski. "How do we know these guys won't just shoot us in the back when we get to their base?" He leaned closer to her ear. "I'm not liking this. I should have never come to this planet and to think I wanted to live the rest of my life here. No way."

Madu smiled broadly at his words. "The distrust is mutual. I assure you, human."

Krysta spun on her. "Stay out of this." Then she addressed Grim. "Hosir Matelija risked his life to save mine, many times. His reputation and his honor are at stake by trusting us. We should return the favor." She flashed a warm smile over at Eski, who nodded back at her.

"But, Krysta," Grim argued. "This guy kidnapped you and you are okay with that?"

"Grim, you of all people should know that it takes a lot for someone to earn my trust. Eski could have left me for dead back in the mountain pass or even amongst those hata. We have a better chance of staying alive with them than with the colony. Dhank Trust is up to no good, and who knows what our replacements may do to us. We do not know what numbers we would be facing. The better the odds, the more likely we are to survive." Krysta feigned confidence but she knew deep down inside that a part of her sided with Grim. Was her confliction in her skewed feelings toward Eski placing a veil over her logic? Her viewpoint didn't completely convince her.

"She's right, Grim," Bear sighed before her doubt made her take back her words. "As much as I hate it. Dhank Trust has no intention of returning us to Earth. We stick it out here until we can get a ride back home."

"Your call…" Grim's voice trailed off. His eyes were deadlocked on the Hlinan soldier in front of him. "We keep our eyes open the whole time."

Wolf patted Bear on the back while they walked to their ride. "I'm glad to be back. I missed you guys." As she watched Eski and his team depart, she frowned. In her head, she relived the taste of his lips lingering on her own. She removed one of her gloves and slowly touched her lips with a fingertip, pressing the skin against the lower lip. A shudder ran down her mouth as her eyes fluttered shut, her lips craving another drink. She opened her eyes to see Grim's baffled expression. He lifted an eyebrow, glancing between her and where Eski had disappeared. Returning her hand to the glove, she looked away.

"You missed Carson wet himself," Bear snickered. "I even threw out a fake code to put me in charge. He almost went with it."

"I always miss the fun shit. Did he have to look it up?" Krysta was thankful that he cracked a witty comment to ease the mood. She still couldn't make eye contact with Grim.

"Yep. I stashed some beer in the rover with our supplies. I need one badly."

"That makes two of us, Papa Bear. After what I went through, I need three."

Chapter 24

Boredom overcame Krysta hours later at the confined base. The Hlinan gave the Peacekeepers a small space to stay and there was barely enough room for all their sleep pods. Grim was sleeping in his pod while Bear sat up against the wall nearby with his emerald eyes trained on the entrance. "Lone Wolf, this is not good. They posted guards right outside our door, which means we have limited access to this base. Something is not right." He glanced around at the others. "I have no intentions of living here."

Krysta glimpsed at the other mercs who were sleeping or chatting to pass the time. She walked over and sat down next to Bear. "I'm right there with you. I don't know where the hell Eski is."

"We've been tricked."

Unease circulated throughout her mind. She had to admit that she was thinking the same thing right along with him. Standing back up, she moved toward the door. "I'll be right back."

"Where are you going?"

"To get answers." Her emergence prompted both guards outside to assess her appearance. Their judging gazes immediately landed on her. She held up her hand. "Hold up. I got paged by Hosir Madu. Okay?" Both guards exchanged puzzled glances and then one reached for his comm link. Krysta motioned for him to pause. "I wouldn't do that. With us being Arlandr and all, I don't think the Hosir really wants the entire base to know that she wants to speak with us. Earn yourself a cookie and keep it confidential. Just point me in the right direction of the Hosir's office and I'll go quietly my way."

The officer remained speechless and pointed to his right. Krysta's serious expression didn't waver, but she was relieved the trick had succeeded and quickened her pace before he could change his mind. With a mischievous smile, she sharply rounded the corner and nearly bumped into another person. She tensed when she realized it was Hosir Madu herself. "Shit."

"Watch it, human," Madu berated her.

Krysta rolled her eyes. "You're the last person I wanted to see right now."

"What are you doing outside your designated area? We did not permit you anywhere else on the base."

"I'm looking for Hosir Matelija. Where is he?"

"The Hosir is tending to his duties. He and I command this base and see to its operations. This does not include entertaining Arlandr."

Krysta fumed. As much as she loathed her, she knew that picking a fight would not help matters. "Fine. Hosir Madu, the Peacekeepers formally request that you grant us communication with the Bakht Colony immediately. We want to know the progress in discussions between the Hlinan and Director Carson regarding our flight off this world." Under her breath, she said, "And away from you."

Madu slanted her eyes at her. "Your request has been noted. Return to your area now."

"I'm going." Krysta mumbled as she went back to her bunk. "Well, that was a wasted trip." She glanced over her shoulder to see that Madu trailed behind her but kept at a distance. "Shit, she's following me." The two guards tilted their heads to the right as they spotted her coming back. "See, boys? I'm back like a good little Arlandr." Sighing, she retreated into the bunk. In a nearby corner,

Krysta quickly noticed Grim and Bear having a private conversation, both wearing serious expressions. They locked eyes upon her when she came closer to their view. The men ignored her return, and she couldn't understand what they were saying. "Something I missed?"

The two ceased their chat. "What did you find out?"

"I looked for Eski to figure out when we could finally call Carson. Madu intercepted me before I could get far." She leaned against the wall with her one boot pressing against it. She folded her arms. "I don't understand why suddenly he's giving us the cold shoulder. Something doesn't add up." Krysta ground her teeth. Was he playing with her?

"Your pal screwed up," Bear grunted from where he stood. "These guys will not cater to us. Why would they? Now, he's turned tail, mind the pun."

Krysta shook her head in protest. "No way. Hosir Matelija is not like that. He gave me his word."

"I'm with Jack on this one, Wolf. No offense," Grim chimed in. "Intentionally or not, Eski will not do us any favors. I never bought it for a second. I'm just waiting for our eviction notice."

"That or they will just turn us over to the new hires, whenever that is. No way in hell that I'm staying here that long. I'm not that gullible." Bear clenched his jaw tightly. "The Reptilia were here before us, Krysta. They don't want to share it as much as Dhank Trust doesn't want to."

With a pained expression, Krysta sighed. "Maybe you're both right on this. We don't know what kind of backroom deals were made. I can't believe I fell for all of this crap. So much for thinking we had the advantage over Carson. The stupid prick. We have all the muscle and weapons right now for the humans and Carson has what?"

"A few armed freaked out civilians that lack any military training," Bear answered. "At least that's what he tried to throw at us when we left to find you."

"For now," Grim added. "Our replacements could show up at any time. I'm guessing that they were on order as soon as your teams departed Earth. Your group was just a temporary fix. Dhank Trust had no intention of extending our contract. Our window of opportunity is closing more. We need to figure out what to do."

"I'd rather go out into the wilderness and face whatever this hellhole of a planet can throw at us than remain here. We are fish in a barrel." Bear squared his shoulders and faced them. "We assume that Dhank Trust has no intention of taking us back to Earth. Our tech here won't be able to contact Captain Masters; Bakht has what we need. The colony doesn't have the means to go up against us."

"And what if Carson throws armed civilians at us?" Grim argued against him. "We just shoot them?"

"I have a better idea. T   he Hlinan may have the means to get us back to Earth on one of their own ships. It may take some time for modifications, but that's an option." Krysta jumped back in, though she knew they couldn't scrap Bear's idea if her plan didn't work out. There were no other choices out there.

"No offense, Krysta. I'm not too keen on giving the Reptilia the coordinates to Earth. Plus, you really think that our militaries will allow an alien vessel to just move inside our planet's orbit?" Grim questioned. "The only contact we had with an alien race was with the Achli and you saw how that turned out. We show up with the Hlinan and they will think we were all brainwashed by these lizards."

"Face it, Lone Wolf," Bear agreed. "Your guy is hiding because he knows we are screwed and all that bullshit he spouted is now biting him in the ass. He may not even be on this base anymore. Did you spot him while you were out there?"

"Negative, but Madu said he was." As much as Krysta hated to admit it, the two men were right.

"So, what if he is?" Grim fired back. "What if the guy above him orders our deaths? You think he's going to choose us over his race?

I've seen how he looks at you, Krysta. Something about it isn't right. I don't trust that slimy reptile."

Krysta turned crisply on him. "He's a Hlinan, Grim. Just give him a chance. Quit being so paranoid."

"Settle down, Wolf. Let's hunker in here and make a plan." Bear stared intently at her. "We get with the captain, then leave this place before they come for us."

"Understood, Papa Bear." Grim agreed. "After the first attack, Earth hasn't looked so good. I'll take the freezing weather on Manitoba any day."

Krysta frowned at her mentor's decision. Her closest colleagues were so paranoid about the Hlinan turning their backs on them or Eski turning tail if pressed to choose sides. Their arguments were valid, as much as she didn't want to admit it. The same question nagged in her gut. What would she do if war broke out between the only ones she knew as family, and the Hlinan? Would she be able to hold a gun against Eski? She had nothing against him personally and still wanted to believe in him. Her mind flashed to what happened back in their city and how he came to her defense against Carson. Did he harbor feelings for her? Would he be able to hold his weapon against her without hesitation?

Chapter 25

Several days passed and the pods that the Hlinan provided for the Peacekeepers to sleep in temporarily were not a welcoming sight to Krysta that evening. She found the ivory white oval-shaped pods uncomfortable, and she almost preferred the cold metal floor. The heating lamps on top made it difficult to rest. Bear didn't even bother and was sleeping loudly on the floor outside his pod. With her pants and tank on, Krysta tried to get situated, but was tempted to choose the floor instead. She felt the pod's low hum rumbling underneath her; it almost drowned out Bear's snoring. Picking up her tags, she fidgeted with them gently. There was still no sign of Eski. She wondered if her snoring friend was correct. What if their only ally on the base was gone? Slumber escaped her. She crouched down to her personal pack and dug through it to pick out a small ration bar. Taking a bite, she sat with her back facing the bunk door.

From his nearby pod, Grim let out a loud yawn, then looked down at her. "Wolf? You alright?"

"Hard as hell to sleep in this place," she grumbled in between chews. "I'm going for a walk. Need to clear my head."

"This time of night?" Another yawn escaped Grim's lips. "I wouldn't recommend it. You know what Jack said."

Krysta gestured toward the burly man. "He's snoring like crazy over there. I don't think he would even realize it." With her mind set, she shoved her ration bar back into her pack and slipped on her boots.

"Hold up," Grim crawled out of his pod. "Let me get my pants. I'll go with you. Two of us out there are better than one."

She rolled her eyes at his offer. "I'll be fine, Grim. You know I would really prefer to be alone."

"You know it's not safe out there." Grim latched his buckle. "I'll remain at a distance, if you need it. I learned." His expression twisted in pain. "You just need an escort."

"Escort for what?" She slipped outside first and shivered, feeling the cooler night air brush along her bare arms. Two new guards were posted out there, and she noted that this time they were female. Both reacted defensively to her abrupt exit, and she held up her hands at them. "Ease up, I just need some air."

"Child of Sani, you are not permitted to any sector outside this zone. Return at once," one of them snipped at her.

"Cool your jets, lady," Grim intervened. "Krysta is feeling sick. Too much beer. I don't think you want vomit inside your pristine bunk, do you?"

Krysta held her mouth to go along with the act and stumbled a bit. "Ugh, Grim. I need to find some grass, man." She sprinted off while holding her mouth. She didn't hear any commotion by her bolt out of there and was relieved to hear Grim panting as he jogged after her. When she reached the edge of the metal base flooring and the natural grassy terrain, she held her hands on her knees and chuckled under her breath. "That was great. The guards bought it."

"Hooked, line and sinker." Grim tossed a playful wink. "You played your part well, Krysta." He wiped the tears from his eyes as he laughed. "I'm just glad it's still you in there."

His words stopped her, then she resumed her position. "What do you mean by that?"

Grim shrugged. "You know, like the fear humans always had with aliens. Doing strange shit to you; weird tests."

"Weird tests?" She rolled her eyes.

"Cloning you or making you come back as part alien, wanting to kill us all." A devilish smirk moved across his lips. "Erotic sexual experiments?"

"Give me a fucking break, Grim. That's just sick and not even funny."

"Hey, I have no idea what they did to you while you were with them. Even Jack was concerned about it. How do we know they didn't chip you?"

"Chip me?" Krysta gave him an incredulous look. "Jack thinks this shit too?" With a sharp pivot and a frustrated growl, she stomped off to her right. It felt like a betrayal. Bear and Grim were talking about her behind her back.

Grim caught up to her. He gingerly reached out and touched her arm to stop her. "Ease up, Krysta. You know all the freaky stuff that was on the vids back home about aliens and humans. All I'm saying is that right now, you could be part reptile without you even realizing it. Pretty soon you may start slithering." He teasingly flickered his tongue and then tossed out another bout of snickering. "Will you molt your skin? Or grow an extra pair of eyes to be like them? That would be freaky."

"Just leave me the hell alone, Grim." She stormed off. Has she turned into a big joke to him and Bear now? Approaching the base's back entrance, she observed the planet's two moons positioned closely together in the night sky. The larger moon hung higher. Moonlight offered her some visibility. She then heard Grim's panting breaths as he sprinted to catch up to her. His closeness angered her more; despite her best efforts to leave him behind, he maintained the same speed. "Go away, Grim. I think you have said enough. You wouldn't want to be near the psychotic abductee."

"Krysta, look, I'm sorry if I took it too far." Grim's playfulness gave way to seriousness. "What happened to you while you were gone? Do you want to talk about it? For real."

Feeling cross, she turned on him with her finger jabbed tightly into his chest. "You would be the last person I would want to talk to about it. We broke up, remember? You didn't get me then and you don't get me now."

A sharp glare emanated from him. "You're right. I don't get you. You are not the same person. Back on Earth, I knew it was hard to get inside your circle. You trusted no one and relied only on yourself. There was a time when I'd do anything for you, Krysta. Now, I'm not sure. You fully put your trust in one of these Hlinan. That's all you talk about now. It's out of pattern. What if these guys truly did something to you? Were you unconscious at any time?"

Krysta wrinkled her nose at what he implied. "This shit again?" Her eyes rolled again. "Listen to yourself, Grim. You are grasping at straws."

"Just answer me."

"Right before they brought me to their city." Her thoughts shifted to the breathing treatment and her kiss with Eski. Her solid disposition was cracking at the fault line. "They gave me a breathing treatment to cure the inflammation in my lungs, saving my life."

"What if they altered you somehow during that time? You wouldn't have a clue."

"So, what are you saying? That I'm some kind of lizard puppet? Seriously, Grim, lay off the damn sci-fi vids." Without another word, she walked on. His accusing words tussled inside her head, putting her more on edge.

"Wolf, wait." Grim grabbed her arm.

She jerked away from him. "Let go, Xavier. Give me some damn space."

"Just talk to me. Quit running away." He reached out for her again.

Suddenly, a shadow whirred past Krysta, and she barely made out a Hlinan shape until the being was right on Grim. Eski shoved the man hard to the ground. "Krysta told you to let her be human." Poised with sharp fangs, he hissed a hostile warning to the man.

Realizing the quick escalation between the two, Krysta moved to stop Eski, but Grim leaped back on his feet and charged at the Hlinan. The two stumbled onto the ground with Grim on top. He delivered a punch to the Reptilia's face before Eski got his boot up against Grim's abdomen and used it as leverage to throw the man onto his back away from him. Both stood up to face off again, but the Hlinan was faster. He struck the man hard with two swift punches to the face, busting the merc's bottom lip. The disruption provoked an alarm on the base. Nearby soldiers raced in to assist along with awakened Peacekeepers, who came charging out of their bunk with Bear in the lead.

Krysta locked both of Grim's arms behind his back and held him. "Enough, Grim! It's over!" Meanwhile, around them, both sides drew weapons on one another.

Blood trickled from Grim's split lip; he glared angrily at Wolf. "Krysta! Whose side are you on?"

"I'm on *yours* if you calm the fuck down."

Wearing only his pants with no shirt, Bear moved to place himself between Grim and Eski. His two eyes squared up into the Reptilia's four, defiantly. "That's enough, lizard. You want a go at one of my men, you start with me. Got it?" His attention then shifted to Grim. "Get your ass back to bed and that goes for all of you," he ordered the remaining mercenaries.

Aggravated, Krysta swiped her fingers through her bangs while she watched Grim and the others walk away. "One hell of a night already."

Bear kept his eyes on Eski, who didn't budge from his stance. "Slither back to your hole. This doesn't concern you."

Eski tore his defiant gaze from Bear, turning towards Krysta. "Will you be okay out here, Lone Wolf?"

Krysta patted him on the arm and nodded. "I'm fine, Eski. Thank you. Just go on." After the Hlinan moved out of sight, she allowed herself to meet Bear's judging frown. "Grim wouldn't ease up," she spat back in defense. "You know, when I want to be alone, I want to be the hell *alone.* He wouldn't take the hint and kept blabbing out crazy shit and conspiracies about me. He thinks I'm one of *them.*" She pointed at the Hlinan walking away.

"Aye, I know when you want to be alone, but I also remember advising everyone to stay hunkered down together." He motioned to Eski's back. "Why was *he* out here?" When she said nothing, he sighed. "They are watching us like inmates, Wolf. None of us like it. At least now we know he's still around and avoiding us on purpose."

"I don't think he's behind the avoidance, Jack." She furrowed her brow. "Grim said you believe that I'm chipped. Is that true?"

"Come again?"

"Don't play stupid. You both believe that the Hlinan chipped me to make me one of their spies. Or are you waiting for me to stab you in the back?"

Jack rubbed at his haggard face with his hand. "You and I both know that there is a possibility the Hlinan are controlling those hounds. There have been no attacks here yet, in case you didn't notice. You were with these guys for days. Plenty of time for them to implant some crazy tech inside you."

Even though she expected the same answer, Krysta backed up to put more distance between them. Fear crept through her mind, like a parasite, feeding on her emotions. "That can't be true, Jack." But doubt surged inside her, against her anger. Maybe they were right.

"Krysta," He stepped toward her. "Look, I know you went through some messed up shit losing your dad because of the Achli. These guys had a run in too. So what? Pure coincidence. Eski has been feeding you information about the Achli, making up some bullshit to just tell you what you want to hear. Be levelheaded about this and don't let your emotions override the obvious manipulation." He motioned to the base with his arms wide. "These guys are not our friends and infiltrating us through you is the perfect entrapment."

Krysta's hot tears flowed down her face like little streams. "I am going to get my revenge against the Achli one day, Jack. No child should lose their parents like that. You can say that I'm messed up because of it, but there is no way that Eski is playing me. I'll fight my battle alone if I must. Just say I'm out. Do it."

"Wolf," Bear's voice grew softer. "Look, I'm sorry. Things got a little heated. This whole planet is fucked up. I want you here with us. You are one hell of a soldier and a Peacekeeper to me. Just take fifteen minutes to yourself, then get back here. I'll be waiting for you."

While wiping her tears, Krysta walked away. "Get it together, Marine. Tears don't get you anywhere." Rounding the corner, she arrived at a more isolated area of the base, inhaling the night air. Her eyes lifted toward the twin moons hanging in the sky. Her heart lurched inside her chest, and she chewed her lip as she thought back to how Eski kissed her. A part of her desired his embrace again, but the sensation was so strange it was hard for her to accept that even happened. Suddenly, a blur in her peripheral vision captured her attention. Krysta turned her head but saw nothing in the shadows, no movement at all. A chill crept down her spine. She got the sensation that someone or something was watching her.

"Hah, nice try Hosir Madu. Go sulk somewhere else." When there was no answer, she diverted back to the bunk. "I need some damn sleep. Now, my mind is playing tricks on me." Despite leaving the area, she couldn't shake the feeling of eyes upon her.

Chapter 26

The next day started off like nothing out of the usual happened the night before, except that Grim was keeping his distance from Krysta. The Peacekeepers were knee deep in their routine exercises to pass the time. Bear *politely* told the guards what they were going to do despite the protests, which caused the Hlinan security outfit to increase around them. "Wolf, you were off by a second," Bear teased as she crossed their invisible finish line for their afternoon jog. "Care to explain yourself?"

Krysta panted, catching her breath as sweat poured down her face and chest. The late afternoon sun's rays hit her exposed skin under her sports bra and pants. "I think your counting is just off. I know I was faster that time," she gasped between breaths.

A teasing grin played on the man's lips as he shook his head at her. "Face it, Wolf. Either you are getting old or out of shape because of this trip."

She pursed her lips at his remark. "Talk about getting old. What was your age again? Sixty-five? I see a few gray strands in your beard." To emphasize her point, she mockingly pointed to the hair on his face.

Bear batted her hand away, his gaze sweeping over the remaining mercenaries who had completed their laps behind Krysta. "None of you beat her, so you know what that means? One more lap, ladies." The mercs groaned and trudged on.

Grim stopped. His painful expression reminded Krysta of the fallout from the night before. Without a word, he jogged on to catch up with the others. Wolf followed him out with her gaze and sighed sadly to herself. "He's still pissed."

"Let him be," Bear interrupted as if reading her thoughts. "He'll work through it." A rumble overhead drew both their heads up to the sky. "Great. Dark clouds rolling in, how fitting."

"A severe storm could be on its way." Krysta worriedly watched the mercs circle around ahead. A louder rumble soon followed. "Damn, it's moving in fast. We should probably bring everyone in."

"Hold up. Looks like we got company," Bear pointed to a Hlinan soldier hurrying over to them. "Finally, they talk to us."

When the soldier reached them, he faced Krysta. "Hosir Matelija has asked for your assistance, Lone Wolf. He has found something that he wants you to see just outside Bakht. He expresses it is urgent. I am to escort you via my cycle." He indicated over to the two-seater slim hover cycle parked near the base entrance.

Several rain droplets crashed down upon Krysta's head from above and she shivered. "I better go see what's up before this place becomes a washout." She turned to the Hlinan before them. "Near Bakht you said?"

"Yes. The cycle is our fastest transportation."

Bear protectively held his hand out to stop her from proceeding ahead. "Hold up. You went with them one time alone and look where that led us. I'll go with you."

"There is only enough room for her and I. We must hurry," the Hlinan pressed.

Krysta saw the distrust brewing in the older man's eyes. "Jack, I got this. You want me back before this storm? I need to hurry my ass to that cycle." Her hair became wet as the droplets picked up.

"Fine. Comms open and gear up." He stared right at the reptile before him. "If the storm gets worse, I'm setting out to find you."

"I assure you, Peacekeeper, it will be a quick trip out there," The Hlinan didn't flinch.

"Don't assure me of anything."

Ignoring the threatening clouds, Krysta ran to the bunk to get her things. What did Eski find out there near Bakht? Was something going on that they didn't know about? Why was it so urgent?

Chapter 27

The wind whipped around Krysta as the heavy rain from the storm ensuing soaked her helmet and armor. The Hlinan driver remained silent after leaving the base. She held onto the passenger hooks as the cycle swiftly maneuvered around the trees. To her right, she recognized the mountain where she'd first met Eski and his team, watching it shrink in the distance with every passing second. Something wasn't right. Her gaze swept across the scene, finding nothing she recognized. She risked a fall from the cycle if she tried to use the navigation on her gauntlet. Wolf tapped the Hlinan in front of her on the shoulder. "Hey, are you sure Eski is out this way? I thought we weren't taking the scenic route to the colony." When he didn't respond, she tapped his shoulder even harder with her gloved fingertip to get his attention. "Hey!" She shouted over the gushing rain. "I'm talking to you! I think you are lost!" The unsettling silence unnerved her, causing her to draw her pistol. She bent close enough for him to see the gun aimed at his temple. "Can you hear this? I said stop the damn cycle! Now!"

Without an auditory response, the driver slowed the cycle down till it came to a halt. He subtly shifted his gaze towards her. "We are here, Peacekeeper."

Guardedly, Krysta unsaddled the cycle seat and trained her pistol on him. She anxiously glanced around her surroundings. They were in a wooded enclave, however, neither the colony nor Eski were in sight. "Hosir Matelija?" She removed her helmet and called out while she kept her attention fixated on the driver. He exited the cycle and stood motionless.

"Lone Wolf." With a taunting coo, Hosir Madu and two other Hlinan members appeared on her left, fully armed and armored. "It is dangerous to be alone this far out of our base."

Krysta cocked her pistol at Madu. "Where the hell is Eski?" She watched Madu and the three Hlinan form a circle surrounding her. Rain poured down from the gray clouds above as a flash of lightning created a brief white out.

"Hosir Matelija is at the base, Lone Wolf. I wanted to talk to you in private, and this was the best way to pull you away from observant eyes."

"Couldn't you have picked a better time than to drag me out into the middle of a goddamn storm?" Keeping a close eye on the Hlinan flanking her, Krysta held her pistol more tightly. A crackle of lightning flashed upon the Hlinan's helmeted faces. The heavy saturation churned the soil into mud, and she dug her boot heels in.

"The humans of this world are a pestilence. Despite what others like Matelija wanted to hope for, Hlidar did not create you and you are not our ally. Your deception has clouded Eski's mind and our Hevding. Your existence has created Slaroars, and your poisonous words have spread the infection from Emble to here on Ljosa. I will not allow this to continue, Child of Sani."

"Didn't think you were calling the shots," Wolf derided her. "So, you brought me out this far to just voice a complaint? Unbelievable." She huffed, "You have issues."

A hiss escaped Madu's lips as her fangs emerged; "I did not bring you here to just talk, Peacekeeper." She raised her hand and the other Hlinan trained their rifles on Krysta.

Wolf felt her heart pounding as adrenaline rushed through her. The fight-or-flight response kicked in. She didn't break her hold on her pistol with the barrel directly still on Madu. "You may kill me, but I'm taking you down with me. I don't miss my target."

Madu beamed boastfully. "Activate shields." Seconds later, a glowing aurora basked all four of the Hlinan's bodies.

Krysta narrowed her eyes at their defense mechanisms. *Well, shit. She called my bluff. I forgot about their damn shields.* Remembering Bear's lecture, she moved her free hand up towards her ear comm piece to place a call to him.

Madu quickly noticed this and laughed mockingly. "Calling for backup so soon? Are you that weak, Peacekeeper?"

Krysta stopped and put her hand down. She glowered at Madu. "I'm never weak, bitch. You kill me and you start a war. The Hlinan blood spilled will be only on your hands. I'm sure your Hevding will be unhappy."

"Perhaps you are right, deceiver." Madu grinned menacingly. "Killing you may not be the best approach to this. We should send a clear message to the rest of Sani's children." She flagged the others at her side. "No weapons. Make sure we get the message across that the Hlinan worship only Hlidar and the offspring of Sani will not defile us. We will avenge our ancestors."

Before Krysta anticipated their next move, all three Hlinan soldiers rushed at her with their weapons strapped back to their armor. Their quickness made it impossible for her to get a clean shot. One swiftly kicked the pistol out of her hand while another struck at her torso. She blocked the strike to her chest, but a hard kick to her back caused her to lose her footing in the murky mud and stumble forward.

After she regained her traction, she delivered a powerful front kick to the nearest Hlinan soldier, before striking another with a sidekick. Krysta pivoted on her heel to confront Madu just in time to see the Hlinan's gloved claws coming right at her face. The blow made the entire area spin before Krysta's eyes. Shaking her head to suppress the sharp pain, she spat, "Cheap shot," "Only one you get."

She lunged out at Madu with a hook, but the Hlinan blocked it with ease and even seized the opening that Krysta left on her upper torso. Simultaneously, another lizard to her left kicked at her legs, tripping her. Wolf's entire front slammed into the pool of mud with her face completely covered.

Krysta tasted the grainy concoction inside her mouth and spat out the brownish red fluid. Mud drenched her hair. Before she could regain her balance, the Hlinan moved in and delivered powerful kicks to both of her sides. Ignoring the pain, she angrily grabbed one's boot, twisting the leg and throwing them onto their backside into the splashy mud.

The mixture of mud and rainwater seeped down Krysta's face and she wiped away some of it. A clap of thunder roared, then another flash of lightning lit up the darkness as evening approached. Her body ached by the multiple blows, and she heard Madu's cackle of delight over the storm. "Yield, human."

"Never." Krysta staggered to a standing position and spat another gritty taste of blood and mud from her mouth. She held up her fists in a guard position. "I'm not done yet!" She charged at Madu with her fist reared back. She thrusted forward with the attack, but Madu easily dodged, then grabbed Krysta's arm, and flipped her onto the sludge with a splash. The rain poured over Krysta's face, and she heard the Hlinan's boots trudging through the murky slop to her.

The rumble of a nearby, approaching cycle caused her to lift her head and look up. Another fully armored Hlinan dismounted the cycle and stormed to the surrounding four Reptilia, punching the closest one before kicking the next. His confrontation caught all of them completely off-guard. Krysta picked up on the upside-down triangle across her defender's arm. "Eski?"

The remaining Hlinan soldier held up their hands to surrender and Hosir Madu threw off her helmet in fury. "Hosir Matelija! What are you doing?"

Eski jerked off his helmet and moved to help Krysta back up. Mud drenched both sides of her armor, hair, and face. Another flash of lightning in the distance brightly lit up his face. "Krysta, are you alright?"

"Never better. I just love your species' hospitality." Wolf wiped the dirt off her face.

Enraged, Madu stormed over to them. "Hosir, explain yourself! Why do you fight us?"

"I should ask you the same!" Eski fired back. "Whose order was it to ambush Lone Wolf out here? This is not a fair fight!" When Madu did not respond, he positioned himself between her and Krysta, protectively. "The Hevding wants us to be allies. Is this how we treat such a friend?"

"No, Hosir Matelija." Madu glared at him. "You are wrong. The alliance is only with the Bakht Colony, not with these exiles. These Peacekeepers are a threat to them and us."

"If they are, then why select only Lone Wolf for your hostility? Is she your only foe?"

"I was sending a message to *them*, Eski."

"What message is that, Hosir?" he gritted out. "That we dishonor ourselves by going after just one? You did this act on your own. I will make sure the Hevding is aware of this transgression against the Peacekeepers." His gaze shifted toward the other Hlinan. "Hosir Madu is to be restrained for her betrayal against our divine leader's wisdom. Escort her back to the base and see that she remains confined. I will deal with her once I seek Hlidar's guidance on how to further handle the matter." Krysta held her breath when she observed the other three soldiers not acting on the order given out. Eski's voice grew more stern. "Did you not hear me?" They remained still.

"Oh, shit." A whisper full of dread escaped Krysta's mouth. Madu was making a power play.

With a wide grin, Madu triumphantly approached Eski. "They see you for what you are now, Hosir Matelija; a Slaroar. You are the one who has betrayed us—betrayed *your* kind with your protection over these—" Her finger pointed at Krysta. "—children of Sani. Today, you have shown us your true colors."

His expression did not waver. Krysta saw tension rise as their faces drew near. "You are only against me, Hosir Madu; not them."

Madu chuckled and reached out to caress the side of his face with her gloved fingertips; both of their scaley faces glistening in the rain. "You cannot let me go, can you, Matelija? Are you blaming your own blasphemous actions on me?"

"No, Madu." He didn't budge. "You let the power of being a Hosir get to your head. Years ago, I wanted to spawn with you, and we were on the list for approval. You changed, and I moved on. I cannot be with someone as cold as you."

She balked at him. "Eski, why would I ever want to mate with a Slaroar? Take your precious human. Go to the Hevding if you wish. Just know that there is growing discontent throughout the base about your intentions. You are no longer a genuine believer of our faith." With a frown, Madu got on a cycle with one of her soldiers' and sped off, while the other two scampered out of sight through the trees to trail behind them.

Immediately, Eski faced Krysta and brushed the matted hair from her face. "Lone Wolf, you must seek medical attention."

"I should have known this whole thing was a setup." She winced in pain and figured her body had probably a few colorful bruises.

He dragged her over to his own cycle. "Come. We need to get out of this area without delay. The smell of your blood is risky for the hata lurking all over this territory. It was foolish for even Hosir Madu to be out here with the others."

Krysta remained still as she watched him straddle behind the cycle's handlebars. His repeated protection gnawed away at her. "How did you know where I was?"

From his seat, Eski glanced at her. "I left my office to tend to my perimeter duties and saw your friends outside of their bunk with you nowhere in sight. When I went over to ask your friend, Grim, was it? He said that you went out with another Hlinan to find me. Each cycle has a tracking device, and I traced you here. Believe me, Wolf, I did not know that Madu would go this extreme to rid your group from the base. I now fear for your life."

Krysta walked over to him and gingerly sat down behind him. Deep down inside, the suggestion of him being ousted by his race was not a good sign. "Eski, I know you are trying to look after me, but it sounds like you are losing your status on the base. This was more than a shakedown."

Eski held his helmet in his hand and turned in his seat to look more at her. "Hlidar is testing my resolve. He has granted me the purpose of being your guardian. I hear his words now."

"Eski, you know why I called myself the Lone Wolf. I'm fated to be alone. The Achli murdered my father, and my mother ended her own life because of the shock of his death when I was only ten. I bounced from foster home to foster home until I could enlist in the military. I saw my comrades die in missions. Death is all around me. I do not want it to happen to you."

"Death is hard to understand in my culture as well, Krysta. As a Hlinan, I am reminded daily of my purpose for life, but the focus is never on what happens when my time being alive has expired." His eyes drifted towards the mountainous landscape. "Some of my kin and friends were among the first Hlinan to set forth on this planet. Many believed that the selections for the first colony were by divine intervention. They all perished by the Children of Sani."

"You mean the Achli."

He nodded to her correction. "Yes. You and I share similar tragic tales, and yet here we are on this very planet. We were both reluctant to trust one another at the very beginning."

"And now?" She playfully lifted an eyebrow.

He smiled at her, almost fondly. "And now, Lone Wolf, I will do everything that I can to keep you alive. I admit that I have developed feelings toward you, unlike the bond I shared with Madu. It is not by the will of my faith nor my government, but by what I desire."

Krysta's lower lip quivered a little. She leaned forward and gently cradled his face. Ignoring the pain in her body, she closed her eyes and gently kissed him. His cold, wet lips pressed against hers and the light touch of his gloved fingertips danced upon her face. When their mouths parted, Krysta slowly pulled back into her seat. He never took his eyes off her. "Thanks for saving my ass back there. As confusing and odd as this is, I can't deny what I feel toward you, Eski."

"Another factor that we share in common." With a smile, he turned around in his seat. With a rev of the engine, the cycle darted back toward the base.

The air grew chillier by the evening taking over. Krysta made a face at the dried caked mud all over her. With her helmet on, she stared at the back of his body. Her heart raced. A warm, but serene sensation wrapped around her like a blanket, and she rested her head on his back. For once in her life, she felt at peace.

Chapter 28

A rumble of thunder set the stage for the scene ahead. Bear and Grim were already walking toward them as Eski's cycle approached the base. Krysta grimaced, "This is going to be fun." The Hlinan driver in front of her didn't react to the expected hostility coming their way. Krysta knew Bear was pissed, and she didn't have to see his face to figure it out. "It's best to let me handle this."

Eski parked the cycle inside the base's interior and moved to get off first. Bear was up on him in seconds. The bearded man came at him, swinging. "You scaly son of a bitch!" He delivered a hook, catching Eski right in the face, sending him careening into the wet mud.

"Jack, wait!" Krysta snatched off her helmet and hopped off the hover bike to place herself between Eski and her old mentor. "He didn't do this! Just calm down!" Grim rushed to Bear's side along with several others.

"I knew it was a trick!" Bear fumed. His frantic eyes watched the Hlinan roll back on his feet.

Grim moved over to examine her face. "Are you alright?" The rain was slowly washing the caked dirt off her body.

Not waiting for a response, Bear rushed in again for another strike. This time, the Hlinan soldier was ready for him. Eski blocked the attack and delivered a powerful cross punch that made the man stumble backwards.

"She speaks the truth." Eski jerked his own helmet off. Amidst the commotion, Hlinan soldiers ran in to assist their leader. Eski spun on his heel and held up his hand to stop them. "Stand down. Weapons are unnecessary." His head then whipped back to the Peacekeepers. "Restrain yourselves or we will ask you to leave this base." Painfully, his eyes drifted to Lone Wolf. "*All* of you."

"Fine by us, lizard boy," Bear spat. "Peacekeepers, inside now."

Grim urged Krysta to follow him back into their designated space with the rest of the group. "Come on. Let's get you patched up."

Bear moved over to them. "*None* of us will separate from now on." Wolf flinched under his scolding gaze, and he let out a heavy sigh. "Enough is enough. Trust is over."

"Krysta, what happened?" Grim asked gently as they moved inside their bunk.

"Hosir Madu ambushed me with some of her minions. They gave us a false story. Eski was still on the base."

"Yeah, he came over and asked where you were, then sped off before we knew where he went. We've been on pins and needles since." His face soured. "That's three times, Krysta. Do you believe us now?"

"Let it go," she harshly corrected him. "Eski is on our side. He saved me and I think it's what we all feared. The Hlinan are going up against him."

"Which is why we are packing our shit and leaving." Bear surged ahead. "The Peacekeepers will handle things on our own. Everyone, grab your gear and eat one ration pack."

Eyes wide, Krysta ran to catch up with him. "Hold up, Papa Bear. Are you sure that's wise?"

"You suggest we wait until these greenies come after us during our sleep? Have you seen yourself, Krysta? You are bleeding and bruised up. They could have killed you."

"I've looked a lot worse before. It's not right to let Eski take the fall for this."

"He's not one of us, Krysta," Grim pointed out. "I'm with Jack on this. We send a few scouts out to see if we can find a place to camp out at, then we hightail it out of here."

"Good idea," Bear concurred. "Grim, you lead that group. Take three men. I want a fifty-meter perimeter sweep. If anything is unusual, even if a squirrel looks at you funny, you bring your asses back here, got it?" Grim jogged off to carry out the order.

"Really?" Krysta mocked him. "A squirrel, Jack?"

He ignored her shot. "At least Grim is smart about this and already thinking about our exit strategy." He thumbed towards the others. "Grab a med pack and get yourself cleaned up. We are moving out when Grim returns."

As things rapidly worsened around her, Krysta groaned loudly before gathering her belongings rather aggressively. She opened her medical kit and then glimpsed her travel pack. Closing the kit door, she opened her pack to take stock of her items, including ammo clips. She closed her eyes and thought back to her time with Eski. Her fingers trembled in her pack. Was she really going to do this?

Chapter 29

Bear looked up from where he sat when Krysta approached him twenty minutes later. She cleaned up and fully geared up, with her pack on her back. He nodded his head in approval. "At least you came to your senses there, Krysta. Be ready. Grim should contact us any minute."

"Jack, I'm not going with you. I'm staying here with the Hlinan." Her bold words fell into place as she clenched her jaw tightly.

Her announcement made the larger man give her a second look. "Come again?" he scoffed. "Wolf, don't start this shit."

"You heard what I said. I've got my things and I'm going to tell Eski that I'm staying here. He's not facing this witch hunt alone."

Bear slammed the interface tablet that he had in his hand against the table, then stood. He towered over her. "You took the oath. You are a Peacekeeper, Krysta."

"I will break my oath to save someone's life if I have to."

"For a lizard?" He gaped at her angrily.

"For a Hlinan," she snapped back at him. "For a friend." Her loud words provoked the attention of the other mercenaries in the room, and they all paused from their bunks to watch the unfolding exchange.

Bear noted the attention and swore under his breath. "Krysta, you've been under my wing for how many years now? If anyone in this room knows you better, it's me. Don't do this."

The wail of a klaxon outside set a deathly tone, causing Bear and Krysta to halt their words. Fear clutched at the bearded man's face, and he bolted out the door with Krysta right on his heels with the rest of the mercenaries. Wolf walked into chaos as she spotted Hlinan soldiers racing in the southernmost direction. She snatched one's arm as he passed by to stop him. "What the hell is going on?"

"Hata are in the area." The soldier yanked away his arm to continue.

Krysta bit her lip. "Grim and the others." Throwing her pack off, she snatched her pistol and fell in line behind the Hlinan soldiers along with the Peacekeepers. Up ahead, Eski was giving out orders. "Eski!"

Seeing her, the Hlinan base leader moved through the crowd to get to her. "Stay close, Krysta. The hata are moving in and we are going to activate the base's barrier to prevent entry."

"Eski, Grim and the others are out there!"

His eyes widened at the disclosure. "What? I fear they may be lost."

"Those are my men out there you're talking about," Bear snarled next to Wolf. "Do not activate that shield until they are back."

"I'll go with you to find them." Eski flagged a few of his soldiers to accompany him as he, Krysta and Bear charged out to search for their friends.

Krysta tapped her comm link. "Grim, this is Lone Wolf. Do you copy?" The silence was heart-clenching, and she tried again, hoping that her voice would not crack. "Grim, this is Lone Wolf. You have hata in the vicinity. Fall back to the base."

"Wolf, Grim's armor beacon is pinging one hundred twenty meters ahead." Bear glanced down at his wrist gauntlet.

"Then we must not delay our steps, Peacekeepers, because our drones detected the hata near the same area." Eski moved beside them in a sprint.

Busting through bramble and overgrowth, Krysta's blood froze when she heard demonic howling up ahead, then the agonizing sound of someone being torn apart. "No!" She pushed harder with her legs. Eski and his kind did the same, and they moved ahead.

"Damnit," Bear huffed behind her. "They are faster than us. I don't like what I'm hearing ahead, Wolf."

"Neither do I." Krysta remained focused, ignoring the savage sounds. The Hlinan left her field of vision, and she prayed they made it in time to save who they could from imminent slaughter. When they caught up with Eski's team, Lone Wolf stopped cold. The top half of a Peacekeeper's corpse was on the ground with the bottom half nowhere in sight. Grim was on the ground in a sitting position with bloodied scratch marks on his face. He was firing wildly at three hata in the vicinity. With the Hlinan present, one hound turned to threaten them while the other two remained tightly on Grim.

"Holy hell." Bear remarked on the horrific display.

Krysta targeted a beast and fired her weapon. The hata wailed loudly by the strike in its torso and it snapped its jaws in her direction to defend its intended prey. The second hata charged at Grim for the kill. Krysta watched in horror. "No!"

Just as the beast pounced toward Grim, Eski lunged at the creature, crashing into it from the side, sending both tumbling onto the ground. Enraged, the hata attacked Eski, snapping its fangs near his face while holding him down with its paw pressing against his chest plate.

Krysta heard Eski grunting loudly to push back, his hands holding onto the canine's jaws to prevent the death blow. Switching her targets, Krysta aimed her pistol at the hata and squeezed the trigger multiple times. The rounds pummeled the creature's torso, causing it to twitch before it collapsed dead on the ground next to the Hlinan leader.

Eski craned his crimson visor straight at her. Krysta smiled, then moved over to Grim to check on him. The man trembled as if he saw a ghost, with blood still trickling from the nasty scratches on his right cheek. His dark eyes set upon Eski, and he blinked in disbelief. "That lizard saved me. I thought I was dead. Those wolves busted my helmet."

"Easy, Grim, we will get you another one. We need to get out of here. Can you walk?" Krysta moved to his side in an attempt to assist.

"Yeah. They tore Ace apart, and I have no idea what happened to Blitz. He was ahead of us. We heard him cry out and by the time I got there, one of those things was dragging him away."

Bear moved over to Grim's other side. "The rest of the wolves are down. Let's move out of here." He hoisted Grim up on his feet and Krysta moved over to hold his other arm.

Grim shook his head. "I don't need help. Let's get out of here." His eyes shifted over to the Hlinan that ran up to provide aid. "I'm glad you guys showed up. I take back everything I said about not trusting you."

"You do not need to thank us, Peacekeeper." Eski redirected his attention squarely on Bear. "As I have said before, we need to work together."

Distant howls sprung from their east. Krysta tensed. "That's not a good sign. Let's get back to the base." She glimpsed sadly at her mentor. "We can't save Blitz."

Bear sighed in defeat. "Yeah, nor what is left of Ace. They shouldn't have died like this."

It was only when they arrived back at the safety of the base, did Krysta allow herself to relax her body, rolling her shoulders back. A translucent yellow lit dome capped over the entire base behind them. The defense shield hummed loudly and sizzled from the electricity passing through it. She glanced over at Eski. "This thing will protect us?"

"The barrier has successfully thwarted their attempts thus far."

A chilling howl echoed from the trees nearby and all heads turned towards where it came from. Hlinan soldiers formed a horizontal line four meters from the barrier's edge. The Peacekeepers moved to follow suit and fell in behind them. "We need to work together as a team," Bear called out to the mercs.

Krysta heard the wolves' paws striking the ground in rapid succession from their charge towards the base. She threw a nervous look at Eski. "How does this barrier work?" She winced in discomfort as she propped the butt of her rifle up against her previously injured shoulder from Madu's ambush.

"It charges fully with the sun's energy during the day, and we can use it at night to protect ourselves from the hata. They have tested the durability several times despite the electrical shock it poses on their bodies," the Hlinan explained.

"Is the shock fatal?"

"No, but it has kept them at bay for years now."

The new hata pack emerged from within the trees, but unlike the others, it contained three large black ones along with three brown ones. The feral beasts hesitated just meters away from the barrier and stared through the luminous protective cover to their queries inside. "Do not fire unless the beasts puncture the shield," Eski instructed his team.

"Shit. There are three alphas?" Grim asked, "How is that possible? This is bad news." A gloomy expression crossed his bloodied scratched face as he looked at Krysta. "Déjà vu all over again with Bakht."

"Grim, you are hurt. Stay back to the bunk." Krysta gestured with her rifle.

He shook his head and kept his sniper rifle poised. "No way. I'm still in this fight."

"Your friend speaks the truth, Lone Wolf. We have never come across a pack that contained over two alphas. This is rare." Eski concurred ahead of them. From the revelation, Krysta overheard the Hlinan's breathing increase in trepidation.

The center black hata viciously snapped its jaws to one of the smaller brown ones on its right. It lurched toward the barrier, but after the impact seconds later, it whimpered loudly in pain. It sprawled onto the ground, briefly twitching from the electrical charge it endured. The remaining canines growled louder by the outcome.

The three large black beasts broke apart and stood right outside the shield. Krysta watched on and held her breath. "They are going to punch it all at once."

"These fuckers are smart," Bear murmured to her right. "No way an animal can be this smart, Wolf."

"Stand ready!" Eski sounded the order.

The three alphas rushed at the barrier's perimeter, but instead of lunging at it like their counterpart, they viciously swiped at it over and over with their claws. Light from the shield flickered with each hit but did not phase out. The alphas whimpered loudly by the jolt they were receiving but would not back down. Everyone stood on pins and needles as they watched on. Krysta's finger twitched on her pistol's trigger. Unflinching, Eski kept his eyes fixed ahead. "Eski, are you sure about that barrier?" Beads of sweat dripped down from her forehead.

After a few intense seconds, the hata gave up and backed off from their approach. The alphas gave one last look to their prey, then rushed back through the trees into the darkness of the night. Eski held up his hand to signal the all clear, and it was only then that Krysta released the breath she had been holding. Her heart thumped loudly in her chest, and her eyes met Bear. "Too close for comfort."

Eski turned to one of his officers. "Get a drone in the sky and follow them. We must alert the human's colony should the hata go in that direction." The officer saluted, then rushed off to carry out the order. He then turned to the Peacekeepers. "Thank you for the assistance."

Bear rubbed his beard thoughtfully. "That just wasn't a random attack. Something about this is not right."

"I agree, Peacekeeper." Eski glanced quickly at the barrier. "That was a strategic move. The hata were not here when our first colony arrived. They do not act like any wild beast we have encountered. Their ability to solve complex problems is unlike what we have seen before."

"We figured you had a hand in their control earlier on when they attacked whenever you were around," Krysta admitted remorsefully.

"A logical perception and an excusable one. Control is our assumption as well, but we do not know how or who it is."

"Hlinan, er, I mean Hosir Matelija. Thank you again for saving me back there. I owe you my life." Grim spoke up. He looked over at Bear. "I was wrong a lot about you. I trust you."

"Such payment is unnecessary. My trust in your group is mutual. The situation with the hata in the region is becoming a greater concern. I implore you to remain here. I must assess the situation with Hosir Madu. Please excuse me." He bowed slightly before walking away from the group.

"Okay, he's right," Bear admitted. "We stay here. Grim, let's go patch you up." He grinned at Krysta. "Wolf, you look like shit. Get a damn shower."

Krysta ran her fingers through the hardened mud on her hair and nodded. "Don't have to ask me twice."

"Still need to figure out a ride off this planet," He brought up as they walked back inside their bunk. "Eski has said nothing about us getting a ride from the Hlinan. May have to have another talk with Carson as much as I hate it."

"So, we just go back and kiss Carson's ring and act like nothing happened?" Krysta grumbled with a shake of her head. "No way in hell am I doing that."

"Wolf, the longer we pussyfoot around here, the more time we lose with our window of opportunity. If push comes to shove, then we barge our way in."

Grim cringed at the suggestion. "I'm not too keen on that, Papa Bear. What if the colonists try to go up against us? We just shoot them?" The brawnier man did not respond.

"If we go up against the colony, then we can't ask the Hlinan to help, Bear. Dhank Trust will use that as an excuse to wipe them all out. Earth's militaries are not involved yet, but you get filtered information with the hint of a hostile alien race, and everyone back home will be up in arms. The fact of the matter is that they wanted to be left the hell alone and Dhank Trust chose to still build a luxury resort on this planet. I don't like where this is going and we can't just leave the Hlinan here to deal with it alone."

Grim disagreed. "It sucks. I know, Krysta. But it's not for us. We have no damn business getting involved."

"Coming from the man whose life was just saved by one of the Hlinan? Heh, some gratitude."

Bear stepped in. "The Hlinan is partly to blame too. Their screwed-up religion messed them up. They believe we are their mortal enemies and even ambushed you."

"Not all of them believe that."

"Fine. Most of them do. They will crucify Eski by the end of this."

Krysta sighed hard and held her head. "Okay, okay. Let me at least go talk to Eski. One last shot. We owe him that much."

"One last shot, Krysta. That's it, but after you clean up."

"I'm going, I'm going." She moved toward the washroom facility near the back of the bunk.

"Wolf?" Bear called her.

Krysta paused in her step. "Yeah?"

"I'll hang outside his office while you talk. They may target you, and I'm not allowing it."

Taking in the warm air through her nose, Krysta did not respond while she moved into the bath house. Her eyes glimpsed over the hexagon shaped mirror to stare into her exhausted soiled face. She activated the waterspout with a wave of her hand to splash her face. What was she going to do?

Chapter 30

Soon after, Bear met Krysta outside the bunk, dressed in his full body armor. "You look better. How many bruises do you have?"

"Plenty." She noted that the usual guards at the door were missing. "What happened to our lockdown?"

Bear shrugged. "No one was here when I came out. Ruined my fun."

"That's odd. Maybe Eski called them back?" She strolled along with him to the center of the Hlinan base where the Hlinan's office was located. She figured she would have more of a chance to find him there. "How's the leg?"

"Strangely, whatever these reptiles did to it with their scan after we arrived here, fixed it. No residual pain at all."

"I wonder what the chance would be for me to get some of that special treatment. Grim patched up?"

"He will have a slight scar."

A few guards outside the main building approached them cautiously. "This is a restricted area, Arlandr. Move back into your designated zone."

"Did Hosir Madu give you that bullshit order? I don't recall Hosir Matelija prohibiting us from walking around." Krysta argued. The two guards exchanged uncertain looks, and she caught on. "Look, I have business with Hosir Matelija, so call it in."

One guard hesitantly followed through with the request and tapped a section on his shoulder. "Hosir Matelija. There are two humans outside to see you. Shall we provide them clearance?"

"Just Lone Wolf," Bear chimed in loudly. "I'm staying back just in case you try to jump her." A leer twisted his face as he slammed his fist into his palm.

"*Let her proceed,*" Eski's voice came over the tiny speaker on the guard's armor. Then one of them motioned her inside to follow him.

Bear flashed her a serious look. "Stay safe in there."

Krysta watched the door close behind her as she followed her escort through the dark, red-lit hallway. There were several closed doors to the hallway sides; none of them labeled. After a few turns, her escort stopped and swiped his hand under a sensor to activate the door opening.

Eski glanced up from his screen. "Thank you for bringing her here. Return to your post." He rose from his chair and motioned the guard along. The soldier dutifully saluted his Hosir and then exited, leaving Krysta alone with Eski. "Forgive me. I must keep this conversation short. Hosir Madu is in her office, and I fear she will not like you within our primary operations."

"I'm sorry for Jack hitting you. At least you had your helmet on." She frowned at him. "Any chance we can bum a ride from you guys back to Earth?"

He sat back down and flagged her to sit in the small, curved chair in front of his desk. "Krysta, you know that is something that I cannot request. The alliance with your colony is new and not solidified. The Hevding wants the Peacekeepers and Bakht Colony to reconcile."

Krysta rolled her eyes. "There's no way in hell that is happening right now. I assure you. Look, both sides want us to go. Just give us a ship and we will be on our way. If you don't, you may have another problem on your hands."

"Oh?"

"The only option we have left is to barge our way back into the colony to contact our captain or commandeer the arriving transport ship."

"It is not that simple," Eski muttered.

"It is." In frustration, Krysta's voice rose. "Just make a damn call or whatever you do to get your Hevding's attention."

"The Hlinan Hierarchy is intricate, Krysta. A transport ship capable of such a journey to your home world in another system is not something that the Hevding can obtain. I assure you that I have made a formal request to Emble. It takes time. You must exert patience here."

"Intricate? You mean like the chain of command?" Krysta fired back. "You act like I am a simpleton. Why don't you dub it down for me?"

"Krysta, you are overreacting. Any rash decisions-"

"It sounds like you and your Hevding are just jerking our chains."

"Lone Wolf, enough." With a furious shout, Eski pounded the desk with both fists and sprang up from his chair. His sudden aggressive behavior startled Krysta. She never heard him raise his voice this way.

Angry and disbelieving, she rose to meet his gaze. "I can't believe I trusted you." She threw up her hands. "I'm an idiot. I thought I had feelings for you and fell for whatever deception you threw at me."

Her harsh words caused his eyes to widen, and his expression darkened. "I may have risked my entire life to help you, Krysta; rumors of me turning into a Slaroar will spread. Madu will make sure that your group remains hostile as long as you are here. My time as an acting Hosir is limited. Perhaps you should return to your colony. It would be in your best interest and the safest option."

"Fuck her!" Krysta moved around the desk to where he was. "Are you really going to let Madu undermine you?"

"I will not," his words bled with venom. His chest heaved with a labored breath. "There's more to it than that. Lone Wolf. I cannot give you the timeframe that you need. I am sorry." Slowly sinking back into his seat, his voice trembled.

Her anger diminished by the look of turmoil and pain on his face. Something was really eating him up. "Eski? What is it?"

His eyes avoided hers and he held his hand on the top of his fringe to keep his face pointed downward. He was cowering inside. "I must tend to my duties, Lone Wolf. I am sorry."

Krysta crouched down right before him. "Don't give me that crap. You're acting like a rookie in his first war."

He slowly turned his head to look at her. "What if your words ring true, Krysta? What if my kind's religion is false? All these centuries, everything we were told. Then what if Madu and the others are correct? You could be merely a deception of Sani sent to test me. Or perhaps I am slated to be the catalyst for the destruction of my race."

Right before her eyes, she was seeing him break. The whole concept of the humans' existence was on a much higher level than she presumed. Empathy seized her, and she delicately grazed his face. "Hey, it will be okay."

Her touch caused his eyes to flutter shut; a calming hiss escaped his lips. His lips brushed her gloved fingers in a gentle kiss. "Krysta, I want to be more than a protector to you. I will risk my very existence in doing so."

Krysta's heart skipped a beat at his words; her thoughts trembled, wanting to respond to his affection. "Eski, let's forget about what is happening around us for a moment. Forget about my past and forget about what your faith tells you to do. Let it just be me and you."

His voice dropped to a low gravel. "I desire you." Eski leaned in and pressed his wet cold lips against her warm soft ones.

His hands pulled her into a tighter embrace. An urge of want soared through her and she reciprocated by intensifying the kiss with a more passionate one. Her body relaxed and her subconscious escaped her. Her breaths grew heavier. She wrapped her arms around his neck, leaning her body into his. His kiss was unlike any other, sweeter than any she had ever experienced, which was unsurprising given he was not human.

She began to trace the scales on the back of his head with her fingers, curiously.

Pulling away after a moment, his breath left the warmth lingering on her skin. He wrung his hands in distress. "By Hlidar's mercy, what has come over me?" His eyes broke away in shame.

With his taste lingering on her lips, Krysta desired him more. She leaned in and captured his mouth once again. Feeling his abrasive tongue flicker against her own, she moaned softly, then slid onto his lap in the chair as his hands caressed the small of her back.

He broke away again and shifted her body off his. "I cannot do this. I must pray to Hlidar for understanding." His solid disposition regained control. "An urgent message will be sent per your request. Please remain here until there is a response." His eyes pleaded with her own. "Is that all for today, Lone Wolf?"

She saw the mounting fear inside him. "I don't know what's coming over me, Eski. We need to talk about this… about us."

"Another time." Nervously, his eyes darted to the wall behind her. "I have a meeting shortly with Hosir Madu and need time to prepare."

Krysta glared at the wall. Was she feeling jealous? The emotion startled her. "You can't get over her, can you? Does what just happened mean nothing to you?"

He clenched his hands into fists and stood to face her. "It means everything to me." His eyes flickered, and he slowly sat back down. Unable to meet her gaze, he forced out, "Thank you for stopping by."

The strength of her affection confused and shocked her; she backed away slowly, taking deep breaths to steady herself. Hurrying out of the door, her boots clattered loudly on the metal floor. *What the heck is happening to me? What was that?* Her face felt hot. As she rushed out of the building, she almost collided with Bear.

"Whoa! Wolf, what is it?" A worried look crossed his face before his gaze fell upon the door she just exited. "What spooked you?"

Krysta avoided facing him. "Nothing." She fought the urge to reach under her armor collar to find her dog tags. "Let's head back to the others. Hosir Matelija said that he would send a message." She left him where he stood and nearly broke out into a sprint to their bunk. The world around her spun, orbiting over her own thoughts.

Huffing under his breath, Bear caught up to her. "Damnit, Wolf. You are moving fast. What is it? I know something is up. What happened there?"

Her eyes widened. "Nothing, Jack." She desperately sought a lie, but her words failed her. She felt hot inside her armor as her mind lingered on her intimate session with the Hlinan. "Just another flashback. I can handle it." She heard the man murmur under his breath, but she ignored it. *How can I admit to Jack that I am attracted to an alien when I can't even admit it to myself? What is wrong with me?*

Chapter 31

The following morning, Bear roused her by kicking her boot. "Wolf, wake up. Your pal is back."

Krysta yawned and stretched as she rose from her spot on the floor. "Good news I hope."

"Depends on how you take it. Our ride may have shown up." Bear waited for her, then led her back to the front of the bunk where Eski and Madu stood.

Madu's four eyes bore down on her coldly while Eski kept his eye contact away. Krysta glanced at her bearded colleague. "How come I don't like the sound when *she* is here with the news?"

"Like I said," he muttered quietly. "Depends on how you take it."

"Peacekeepers," Madu approached the group. "Our satellites detected a vessel inbound over your colony during the night. Your ship for off-world has arrived, so we ask that you take your leave from here. Now."

"Any word from the ship or from Director Carson?" Bear inquired first.

"None," Madu spat back. "Our fighters remained on standby until the area was clear of your craft."

"Doesn't sound like that ship is for us." The merc uneasily tossed a glance over at Wolf. "I wonder who came onboard."

"Could be just a supply ship," Krysta ruminated.

"We dispatched drones for surveillance." Eski finally broke his silence.

"And?" Bear motioned with his hand for the Hlinan to continue. "Get to the point. What?"

"Our scans showed several cargo containers outside the docked craft. We did not see any other armed forces on the ground. However, the colony shot down one of our drones, so we called the other back before we could make another pass to confirm."

"Shot down?" Bear gaped at the reveal.

"Since when are civilians sharpshooters?" Krysta followed along.

"This action violates our treaty with them," Madu hissed. "The Hevding is not pleased."

"Things just became interesting," Bear mused to the group. "I doubt that craft only brought supplies."

"I'm with you, Papa Bear," Wolf nodded her head. "Can't believe they would fire at a Hlinan drone when they have an alliance in place. They were faking this whole time, I bet."

"Why would they do that?" Eski blurted out. Their eyes finally met. His state of distress was unchanged from the day before. "Are they that eager to break their treaty?"

Krysta chortled. "Humanity has broken a lot of alliances throughout history. Please remind me to give you a lesson later. Hosirs, Dhank Trust will come for us and your Hevding will order you to surrender us over to prevent open war." The atmosphere surrounding them became dire.

"Then you should leave now," Madu interjected icily. "Come, Hosir Matelija. We need to put the base on full alert." She exited the bunker with purposeful strides.

Eski stayed behind and sadly looked on at the Peacekeepers. "It may be unsafe for you to leave. You should wait until you know what you will face at the colony. I will find out what I can."

Krysta shook her head sadly. "You have exposed yourself enough. We don't belong here, Eski. You can die because of us."

"Then I will die." His four eyes remained transfixed on her. "For you."

Her eyes burned. It took every fiber of her being to not break down in the room. The Hlinan base leader grew silent and followed his colleague outside without another word. Krysta remained frozen in place. *Eski, don't do this.*

Next to her, Bear scratched his head. "What did he mean by that?"

Krysta's bottom lip quivered. "He will sacrifice himself to save us."

Chapter 32

After everyone gathered around in the bunk, Bear and Krysta moved to the front. The room was buzzing about the alarming news they received from their Hlinan partners. Bear leaned against the table casually, arms folded. "Wolf, how do you want to play this out? I know what I want to do."

"Our brain waves normally click. I say we don't sit around here and wait for scans to show what we are up against. I hate to say it, but his superiors will hold Eski back, then it will be too damn late to stop it." Krysta frowned at her own words; the cold reality settled in.

"Agreed." Jack unfolded his arms and stood straighter.

"Infiltration party."

"Team of four, form up and stash two clips; things could get messy out there." Bear pulled his armor out of his locker hold and slipped it on, then attached the pistol and rifle.

"I got an extra clip if someone is out," Wolf added after she took stock of her own pistol's chamber to ensure it was ready to go before holstering it. There was no way she was going to miss this. She slipped on her own personal armor.

"Company." Grim flagged the others. All eyes turned to the doorway where Eski and another male Hlinan officer walked in.

Unlike the familiar facial features of Eski, the other notably had black spots around three millimeters, each in diameter that ran up the right side of his face.

"Are you leaving the base?" Startled, Eski sought an explanation from Krysta.

"We know they are gunnin' for us." Bear pulled his pack over his other shoulder. "Best that we bring the fight to them on our terms."

"How will you do that?"

"We've been here longer and have a gist of the land. That's our advantage," Krysta simply stated with a mischievous grin. "We might send them Ikol's way."

A sterner look settled on Eski's face. "I hope you are joking, Wolf. To entangle with Ikol is deadly. Perhaps I may offer help? Recon would be the best approach."

Grim nodded his head in appreciation at the suggestion. "I'm all in for stealth mode. What were you thinking?"

Eski glanced at his companion and walked closer into the room with the other following him. "This is Korlur Lers, a long-time friend and someone I can trust completely. The news of more military soldiers in your colony is unsettling. It is a threat to this base since we are in the closest spectrum of proximity and the first line of defense for any assault against our colony. Although our reasons may differ, we, too, are interested in learning more about their intentions."

"I know you like to send drones and shit, but we don't have time to do that," Bear gruffly argued. "It needs to be up close and personal."

"I was thinking of a new tactic," Eski dryly grinned. "Two of you may accompany Lers to an area outside the colony's perimeter. With the current alliance intact, they will not be on full alert for a Hlinan vehicle in the area. This could give you time to gather the intel you need and a ride back. In return, I ask that you disclose all your findings."

"Why don't *you* come along?" Bear grunted. "Aren't you friends with Wolf?"

"My absence will not sit well with Hosir Madu. I must tread carefully. I do not recommend a journey on foot. As you are presently aware, there is an increase in hata activity outside the base."

"Good idea. Bear and I will head out with your friend here." Krysta nodded at him.

Bear's eyes widened at her decision. "Negative, Wolf. I'll take Grim with me. I wouldn't say I enjoy leaving my guys here unprotected. At least this one is nice to you, and I know you won't let them mess up."

"No way," Krysta argued against it. "I'm not missing out on this. I'm going. You know I won't take no for an answer."

"Then it's settled," Eski concurred. "You will leave when night falls."

"Good idea. No colonist will be outside at night and the fear of the hata will keep them hunkered in." Krysta agreed to the plan.

"I hope you are right," Bear mumbled.

Hours later, after the dark completely engulfed the sky, the small hovercraft similar to Eski's sped from the Hlinan base towards the Bakht Colony. "You think these guys will buy the whole hata tracking scheme?" Bear shifted uncomfortably in the front passenger seat. Krysta managed to fit herself into the small storage space behind the front seats.

"The hata do hunt at night, and their packs have been moving closer to your colony over the past few days," Lers said matter-of-factly from behind the driver's control dashboard.

"What if those dogs are *here,* then? We are playing hide and seek in the bushes for them to find us."

"I have brought my rifle should the threat come. I will remain near the vehicle for your pickup."

"Wolf and I could only bring our pistols. You can use your rifle all you want, pal. If those things come, she and I will confiscate your ride back."

With the same serious, unemotional expression as Eski, Lers looked over at him. "I do not fear death. My creator, Hlidar, watches over me."

"Your other buddies didn't make it. I guess your god didn't like them too much," Bear jabbed at the mention of the reptile's faith.

"You think these guys are some government's military?" Krysta switched subjects and leaned in more from where she sat.

"No way. Space was hands off for all global governments when we left Earth, and I doubt they agreed to terms to police it since then. If one country sent up arms, there would be a tremendous uproar. Could it be a bunch of cruisers' security details?" Bear chuckled at the notion.

Wolf shook her head at the joke. "Don't think so. Eski said these guys had containers. Cruisers don't have that type of luggage."

"We pissed them off, remember? You think Dhank Trust would hire another ex-military group?" Bear remained unconvinced and straightened up in his seat.

After the vehicle came to a rest, the door on the passenger side lifted entirely up to allow Bear to exit first, followed by Krysta, who clambered over the back of the seat to get to him. Both sets of Lers' eyes trailed them out. He called to them, "The colony is ahead forty-five meters in the northern direction. The trees should be able to provide you with cover within their perimeter. You have the communication apparatus?"

Krysta tapped her pocket. "Affirmative."

"May Hlidar watch over you. I will proceed with my duty." He exited his side and moved to the back of the cargo hold to retrieve his rifle.

Bear rolled his eyes at him before moving out with Wolf. "Why would their lizard god give a shit about me? Lers just dumped us out, and he is carrying the rifle."

A gentle laugh escaped Wolf's lips at his complaints; then she eagerly dashed forward. Their boots passed over the fallen leaves and dirt floor while the duo darted through the foliage until the light from the colony's boundary greeted them ahead. Bear was first and held his right arm out to swiftly stop her in her tracks. She glanced his way, and he used his other hand to put a finger on his lips to signal her to remain quiet. His eyes darted around before focusing on what lay ahead. With two fingers, he pointed towards a cluster of bushes to his right that had a better view of the colony structure. They crept over, and Wolf kneeled into position, then slipped out her infrared binoculars. Bear did the same. Tapping the controls on top of the small handheld device, Krysta zoomed in and saw several heavily armed soldiers wearing all black, patrolling various routes within the structure's exterior walls. Two manned the main entrance, guarded by an extensive fixed artillery gun.

"Heavy upgrades," Bear whispered. "Puts us to shame. You see, the barrel extension of that artillery gun?"

"You getting aroused over there, Jack?" Wolf snickered.

The man swore under his breath. "Any insignias?"

Wolf followed one guard with her eyes when he moved in the other direction. She recognized a familiar graphic on the soldier's body armor: a tribal artistic version of a fully inflamed sun. "Hell Suns." Her mind flashed to the mission on the Mars shipping freighter. "Holy shit. What are they doing here?" She didn't like the déjà vu feeling settling in.

"Well, this just got interesting," Bear said beside her in a hushed tone.

"Why the heavy equipment?"

"Someone didn't send them here just for us and I bet there will be more arrivals."

Wolf narrowed her eyes at what he was digging at and lowered her binoculars. "We need to warn the Hlinan. This situation just became even more dangerous now that the Hell Suns are involved."

"You think their Hevding will believe us? That guy is naïve."

"I would love to see Carson talk his way out of this."

Suddenly, there was a zip through the air past their heads, followed by the sound of a sudden impact of a round striking a tree deadly in the center to Bear's right. Wolf and Bear became alert and froze while they slowly moved their heads toward the direction of the round's origin. A Hell Suns soldier faced them with his sniper rifle poised in a ready position. A familiar soldier with coal black hair stood next to him without a weapon drawn. The soldier shouted out, "Welcome back, Peacekeepers!" He tauntingly chuckled, "I hope there are no hard feelings; that's how business goes."

Wolf growled and clenched her fists. "It's Jones." She placed both fists on the ground to push herself out of cover.

"Hold." Bear prevented her from proceeding ahead because of the bait. "We need to head back." He furrowed his brow and his body became tense. "Now is not the time for round two, Lone Wolf."

Krysta crept low behind him. The look in her friend's eyes was the same as it was when she led her first mission against the notorious mercenary group. Was her short fall a precursor of what was to come?

Chapter 33

Back at the base, an hour later, Eski jogged over to greet Krysta, Bear and Lers as they got out of their vehicle. "Hosir Matelija, this is bad," Wolf stated, voicing her concern first.

"We can discuss more in the conference room. I will take you there," Eski quickly whispered to them.

"It's time to see what the Hlinan are really made of." Bear followed in a line behind Krysta. The specified conference room was just large enough to accommodate eight attendees around a thin metal-framed square table with two chairs on each side. The red lighting made Bear rub his eyes to adjust to it. "Don't you have normal lights?"

"You get used to it," Krysta commented in amusement. The two Peacekeepers sat in the chairs closest to them. Eski grabbed one seat to their right at the head of the table and Lers sat down next to him. Hosir Madu stormed in before they continued their conversation.

"Hosir Matelija," the furious female snarled. "What is the meaning of this?"

Lers shot up in defense of his friend, but Eski tapped his arm to stop him. The Hlinan base leader rose from his chair. "Hosir Madu, there has been a development at the human colony and the Peacekeepers provided surveillance for us. Please sit."

Madu glared angrily at the two humans in the room before she sat across from them. "How do we trust anything they say?"

"Because, Hosir," Eski began calmly, "I instructed Lers to accompany them to make sure their findings were not biased."

"Proceed then." She gestured with her hand. "Though, I am sure you know fully that the Hevding declined your outlandish request to use one of our own ships from Emble to send these exiles back to their home world."

Bear snorted at the disclosure. "I wasn't holding my breath."

"I am aware," Eski acknowledged. "He fears that the volume of aid would be a sign of intervention in the current situation. The Honegar, our divine overseer, is troubled about the Peacekeepers' exile status and emphasizes the need for adherence to their own species' rules."

He paused for a moment, then continued, "However, Hosir Madu, the Hevding *is* unsettled by the potential threat in the colony and will come here in the morning to arrange a visit to Bakht. He believes transparency should be expected on both sides as part of the alliance. We permitted their leader to enter our boundaries, and we expect the same action to be reciprocated on his part. The Peacekeepers have now confirmed that there is a new military force on the colony."

"And lady," Bear turned his head directly to Madu. "This is serious so get your head out of your ass and listen to what we have to say." He stood. "I highly recommend that your Hevding does not go near here. While Carson is too stupid to do a headcount, he has access to your base and information on the layout. All of this intelligence, I'm sure, he divulged to the new group in town."

Krysta piped in, "The new group is called the 'Hell Suns.' They are nothing to scoff at. Each of you now has a bullet with your name on it."

"Your Hevding should expect nothing to gain from this visit. Do you think the Hell Suns will just uncover every little weapon they have?" Bear grunted contemptuously and relaxed more in his seat. "Dhank Trust avoided you before and don't expect them to just be buddy-buddy with you over a handshake."

"Hell? Suns?" Eski lifted an eyeridge at the name. "What do you know about them?"

"Ex-military as well," Wolf elaborated first. "And I mean '*ex.*'"

"Dishonorable discharge, convicted felons, including a few murderers, mixed in," Bear added. "You need someone to do your dirty work and not feel a damn thing about it, then you call these guys."

"I just don't understand why Dhank Trust dispatched them." Krysta reflected over to her old mentor for insight. "These guys mostly handled civil unrest, trafficking, or coups in unstable countries. The Martian transport must have been an anomaly. If word got out that a high-ranking financial institution deployed them, it would not look good at all."

"Think about it, Lone Wolf." Bear avidly leaned over the table's edge with both arms. "Out here, there are no laws. How is anything going to get back to Earth unfiltered? You have guys like the Hell Suns keeping everything shut, and no one will question a thing. Dhank Trust will not be happy with just that one spot. This place is money to them; every single rock of it, and they own the full rights."

"Full rights per *your* world," Madu snapped in.

Eski sounded next. "What does this mean for our city?"

"A countdown till the party's over," Wolf sighed. "Dhank Trust takes the Hlinan out, so they can have this planet."

"The Children of Sani," Lers spoke to his kin nearby. "They have returned just as the others feared."

Both sets of Eski's eyes hardened on Lone Wolf. He exhaled loudly through his nose before he addressed his comrades. "The Peacekeepers are *not* them." He pivoted back to Bear and Krysta. "However, it troubles me if what you say is accurate. This base will be on complete lockdown because of the high priority target coming in. We should remain neutral in your conflict with the colony, but I worry we will ultimately have to choose sides."

"As much as I do not trust these humans, Hosir Matelija, it would be foolish to not use them in a temporary alliance against these newcomers," Madu surprisingly suggested with a sneer. "And only temporary."

Krysta blinked in shock at her words. "I am willing to suffer by forging an alliance with you, Hosir Madu." She redirected her gaze to Bear. "We have to reach Captain Masters and see what he thinks about the Hell Suns being here."

"Aye, and we need a damn ship. Even if Carson agrees to let us go, I wouldn't trust whatever he gives us. It would be bloody booby-trapped, for sure," Bear agreed.

"Hosir Matelija, you guys don't need to go alone," Wolf turned back to the Hlinan. "Let us accompany you."

"I am not sure if your appearance will be permissible." Lers differed.

"*I* will make it permissible." Eski sharply argued.

Lers activated the holo graphics interface at the center of the table. "Hosirs, our latest dispatch of drones uncovered more activity by the colonists outside their border."

"Expansion?" Eski directed his question to the two humans in the room.

"Of course it is," Hosir Madu pointed out harshly. "Hosir Matelija has weakened our position against them by his deteriorating faith."

"With all due respect, Hosir, Eski, is a full believer," Lers interjected.

"Has he corrupted you as well?" Madu hissed. "This entire base is compromised. The Hevding will see for himself when he arrives."

"Back off." Krysta jumped from her seat. "You have a serious chip on your shoulder. Lay off Eski or you will have to deal with me."

Madu glared at her, before relaxing into a smirk. "I have already dealt with you, human. You were no challenge."

"Be careful there," Bear growled. "You haven't dealt with me."

"Enough." Eski's voice thundered over them. "Hosir, your rivalry with Lone Wolf is superfluous. War is on our doorstep. We must prepare for the Hevding's arrival."

"Fine, then we can see what he thinks of an alliance with these exiles." Madu gestured to the humans in the room. "Come to my office, Hosir Matelija. We need to discuss this more in private." She abruptly left.

Inflamed, Eski's focus followed her out, then he turned to Lers. "Alert the base. I will see you once I have spoken with Hosir Madu."

"I'll get everyone ready on our end," Bear stood. "No offense, but Hosir Madu needs to tone it down a notch."

Krysta lightly touched Eski's arm. "Are you going to be okay in there with her?" Without a word, he left the room, somber. Wolf didn't like where the conversation left off; things were spiraling out of control. Getting off the planet was one thing, but that would leave the Hlinan in an inevitable open war with the colony and it appeared Madu was determined to remove Eski from power. Would the risk of returning to Earth be worth it in the long run?

Chapter 34

The next morning, Krysta and the other mercs arranged outside in their full body armor and weapons with the Hlinan soldiers. A sleek hover craft arrived, and Krysta presumed it was the Hevding. She was correct. Upon his exit from the craft, four turquoise armored Hlinan soldiers accompanied the planetary dignitary. Hosir Matelija and Hosir Madu stood at the front of the mixed groups donned in full body armor, without helmets. Krysta stared at the two of them and wondered what words they exchanged during their private conversation the evening before. It was difficult to tell when Eski and Madu's faces were devoid of expression.

When the entourage was three meters away from the Hosirs, the two front guards side-stepped to grant the Hevding passage ahead. Krysta remembered his clothes from their first city meeting; however, this time a prominent silver pendant, engraved with a Hlinan's head, glittered below his collarbone.

Bear tittered at the reptile's fashion statement. "Is he their Pope?"

"He's their Hevding, the religious and political head on this planet," Wolf whispered.

Eski saluted his leader. "The base is now yours. It is an honor that you bless us with your esteemed presence."

The Hevding's eyes skimmed around the natural view and forestry in the distance. "You would think that as one chosen to lead on this world, I would be privileged in all things, and yet I have been denied access to this tranquil wonder," he hissed in delight. "I have been a prisoner of the city for far too long. This place is above what Sani made for us. This is Hlidar's creation; I can sense it."

"Stay here for as long as you would like, then, your esteemed excellency. We shall pacify the humans to ensure your safety," Madu said firmly.

Krysta rolled her eyes. Bear snickered under his breath to her, "I'd like to see her try."

The planet ruler frowned at Madu. "Hosir, it troubles me that you expect me to want the downfall of the humans. I would like to travel here again, but I do not wish violence against a neighbor. Hosir Matelija has stated that the Peacekeepers provided aid for us, and I am grateful for their unconditional servitude." He partially saluted the mercenaries with closed eyes. The rest of the Hlinan followed suit in unison as if on cue. He then continued, "I hope my dialogue in the Bakht Colony will cause the Peacekeepers' safe return in terms of friendship and peace, for that is the way of our creator, Hlidar. He does not wish destruction nor death, unlike his brother, Sani, and yet we must be vigilant should the time come for such unwanted carnage."

Grim shook his head at the statement and whispered to Krysta, "They don't *want* us back."

"I agree with you on that," Krysta uttered through her feigned polite smile.

"Perhaps we should talk then," Eski urged the Hevding to follow him. "Darkness draws upon us."

"One moment." The Hlinan superior did not move his step. "Before discussing such vile matters, we should ask for Hlidar's guidance and wisdom, as we do in everything." He bowed his head, and the rest of his kind did the same. The Peacekeepers did not partake in the religious ceremony and kept their eyes locked on the figures ahead. "Hlidar, our architect," The Hevding began. "We pray for your guidance, patience, wisdom, and understanding. For I am your tool, and my actions are your actions." Reopening his eyes, he smiled wider. "It is done. Let us continue, Hosirs."

Madu glared mockingly at the mercs. "Peacekeepers, I ask that you remain here. This is a *private* matter."

"Hosir Matelija," Wolf called to him, ignoring her words. "Perhaps it would be best that one of us accommodate you in these discussions to provide our perspective."

Eski continued to guide the Hevding and his entourage towards the building. "That will not be necessary, Peacekeeper." Krysta saw his eyes flick away from Madu as if uncomfortable.

His answer surprised her, and she watched him disappear into the building. Arms crossed, she cast a disappointed look at her team. "What is he thinking?" She had to admit that the tone in his voice provoked suspicion within her. Eski's words felt distant, making it difficult for Krysta to trust him. Was he falling in line with Madu? Was he really over his past lover? Krysta's mind switched to their intimate moment in his office. *Was it all a lie?*

"Wolf, I really want to trust these guys as much as you do, but something about this isn't right." Bear peered around at all the reptilian soldiers dutifully standing at their positions. "We need to think about what *we* will do should things get hot."

"I'm with Papa Bear on this," Grim whispered. "Even if they are on our side, these guys will be cooked if the Hell Suns brought more weapons here."

"Our comms won't get to Earth. We need the colony's linkup; that means getting inside Bakht and bypassing the Hell Suns." Bear's eyes darted to the rest of the mercenary group, then to the Hlinan.

"No way the Suns will just let us waltz right in and ask." Krysta chewed her lip.

"I say we come up with a plan before they exit their meeting," Grim stressed.

"Anyone feel like we are a damn bargaining chip?" Bear tossed out into the fray.

"What do you mean?" The question threw Krysta off. She could almost imagine the gears grinding away inside his head.

"I mean, what if there is something that the Hlinan want from Bakht and our demise is a way to gain that?"

Grim nodded along. "Yeah, I can see that."

Bear side-eyed the nearby Hlinan, carefully. "It's time to stop playing dumb. If they come out with demands for us to leave, then we make demands of our own. We get a message to Earth, and I mean a *direct* one. I'm not going through anybody."

"If they refuse?" Grim crossed his arms. "Because I kind of see them saying no."

The red bearded man before them didn't flinch. "Then we *force* our demand. If we willingly go back to the colony, then we are all dead. I would rather make my stand here."

Having patiently awaited the meeting's conclusion, the Peacekeepers watched as Eski exited the building. Krysta didn't like the troubled expression the Reptilia had on his face as she hurried over to him. "What is it?"

"I have persuaded the Hevding to allow two of you to accompany us in the Bakht Colony for this meeting."

"You don't sound very thrilled." Grim moved in next to Krysta.

"I fear he has a lack of confidence with your group because of your banishment. He first attested to the idea of you accompanying us."

"That's your fault, buddy," Bear approached them. "You kid-napped Wolf. What the hell did you think we were going to do? Get on our knees and beg for her release?"

"Easy, Jack," Krysta coaxed him. She didn't miss Eski's nervous glance thrown toward Madu. "What is it, Eski?"

Silent, the Hosir watched the Hevding leave with his entourage, then glanced back at the Peacekeepers. "Emble's Slaroars have grown in number because of a fascination with your species and reference to the Children of Sani. The Hevding fears the extreme beliefs will spread to this planet and create a partition between both ideologies." He stared directly into Krysta's eyes, easing into a softer tone. "There will be a lot of alterations to how we *feel* toward you." A tender smile touched her lips as she grasped his unspoken message. His focus lingered as if there were more words resting on the tip of his tongue. A questioning look from Bear caused Krysta to avert her gaze and clear her throat.

"Hosir Matelija." The Hevding's call interrupted their private conversation. "I am ready to proceed. Please have the Peacekeepers' emissaries join us."

"Papa Bear, you and I can go," Krysta quickly chose for the group. "I have experience in speaking with the Hlinan and their Hevding. If anyone can keep them on our side, it will be me."

"That's a good point," Bear conceded. "But we are going to be outnumbered." His emerald eyes swept across the remaining mercenaries. "Stay alert and if anything looks funny, call it in. Keep comms open." He redirected his attention to her. "Keep a level head about you. Don't let Jones dig under your skin. He will make sure to use us as a spectacle if we are not careful. Carson will feed off that."

Krysta's face twisted in displeasure. "We are walking right into the lions' den. I still can't believe Dhank Trust bought the Hell Suns. Why them, of all groups?"

With a sigh, Bear folded his arms. "I'm with you on that one, Wolf. Something about that doesn't settle right. There's more to this than a simple replacement. At least Jones will be on a leash, and it's not just their operation."

"Ditto that. Just hope it's a very short leash."

Chapter 35

Upon exiting their Hlinan vehicle at Bakht Colony an hour later, the two Peacekeepers heard the director's frantic complaints. "Wait a minute!" The man waved his arms to alert the head of the Hell Suns that lurked nearby with his armed men. "This meeting did not include any member of the Peacekeepers. That's *not* what I agreed upon." His words scorching with resentment. "Per Dhank Trust's order, we have expelled them, and we do not permit them within the walls of our colony." He flashed the interface tablet in his hand.

"Screw you, Carson, and shove that tablet right up your corporate ass," Krysta barked back viciously. "I can't believe your employer sold us out to *them*." She pointed to Jones.

"The Peacekeepers are part of the negotiations, Mister Carson," The Hevding addressed the elephant in the room. "I hope you can resolve your quarrels and lower your hostility." His eyes lifted over to Eski. "As you well know, the error is on our part, and we want to make amends."

Hunter glared at Bear and Krysta. "Fine." He motioned them to follow him. "Let us proceed. I agree that the colonists have been terrified ever since the Peacekeepers violated the *terms* of their contract.

I only look out for my people, and you must understand where I am coming from."

"Straight to that again, eh?" Bear rebuked him. He proceeded forward with Wolf at his side and with the Hlinan presiding after them. A line of Hell Suns walked parallel to their right.

Krysta glanced from side to side while they passed through the main gate into the walled settlement. She noted the security cameras placed in various spots and at least one guard on patrol on every route. The place appeared familiar, yet unknown. She mentally counted every guard she noticed, but quickly halted when she caught Jones' judging look. His proximity gave her a better view of him. The man appeared to be in his forties, with rough tan skin from blunt exposure to the sun and coal black buzz-cut hair, followed by a prickly shortened beard without a trace of gray in it at all. On his neck, he bared a tattoo of their group's emblem. He slowed his pace to where he was next to her, edging closer on purpose. She nearly gagged at his aftershave cologne.

"Good to see you again, baby. Admiring what we have? Does it turn you on?" He leered in his familiar, thick Australian accent before chuckling in delight. "Don't be getting any wild ideas, or I may have to shoot you right now." He held a shiny handheld pistol to show off before her. "I bought this with Dhank Trust's money right before we took off. Fires like a dream."

Krysta rolled her eyes in disinterest. "Small. Does that reflect another part of your body?" She beamed devilishly from ear to ear. Even Bear snickered loudly from the quip.

The man shoved his pistol back into its harness. "Bitch." He redirected his focus ahead and then he glanced over his shoulder at the Hlinan walking behind them quietly. "Did your group get cozy with the natives? I heard that deep space travel can do some weird shit to your head; mess you up for life." He leaned in closer, and she smelled the obvious tobacco use off his breath that mixed in with the cologne. "Can make you become less human and more animal.

Maybe even make you want to fuck one of these lizards. Which one of you did?" Lustfully, his gaze traveled the length of her body. Krysta didn't dare to catch his eyes to give him the satisfaction and simply tried to block out his words. "You're too pretty for that. Maybe Jack did."

She shot him with an icy glare. "Your words are just like your cologne."

His dark eyes met hers challengingly. "Oh? How so?"

"Cheap and useless."

"You little vicious—" He growled, but Bear's voice tore his attention away.

"Back off from Wolf. How much did they pay you, Jones?" Bear beckoned to him.

"Jack, Jack," Jones chuckled in delight. "Surprised to see your face again after your group retreated like a bunch of pussies out on that Mars' ship. Didn't know that the Peacekeepers declined to a level one."

"Heh, didn't know your group turned into mall cops with us lowly level ones. Figured you had more class than that."

"You think your group is all cute by having codenames? I know all the dirty secrets about you just as much as you know about me. Your callsign is as adorable as a teenage girl's holo avatar name." The Hell Suns' leader coldly glowered. "At least I didn't sell out against my kind." He raised his pistol at him threateningly. "Sucks to be you. With the money I will rake in, I plan on retiring after this gig. It will set me up for life. I may even buy some land here. There's plenty to go around."

"Do you think Dhank Trust will allow you to stay here?" Krysta taunted. "I don't think you fit their clientele."

"More than you exiles." He glanced at Bear, who was next to her. "Keep your doggy here on a leash, *Bear*." Jones broke the conversation and moved on to the very front.

"Bastard." Krysta increased her pace after him, but Bear clenched her shoulder to pull her back quickly.

"Wolf, remember what I said. Let him go for now." He turned to see that the Hlinan watched the entire discord with drawn looks. "These guys will do everything they can to make us look bad. Don't give them any ammunition."

Rounding the last corner, the procession entered the meeting room. The area was brightly lit, and Krysta noticed the Hlinan stopped briefly to adjust to the lighting. Carson paused behind a large circular table and motioned for them to sit. He took his place at the head with Jones on his right while two more armed Hell Suns remained protectively behind him. The Hevding and Eski sat to Jones' left with the other armed Hlinan poised next to them. Meanwhile, the Peacekeepers found seats across from the Hlinan.

"Hopefully, these are suitable accommodations for our agenda." The head of the colony held center stage right away. "I'm sure the staff change is startling," Carson laughed light-heartedly. "I'm not sure how the Hlinan govern their economy in your bustling metropolis, but change is the norm for corporations on Earth. Our new security detail is *purely* for protection."

Wolf boiled in her seat at his opening statement. "Protection against us *only*, Director Carson? You have double the men here, an enormous gun, and crates filled with armaments, no doubt."

"He fears us, Wolf," Bear mocked. "I don't recall us bringing any aircraft for them to need a surface-to-air gun. Did we, Wolf?"

"No." Krysta shrugged. "I think we forgot them back at home. Whoops."

Their comment dissipated Carson's bright-eyed, flashy smile, and he clenched his jaw. "I do hope there are no hard feelings, Peacekeepers. Our colony has every right to defend itself." Another strained, fake smile stretched across his face as he looked directly at Krysta. "I'm so glad you are alive and well, Lone Wolf. I'm sorry that the result of your disappearance led to the early termination of your group's contract." His eyes gleamed happily. "Fortunately for our colonists here at Bakht, the transition of our security detail was seamless. Dhank Trust had already dispatched their permanent security group prior to the Peacekeepers' betrayal. If my employer solely relied on these exiles, then I'm afraid that the planet's hostile wildlife would have doomed us all."

"Permanent?" Bear nearly choked under his breath at the label.

Krysta picked up on this. The disclosure was unexpected. "How fortuitous for Bakht."

"Lone Wolf is not to blame for her disappearance, Colony Director Carson." Eski's eyes fixed on him. "Your action to fault the Peacekeepers was premature."

"Yes, on the contrary, colony director, I would like to speak about that." The Hevding rose from his seat and glanced down at where his Hosir sat. "Hosir Matelija has been providing the Peacekeepers sanctuary at our base. This world can be unforgiving, especially by the hata, which your colony sadly learned firsthand. I understand through him that Lone Wolf saved his life from Ikol, the demon arachnid that guards the mountain pass."

"A spider?" Jones teased loudly. "She saved him from a *damn* spider?"

Krysta figured the merc boss's remark did not sit right with Carson, for he flashed an irritated glare over at Jones. Then the director composed himself and reinserted his same wide smile, "Yes, well, we call that humanity. The Peacekeepers' other negative actions do not reflect the Bakht Colony or Dhank Trust. I assure you."

Krysta mouthed the words, "Fuck you," over to him. Bear lightly jabbed her in the side when he picked up on her rebuttal.

"I know there is disharmony amongst you." The Hlinan overseer continued. "Our erroneous action is the catalyst for it. To solidify our partnership, I would like the Peacekeepers to be reintegrated safely back here to start anew. After all, our creator, Hlidar, asks that we provide second chances."

Carson kept his smile on his face longer. "As much as I would like to grant you this request, Hevding, I'm sorry to say that allowing them within our colony's walls is not an option. If it were so simple, I would graciously consider your words. As you can see, Dhank Trust has employed additional security, and we certainly cannot pay for both."

"May I suggest something?" Rising from his seat, Bear surveyed the others.

Carson blinked at the request, but he gestured for the bearded man before him to continue, then sat down. "By all means, sir. The floor is yours."

Bear glowered at him. "I'll make this simple for all of you. Just get me a direct call to Captain Masters. He can handle our ride to Earth. We will get out of your hair, and you can hash it out between yourselves."

An eerie silence fell over the room, then Jones let out a loud chuckle. Carson blinked several times, then asked, placidly. "You haven't heard?"

"Heard what?"

"Dhank Trust informed the authorities on Earth about the hostile actions toward the colony. Multiple media outlets labeled the Peacekeepers as a global terrorist group, and the Canadian military issued a strike on the compound in Manitoba." Carson grimly continued, "I'm so sorry to break this tragedy to you this way, but I know the airstrike produced several casualties. Isn't that where you guys came from?"

"What did you fucking tell them?" Wolf sprung up with her fists at the ready. "You are a damn liar." She kicked her chair out to lunge forward, but before she could, the Hell Suns drew their guns on her. Jones placed himself between her and Carson.

"Nuh-uh, girly," Jones teasingly scolded her with his finger. "Play nice here, and you can play rough with me later."

In a flash, Eski moved in between Jones and Krysta. He squared up closely to the man's face. A low, threatening growl rose from his chest, and he bared his sharp fangs. "You will have to go through me, human, to get to her."

"I knew it was you," Carson accused Eski. "You were in the meeting with the Hevding and took her side last time." He crooked his finger over at the Hlinan soldier while he remained cowardly behind Jones.

"Hosir, stand down," the Hevding shouted scornfully at his companion.

Unflinching, Eski maintained eye contact with Jones. The man tilted his head side to side to release several cracks of his neck, then smirked sadistically, "What will you do, four-eyes?" The Hosir produced a hiss from his mouth and his upper lip raised higher to reveal more of his fangs.

Bear moved beside Wolf and cracked his knuckles. "Hey, Carson. Tell your pet to calm down, and you better explain yourself right now."

Above the chaos, the Hevding's voice roared, "Please, I want us to have peace!" Fear laced his words as he watched in dread.

Jones raised his pistol toward the leader of the Hlinan. His eyes followed suit from Eski to his new intended target. "Fuck peace." He squeezed the trigger, and the bullet hit the Hlinan right in the center of his forehead. The Hevding's eyes widened at the fatal shot, his lips slowly parting. Blood trickled out of the hole in his head, then, seconds later, his body fell backward and onto the floor. Carson dove to the ground with a scream of fear, holding his hands over his head for protection. One of the Hlinan guards behind the Hevding fired his weapon at Jones to retaliate, but the man rolled away to avoid.

"Engage shields!" Eski ordered. Before the turquoise armored guards reacted, Jones fired, striking one in the upper right chest. The force of the impact slammed the soldier against the wall; he slumped to the ground, blood seeping from a damaged section of his armor.

The other Hlinan guard took out a Hell Suns soldier with a single, precise shot to the head. Jones leaped up from where he was on the floor and fired fast on him; the round struck the exposed neck. The armored Hlinan immediately dropped his weapon and clawed at his neck as dark blood poured. A sickening gurgle escaped his lips before he fell to his knees, then collapsed face-first onto the floor.

With his armor's shield fully active, Eski unleashed several shots from his pistol at the last Hell Suns soldier near Jones, hitting him squarely in the face. The man's body convulsed violently, face contorting beyond recognition before he collapsed, dead.

Jones shifted his chrome pistol to fire at Eski, but a sharp click behind him stopped him in his tracks. Wolf stood in his peripheral vision, and her pistol barrel was right against his temple. "Don't even fucking try it. You know goddamn well at this range that I will send you quickly to hell, where you belong, if you pull that trigger."

The Hell Suns' leader briefly looked at Eski before returning to Wolf, but kept his pistol trained on the lone Hlinan. "I have heavy armor-piercing rounds, baby, and can still take him out."

"I guess we think alike, jerk-off, because I have the same in my gun."

"You're bluffing."

"Try me."

Carson clambered onto his knees to peek over the table at the stand-off. "Jones, what the hell are you doing?" With a sickening expression, he stared at the body of the Hevding. "I didn't tell you to shoot him!"

Jones remained steady where he stood. "Not your orders." He smiled at the sound of his men outside the room. "None of you exiles will make it out of here alive. The Peacekeepers are gone off Earth and your group here is all that remains. You two can be first. Fitting end for you, Jack."

Eski risked the opportunity to check on his fallen comrades, including his leader. He hung his head somberly, when he confirmed there was no more life in any of their bodies. Slowly, he rose to face the murderer. Krysta watched on and kept her pistol trained on Jones since she deduced he was the only remaining threat in the room. "Do you realize you signed your death warrant, Jones, including everyone in this colony? The Hlinan will seek retribution for your actions, and we won't stop them."

Jones didn't even recoil at the threat. "No, Lone Wolf, the Peacekeepers are the ones that have targets on their backs. Dhank Trust wants this entire planet, and these lizards gone for good."

Eski pointed his pistol toward Jones; his muscles tensed tightly in his arm. "We will never leave."

Horrified, Carson staggered to his feet. "Wait! I don't want to be part of this! Earth's governments would never approve of what just happened. I will take it up with them!"

A mocking chuckle escaped Jones' lips as he watched the trembling man. "Who are they going to believe? A large, wealthy, reputable financial institute that invested millions while keeping politicians in their pocket... or some global terrorist organization not even on Earth?"

"They will believe me. I'm not some hired mercenary. I'm in control of this facility."

"We have locked down comms until further notice. We are following Dhank Trust's orders."

Bear fearfully glanced over at Wolf. "We need to go."

Krysta nodded and motioned Jones with her gun. "You and Carson will be our tickets out of here."

With a sigh of reluctance, Eski carefully hoisted the Hevding's body onto his shoulder, leaving the other dead Hlinan behind. He held his leader's limp corpse with one hand and sported his gun with the other. "I am ready."

Jones glared fiercely at the Peacekeepers. "Are you going to side with those four eyes?" He spoke directly to Bear. "Go against your kind? That isn't like you, Jack. Her maybe, but not you."

With his gun pressed against Carson's back, Bear motioned for the director to move towards the door first. "Better them than with you. I may live just a little longer. Carson, you're the guinea pig."

"Drop your gun, asshole," Krysta ordered Jones in front of her. "The other on the side, too." Jones reluctantly complied and tossed both weapons onto the floor. With a taunting leer, Krysta deliberately kicked his cherished new firearm out of reach. She then waited for the leader of the Hell Suns to follow Bear out, and Eski took up the rear. Exiting the room, they noticed armed Hell Suns packing into the hallway.

Jones grunted to his men. "At the ready."

"Get the hell out of our way!" Carson waved his arms madly at the crammed soldiers. The Hell Suns backed up to allow a path forward. The newly hired mercenaries snubbed their noses disrespectfully at the Peacekeepers. One spat saliva down at their feet as they walked by, while a few tossed out their middle fingers. Krysta tightly kept her distance in line with Jones, anticipating that he would underhand them before their destination. After a few tense minutes, they were outside and within visible range of their escape vehicle. A few colonists shuffled out to see what was going on. The Hell Suns kept the onlookers back, while a half-circle of the armed mercenaries formed behind the Peacekeepers.

Noticing the nearby audience, Carson glared at Bear and Krysta. "Do you see how bad you look? You're taking a hostage."

Wolf risked a glance at them. The colonists stared back in sheer terror. "You stay here, and you will die!" Krysta shouted to them. "And we'll not be the ones to take your lives. Dhank Trust has betrayed you all."

"You Peacekeepers are finished," Jones retaliated against her. "You may as well give up now."

It felt like the walk would never end, and a spine-chilling coldness caused the hair on the back of Krysta's to prickle. There would be a pocket of vulnerability when they moved inside the vehicle; she expected Jones to give the signal at any moment. The semi-circle of armed Hell Suns tightened around them. Wolf angled her body slightly to have a better look at her hostage and the threat from the rear. Upon reaching their vehicle, Eski opened the door and tentatively placed the deceased Hevding down in the back while Wolf and Bear remained still with their weapons drawn on Carson and Jones. Eski then moved into the driver's seat and turned on the system to activate it. He nodded to Wolf.

Bear shoved Carson hard before taking his turn to get into the front passenger seat. The colony director scrambled away; his hands tore at the ground to crawl to safety behind the armed troops.

Wolf waved her gun to Jones. She backed up a few steps and met his gaze head on. Hatred flickered in his eyes like flames. A sly smirk played on her lips in return. "I guess I'm damn good at bluffing. I have regular rounds." Then, she leaped into the small back cargo hold behind the front seats and Eski closed the door behind her. Jones withdrew a hidden sidearm and fired a shot at the exterior hull just as the vehicle sped away from the colony. A dust cloud formed behind it in its wake.

Krysta heard Jones' rage fueled scream from behind them, "Fire!"

"Now you really pissed him off." Bear dipped his head down as the rounds pinged off the hull. Krysta lowered her body into the back of the vehicle.

"Hold on." Eski switched to manual guidance, diverted sharply to the right to take a tighter path. Alarms blared inside the cabin from the exterior damage, but his claws engaged the interface to silence them. The gunfire faded into the distance.

Krysta craned her head towards the visual display that provided the feed off the vehicle's back camera. The image of Jones and Carson grew distant. "Eski, can this camera zoom in?" The reptilian driver tapped a few options on the screen to comply with her command and the feed changed over to a closed in image of the two men. There was no sound, but they were in a heated argument. Carson was obviously shouting at the other. Then she watched Jones raise his pistol and shoot the man in the head. "Holy shit!" She cupped her mouth at the spectacle of horror.

Bear stared at the screen in disbelief. "Did he just off Carson?"

"Jones just shot Carson!" Krysta's eyes were still wide and her hand stayed pressed against her mouth.

Bear punched the interior door side with his fist. "Son of a bitch! It's a damn coup! What was Dhank Trust thinking by bringing the Hell Suns here?"

"We can discuss that later." Eski butted in from behind the controls. Several pulsing chirps erupted within their craft while they zipped around trees and back on the path towards the Hlinan base. "We are being followed."

Chapter 36

"How many vehicles are on our six?" Krysta shifted her cramped body in the back compartment. Being near a corpse wasn't ideal, but it was a better alternative to being dead herself.

"Drones," Eski corrected her, and then he glanced over his shoulder slightly to where she was. "There is a long-range rifle back there. Hand it to me."

Wolf complied quickly and pulled the weapon between the two front seats. "Do you need someone to drive?"

"That will not be necessary," Eski checked the gun cartridge. "I have engaged the auto-navigation. It looks like only two; simple enough." He waited until the rover passed a cluster of trees before he opened his door. Wolf scrambled over the seat to retake his spot and held on to his waist when he leaned out of the moving vehicle. "Keep me steady."

"I'm more worried about you being sucked out of here." She held onto his hips and kept her eyes fixed upon the console with the unknown language displayed before her eyes. "I don't know how to read any of this shit."

"That guy is nuts." Bear rotated his head back and forth from them and then the console.

Krysta leaned to the side to peek out the open door to look up at what Eski was doing while she gripped his body. The vehicle's autopilot navigated the pathway. Eski had his rifle braced against his shoulder to aim at the incoming drones. "Lone Wolf!" He pulled away from the targeting scope. "We need to de-accelerate. There should be a button on the left side of the interface. That is for controlling speed. Tap the lower half four times to lower our speed." His voice strained over the deafening wind gusts.

Wolf skimmed over the controls to follow the directions, then located the button and tapped it four times. Several digits changed on the screen in front of her, but she did not know what they meant. Her translator's earpiece only interpreted vocal dialogue, not words. The vehicle slowed down, and she breathed a sigh of relief. "I got it."

"Why the hell would we be slowing up to outpace them?" Bear gave her a confused glance.

"I hope you know what you are doing out there, Eski!" Krysta held onto him in blind faith.

Eski repositioned himself and fired out. Seconds later, she heard explosions, followed by the fate of both drones. The Hlinan slowly lowered back into the vehicle while Wolf made her way back to the rear compartment. He handed her his rifle and then closed the door behind him. Only after his onboard radar confirmed no more enemy targets in sight did Eski break his silence. "We are clear of the enemy for now."

"You are one crazy Reptilia," Bear chuckled at him. "Nice shooting out there."

"I'm sure that will not be the last of them. They know the location of this base," Wolf reminded them grimly.

"Agreed." Eski tapped the vehicle's communication control. "This is Hosir Matelija. Implement code: Vyrd."

After a brief pause on the other end, a familiar snide voice replied, *"This is Hosir Madu. code: Vyrd acknowledged. What has happened, Eski?"*

"We got ambushed, just as I feared."

"The Peacekeepers?"

Bear snorted at the remark while Eski continued speaking into the console. "No, the Peacekeepers remain devoted to us and are with me. The human colony has altered its initial plan. They do not want peace between our two races."

"I will implement the base's lockdown. We cannot be naïve, and we will dispose of these deceivers. I hope you have seen your credulousness, Hosir. I will await instruction from Heofen. Hosir Madu, out."

"She really has it out for us," Krysta grumbled from where she sat in the back.

Without a comment, Eski tapped the console with his claw. "Heofen, this is Hosir Matelija. I have implemented the code: Vyrd. The Hevding's body is with me. I request additional soldiers at the base outside the human colony. An ambush targeted the high-priority team, and I am the only one who survived. We must assume a direct strike on the base is forthcoming."

"I have recorded code: Vyrd, Hosir Matelija, and your request is granted." A male Hlinan's voice confirmed over the speakers.

"I have two humans from the Peacekeepers inbound with me. They risked their lives to save me and help me escort the Hevding's body for proper burial rites. I lost two other soldiers and could not take them with us without forfeiting our own lives. I will see that we negotiate a body transfer later."

"I highly doubt Jones will be so generous," Bear objected. "If he agrees, it's a trap."

"Will see you when you get here, Hosir. May Hlidar watch over you." The responder on the other end of the call confirmed Eski's information.

"Okay, I have to ask," Bear immediately jumped in. "What the heck is code: Vyrd?"

"We use it when our leader is killed. It places our military on high alert."

"And how many times have you used it?" Krysta hung her arms over their seats behind them.

"Just today."

Bear peeked back at Krysta. "The shit is going down, Wolf, and we are right in with it." A frown appeared on his face. "I hope that asshole back there was lying. The captain can't be dead."

"We had a lot of good people on Earth," Krysta agreed sadly. "Carson had to be lying and now he's dead." She replayed the last hour in her mind, shaking her head in disbelief. "You think Dhank Trust is moving us like pawns?"

"My money is that the Hell Suns have their own agenda and are just playing along with Dhank Trust. Think about it. They just held the entire place hostage. This is the corpos' gold mine, and those suits will pay a fortune for its return."

"Or Dhank Trust can just be that damn greedy behind closed doors. Either way, we can't just leave the colonists there like that," Krysta reflected on her father during the colony Enlightenment. Unease brewed inside her like a tornado about to form, and she slowed her breathing to quell it.

Bear's face sharply set upon the Hlinan accompanying them. "I'll just put this out here. We are going to get blamed for this entire mess, right?"

Eski shook his head, "I will defend you against any implications that—"

"No offense," Jack cut him off bluntly. "You're only one Hlinan, and how large is your population on this planet? Plus, your entire home world? We are outsiders. You think they are going to believe *you*?"

"I agree with Jack, Eski," Krysta said glumly. "Hosir Madu is already making you out to be one of those radicals. Things are spiraling out of control, and we are going to take the hit for it. You will be burned alongside us if you are not careful."

Eski glanced at them both. "You saved me again, Lone Wolf; you and your companion. That is twice now. I am in your debt and will defend you with my dying breath."

Bear grumbled, barely audible, "That's probably all the help we're getting from you. We are stopping at the base, right?" He redirected his focus back to Krysta, "No way am I going to step into their city with their dead leader's body."

"If you do not accompany me, then I believe the Peacekeepers will be deemed just as hostile as your brethren in the colony," Eski pointed out.

"Not *our* brethren," Wolf corrected him. "Don't compare those assholes to us."

"One quick question," Bear interceded her gripe. "Which one of you guys is in charge next?"

"The Hunegar will designate Hosir Firben to serve as the acting Hevding for fourteen days to allow mourning over our loss, and then the Heidrs back on Emble will select a new one. Therefore, we must go to Hosir Firben immediately," their Hlinan companion explained.

"You guys don't get to vote for your leader?" The idea intrigued the male mercenary.

"No. What about your planet? Do you get a say in who leads?"

"Depends on what part of the planet you are talking about. I always hated damn politics." One thing is common, not everybody is happy with who leads them."

Playfully, Krysta gave the burly man a pat on the shoulder. "And when there's discord in countries where the other governments don't want to step in, that's when they call mercenaries like us."

"Aye, good days," Bear nodded along happily. "I would give up half the money I got from this pisshole to handle that again."

"Any idea how your friend, Firben, will read us?" Krysta switched gears back over to Eski.

"The Hosir is analytical. He will not make any judgments until he comprehensively reviews all facts," he responded.

"Not that much time there," Bear commented. "And we are in the dark on the guy after him. That new Hevding may hate us." He then shifted in his seat to look back at Krysta before grunting. "I wish I could find out what the heck is going on back home."

"The Peacekeepers are getting a bad rep, that's what," Krysta grumbled. "We could be all that's left." She reached over and gently tapped Eski on the shoulder. "We may not have fourteen days for you guys to decide."

"A ceremony must take place to mourn our loss, Lone Wolf."

"The Hell Suns won't care. They don't play by anyone's rules but their own. We didn't have time to see what came in those crates that arrived with them, and we are not exactly sure if this is all that Dhank Trust will throw against us."

Eski's jawline tensed. "Our kind was here first. Even the Achli, the Children of Sani, could not stop our return and growth."

"Hah, your kind was here first. Our history's pattern shows that's one thing humans don't care about," Krysta pointed out matter-of-factly.

Bear furiously stomped on the floorboard in front of him. "The captain fucked around with the wrong people. We have no clue about any allies on Earth. Going there could cause us to be killed or be on the run for the rest of our damn lives." Eski flinched from the more prominent man's outburst right beside him. Both sets of his eyes blinked, and he leered momentarily before returning to his neutral state.

Krysta sat quietly, mulling things over. Things were going to get ugly, and more blood was going to be spilled. With Jones at the helm of the opposition, the feeling of defeat loomed over her. Was this going to be the extinction of the Peacekeepers?

Chapter 37

Krysta peered over the seat top and saw the dawn light bounce off the skyline structure on the console's camera feed in front of them a few hours later. "Are we finally here?"

Eski tapped his interface comm again. "This is Hosir Matelija. My current vector has an approach of within ten minutes. I will pick the southernmost entry point for a direct route there."

"*Welcome back to Heofen. This is Hosir Firben,*" another voice greeted them on the other end. "*The Hunegar did not want to let the news of the Hevding's untimely passing linger too long in the air, so we had to correlate our announcement with Emble's.*"

"When was that?"

"*About an hour ago.*"

"They couldn't bloody wait until we got there?" Bear was on edge.

"*A gathering has formed outside the Hevding's tower, and we have guards in place should it get out of hand. Upon your arrival, one of my guardians will take your vehicle to another place to transfer our leader's body to the funeral rite. We do not need a spectacle.*"

Flabbergasted, Bear threw up his hands. "They claim the Hevding was murdered, but they want to conceal the body? That makes little sense."

"It is out of veneration," Eski explained. "My species believes in transparency, but the funeral rite is a holy, but private procession."

"If you insist."

"The gathering is only composed of mourners?" Eski returned to Firben's original statement.

"*Yes, we believe so,*" the other confirmed. "*They do not sound of any protest like the Slaraors on Emble. However, we did not reveal that you have the Arlandr with you.*"

"Terrific," Krysta grumbled.

Having quickly traversed the city's wide metallic streets, Eski thereafter landed the vehicle next to the tower's plaza. They spotted the sizeable crowd of Hlinan gathered at the base of the city's tallest skyscraper. Krysta recognized the structure of the place where they had taken her earlier to see the Hevding. The crowd became alert of the vehicle's arrival, and their heads turned one by one to see who the newcomers were. Eski secured his pistols from where he stored them in the compartment next to his seat and checked the cartridges. "Stay close."

Bear moved to open his own door. "You want me to think it's okay, and yet you are prepping your guns?"

Eski stepped out first and briefly observed the crowd before he turned to see the humans out. Bear exited next, followed by Krysta. The crowd reacted swiftly to the humans' armored appearance, and hisses of resentment followed by shrieks of fear emitted from the group. "Murderers!" A male voice screamed first in outrage.

"You protect the Children of Sani!" A female voice sprang up next.

"Slaroar!" Another directed his rage toward Eski.

Hlinan guards moved in to barricade the crowd on each side to allow a path for the three to make their way into the building. Goose-bumps rose on Krysta's neck as she walked past the furious group. The reception was a lot different from last time. Before, there was curiosity, but now they did the one thing that she feared: Associate them entirely with losing their planet's religious head.

Bear moved in closer beside Wolf and said, "Stay on guard."

She spotted his hand slowly inching toward his holstered pistol, but she paused his arm. "Don't. They see you going for your weapon, and all hell may break loose."

Bear directed his eyes at Eski ahead of them. "He's a walking dead man, Wolf, and so are we if we linger here too long. We say our peace and then get the hell out."

Wolf nodded her head. "Agreed, but if things turn bad, we take Eski with us. It won't be right to just leave him here. They will hang him."

When they reached the building's entrance, an elevated roar erupted from behind, and the three pivoted around to see the protestors breaking through the line of guards and moving in on them. Their enraged voices filled the air with their battle cries. "Stand with the Hevding! Not the Children of Sani!" Their voices swelled into one, then intensified after they crashed through the barricade.

"Get them inside," a guard yelled as the crowd surged toward the humans.

Two Hlinan soldiers at the door motioned the trio quickly inside and locked the doors behind them, with only seconds remaining before the mob reached the building. The crowd furiously banged on the doors and windows. "Well, that was a wonderful reception, Eski. Thank you," Bear's voice dripped with sarcasm.

A Hlinan moved out of the elevator to greet them with both sets of eyes on the protestors outside, then wrinkled his brow. "Hosir Firben. They are just frightened. There is a lot of unknown right now."

Bear jutted his thumb back in the direction they came from. "I think that's much more than just scared there, pal."

"Come," Firben motioned them to follow him back into the elevator. "We shall speak more in the Hevding's office. However, it feels strange being there without his presence. There is word that our city is at the twilight of its existence." His reptilian eyes glanced at the

Peacekeepers to his right. "I will confess that I am wary of you being here after what transpired. I fully trust Hosir Matelija, but not you."

"Understandable," Wolf responded, before allowing her companion to retaliate. She was the voice of reason for a change. "Yet Jack and I are risking our lives to be here."

Bear grunted from where he stood, "You can say that again."

At their destination, Firben exited the cart first, and led them down the corridor toward the office. "The humans betrayed our trust, Lone Wolf. You offer one hand but hide the other with a weapon."

"The Hell Suns were the ones who pulled the trigger, and not *us*. Dhank Trust is still calling the shots there," Krysta maintained while she followed him into the office.

The temporary Hevding faced them again. His hardened expression gazed into her eyes. "Then what purpose were the Peacekeepers here for? All I have is what Hosir Matelija reported after your first encounter. I want to hear it from you two directly."

"Look," Bear stated exhaustively. "For the hundredth time, we were hired as security only for Bakht. Which means we were to protect the colonists from outsiders. The Peacekeepers got caught up in Dhank Trust's little game, but we want out. You two can fight."

"Yes, I heard what happened at the base before Matelija's return. The lack of communication was the problem, and I am sorry that my kind jumped to assumptions, but there is a shared burden on both sides. The only question is, how do we fix this issue?"

"The Hlinan believe that we are the Children of Sani, and the death of your Hevding will only fuel this labeling," Krysta joined in. "You think the Achli, who decimated your first colony hundreds of years ago, were also the Children of Sani. Let me ask you this, Hosir Firben: What if there are no Children of Sani? What if it's just the Achli and the humans?" The Hlinan leader tipped his head at the question, puzzled. "What are you saying, Lone Wolf?"

"I'm *saying* that what the Achli did was an isolated event to what is happening now. They destroyed our first colony as well on a different planet. Dhank Trust wants most of this land, and they may go to any means to retrieve it. Real estate in space is the next endeavor for these big corporations. They have too much money on their hands. Legacy and greed fuel them, not morals, nor religion. No Sani is guiding them. Sani does not exist for us."

He blinked at her statement. "I do not understand. Our religion shows us that at the beginning of creation, there were two gods: Hlidar and Sani. Hlidar created us, and Sani created Emble. When Sani grew jealous of Hlidar's creation, he left to create his own kind and vowed to destroy us. The battle between the two creations will be the fate of our universe."

"Yes, I know this, from what Eski told me, but what I'm saying is, what if you are *wrong*? I do not know about the Achli, but I can tell you that neither Sani nor Hlidar created humans."

"Then *who* created you?" Hosir Firben countered. "Life simply does not exist without divine intervention."

Bear groaned, "Please, Wolf, let's not get into religion. Humans have many theories."

"Theories?" Firben shook his head. "Preposterous. It cannot be possible. There are no creations besides the Hlinan and the Children of Sani."

"Yet, we are not the Achli," Krysta pushed back. "That's if you believe they are the Children of Sani."

"Perhaps Hlidar sent the humans here to us for guidance and understanding," Eski proposed.

Firben exhaled slowly at his cohort. "Hosir Matelija, any hint of altering our faith is in alignment with the Slaroars. I will not jeopardize my virtue any longer with this blasphemous discussion. However, I am torn by the security of our kind at your base and in this city. *That* is my duty." He strolled over to the desk and sat down behind a monitor interface. "I can dispatch twenty soldiers to your base, Hosir, along with one craft for deployment. I will also risk sending in three armed vehicles if we need to move the troops out. This is the most I can spare. You have your fliers." He peered at the two Peacekeepers again. "Do you have any idea what we are up against?"

Bear exchanged a look with Krysta. "The Hell Suns had at least six hundred global troops on Earth. Most likely, Dhank Trust bought a fraction of that for their venture. The Hells Suns would not pony up so many here and lose what they have back home. Wolf and I could not get a good look inside since we were limited to certain areas."

"And I can tell you, they implemented upgrades after the Peacekeepers were kicked out," Wolf added. "They have a large artillery gun capable of surface-to-air attacks."

"These guys are hardened vets with most having dishonorable discharge records. They won't be easy to take down. They won't play by rules or ethics. There will be no prisoner exchange, if you get my meaning," Bear grimly reminded them.

"Do you expect reinforcements, Hosir Firben?" Arms crossed, Eski rested against a nearby wall.

"Emble has assured me they will send one hundred with seventy-five of that number to remain here to bolster our own defense, and twenty-five will go to the base," Firben confirmed from behind his desk. "We do not predict a substantial human army."

"What kind of timeline are you looking at?" Bear inquired.

The temporary Hevding glimpsed at his monitor display. "At least five to six weeks. Are more soldiers coming to your colony?"

Wolf shrugged. "I do not know of any inbound." She glanced worriedly over at Bear. "Let's hope not, or they may seriously outnumber us before your second wave arrives."

"What she is saying is that you need to move your asses now," Bear warned. "Don't give them any type of advantage."

"I have all of this in the works already." All four of Firben's eyes stared silently at the two human outsiders. "There is no conflict between you going up against your own species?"

Wolf disagreed. "No hesitation whatsoever. But we will try to save the colonists. I doubt any of them wanted this conflict."

"We will attempt to spare innocent lives on both sides," the acting Hevding agreed.

Bear mentioned out loud, "The Hell Suns may use the colonists as hostages if they get cornered, Wolf. Casualties should be expected."

"Then I must speak with the Hunegar for the last discussion." Firben rose from his seat. "I will see you both in another room during this time. It should not take long."

Chapter 38

Bear profusely paced inside the small conference room and stopped in frustration to check his digital holographic watch display. "We have been here for twenty minutes, and I have got to piss. What the hell is taking so long?"

Wolf faced the door with her back propped against the wall. His predicament amused her. "We are asking them to go to war. Kind of a big deal."

"I'm not *asking*. The lizards are at war now," he corrected her in a snort. "I'm going to find a restroom."

"Good luck on asking for one," she chided playfully, watching the impatient man exit the room. She moved over to the window of the skyscraper they were in to look down at the city below. The crowd that ambushed them remained assembled at the plaza with no apparent intention of dispersing soon. A larger presence of military was blocking the tower. It was as if the city became alive like an awakened dragon; filled with fiery rage. She pondered the Hlinan's plan to transport them from the building. peacefully. Hearing the door behind her open, she turned to throw another taunt at her comrade. "No luck?" She paused abruptly when Eski entered. The merc's absence from the room seemed to unsettle him. "Bathroom break."

"We will move out soon. Hosir Firben is finishing up his call now. The Hunegar is pleased to know that you and the rest of your team support us. Your inside help will be beneficial."

"How you guys want to handle this fight is fine, but just know that Jones is mine," she maintained. His involvement gave her another reason to fight alongside the Hlinan. She needed redemption for her past failure. "I can add another tick mark to my rifle." Her eyes flickered down to the chaos below at the plaza. "Not everyone is happy about the support though, Eski."

"They are clouded, Krysta." He moved to her side to view the angry crowd. Then his head turned to her. "They do not know you the way I do." A beat. "I mean the Peacekeepers."

"Why am I not surprised?" Annoyed, Krysta blew air from her nose. "Religion has destroyed many innocent lives throughout humanity's existence. Contradictions that led to bloodshed, with everyone having their own spin on the creation of life and where we go after death, because nothingness makes life meaningless." She groaned slightly and placed her hand on her head. "Now I sound all philosophical."

The solid resolution on Eski's face appeared to be more fragmented as he looked at her. "Lone Wolf, I am affected now more than ever. Ever since our first encounter, there has been a disruption in my soul. I do not know what it means or how to perceive it." Taking off his wrist gauntlet, he gently cupped her face in his hand, a claw lightly stroking her skin. "I should not question my faith, and yet, I do."

Krysta perceived his internal struggle. His trembling words, filled with such sincerity, brought a small smile to her lips. His tender touch warmed her frigid heart. "Eski." His dark yellow eyes held her spellbound, provoking unknown feelings inside her. Her previous life was devoid of emotion. The iceberg built inside her by pain and loss was breaking apart. She nuzzled her face up against his gentle touch, feeling his scaly skin. "Why do you have to say these things now? I need to remain focused for the fight ahead." She wanted to lean up and capture his lips with hers again, to feel safe in his arms, but something was holding her back, chaining her down to the floor. An unfamiliar feeling wished that he would break those chains grounding her, to set her free.

"I cannot help it, Krysta. I am afraid that I will lose you at the end of this, one way or another, and I do not wish that to be."

She closed her eyes to suppress the tsunami of emotions slamming into her. "I do not want you to die because of me." Krysta heard the confession seep out of her mouth; ironically it felt alien to her entire being.

The rough skin of his forehead pressed against hers and the heat of his warm breath fell over her face. She felt a sense of peace from his proximity, causing her to briefly imagine that only they existed within their shared reality. His words cocooned her like a soft blanket, "I do not yearn for death unless my creator demands it. I promise you, Krysta, that I will fight to the very end to protect you. That is the purpose that Hlidar has given me. I know it in my heart."

With a defiant look, she opened her eyes and stared up at him. "I don't give a damn what your creator asks of you. You fight hard against the Hell Suns, but don't give them the satisfaction of your death. You live dammit. Live for me. If you should fall, then I will dive into your afterlife to face Hlidar and demand that he return you back to me."

A quiver moved his thin lips. "Krysta, you make me feel unsettled and uncontrolled. Your fire burns like no other because it is untamed." He leaned closer and devoured her lips. His arms wrapped around her waist to draw her in. Her return kiss was full of suppressed passion pouring out. Tears trickled softly down her cheeks as she wrapped her arms around his neck.

Seconds later, the sound of the door opening made her freeze in place. Bear's familiar voice soon followed. "Hey, Wolf, can we please head back now?" His words trailed off, and an eerie quietness descended on the room as the door closed behind him. Krysta immediately withdrew remorsefully but knew it was pointless to hide her flushed face. Disbelief and revulsion were clear on the bearded man's face as he scrunched his nose and arched an eyebrow. "What the hell?" His hands raised then clenched. "Krysta?"

Krysta saw the shock develop into rage as the unveiling fueled it. Her heart raced eight thousand kilometers per second in her chest. "Jack." Her mouth grew dry, and she forced herself to take a step toward him. "Look, I need to explain something."

"No." A low growl rose from within him. "I don't think you should." He shook his head and stepped backward till the door automatically reopened from behind. Bear hurried out with his back completely turned on her.

"Jack, wait!" Panicked, Krysta didn't glance back at Eski as she hurried after him. She stopped short outside in the hallway when she spotted Hosir Firben approaching.

Wolf's distressed expression caused the planetary leader to pause in bewilderment. "Is there something of matter, Lone Wolf?"

Krysta noticed her merc companion didn't go too far. He stood at the window, his back to her. "Everything is fine."

"Where is Hosir Matelija? I sent him over to you both."

"He's inside the room," she thumbed to the door behind her. "I had to come out to check on my colleague. He was not feeling well. Just the occasional migraines he gets from time to time. How are you doing over there, Papa Bear, um, with your head?"

"Just peachy," He grumbled without facing her.

"I will update the Hosir now," The Hlinan bowed, then proceeded inside the room.

As soon as he was out of sight, Krysta hurried over to her friend. He flashed her a side glance. "More like a pain in the ass." Then he spun on her completely, "What the hell did I see back there, Krysta?" he whispered harshly. "Please tell me that this just happened, and you haven't been keeping it behind your back the whole time. Whose side are you on?"

"I'm on your side, Jack," she whispered defensively. "I always am."

"Are you?" Bear sighed in frustration. "I knew something wasn't right when they jerked you away to their city. It wasn't like you."

"I didn't have a choice, okay? I was unconscious." Her voice rose alongside the heat in her chest.

He glared at her. "With you, Wolf, you always have a choice. I know you," he griped under his breath. "Hard to tell what kind of tech those lizards put in you."

His remark made her recoil, with her lip parting in disbelief. "Is that what you think happened? That I am now some type of alien monstrosity? Here to deceive you and the rest of the Peacekeepers to side with the Hlinan?"

"Looks like it. No wonder you wanted to be all buddy buddy, sneaking off to see *him*." A pained murmur left his lips as he shifted his gaze.

"This isn't easy for me either. Do you think I woke up one day thinking that I should have some kind of attraction to a nonhuman race? Eski cares for me, Jack, in a way I haven't felt before."

"So did Grim." His voice softened. "I knew what was between you and him to be none of my business, but I saw how distracted he became during missions. As a group leader, you pick up on these cues. I don't get why it didn't work, but I really don't see how you prefer Eski over him. Grim's one of your kind."

"Jack." Krysta lowered her voice to mirror his. "I know this is a shock."

"You can say that again."

"Grim's a nice guy and sometimes he pushed the relationship further than I wanted. I just didn't want that." She ran her fingers through the top strands of hair on her head. "Heck, I don't know what I want with Eski either. But he makes me feel safe in a way that I haven't felt before."

"Does his race know? About him and you?"

Wolf halted her response to him when she spotted two Hlinan soldiers moving down the corridor in their direction. Once they passed and far enough to not eavesdrop, she shook her head at Bear's question. "No, they don't and if they find out, it may cost him his life; more so than by aiding us."

"Alright. Let's just drop the subject for now. I'm trying to get the image of you and him out of my head." He pushed up against her shoulder mischievously. "To make sure you are not some type of weird alien clone, answer me this: what kind of ale did we fight over back in Manitoba?"

A sly, triumphant grin spread across her face. "The good shit, the ale you smuggled from Brazil. I recall I beat you at the match."

Her taunt made him chuckle. "Okay, it sounds like you're in there, Wolf." His playful tone quickly morphed into a serious one. "Don't make me regret trusting you. Just keep whatever you have with that guy on the down low. We have a mess as it is to worry about, so keep your head in the game. These guys do not know what to expect from Jones. I bet a week's pay that our warnings to them will fall on deaf ears."

"I agree. We got our asses kicked last time against the Hell Suns. I'm not losing this round."

"When we hit the Hell Suns, you are taking the lead, Wolf."

Krysta tensed at the unexpected move. "No way, Jack. You saw what happened last time I took the reign against those guys. They wiped the floor with our asses. I'm not ready to lead."

"Bullshit," Bear cut her off. "Not all missions go one hundred percent to the plan. Shit falls apart. A good leader knows how to deal with it. If I thought you couldn't handle this, I wouldn't have said a thing." He extended his hand out to her. "I trust you, Lone Wolf."

The kind gesture prompted a small smile from Krysta. She accepted his handshake. "Thank you, Papa Bear. You're right. I can do this."

Chapter 39

That night, Krysta lay in her dark bunk room, staring up at the ceiling with one arm behind her head. For the past two days since she and Bear returned to the base, she could not think straight, and she yearned to glimpse Eski, even if it was for a brief status update. All she saw inside her mind was their kiss and the sound of his words by his confession replaying over and over. She fidgeted with her dog tags. What if he lost his life during the fight against the Hell Suns? How would she take it? As a soldier, death was so common that she grew callous about it, but she feared for him. Their relationship was bound to be revealed, eventually. How would his race view it? Hosir Madu was on the warpath to cast him out as a radical. Would Wolf's lingering presence be Eski's demise? Frustrated, Krysta sighed hard and shifted one bent arm behind her head to prop herself up in the sleeping pod. She turned her head to the right to see where Grim was snoozing away. A frown of remorse spread across her mouth. He was the first to be tossed up in their current hellhole, and she wondered if he agreed to the assignment to only get away from her.

Grim stirred in his pod and rolled over to where he was facing her. His eyes flickered open momentarily, and he caught her looking at him. "Krysta? Something wrong?"

"Just running through scenarios in my head about how to take out the Hell Suns," she fibbed.

He let out a tired yawn. "Wolf, let it go. It's three in the morning. You need to sleep sometime."

"Yeah, I know," she mumbled, but then froze in place when she heard the loud sound of an incoming aircraft. Both she and Grim exchanged nervous looks and then sprang up from their pods. "Peacekeepers, high alert! We got inbound!" She raced to her personal locker. The mercs groaned at the rude awakening and hurried to fetch their gear and weapons. Within minutes, the squads dashed out to catch the sight of an unrecognizable aircraft landing at a designated point south, inside the base's walls. The design was unlike anything Krysta recognized. It was at least twice the size of Earth's largest fighter jet, with a neon green flashing light bar that outlined the craft's perimeter.

Eski walked to them with Madu at his side. "The reinforcements from Heofen."

Grim's mouth opened wide in awe, at the display before him. "Whoa. That's one sweet ride."

Unimpressed, Bear remarked, "Fancy toy you have there. Can't really rely too heavily on air support. What else do you guys have to throw at the Hell Suns?"

"We will have ground troops," Eski explained. "Along with our fighter crafts."

Hosir Madu pugnaciously folded her arms. "We do not need the Peacekeepers, Hosir. As you can see, we are well equipped for the battle against the human colony."

Eski turned to her. "I disagree, Hosir. To reject aid is unwise and Firben believes that the Peacekeepers' willingness to assist us is a good omen."

"What about that barrier we saw the other night against those dogs? Can you use that as well?" Grim suggested.

"I would not recommend usage for over four hours, if only to preserve the power cell's capacity. Our planet's sun charges it during the day. Without the barrier's protection at night, we would be vulnerable to the hata. Though, I find it odd that the hata have not attempted another attack yet."

"Right now, you should be more alarmed about what the Hell Suns will do to you than those hounds," Bear cautioned before he turned to Krysta and Grim. "Wolf, you got the lead. I recommend we keep one team here with the barrier online to prevent ambushes and send the other team to the colony. We stay on the offensive before the Hell Suns bulk up their forces."

"Agreed." Krysta nodded along with the plan. "We assume the colonists are friendly, but if they shoot at us, then they are a target. Got it?"

"May I suggest the colony team go with our transport?" Eski directed them over to the aircraft. "A small strike team can stay within the large cargo hold until the drop off point."

"They have an artillery gun at the colony, remember?" Wolf reminded him. "Their radar will see us coming, and I'm guessing the gun's range is what, twenty-five to thirty kilometers, Jack?"

"At least that," Bear agreed. "I recommend finding a landing zone elsewhere, unless you have that ship protected by some sort of defensive barrier." Eski shook his head at the question.

"Jones will have that place solid in the fortification, but if he wants this base, he will have to pull most of his men away." Concern crested Wolf's brown while contemplating their strategy. "Then we split. Grim, you take one group with the colony team. I think you are seasoned enough to co-lead. Bear and I will hang back here to ensure things don't get rough. Watch the colonists."

Grim saluted back. "Thanks for the confidence there. Just watch your six."

"I will accompany the team to the colony and lead our forces to victory." Hosir Madu spoke up.

"I know we all started off at a wrong start," Grim addressed her. "I'm sorry that I held biased opinions about your people, especially after the initial attack on the colony." Krysta flashed him with a smile of approval.

Eski bowed his head to him after Madu remained quiet, unmoved by the display of friendship. "Thank you, Peacekeeper. We too allowed fear to consume our minds at first. It is an honor to now be fighting alongside you. Hlidar will watch over us. We will move forward in four hours as dusk approaches. That will give us time to prepare. I will make sure everything is ready to go."

Krysta grinned deviously at her mentor. "Jones may not be ready within four hours, so we will get the drop-in on them. If all his guys are there, then I say we join in with Grim's team."

"Not to play devil's advocate." Bear scratched his beard. "But what if we are wrong? What if the Hell Suns' orders are *not* to hit this base but their city instead?"

"Would they have the means to get that far?" Grim asked no one in particular. "That's a lot of unknown for them. I would not risk it."

"I agree," Krysta nodded. "Jones would not be that crazy or stupid. Too far out with no safety net."

"Hosirs!" A Hlinan officer sprinted to the group in a state of hysteria.

"What is it?" Hosir Madu addressed the newcomer first. The officer's face was pale, any color drained.

"We lost contact with one of our scouts about an hour ago. I dispatched two more to assist. They located the missing one's body in the same vicinity as his patrol." The officer's words wobbled with his explanation.

Madu growled out in frustration. "Take me there now on your cycle."

"Hosir Madu, I will accompany you." Eski jogged over to another cycle on standby.

"As will I." Krysta followed him. A gut-wrenching realization struck her. Something about the news didn't feel right. Was Jones already on the move?

"Wolf, comms open. Good luck with what you find," Bear called to her.

Slipping on her helmet, she straddled the seat behind Eski and wrapped her arms around his waist. With his own helmet on, he gave one tiny look over his shoulder to see that she was secure, then hit the throttle. Krysta clutched his torso tight due to the inertia from the acceleration as the cycle raced out from the base toward the two Hlinan soldiers awaiting them.

One of the Hlinan soldiers approached Eski's cycle when he and Krysta arrived at their location nearly ten minutes later. Wolf noted that the second soldier was still at the scout's body. Eski removed his helmet, and she followed suit. "Hosirs," the first Hlinan saluted both Eski and Madu.

"Another hata death?" Madu inquired. Eski walked over to where the body was. Krysta trailed behind him. She saw the scout was face down in the dirt with blood all over where his body lay.

"No, Hosir Madu. I am not sure what to make of this," Wolf overheard the officer reply to the female leader.

Kneeling, Krysta stopped near a mark on the ground. Her fingers dabbed at the impressions. "The Hell Suns," she concluded. "I found several human boot prints here." Her eyes surveyed over the area. "I say at least three to four individuals. Your scout was outnumbered."

Eski tipped the body over and his features winced when he glimpsed the scout's face. Krysta grimaced at the gruesome display. The Hlinan had a deep jagged laceration from his left temple down his cheekbone, and someone brutally cut out his top right eye. A bullet hole burrowed through the center of his head. "This is Jones' handiwork," she deduced. "They tortured your guy and then executed him."

"For information?" Hosir Madu moved to them.

"Possibly. I would bet on it. No other reason they would venture this far out."

Crouching, Madu gently placed her hand on the deceased's chest. For one moment, Wolf noted a different view of the hostile Hlinan. "You see, Hosir Matelija, what kind of brutality do these humans seek to afflict upon us?" Madu fumed up at him.

"Jones is a merciless bastard, and his group mirrors his sadistic energy. We must assume that your scout released sensitive information prior to his death: defense mechanisms, number of men stationed at your base, combat strategies, etc." Krysta ignored the other's remark. "Hate can come from any side, Hosir Madu. The Peacekeepers do not hate you if that is what you make of this."

"We are now one step behind." Eski redirected his colleague's focus to the issue at hand. "We must act quickly."

A dangerous glint appeared in Madu's eyes as she looked at Krysta. "I request we converse in private, Hosir." The pair walked away at a sizeable distance.

The shift made Wolf uneasy, and she reacted by placing her hand on her sidearm but refrained herself from the gesture. Taking a few steps in the opposite direction, she tapped her earpiece communicator. "Bear, this is Wolf."

"*Let me guess. The Hell Suns?*" Bear asked on the other end.

"They tortured the poor guy before killing him," Krysta relayed. "Not good, Jack." She decided not to tell him the cold shoulder she was now getting from their supposed allies, yet she nervously glanced their way to notice that they were still speaking with one another.

"*No, it isn't. Get your ass back to the base. We do not know how hot that area is.*"

"Agreed." She hung up and then called on them. "My recommendation is to hightail it out of here. With the Hell Suns in the same proximity, we will give them a free shot right now."

Eski halted his conversation long enough to acknowledge her warning, then the two spoke a few more seconds in hushed tones before he moved back to his cycle. Krysta made her way over to him and noted that his eyes lingered on the cycle that Madu went on. Envy filled her, and she bit her lip. The private talks between him and his ex didn't help matters. Hesitantly, she moved in behind him on the cycle and held onto his waist. He didn't look her way. "Ready to go, Lone Wolf?"

"Yeah." She averted her eyes from him, unable to shake the uneasiness that was inside her. "Let's go back."

Chapter 40

Grim and Bear walked back over to her when she and the rest of the Hlinan arrived back. "Did you spot any mercs?" Bear was the first to speak up.

Exiting the cycle, Krysta shook her head. "Only tracks." She slipped off her helmet. "Not a good sight. We should leave right away."

"They are close then," Grim confirmed. "So much for the element of surprise."

"Thank you for accompanying me, Lone Wolf. I will prepare for our next phase," Eski tapped her on the shoulder. Krysta felt her breath catch as he held her gaze for a moment before moving away.

She did not let his image leave her until he cleared a building ahead, which obstructed her view. The way he looked at her made her wonder if he wanted to say something else but held back. Bear cleared his throat, which made her snap out of her thoughts, and she turned to her old mentor.

He gave her an uneasy look. "I'm going to get everyone ready to go. Don't dwindle out here too long, Wolf. You are leading, remember?" He moved back to the bunk.

"Wolf?" Grim spoke up next. "A second?"

"Yeah?"

Grim let out a burst of air. "I'm not even sure how to broach this but I can't help it." His strained laughter and the way his eyes darted toward Eski's direction and then back to her made her stand straighter. "This is going to sound wild. Then again, I'm not sure if I'm crazy for even guessing it."

"What are you talking about?"

"You and Eski. Are you two together? And I don't mean just taking sides. I mean *together*. I have noticed how he looks at you. My gut tells me there's more."

Her eyes widened, and she felt her cheeks heat. "Nothing gets by you. I'm not sure what it is yet."

Grim frowned. "The way he speaks to you and how he protects you, is the same way that I used to. You know, before we broke up, I thought you didn't desire a relationship with anyone. I guess I missed only with a non-human qualification.

Annoyed by his last remark, Krysta rolled her eyes. "Oh yeah. Right, Grim. I just woke up one day and decided that bipedal humanoid Reptilia are more my type."

Grim held up his hand. "Look, just never mind. I get it. Well, I really don't, but at least you found someone that fits what you always wanted. I think the months away up here before the nightmare came really helped me get over whatever we had. I'm not hurt as much as I thought I would be."

"Whatever comes of me and Eski doesn't mean I still don't care for you as my friend, or a comrade."

Eski's shape came into her field of vision. "Lone Wolf, the transport for the colony team is ready."

"That's my ride." Grim gave her a sad look. "Take care of yourself out there, Krysta. I'll see you on the other side, got it?"

"You too, Grim. I'll be waiting for you. I need another victory dance," she teased.

A sly grin briefly teased his lips, then a stoic look replaced it as he faced the Hlinan. "Sorry about the other day. You better take care of her. If you don't, there will be a lot more of us after you and even your god won't protect you." He stepped around Eski, then moved ahead to the bunk without even a glance back.

Eski was expressionless. "I interrupted your conversation with him. I apologize."

"Grim knows, Eski," she softly admitted. "About us." Relief washed over her, yet a heavy burden still weighed her down. Krysta reached under her armor's collar to clutch her dog tags.

"If you need a moment to be alone, Krysta, I can return after."

"It's okay." She gazed up at the coral glazed sky as sunset eased in. "There's no guarantee that I will be alive after we set off here. It's ironic that my father died on the first attempt to colonize outer space, and it looks like I may die on the second attempt."

"Tell me about him and your mother, Lone Wolf. I want to learn more about you in what little time we have left."

She hung her head as tears filled her eyes from the stark reminder. "As I said before, my father was in the Enlightenment colony when the Achli hit. He worked in the hydroponics division. I was ten when the news reached Earth about what happened to them. There were no rescue attempts, and we were told that there were no life signs present on the exo-planet. My mother loved my father so much that his death ate away at her. She chose suicide over raising me alone. I think it was because I favored him too much and she couldn't handle the reminder. After their deaths, no one wanted to deal with me; a kid who was angry at the world for what happened." She furiously wiped the tears from her eyes. "I joined the Marines for a few years and then came to the Peacekeepers."

"Most Hlinan are not close to their parents due to our bonding contracts. My mother returned to Hlidar from a viral outbreak when I first entered the academy. My father is still alive on Emble. Though, when my bonding contract was severed with Hosir Madu, my father blamed me for it."

"Why should he care about who you fall in love with? I'm sure you could have done a lot better than her, anyway."

He let out a small chuckle. "Despite my species being for peace, Lone Wolf, we do not bond with someone for love. It is for the establishment in our hierarchy of things. There are restrictions in place due to the high birth rate on Emble. The Hunegar must bless each contract to allow the mating to take place for offspring."

"What if he says no?"

"Then there is no mating. Many Hlinan live out their full lives without a bondmate."

She daringly met his eyes, and a lump formed in her throat. "Do you still care for her? You've both been whispering lately." Jealousy scraped inside her chest like a jagged shard of glass.

He reached out and gently brushed away the hair from her face. "I am a Hosir, Krysta. I must talk with her despite our past lives. This is out of duty. I converse with you because I want to. That is out of love."

Feeling like an ass, Krysta held his hand on her face and looked directly into his eyes. "I'm sorry, Eski, for doubting you. I want to feel solace in all of this, but I don't know where to begin. It's hard for me to even explain the feelings I have or how you are making me feel this way."

"Krysta, your existence unravels my faith to its core. I do not want to accept that you are my mortal enemy." He nuzzled her forehead with his own. "I do not want to give my life so freely in battle for our creator. I want to remain alive with you. If you fall, I want to go where you are." Eski gingerly took her hands into his and pulled her arms closer to his chest. "I fear I will not be allowed to do so."

"Hosir Matelija." Madu's voice from behind him made them both freeze in place. Eski released his grip. Krysta's eyes darted up to Eski in fear, and she stepped back. Her eyes flashed over to the female Hlinan standing at Eski's back about nine meters away. "Why are you back here alone with this human and not with our team?"

Dammit. Krysta stepped to the side and remained perfectly still, with her hands clasped behind her back in a military posture. "Hosir Madu."

Surprisingly, Eski turned calmly around to address his companion. There was not a flicker or sign of worry on his face at all. "Lone Wolf is the active leader for the Peacekeepers on this planet. I came here to inform her we are ready to depart."

Madu rolled her eyes as she approached. "The rank of Hosir is distinguishable, Eski. It is not simply given out. Why must you constantly consult with her and *only* her?" Then a twisted smirk spread across her face. "The way you fuss over her is quite facetious. Is becoming a Slaroar breaking down all sense of logic in you, Eski?"

"Lay off of him," Krysta broke formation, her anger rising up her throat.

"Are you threatening me, Child of Sani?" Madu bared her two front fangs with a snarl in her throat.

"What if I am?" With a menacing gleam, Krysta crossed her arms. "What are you going to do about that, Child of Hlidar?" She played on their religion. "Take your best shot, because this may be the only chance you get."

A piercing alarm sounded from the center of the base, snatching their attention from the heated discussion. "We are too late!" Eski charged forward. "Come, Hosir Madu. I need you with me."

Krysta didn't bother to give the offending female standing before her another second of her time and raced after Eski to see what the emergency was. Moments later, she caught Madu sprinting past her at a rapid pace. Krysta frowned. "Crap, she is faster."

"We got drones!" Bear stood with the gathered Peacekeepers outside their bunk. "Stand ready!"

"Activate the base defense barrier!" Eski ordered one soldier and then seconds later, the sound of the sizzling fluorescent lighting encased them.

Krysta held her breath while her eyes looked upward to the sky. Jones was after the base, after all.

Chapter 41

Three drones that were one meter by one meter flew over the dome barrier. "Peacekeepers, the Hell Suns want to take pictures of us. Shall we?" Bear asked his team. They laughed and flashed their middle fingers up at the mechanized aerials. The Hlinan laser cannon quickly knocked one drone from the sky into multiple shrapnel parts before the other two sharply turned to retreat to their point of origin. The mercs jeered and slapped one another on the back. Their reptilian counterparts exchanged puzzled looks; Krysta found that there was a distinct difference between the two species.

A Hlinan officer darted over to hand Eski a tablet. The Hosir's face soured at whatever was on the device. "What is it?" Krysta watched him mull over at the incoming intel.

"We've repositioned our satellite over your colony. They are a much larger force than what we first perceived." He frowned over at Hosir Madu before handing her the tablet to read for herself. "This will make things more complex."

Hosir Madu swiftly returned the tablet. "Nothing has changed, Hosir Matelija. Our forces will prevail."

Bear snatched the tablet. After reviewing the data, the man's nose twitched from side to side in contemplation. "I don't know. Your satellite's image looks like it was captured during the unloading of their ship. Yeah, there are more mercs walking around, but I don't see any aircraft or ground threats."

"They may have been still on the ship during the capture," Krysta pointed out.

Bear observed the two Reptilia before him. "When can we get a refresh?"

"In three more hours," Eski relayed.

Bear sighed. "I don't enjoy going in blind, but if we wait on that updated image, we may lose our window of opportunity. Their drones already took pictures of us."

"What about your drones?" Krysta inquired the Hlinan.

"We sent them two hours ago, but the colony's artillery fire destroyed them before image acquisition," Eski explained.

The older merc eyed Krysta gravely. "Fantastic. Their cannon's radar can detect the Hlinan's drones. We feel outdated. With no type of intel, this is a risky move. Can we get more men from your head leader, Eski?"

"The Hunegar is hesitant to transfer more numbers to us until we have more logistics to analyze. For now, I will need to make do with what we have. Our craft from Heofen can still take a team to the colony drop off as formerly conferred." Eski tucked the tablet back under his arm.

Bear shook his head at the proposal. "Nay to that. They have a big damn gun. If you go that far in, it will light you up."

"I agree with Bear on this. It's better to see what we are up against than risk that many men, plus your drones can't get through. We split the teams and have the colony team go scout first." Krysta suggested.

"I will still lead the colony team," Madu firmly reminded.

"Grim, go with her and help the colonists if you can. You're the delicate one of our group. Better not to scare the shell-shocked colonists any more than we have to." Bear beckoned him again.

"Alright," Grim sadly turned to Krysta. "Both of you stay safe out there."

Krysta watched his group board the plane with Madu's team. She exhaled slowly to evict the dread building within her. Bear silently moved to her side; his eyes sharpened on the plane. "Are you ready for this, Lone Wolf? I have my full faith in you."

"I am ready. Let's kick some ass."

Chapter 42

"What's our plan for here?" Krysta jogged behind Eski as she and Bear followed him to another location on the Hlinan base after the plane departed with the mixed groups onboard. Eski entered the building first.

Bear groaned from the quick change in the lighting. "Fantastic. Darkness again."

"We can track our friends' path at the communications hub, and I will have my officer patch both frequencies in." The Hlinan base leader moved forward.

"I don't like just sitting and waiting for something to happen. It's like being a sitting duck," Krysta called to him.

Eski faltered in his steps. "My apologies, but what is a duck?"

"A bird that goes quack," Bear chuckled.

"And a bird is?" He looked dubiously at the explanation, lifting an eyeridge.

Krysta held her face with her hand. "Never mind."

After a few twists and turns in the hallways, they approached their destination. Krysta noted the large open room had a large, crystalized display in the center that revealed a detailed outline of the surrounding area outside the base. She spotted a tiny blinking triangle moving across the terrain toward the colony. On top of it was some sort of writing that she struggled to decipher. "Whoa." The setup amazed her. All around her were different Hlinan officers behind transparent interface stations with their claw tips swiping away at the different screens. Eski moved ahead over to one officer. Krysta shook her head in wonder. "Talk about high-end tech."

"And here I assumed holo maps were top of the line." Bear then pointed at the map. "That blip Grim and the others?"

Krysta shrugged. "You are asking the wrong person. I can't read that crap." Then she spotted two smaller blips moving toward the first one and right to it. "Um, Jack?"

"*We have unknown fighters upon us! They came out of nowhere!*" The pilot's scream cracked over the speakers above their heads.

Seconds later, video images of the hostile aircraft popped into view to the right of the map. Krysta instantly recognized their unique sleek design. "They can't be what I think they are."

"Shit. Well, the Hell Suns got them some Koscheis. Those things have one of the top stealth capabilities." Bear jerked his head to Eski. "Please tell me your craft up there has countermeasures."

Eski solemnly shook his head. "It is only for transport." He returned to the officer sitting in front of him. "Summon two fighters."

Bear roughly grabbed Eski's shoulder to get his attention. "Bogey out! Call the mission off!"

"*I am locked on! Taking evasive maneuvers!*" The pilot cried out on the speaker. "*I cannot decipher their location! They keep disappearing from my radar!*"

"Grim." Krysta listened in anxiously.

"Abort the mission! Return here, then activate the barrier as soon as it lands." Eski roughly shrugged off Bear's grasp, refocusing on the officer.

Krysta's heart raced inside her chest. She was powerless just listening in on the comm chatter and hearing Eski's desperate pleas of salvation for the crew onboard the air vessel. Visible tension replaced his usual calm. Her attention shifted to the video feed. The bulky craft banked hard to the right to evade. Behind it, a silver blur streaked into view, eating up the distance. "They won't make it."

With a loud hiss, Eski stormed back over to the officers. "Order the pilot to evacuate everyone there to the nearest safe jump point. Use de-acceleration packs. There should be plenty onboard for them."

"What?" Bear eyed him skeptically. "You are telling them to jump? Those fighters will be all over them."

"If they stay onboard, they will die." Eski's voice choked with emotion. "This is the only option."

Krysta shook her head at the map. "Eski, they are too far out. At least eight kilometers from any designated landing site."

"At jump point. Opening loading doors now," the pilot announced again at the next few uncomfortable minutes later. Krysta overheard the alarms blaring in the cockpit from over the radio. *"They launched a projectile!"*

Eski's mouth made a flickering noise, and he closed his eyes at the pilot's words. "May Hlidar have mercy for my actions."

Seconds later, Krysta heard the pilot come back on the line. *"All crew out. Climbing now. Another launched a projectile! They are fast-aaah!"*

Bear punched his fist against the palm of his other hand. The pilot's scream blared from the speakers, then the feed died, leaving a queasy silence. "What about our teams? Are they clear?"

"Hosir Madu." Eski tapped a button on the map. "All account-ed for?"

"Yes, we are all safe. The humans sent two fighters after us," she stated bitterly.

"And what about the Peacekeepers team? Are they safe?" Eski prided.

There was a brief delay before she responded, *"They made it."*

Krysta finally let go of her breath and flashed Bear a smile of relief. "That was close."

The sound of the base's klaxon wailing like a banshee outside ended their short-lived celebration. "Inbound unidentified flying crafts!" One comms officer shouted from his station.

"Activate the defense barrier." With Lone Wolf, Bear, and the others in tow, Eski quickly exited the room. The commotion of the threat caused Hlinan soldiers to dart to their posts. The sickening sounds of the approaching crafts made everyone tense up. It was the moment of truth. Would the barrier stand up to the human tech?

Outside, Wolf and Bear positioned themselves against the building, rifles at the ready. Both Koscheis flew over and spread apart, going in each direction after the flyby. There was a minute of relief from all around. Stepping away from her position, Wolf tried to see the planes' direction, but the night sky obscured them.

Then there was a silver flash in the black backdrop as one jet screeched toward the base for a second run. When it passed over, a strange device deployed from one of the weapon pods, but it wasn't a missile. Instead, the blinking object merely fell straight towards them and the barrier. Krysta's eyes widened when she realized what it could be. "It's a bomb!" Uncertain of its power, she questioned whether the barrier could withstand such a force. Jumping down to the ground with Bear, she covered her head and tightly closed her eyes shut to brace for impact, but there was no explosion that followed. Instead, an intense electrical sizzle fell over the entire dome till it flickered out of existence. She opened her eyes and saw that the radiating light over them had disappeared.

Stunned, the Hlinan soldiers stared at the result, slowly rising, guns in hand. One of them shouted, "The barrier is offline!"

Eski yelled from where he stood about four meters away. "Projected time on the restore?"

"Assessing now, Hosir."

"Take a team." Eski moved to Krysta and Bear. The sound of the crafts dissipated as the pair escaped the vicinity.

Bear glanced back at the rest of the mercenaries clambering back up to a full stand. "Everyone okay?"

"Why would they bogey out now when we are exposed?" Krysta scratched her head in confusion.

"Lone Wolf, what kind of armament was that?" Eski's eyes were wide in shock.

"I think it was an EMP," Bear explained. "The only thing I would think could take out the barrier."

When Krysta noted the clueless look on the Hlinan's face before them, she chimed in, "Electromagnetic Pulse. The barrier must have absorbed all the shock, and that's why everything else is online."

"How did they know about our barrier's schematics?" The Hlinan was vexed.

"The scout. Jones got that intel from him. Only possible way to know exactly what would knock it offline," Krysta said plainly. "The Hells Suns brought a lot more armaments than we presumed. Hard to tell what other bombs Jones has stashed away."

"Can we discuss this later?" Bear pointed up to the night sky. "If those two Koscheis come back for us, we are fully exposed."

"I will go get our fighters ready." Eski rushed off again.

Bear flagged the Peacekeepers behind him and Wolf. "Everyone be ready. We should have air support shortly." A few moments more and the underground hangar doors opened. No sooner than they did, the sickening sound of bullets from the tree line nearby caught many of the Hlinan off-guard near the hangar doors; their bodies twisted and groaned from the fatal shots.

Amid the chaos, Wolf rolled for cover, trying to pinpoint the shooter's location. "Peacekeepers, eyes up! We have an incoming!" Bear crouched down beside her. She spotted that half of the flight crew's bodies were on the ground, dead from where they stood.

"We are under attack! Take cover!" Eski sprinted towards the hangar doors with his men nearby and unholstered both pistols.

A group of black and green camouflaged, hooded human soldiers slowly moved in a staggered formation position from the easterly tree line, heavily armed with assault rifles. Their powerful guns' rounds tore up the ground nearby and structures to draw the hiding Hlinan out. A few reptiles dashed out to retaliate, but the barrage of ammo quickly took them out. The Peacekeepers fired on the intruders, inflicting casualties but suffering losses themselves.

Jack aimed his rifle and shot at one enemy mercenary. He then dove quickly back into cover when the opposing rounds ripped up the corner side of the building where he and Wolf stood nearby. "Switch!"

Krysta skirted around his body and waited until the bullets stopped before she risked moving out from cover to fire. She pulled the trigger of her assault rifle and nailed two of the men in the frontline. Their comrades nearly stumbled over the enemy's dead bodies. Krysta jumped back into cover when they fired back, narrowly missing her. She winced at the sound of their rounds pummeling the metal structure that blocked their view and squeezed her body tight against the building. "These guys mean business!" Wolf noticed Eski pinned and gestured to the man beside her. "Give me cover! I need to get to him!"

After Bear took her spot, she waited until he held the mercs briefly and raced to where Eski was.

The Hlinan leader noticed her storming towards him, and he fired his pistols at the Hell Suns to distract them until she got to safety. "Some of the flight crew is over there." He motioned his head towards a small building. "I must help them."

"I'm with you." She opened fire and then followed him before crouching and sliding on her upper thigh just as the opposing rounds hit the structure where they stood previously.

The flight crew member fell to a slumped position on the ground, with his head lolling. Eski reached down and checked his pulse, then closed his eyes. "He is gone."

"Hosir, someone hit the control panel at the hangar door, and the damage is too extensive to begin repairs," one of the crew members cried out in a panic.

"Is there another way to get the craft up? We need them."

"There is a manual control down in one tunnel. Access point is the ladder from the top, but there is no way to get there without being fully exposed."

"*We have enemy craft on approach.*" The tower alerted their comms. They were running out of time.

Eski turned to Krysta. "We need to get my fighters up. Can you have your team draw their artillery away?"

"I'll do my best, but you are going to be exposed. How much time do you need?"

"Let me worry about that." Eski motioned two of the flight crew members to follow him. "I shall go first. Wait for the Peacekeepers to draw their fire away. Do not hesitate. Keep running until you make it down the ladder. Lone Wolf, patch me into your frequency."

"Yes, Hosir," both his men replied in unison.

"Papa Bear!" Wolf summoned the link up. "Eski needs cover fire to get their birds in the air. Light 'em up!"

"*I love it when you talk dirty, Wolf. Party time, boys!*" Bear jokingly responded. The Peacekeepers let out a barrage from where they were, dropping several Hell Suns in their wake and keeping the others pressed to their tree line cover. Wolf then opened fire on her side and nailed a few unsuspecting mercs that did not expect a crossfire.

With Eski's departure for the underground hangars, she returned her attention to fighting. Seconds later, she heard the sickening sound of her clip being empty and she dove back into cover to change it. "Shit, I'm out." Her fingers fumbled with the clip, and she glanced over her shoulder in the direction of Eski and his team. No one came up yet. She shoved the replacement clip into place, cocked the rifle, and folded back into position. "Better hurry it up, Eski. We are going to run out of ammo out here."

"We have two," Eski cheerfully confirmed into her earpiece. Suddenly, movement nearby caught her eye, and she peeked around the bend to see two crimson-colored fighter crafts rise from the open hangar doors. A Hlinan piloted each craft, and she barely saw their heads through the tinted cockpit shield. The engines roared to life with a piercing, whirring sound and steam moved off from beneath the craft. With hover mode activated, both propelled themselves upward off the ground.

The Peacekeepers nearby rooted loudly in celebration and Krysta returned to her cover to take a breath. "About damn time."

"The Hell Suns are backing away." Bear laughed over the comm. As if on cue next, the sound of the inbound enemy jets erupted into the sky. *"Well, craptastic."*

"I really hope this is a dogfight," Krysta swallowed hard at spotting the hostile aircraft. "Time to see what the Hlinan are made of."

One of the two Hlinan planes gained altitude, then turned toward the enemy planes for an intercept. Each of the Koscheis matched up with one of the Hlinan fighters. The Hell Suns' jet used its artillery gun. The Hlinan fighter twisted and turned in a scissor maneuver until it was out of the gun's range. Then it stopped mid-air with its nose pointing upwards. The craft looped over the Koscheis, placing the human pilot at the disadvantage of being at the front. A bright blue wave of forced bright energy fired from underneath the Hlinan craft. The strike slammed into Koscheis' tail and left wing, demolishing both areas as if they were made of paper, sending the craft into a fatal nosedive. Wolf cheered loudly as she watched the impressive display. "Yeah! That's what I'm talking about it!"

Eski ran back to her. "Are you alright, Krysta?"

"Yeah, your pilots are kicking ass." Krysta flashed a thumbs up.

The remaining hostile jet broke to disengage, but the Hlinan crafts were faster and on it within seconds. Both used the same intense laser and completely obliterated the human jet into a burning fireball. One pilot paged the comms, *"Sky is clear, Hosir. We will take out the next target."* The planes then moved towards the small group of armed soldiers near the base's perimeter. One craft released a small, infused bomb as it passed over them. A massive plume of fire and smoke instantly erupted from the ground, incinerating everything at ground zero with the blast's immense energy. The only remnant was a crater where the Hells Suns had been standing.

The base erupted with applause of joy. Eski smiled with relief. "Thank you, both." He spoke to the pilots. "Head to the colony to provide air support for Hosir Madu's team."

"This was easy." Bear moved over to Krysta and Eski. "I figured there would be more than that." He grinned widely from ear to ear.

"That's what I'm afraid of." Krysta frowned at him. She wondered how Grim and the others were faring on their end. Did Jones hold most of his forces back at the colony? She tapped her ear communicator. "Grim, sending two birds your way."

"Lovely. We landed in hata territory and the Hlinan are leaving us in the dirt. Thankfully, no sign of those feral wolves," he sighed, his breaths punctuating his words.

Krysta rolled her eyes at the news. She wondered if Madu would even try to sabotage the mission altogether to prove a point. "Watch your six out there, Grim. Could be even friendly fire."

"Already crossed my mind. Didn't take long for the cold shoulder to come our way." An explosion to the left of the base snubbed out more words from Krysta and the shockwave made her nearly lose her balance. A bright plume of smoke filled the air and flames flickered out from the Hlinan's storage facility. Burning shrapnel rained down, hitting some of the Hlinan soldiers nearby. *"What the hell was that?"* Grim panicked in her ear. *"Wolf? Bear? You guys okay?"* The fire danced in Krysta's eyes. Stunned, she lost her words. *"Wolf?"* Her eyes scouted the area near the structure and spotted a sizable, armored rover tank breaking through the tree line with its barrel straight upon them.

"Holy shit," she finally mustered out. "They have a tank."

Chapter 43

"Eski, we got a tank! Peacekeepers, look alive!" Krysta flagged the Hlinan leader while she and the others put more distance between themselves and the severe threat heading their way. She knew that their body armor wouldn't withstand a tank, and the EMP knocked out the base's defense shield early.

"It must be Jones. Only he can be this desperate and insecure." Bear clutched his rifle up against his torso.

Eski and his men opened fire on the tank from the left while they backed up in their step. Their ammo only pinged the exterior and caused no significant structural incapacitating damage. The tank's primary gun rotated on its axis towards them, and the Hlinan scrambled out of the way just as it fired. Another building crumbled. Wolf chewed her lip, watching in a mix of horror and awe. "Its hull must be made of titanium; a well-fortified 'ass.'"

Bear shook his head. "More like Tungsten. Any ideas on how we go up against a tank, fearless leader?"

"I'm working on ideas." Krysta squeezed the trigger at their impossible foe. More Hlinan to their right fell by the incoming Hell Suns that raced from the tree line in another wave. Lone Wolf charged to help and opened fire against the new threat. "Incoming!"

She alarmed her group nearby. "Watch your flank!" Krysta peered over the pile of rubble that they used as cover to see Eski racing to the second hangar doors. The tank fired again at another building. The hangar doors opened, and the lift brought up another one of his fighters. His men followed him.

The tank's central weapon rotated in Eski's direction. Bear shook his head in disbelief. "Your friend is going to get himself killed over there!" He watched one of the reptilian beings move into the fighter craft.

"Eski! Get out of there now!" Krysta shouted at him. The helmeted Hlinan leader spied her way and then back at the tank. He wildly waved his arm to flag the pilot inside the craft, then leaped to his left to roll away just as the tank opened fire. The projectile hit the plane, exploding it into a fireball. Overwhelmed by the intense heat of the plane, the bewildered pilot could not escape in time. The force of the blast pushed Eski hard along the metal base floor, and he tumbled onto his stomach about nine meters from where he was previously. "Dammit!" Wolf stared in horror to see him not moving. Her heart lurched inside her chest. Was he dead?

Bear tapped her shoulder. "Go! I got your six!"

Wolf broke cover and fired at the mercs before she raced toward Eski's unmoving body. When she was near enough, she held her rifle with one hand and slid on her side next to him. She clutched him with her other arm and dragged him behind a charred piece of the fighter craft. "Eski?"

He groaned from the brief unconscious state, and he groggily lifted his head. The intensity of the blast charred his armor and helmet. "Krysta?"

"You cut it way too close there."

His head slowly turned towards the inferno nearby. "That thing will flatten this place, structure by structure."

"Do you have anything to go up against Jones?"

"Not here." His covered head moved towards a smaller building that was still standing ahead, then he grabbed her hand. "This way." He stumbled the first few steps of his sprint.

She followed him in confusion. "Where are we going?"

"We will need to give him multiple targets." He flagged a few of his soldiers over while she motioned Bear to join. "The others and I will draw him away from the base before he causes any more destruction and death."

Shocked, she paused at the garage entrance, seeing three small rover vehicles. "Please tell me these things have weapons." She removed her helmet to gape in disbelief.

"We cannot take on a tank with those soldiers out there, Wolf." Eski moved to the one he chose. "We will remove it from the equation for now. Your group can remain with my soldiers to handle the other threat."

Wolf held his arm up to stop him. "Eski, this is suicide. You're talking about joyriding around a damn tank." Then her eyes sparked to life. "I got an even crazier idea." She directed an amused smile toward Bear. "Shall we go say hi to Jones?"

He removed his helmet and returned the same devious look. "I think we shall."

Bewildered, Eski cocked his head at her. "Wolf?"

"Do you have room for passengers?" Krysta grinned.

Chapter 44

Three Hlinan hover-rovers sped from the base towards the tank. Bear and Krysta rode in one with Eski, while other Hlinan soldiers piloted the other two. "Now!" Eski ordered. The one in front of them broke left while he and the other went toward the right.

Krysta watched the outside camera display to see Jones steer the tank to pursue the solo vehicle that went left. "Eski."

"On it." Eski drove their vehicle away from the other one and toward the back of the tank. Slipping her helmet back on, Krysta opened the unloading side door and held onto the side's edge to see the tank coming closer to where they were.

Bear moved to take over the controls. "Go with her. I got this." He slid into the driver's seat and glanced at the foreign console with the control stick in front. "Simple enough," he sarcastically joked to them.

"The lever steers and the two buttons to your right maintain the speed." With his helmet on, Eski gave him the quick run-down before he took to Krysta's side at the door.

Bear eased behind the tank's midway left side to maintain a close distance. "Go now!"

Eski eyeballed the top of the tank that housed the cannon and then lurched out to grip the tank's top ledge for dear life. He used his upper arm strength to pull himself to the safety of the rooftop. Crouching low, he slowly turned to Wolf. "Come on!"

Slipping on her helmet, Wolf moved up to the doorway next. Looking down, she glimpsed a narrow space beneath her feet. Suddenly, the tank fired at the solo rover ahead and caused the entire shell of the outer hull to shudder. The blast's shockwave slammed Eski down hard; his hands clambered to grab the metal, desperately trying to prevent himself from being hurled off. Wolf staggered back inside the vessel and watched him struggle to stay on. Fortunately, the tank missed its intended target. Krysta jumped towards him, and he reached out to catch her hand. Just as she did, the tank turned to the right to follow its query. This made Wolf lose some of her distance, and she barely made it. Her body swung into the side of the tank, and she groaned out loudly in pain.

Eski clutched her arm tightly with his hand. "Krysta, I got you!" He used the tank's mount to steady himself and gripped more of her arm to hoist her up.

She clung to him, to catch her breath. "Thanks."

He leaned the forehead part of his helmet against hers. "You alright?"

"Yeah, let's get that bastard."

A whirring noise near them gained their attention and Krysta saw the smaller short-range gun near the front of the tank rotate in the same direction that her Peacekeeper comrade was in. "Oh, God—Bear, break!"

Bear closed the door and then the vehicle sharply broke to the left, away from the tank. It sped up to get out of the gun's range. The tank fired, but it missed by several degrees. "He lacks aim," Eski yelled over the wind that roared all around them by the speed and the sound of the machinery. He motioned Wolf over to the hatch to enter inside, but his arm braced against her chest to stop her when the hatch slid open on its own.

A Hell Sun's mercenary opened the circular door; however, as soon as he saw the night sky, a large black combat boot approached his face. Krysta kicked the unsuspecting soldier straight in the head to send him back through the portal hole and into the tank inside. She moved fast through the hatch and punched the Hell Sun hard straight in the face, knocking him out cold. Spinning to face any remaining enemies, she felt a sharp pain in her arm. A cry escaped her lips as she saw Jones' pistol trained on her. She gritted her teeth from the pain; a warm sensation of blood trickled out of her armor's bullet hole. Even with her armor plating, close range with armor-piercing rounds trumped.

A sneer twisted Jones's lips as he looked at her. "The bitch is back," he spat bitterly. "I should have known you would come down here to get me. Those lizards don't have the balls like you do." Jones stepped forward with his pistol still aimed. The coal black haired man licked his lips devilishly, "Oh, I'm going to have fun with you first, baby."

A knowing smirk played on Krysta's lips. "You sure about that, Jones?"

Eski swung down the opening with both feet and struck Jones' chest hard. The man staggered onto the floor by the force, and the pistol bounced from his hand. With his fists up, Eski spoke through his helmet. "You were saying, human?"

Krysta charged at Jones and tackled him back down while Eski made his way over to the controls. She overheard him mimic Bear's earlier comment. "Simple enough."

Jones roared in frustration, then kicked Krysta onto her back. Pure rage burned in his eyes. "I will end you first, Lone Wolf!"

"I do not think so," Eski jerked sharply at the u-shaped steering wheel to the right and caused Jones to lose his footing. The man careened into the side, giving Wolf time to get back on her feet. Eski then changed direction of the craft toward the tank headed for the mountains, further away from the base. "I need to get this thing away from my people."

Wolf delivered a cross punch with her uninjured arm and followed up with a roundhouse kick to knock Jones back onto the floor on all fours. The man spat out blood from his busted lip, and he wiped the remains off his mouth. He stood to face her, then threw a fake punch before striking her straight in the front of her helmet. Her body slammed against the side, and Jones seized the opportunity to knock her down. He jerked off her helmet, then his hands moved towards her throat to choke her.

"Wolf!" Eski caught Krysta's deadly predicament. She heard him shout into the transponder, "Human, ram this apparatus on the left side!"

"*Ram, you?*" Bear asked with apparent doubt.

"Krysta is in danger! Trust me!"

"*Say no more!*"

As she struggled to free herself from the deadly vice, Krysta twisted her head, slightly, to discover Bear's vehicle charging right at them, full throttle. She grinned widely up at Jones, then shut her eyes tightly. A violent jolt came seconds later, and Jones stumbled by the inertia, losing his grip around her neck. The Hell Suns' leader crashed hard on top of the floor, and Wolf's body tumbled.

With blood streaming from a facial wound, Jones stumbled to regain his balance. "You want your little girlfriend?" He snickered at Eski, who bolted out of his seat to come to her rescue. The man roughly picked Krysta up by the hair on her scalp, then shoved her hard into the Hlinan, causing both to fall backwards onto the tank floor. The Hell Suns' leader limped over to the ladder and cursed under his breath while he climbed out first.

Krysta grimaced through the pain while she used her injured arm to push herself up. Her head throbbed from the jolts. "You alright?" She was still in a daze. Then she remembered Bear rammed his vehicle into them! "Jack!" She scurried out to check on him.

The blood drained from her face when she saw the condition that his rover was in. The impact smashed the entire front end like an accordion, while the tank only sustained minor cosmetic damage. She struggled to see inside the front because of the twisted metal. "Jack!" Her eyes spotted him finally in the middle of the vehicle on his back. His arm was in an unnatural position and his face was littered with cuts. There was a larger cut marring the skin above his right eye from which blood streamed down his face. "Shit! Bear!" In desperation, Krysta scrambled to stifle it. He groaned softly as she arrived. "Hang in there. You are going to make it. I know you hate helmets, but your face looks like shit." She teased and wiped the tear from her cheek. Reaching into the small med pack on her armor, she administered the temporary clotting agent on her arm. "No time to bleed out here." Her head pivoted around the area. "Where the hell is Jones?" She then saw the bloody-faced and bruised Hell Suns' leader limping around the back corner of the tank near Eski.

Leveling his pistol at the Hlinan, the man glared down menacingly. "Die lizard."

"Eski, watch out!" Krysta tried to warn him.

Jones fired, but the Hlinan swiftly reacted, preventing a fatal shot. Instead, the round hit the space between the shoulder blade and collarbone as he turned, sending Eski crashing to the ground. "No, Eski!" Krysta screamed. Jones pivoted on his heel to take her out next, but she dove behind the metal carnage and heard the round ricochet off. She glanced down and realized in the disarray she had lost her weapons, and they were still in the tank. Another soft groan came from Bear's mouth, and she lightly tapped his head. "Don't move, Papa Bear. I'll be right back. I must handle something first." Jones fired again, and she winced. Eski was not visible from her position and the darkness of the night made the task even more difficult. Was he dead? Despair caused her to clench her fists as hot tears welled in her eyes. "Goddamn you, Jones!"

Then the comforting sound of Jones' clip hitting empty gave her newfound energy. He bellowed out in irritation, "Come on!"

She heard him struggling to change out the clip; it was a small window of time. Wolf was reminded suddenly of the mountain pass. She bolted out of cover and raced in that direction. "Come and get me, asshole!" She kept her head low and dared to look back only briefly to see if he would take the bait; if he didn't, then she would have left her old mentor and Eski there defenseless.

With a cackle, Jones gave chase. "You better run, Peacekeeper. When I am done with you, I plan on skinning all the scales off your lizard friend back there. I'll handle Jack last. It's personal with him."

"Don't count on it." Krysta slowed her pace to allow the man to keep up with her. She turned the rocky bend and slid down with her heel towards the cave's entrance. She paused just long enough to make sure she could hear Jones' boots coming up from behind. Satisfied that the Hell Sun was still hot on her heels, she dashed inside. From the dark passageway, she heard the man's grumbling and curses. "You scared?" she taunted out to him. Krysta kept her breath low to prevent her from revealing her position. She heard his boots scuffing against the gravel floor as he desperately sought her out. Krysta held her arm to create a temporary vice around the wound.

Jones' voice echoed off the cavern walls, "No, but you will be when I find you. You know our reputation, Lone Wolf. No one screws with the Hell Suns."

A voice from the dead rose near the entrance. "Krysta!" It was Eski. She smiled widely but withheld herself from answering him. Wolf was unarmed, and Jones had the advantage. She remained quiet.

Jones let out a joyous bellow. "Well, well. The Lizard boy is still alive. Which one of you should I kill first?"

Chapter 45

"Come on out," Jones goaded and fired twice into the air. "I don't care which one takes the bullet first."

With her head down, Krysta navigated the cavern's tall stalagmites. "Not a chance," she whispered, and was relieved the egotistical maniac practically revealed his position. She did not know where Eski went. His stillness was unsettling. Movement caught her eye about eighteen meters to her right and she squatted down to head in that direction, barely touching the cavern floor with the tiptoe of her boot to avoid making a sound. As she drew nearer, she spotted Eski sitting down with his helmet pressed up against the rock formation. He was holding his hand over the same area that had received the bullet earlier. Afraid, she longed to call out to him, but worried the sound would betray their hiding place. As she watched, Eski silently took off his helmet and damaged armor piece, using his fangs to rip away a piece of his black undershirt. He used the tight material for a compression wrap around the wound, then his teeth bit down on the wrap to serve as another hand to tie it off. He retrieved a small capsule from his armor and it appeared to have contained the same black ooze she saw him use before.

She needed to lure Jones away from him. Remaining close to one another was not wise in the lethal game of hide-and-go-seek. Risking it, Krysta darted to Eski, a finger to her lips, urging him to be quiet. Spying one of his pistols, she slowly reached down on his side to seize hold of it. His eyes widened at her action and when he opened his lips to speak, she shook her side to side rapidly. Moving away, Wolf cautiously peered around a large boulderous ridge. Jones' back was to her as he pursued them. There was a safe buffer zone between him and her. Taking a breath, she was about to step out of cover to distract him, but froze mid-step when she heard his voice beckoning out, "Where are you at, lizard boy? I'll take you out first." Bending down, Krysta picked up a small rock by her side and threw it right into Jones' back. Spinning around, he shot at the stalagmite she'd hidden behind; she flinched as the bullets shattered the rock. "So, the girl wants to play first." Jones mocked sadistically.

Hearing his boots near, her eyes briefly fell upon Eski's borrowed pistol. Unlike most human-made weapons, it was exceptionally lightweight and operated not with a trigger, but with a pressure pad located beside the barrel. With the barrel pointed downward, her finger hesitating above the pad and three other fingers holding the grip, she quietly inhaled a quick breath. "Okay, bastard, let's play."

"I figured the military drop-outs would betray their own race," Jones called to her. "For what? A bunch of cowardly reptiles? You want to be a coward with them, Peacekeeper? Or do you want to die with some type of dignity?"

Krysta finally saw Eski's helmeted face emerge from cover to Jones' left. "I'm not hiding from you, human," the Hlinan taunted the merc. Jones spun, firing at Eski. Eski darted out of the way just in time. The bullet struck a stalagmite, and the ground trembled from the impact.

Krysta froze as part of the rock wall collapsed into the cavern, sending debris crashing to the floor. She glanced toward the dark tunnel entrance, a chill raced down her spine. "Ikol."

Using the distraction to his advantage, Eski unleashed a rapid fire. One shot found its mark, striking Jones in the upper leg. Jones let out a pained cry, clutching at the injury as he stumbled back. "You are a lousy shot!" He fumed, his teeth clenched in anger.

Krysta smiled to herself by the sight. *The Hlinan's ammo can pierce our armor material. Good.*

Eski's mocking laughter further enraged the furious man. "My objective was not to be fatal, human. You will live." Krysta didn't see Eski, but narrowed down his location near the tunnel opening, as indicated by his voice. What was he planning on doing?

She sprinted ahead to where the two were. The familiar dark tunnel opening was ominous and foreboding. "Someone tell me why I'm running towards the tunnel. This is suicide," Krysta muttered under her breath. She knew what lurked in the darkened space and their fight awakened it. If she guessed Eski's intent correctly, then it was a very dangerous one. One false move would be game over.

"Hah." Jones ragged back. "You think you are going to bleed me to death?" He aimlessly fired several shots where Eski's pinpointed location was, blasting away the rock.

When Eski emerged from cover again, Wolf saw him shoot Jones in the right knee. The man yelled out in pain but fired back and the shot grazed Eski's left armor shoulder. With a loud groan, Jones clenched his teeth. He was partially bent over, applying more weight on the left knee. Blood poured out from under his hand as he tried to cover the wound up. "Fuck you both!" Jones screamed in agony. Limping, the Hell Suns' leader turned and fired his assault rifle relentlessly where Eski previously stood, blasting away the rock protection. He then moved his shots laterally, going across from left to right. Another volley of wild shots sent a deafening roar through the cavern, making Krysta nervously look toward the tunnel. Where was Eski?

Krysta fired at the man in the arm to distract him from where the Hlinan had gone. Her miss cost her the element of surprise. Jones recognized her location immediately, and he limped her way some with his rifle sights right on her. "You're dead, Peacekeeper!" Before the coal black haired man fired back at her, Eski raced out from his hiding spot to charge at him, but Jones pivoted towards him. Dropping her pistol, Krysta seized the advantage of the merc's back to her and lunged forward to tackle him. Her element of surprise caught him off guard and she used his abnormal gait to knock him off balance. The two crashed onto the hard cavern floor. Jones growled loudly and tossed Krysta over onto her back. He then huffed in pain as he clambered over her and smacked her hard across the face. The stinging blow caused Krysta to cry out. Instinctively, she kicked him hard in his already injured right knee with her boot. Jones yelled out and then Eski came over him from behind. Using his forearm around the man's neck as leverage, he pried the Hell Sun off Lone Wolf, and he flipped him back onto the cavern floor again.

Eski helped Krysta up and touched the injured side of her face with his fingertip. "Are you alright?"

"I'm fine." She panted hard from the fight and glared at where Jones struggled to get up with the lack of the ability to bear weight on his right knee.

"You betrayed your race, Peacekeeper!" The man spat at her on all fours. His back was to the tunnel. "I will see you all in hell!"

Krysta noticed Ikol's terrifying face emerging from behind the furious man. The monstrous spider that haunted the cavern was slowly stalking her prey. Wolf tried her best not to look frightened as she and Eski slowly took a few steps back to put more distance from her. "No, Jones, I think you're only going there."

With a loud grunt, Jones pulled himself to his feet. "Yeah?" he snapped back. "You are backing away. You fear me."

"There are deadlier things in this place than you," Eski flatly answered.

"What the hell does *that* mean?"

Krysta motioned with her hand to Ikol scurrying near the tunnel entrance. "It means you are screwed. Look behind you, asshole."

Perplexed, the man turned to see the spider's glowing blue eyes looking hungrily down at him; her hair-covered legs moved out of the tunnel's mouth to grip the cavern's sides for support. Jones screamed and fired his gun at the beast. His injuries prevented him from fleeing fast enough. Ikol shrieked and leaped out of the tunnel onto her prey. Jones let out another scream as her large body shifted over his, followed by her stinger piercing him. His wails shattered soon, and his life ended.

Eski yanked on Krysta's hand. "Let us move now!"

"Don't have to tell me twice." She wasn't planning on being the spider's second meal or third. While she scurried out with the Hlinan, she winced at the sound of Ikol tearing apart Jones' flesh to devour her meal.

Chapter 46

"I thought you were dead earlier," Wolf squeezed Eski's hand. The pair walked out of the mountain pass towards where they left the rover and tank.

"I did as well." With his helmet off, he frowned at her injured arm. "I will ensure that you heal immediately."

Krysta reacted by pressing her hand back against her arm. She pointed out his own gunshot wound near his clavicle. "You first." She smiled at him. "You're one hell of a fighter."

He chuckled. "I did not know that you planned on feeding the Hell Suns' leader to Ikol. You surprised me."

She shrugged innocently. "Actually, that wasn't my intent. I just wanted to keep him away from you and Jack. Did you plan on Ikol taking him out like that?"

He grinned sneakily. "Not at first."

"You're badass for sure," she laughed, then the tank came into sight, and she broke his grasp. "Jack!" She raced forward. Her heart pounded in her chest. She nearly forgot about his serious injury.

Bear managed a painful smile. "Hey, look who it is." Then his eyes widened at the mangling of her arm. "Shit, Wolf. You've been shot."

"Jones is dead," Wolf announced triumphantly, then thumbed back to Eski, who took up the rear. "This guy had the giant spider handle his ass."

"We both did our part to see to his end," Eski gently corrected her.

Bear shuddered at the gruesome image. "What a way to go; definitely what the bastard deserved." Slowly rising, he unfastened his armor's med pack. "Let's patch you up, Wolf."

She swatted his hand away while he sprayed a disinfectant on the wound. "I got a clotting agent on it. Easy, dad. I'll live for now."

He grunted, "Well, Dhank Trust owes us big time for this job."

Eski politely bowed to the two of them. "You helped save my people. I will be forever grateful for what the Peacekeepers did today."

"Does your gratitude go a long way?" Bear glanced back at Krysta. "I'm ready to get the hell off this rock."

"Jack," Krysta lightly said. "You don't want to stay a little longer?"

The red-bearded older man frowned at her. "Look, kid—"

"Kid?"

"Fine, Lone Wolf," he chortled. "I know you are now into him and all, but you really want to stay here? With all that has happened, I doubt this colony will stay here much longer. Someone will pull the funding and there goes our pay. Can't work for nothing."

"Bear, if Carson's Earth-based report is accurate, the Peacekeepers are gone, and we could be the last of our kind."

"Lone Wolf is welcome to stay with me," Eski gently suggested. "I would guarantee her safety under my protection."

Bear shook his head. "She's one of us." Her unhappy face caused him to roll his eyes. "But it's her call. Are you staying here with the Hlinan?"

Krysta playfully smirked, her arms encircling the Hlinan's neck as she pulled him closer. "The idea is very tempting."

Bear groaned. "I don't want to see this."

Eski smirked back at her, and moved in to kiss her, but then froze when the sound of a transport's approach hummed above them. He quickly drew away and cleared his throat before walking forward to greet the incomers. Krysta recognized it to be of the Hlinan. She frowned at his reaction. He hesitated as soon as he saw that his kind was near. If she stayed to make some type of relationship with him, would anything bloom from it? Convincing his kind was more of a challenge than for hers. Unsure, she flashed a side glance over at Bear, who didn't seem to notice her concern. Was she better off leaving the planet like the others?

The hover vehicle landed, and a few Hlinan soldiers moved out, including Lers and Madu, followed by Grim and a few more of the Peacekeepers. "Grim!" Krysta rushed forward and hugged him. "Glad you made it!"

He gave her a thumbs-up. "Colony secured and the colonists have regained control. Their new head honcho at the place will now be Amir Reddy, the Financial Director. He's ready for peace, unlike the other corporate types."

"We lost many today and suffered severe damage to our base." Hosir Madu rushed over to Eski. "We must seek retribution from the humans for this."

"The war just ended against the Hell Suns, lady." Bear glared at her dubiously. "And you are talking about us paying you?"

"Yeah, if you want cash, go find Jones' wallet." Krysta pointed to the mountain pass entrance. "It's probably in the bowels of Ikol by now."

"The Peacekeepers are correct, Hosir Madu. They did not cause this war and we cannot blame the colonists for what their leaders chose for them. Punishing them would only provoke more hostile relations. Is that what you want?" Eski countered. "We will consult with our new Hevding on action. For now, we shall mourn our dead." He flagged the assembled mercs to follow him back into the transport. "Let us head back."

Madu cursed loudly and stomped past them to go in first. Krysta watched on cautiously. As long as Madu remained nearby, they would always have conflict before any relationship could even begin. Her gaze anxiously shifted to Eski as he walked to her side. What would happen to him in the aftermath? The war with the humans was over, but perhaps another war was dawning.

Chapter 47

The following day, Krysta, the Peacekeepers, and the other colonists stood beside the new colony director outside Bakht's designated courtyard. The Hlinan accompanied them. A small cargo container at the front served as a temporary casket for those who lost their lives during the incursion: Fallen Hlinan soldiers and Peacekeepers together. Off to the side of the courtyard, in another crate, were the dead Hell Suns' soldiers; there were no survivors. Krysta observed Hosir Madu was not at the memorial.

The morning breeze gently bathed over the gathering. A few colonists sobbed. The Hlinan remained still, their hands clasped at their waists, and their eyes stared straight ahead. Hosir Matelija broke formation to walk to where the new director stood to greet him. "We will provide whatever aid we can to you and your colonists. I will also discuss how to help construct a defense barrier against the hata with our new Hevding. We want to live in unity, if that is still feasible."

The director's outstretched hand puzzled Eski, but as he reached out to reciprocate, the director grasped his hand in a handshake. "The name is Amir Reddy and thank you. I will discuss this with Dhank Trust by tomorrow. I want time for the colony to heal; the colonists went through so much. Many want to return to Earth, and

I do not blame them. I also want peace with the Hlinan. Unlike my predecessor, I do not want a corporate agenda. Whatever supplies or material the Hlinan would like from us in return for your aid, please ask of me."

Bear cleared his throat to intercede. "Dhank Trust will come back to this colony. I do not know how they will handle things going forward."

The warning didn't faze the director. "I will ensure to get the word out to the world leaders. Of course, it will take time to bypass Dhank Trust's controls."

Bear dusted off his hands. "Then the Peacekeepers are finished here. As soon as a ship to Earth arrives, we will head back. With the Hlinan's aid, you should be able to adapt to the land. I hope we get paid good for all this crap that we went through." Krysta jabbed him in the ribs and tossed a playful scorning look by his latter comment.

Reddy turned directly to him. "As the new leader of this colony, with the understanding that you are all now free agents, I would like to propose a new contract for continued work here if you are interested. There's no guarantee that the Hlinan will provide us all that we need to remain safe here. The colonists will rest easier knowing that you are still around to protect them."

Bear examined his comrades uneasily. "I'm not sure about that. This is not what I expected. I know you guys don't have the funds to pay us out here."

Grim shook his head. "These people need us right now, Bear." His dark eyes moved over to Eski. "I trust the Hlinan and they may need our help too."

"You have our trust as well, Peacekeepers," the director assured him. "*I* trust you."

Wolf nudged the red-headed man beside her and grinned. "What do you say? Want to stay a little longer? I can arm wrestle you for command if that makes you feel better."

Bear chuckled, "Fine, *only* temporary. We get replacements and we are out. Deal?"

Reddy nodded his hand. "Deal. Welcome back to the Bakht Colony, Peacekeepers."

Epilogue

Achli Ship

Anticipation brought a smile to Xariala's face as her jade eyes scanned the view from her interstellar space cabin's large panoramic window. The darkness of space was not appealing to most, but to her it meant opportunity: the Achli were on the move.

A gentle bell chimed, drawing her to the room's lavender-hued, energy-powered door, which acted like a curtain, shielding the interior from hallway onlookers. "Enter," she beckoned to her guest. Seconds later, the veil lifted into nothingness and an Achli adorned in pearl-colored body armor approached.

"Your Exaltedness," he addressed her.

She simpered inwardly at the self-proclaimed title. "How much further to the planet? I am growing disinterested in this journey."

"The planet Delias is on the far rim of our empire." The soldier walked over to a control panel mounted on the wall.

"That is not what I asked you," she shot back in an icy voice.

Seconds later, the lights dimmed, and the center of the room became the holographic crisp, clear image of the planet, al-sufi C. The soldier moved over next to her in front of the projected representation. "Delias is remote and there have been alterations since your predecessor's arrival there."

"Alterations?" The conversation's direction displeased her. "Clarify." The Achli soldier tapped the planet, and then the display changed to an image of the Bakht Colony layout. Xariala narrowed her eyes at the structure; then a sadistic smile oozed across her pale lips. "So, the pathetic Hlinan rebuilt? They were always so satisfying and resilient; it is almost alluring."

"No, Your Excellency. This settlement is not the Hlinan's." He swiped the image away briefly to reveal the Hlinan City and a smaller image of their base. "Although they have proclaimed our land in defiance."

"A new race?" Xariala salivated at the notion. "Continue."

"It is the humans," he explained, and flipped the image to the colony Bakht. "The ones that inhabited the planet Arcaria."

"Ah, yes. They went down too swiftly to my predecessor, Zenoi. I could barely retrieve adequate specimens. He was always a destroyer of opportunity," she ruminated. "Perhaps the gods have shined fortune upon me, for we have two species to contend with."

"There is something else."

"What?"

"The rynas that Zenoi left are not as strong as we thought. Despite our control, the beasts' population continues to decline."

"Another failed experiment," Xariala mused. "Conduct another genome scan for viable modifications and stay the course to Delias. I am now enthralled by what we will discover there. I hope with the time passed, the humans or the Hlinan have advanced and will give us more of a challenge. The last ones were too primitive."

The soldier bowed to her. "It is done for you, Esteemed One." He exited the room, leaving her to her thoughts.

Xariala sulked. "The Achli have been so stagnant by my precursors. They did not see the full potential of what these lesser races could offer us. I am ascending my race to greatness. My work will continue and perhaps these insignificant lifeforms on Delias will be what I require." Her placid, pale fingers danced around the top of a skull that sat on her desk like a trophy. A sadistic grin spread across her face, and she amusedly held the skull fully in her hand to gaze at it. Her fingertips brushed across the skull's sharp fangs, then away from the mandible to the back of the cranium. "What will you Hlinan offer me this time? Or will it be the humans?"

To be continued…

Melinda Brown

is a history major and author of *Peacekeeper*. Melinda has always enjoyed writing short stories since she was little and has expanded her skills throughout the years. *Peacekeeper* is her debut science fiction novel, and she loves dabbling in that genre. When she's not writing, she enjoys spending time with her family and traveling. She hopes that her passion for writing will be passed down to her daughter along with her love for science fiction.